'Nobody does unsettling undercurrents bett.. ... ..
Cleeves'   Val McDermid

'Cleeves sets a good scene, this time in Northumberland during a heatwave, and she brings a large cast to life, shifting points of view between bereaved relatives, victims and suspects in a straightforward, satisfyingly traditional detective novel'   *Literary Review*

'Ann Cleeves . . . is another fine author with a strong, credible female protagonist . . . It's a dark, interesting novel with considerable emotional force behind it'
                                        Spectator

'Cleeves has a way of making unlikely murders plausible by grounding them in recognizable communities. In this world, neighbours are close-knit, and close ranks'
                                        Financial Times

'Cleeves weaves an absorbingly cunning mystery and fans of Vera, the messy, overweight, man-less heroine of this crime series, will soon have a face to put to her, as the actress Brenda Blethyn takes on her endearing character in a forthcoming television series, *Vera*, based on the books'   *Daily Mail*

'Ann Cleeves is a skilful technician, keeping our interest alive and building slowly up to the denouement. Her easy use of language and clever story construction make her one of the best natural writ.. .. ..tion'
                                        ..y *Express*

Praise for the Shetland series

'*Raven Black* breaks the conventional mould of British crime-writing, while retaining the traditional virtues of strong narrative and careful plotting'   *Independent*

'Like a smoky Shetland peat fire, this elegantly written, slow-burning intrigue shrouds you in mystery and crackles with inner heat'   **Peter James**

'Beautifully constructed . . . a lively and surprising addition to a genre that once seemed moribund'
     Times Literary Supplement

'*Raven Black* shows what a fine writer Cleeves is . . . an accomplished and thoughtful book'   *Sunday Telegraph*

'Ann's characterization is worthy of the best writers in the field . . . Rarely has a sense of place been so evocatively conveyed in a crime novel'   *Daily Express*

'In true Agatha Christie style, Cleeves once again pulls the wool over our eyes with cunning and conviction'
     Colin Dexter

'The setting is Fair Isle, full of birds and beauty, but, in Cleeves' hands, deeply sinister'   *The Times*

'A most satisfying mystery set in an isolated and intriguing location. Jimmy Perez is a fine creation, and I hope Ann Cleeves' Shetland series will be with us for a long time to come'   **Peter Robinson**

TELLING TALES

Ann Cleeves is the author behind ITV's *Vera* and BBC One's *Shetland*. She has written over twenty-five novels, and is the creator of detectives Vera Stanhope and Jimmy Perez – characters loved both on screen and in print. Both series are international bestsellers.

In 2006 Ann was awarded the Duncan Lawrie Dagger (CWA Gold Dagger) for Best Crime Novel, for *Raven Black*, the first book in her Shetland series. In 2012 she was inducted into the CWA Crime Thriller Awards Hall of Fame. Ann lives in North Tyneside.

www.anncleeves.com
@anncleeves
facebook.com/anncleeves

By Ann Cleeves

A Bird in the Hand   Come Death and High Water

Murder in Paradise   A Prey to Murder

A Lesson in Dying   Murder in My Backyard

A Day in the Death of Dorothea Cassidy

Another Man's Poison   Killjoy

The Mill on the Shore   Sea Fever

The Healers   High Island Blues

The Baby-Snatcher   The Sleeping and the Dead

Burial of Ghosts

The Vera Stanhope series

The Crow Trap   Telling Tales   Hidden Depths

Silent Voices   The Glass Room   Harbour Street

The Moth Catcher

The Shetland series

Raven Black   White Nights   Red Bones

Blue Lightning   Dead Water   Thin Air

Ann Cleeves

TELLING TALES

First published 2005 by Macmillan

This edition published 2016 by Pan Books
an imprint of Pan Macmillan
20 New Wharf Road, London N1 9RR
Associated companies throughout the world
www.panmacmillan.com

ISBN 978-1-5098-1590-6

CITY AND COUNTY OF
SWANSEA LIBRARIES

6000269491	
Askews & Holts	12-May-2016
	£7.99
PD	

Typeset by Intype Libra Ltd
Printed and bound by CPI Group (UK) Ltd, Croydon, CR0 4YY

This book is sold subject to the condition that it shall not, by way of
trade or otherwise, be lent, hired out, or otherwise circulated without
the publisher's prior consent in any form of binding or cover other than
that in which it is published and without a similar condition including
this condition being imposed on the subsequent purchaser.

Visit www.panmacmillan.com to read more about all our books
and to buy them. You will also find features, author interviews and
news of any author events, and you can sign up for e-newsletters
so that you're always first to hear about our new releases.

Part One

Chapter One

Sitting at the bedroom window, Emma looks out at the night-time square. The wind rattles a roof tile and hisses out from the churchyard, spitting a Coke can onto the street. There was a gale the afternoon Abigail Mantel died and it seems to Emma that it's been windy ever since, that there have been ten years of storms, of hailstones like bullets blown against her windows and trees ripped from the earth by their roots. It must be true at least since the baby was born. Since then, whenever she wakes at night – to feed the baby or when James comes in late from work – the noise of the wind is there, rolling round her head like the sound of a seashell when you hold it to your ear.

James, her husband, isn't home yet, but she's not waiting up for *him*. Her gaze is fixed on the Old Forge where Dan Greenwood makes pots. There's a light at the window and occasionally she fancies she sees a shadow. She imagines that Dan is still working there, dressed in his blue canvas smock, his eyes narrowed as he shapes the clay with his strong, brown hands. Then she imagines leaving the baby, who is fast asleep, tucked up in his carrycot. She sees herself slipping out into the square and keeping to the shadows, walking across to the forge. She pushes open one of the big doors which form an arch, like the door of a church, and stands inside. The roof is high and she can see through the curved rafters to the tiles. In her mind she feels the heat of the kiln and sees the dusty shelves holding unglazed pots.

Dan Greenwood looks up. His face is flushed and there is red dust in the furrows of his forehead. He isn't surprised to see her. He moves away from the bench where he's working and stands in front of her. She feels her breath quicken. He kisses her forehead and then begins to unbutton her shirt. He touches her breasts, stroking them, so he leaves lines of red clay like warpaint. She feels the clay drying on her skin and her breasts become tight, slightly itchy.

Then the image fades and she's back in the bedroom she shares with her husband. She knows her breasts are heavy with milk, not tight with drying clay. At the same time the baby begins to grizzle and to claw blindly in the air with both hands. Emma lifts him out of the cot and begins to feed him. Dan Greenwood has never touched her and probably never will, no matter how often she dreams of it. The church clock strikes midnight. By now, James should have his ship safely into port.

That was the story Emma told herself as she sat by her window in the village of Elvet. A running commentary on her feelings, as if she was an outsider looking in. It was how it had always been – her life as a series of fairy tales. Before Matthew had been born she'd wondered if his birth would make her more engaged. There was nothing more real, was there, than labour? But

4

now, running her little finger between his mouth and her nipple to break the suction, she thought that wasn't true. She was no more emotionally involved with him than she was with James. Had she been different before she found Abigail Mantel's body? Probably not. She lifted her son onto her shoulder and rubbed his back. He reached out and grasped a strand of her hair.

The room was at the top of a neat Georgian house, built of red brick and red tile. It was double-fronted and symmetrical with rectangular windows and a door in the middle. It had been built by a seafarer who'd traded with Holland, and James had liked that. 'We're carrying on a tradition,' he'd said when he showed her round. 'It's like keeping it in the family.' Emma had thought it was too close to home, to the memories of Abigail Mantel and Jeanie Long, and had suggested that Hull might be more convenient for his work. Or Beverley. Beverley was a pleasant town. But he'd said Elvet was just as good for him.

'It'll be nice for you to be so close to your parents,' he'd said and she'd smiled and agreed, because that was what she did with James. She liked to please him. In fact she didn't much care for Robert and Mary's company. Despite all the help they offered, they made her feel uncomfortable and for some reason guilty.

Above the rumble of the wind there came another sound – a car engine; headlights swept onto the square, briefly lighting up the church gate, where dead leaves were blown into a drift. James parked on the cobbles, got out and shut the door with a solid thud. At the same time Dan Greenwood emerged from the Old Forge. He was dressed as Emma had imagined, in jeans and the blue smock. She expected him to pull together the big double doors and fasten them with a key he kept on a ring clipped to his belt on a chain. Then he would push a heavy brass padlock through the iron rings bolted to each door and shove the hasp in place. She had watched this ritual from the window many times. Instead he crossed the square towards James. He wore heavy work boots which rapped loudly on the paving stones and made James turn round.

Seeing them together, it occurred to her how different they were. Dan was so dark that he should have been a foreigner. He could play the villain in a gothic melodrama. And James was a pale, polite Englishman. She felt suddenly anxious about the two men meeting, though there was no reason. It wasn't as if Dan could guess at her fantasies. She had done nothing to give herself away. Carefully, she raised the sash window so she could hear their words. The curtains billowed. There was wind in the room with a taste of salt on it. She felt like a child listening in to an adult conversation, a parent and teacher, perhaps, discussing her academic progress. Neither of the men had seen her.

'Have you seen the news?' Dan asked.

James shook his head. 'I've come off a Latvian container. Hull to sign off, then I drove straight home.'

'You've not heard from Emma, then?'

'She's not much one for the news.'

'Jeanie Long committed suicide. She'd been turned down for parole again. It happened a couple of days ago. They kept it quiet over the weekend.'

James stood, poised to click the fob of his car key to lock up. He was still wearing his uniform and looked dashing in an old-fashioned way, as if he belonged to the time the house was built. The brass buttons on his jacket gleamed dully in the unnatural light. His head was bare. He carried his cap under his arm. Emma was reminded of when she had once had fantasies about *him*.

'I don't suppose it'll make much difference to Em. Not after all this time. I mean it's not as if she knew Jeanie, not so much. She was very young when all that was going on.'

'They're going to reopen the Abigail Mantel case,' Dan Greenwood said.

There was a moment of silence. Emma wondered what Dan could know about all that. Had the two men discussed her on other occasions when she hadn't been watching?

'Because of the suicide?' James asked.

'Because a new witness had just come forward. It seems Jeanie Long couldn't have murdered that lass.' He paused. Emma watched him rub his forehead with his broad, stubby fingers. It was as if he was trying to rub away the exhaustion. She wondered why he cared so deeply about a ten-year-old murder case. She could tell that he did care, that he had lain awake worrying about it. But he hadn't even been living in the village then. He dropped his hands from his face. No traces of clay were left on his skin. He must have washed his hands before leaving the forge. 'Shame no one bothered to tell Jeanie, huh?' he said. 'Or she might still be alive.'

A sudden gust of wind seemed to blow the men apart. Dan scurried back to the Old Forge to close the doors. The Volvo locked itself with a click and a flash of side lights and James climbed the steps to the front door. Emma moved away from the window and sat on the chair beside the bed. She cradled the baby in one arm and held him to the other breast.

She was still sitting there when James walked in. She'd switched on a small lamp beside her; the rest of the big attic room was a pool of shadow. The baby had finished feeding and his eyes were closed, but she still held him, and he sucked occasionally in his sleep. A dribble of milk ran across his cheek. She had heard James moving around carefully downstairs, and the creaking stairs had prepared her for his entrance. She was composed with a smile on her face. Mother and child. Like one of the Dutch paintings he'd dragged her to see. He'd bought a print for the house, put it in a big gilt frame. She could tell the effect wasn't lost on him, and he smiled too, looked suddenly wonderfully happy. She wondered why she had become more attracted to Dan Greenwood who could be slovenly in his appearance, and rolled thin little cigarettes from strings of tobacco.

Gently she lifted the baby into his cot. He puckered his mouth as if still looking for the nipple, sighed deeply in disappointment but didn't wake. Emma fastened the flap in the unflattering maternity bra and pulled her dressing gown around her. The heating was on but in this house there were always draughts. James bent to kiss her, feeling for her mouth with the tip of his tongue, as insistent as the baby wanting food. He would have liked sex but she knew he wouldn't push for it. Nothing was so important to him that it warranted a scene, and she'd been unpredictable lately. He wouldn't risk her ending up in tears. She pushed him gently away. He had poured himself a small glass of whisky downstairs and still had it with him. He took a sip from it before setting the glass on the bedside table.

'Was everything all right this evening?' she asked to soften the rejection. 'It's been so windy. I imagine you out there in the dark, the waves so high.'

She had imagined nothing of the sort. Not tonight. When she had first met him she had dreamed of him out on the dark sea. Somehow now, the romance had gone out of it.

'It was easterly,' he said. 'On shore. Helping us in.' He smiled fondly at her and she was pleased that she had said the right thing.

He began to undress slowly, easing the tension from his stiff muscles. He was a pilot. He joined ships at the mouth of the Humber and brought them safely into the dock at Hull, Goole or Immingham, or he guided them out of the river. He took his work seriously, felt the responsibility. He was one of the youngest, fully qualified pilots working the Humber. She was very proud of him.

That was what she told herself, but the words ran meaninglessly through her head. She was trying to fend off the panic which had been building since she had heard the men talking on the square, growing like a huge wave which rises from nothing out at sea.

'I heard you talking to Dan Greenwood outside. What was so important at this time of night?'

He sat on the bed. He was bare chested, his body coated with fine blond hair. Although he was fifteen years older than her, you'd never have guessed, he was so fit.

'Jeanie Long committed suicide last week. You know, Jeanie Long. Her father used to be coxswain on

9

the launch at the point. The woman who was convicted of strangling Abigail.'

She wanted to shout at him, *Of course I know. I know more about this case than you ever could.* But she just looked at him.

'It was unfortunate, a terrible coincidence. Dan says a new witness has come forward. The case has been reopened. Jeanie might have been released.'

'How does Dan Greenwood know all that?'

He didn't answer. She decided he was thinking already of other things, a tricky tide perhaps, an overloaded ship, a hostile skipper. He unbuckled his belt and stood to step out of his trousers. He folded them precisely and hung them over a hanger in the wardrobe.

'Come to bed,' he said. 'Get some sleep while you can.' She thought he had already put Abigail Mantel and Jeanie Long out of his mind.

Chapter Two

For ten years Emma had tried to forget the day she'd discovered Abigail's body. Now she forced herself to remember it, to tell it as a story.

It was November and Emma was fifteen. The landscape was shadowed by storm clouds. It was the colour of mud and wind-blackened beanstalks. Emma had made one friend in Elvet. Her name was Abigail Mantel. She had flame-red hair. Her mother had died of breast cancer when Abigail was six. Emma, who had secret dreams of her father dying, was shocked to find herself a little envious of the sympathy this generated. Abigail didn't live in a damp and draughty house and she wasn't dragged to church every Sunday. Abigail's father was as rich as it was possible to be.

Emma wondered if this was the story she had told herself at the time, but couldn't remember. What *did* she remember of that autumn? The big, black sky and the wind laden with sand which scoured her face as she waited for the bus to school. Her anger at her father for bringing them there.

And Abigail Mantel, exotic as a television star, with her wild hair and her expensive clothes, her poses and her pouting. Abigail, who sat next to her in class and copied her work and tossed her hair in disdain at all the lads who fancied her. So two contrasting memories: a cold, monochrome landscape and a fifteen-year-old girl, so intensely coloured that it would warm you just to look at her. When she was alive, of course. When she was dead she'd looked as cold as the frozen ditch where Emma had found her.

Emma made herself remember the moment of finding Abigail's body. She owed Abigail that, at least. In the room in the Dutch captain's house, the baby snuffled, James breathed slowly and evenly and she retraced her footsteps along the side of a bean field, making every effort to keep the recollection real. No fantasies here, please.

The wind was so strong that she had to force out each breath in a series of pants, much as she would later be taught to do during labour before it became time to push. There was no shelter. In the distance the horizon was broken by one of the ridiculously grand church spires which were a feature of this part of the county, but the sky seemed enormous and she imagined herself the only person under it.

'What were you doing there, out on your own in the storm?' the policewoman would ask later, gently, as if she really wanted to know, as if the question wasn't part of the investigation at all.

But lying beside her husband, Emma knew that *this* memory, the memory of her mother and the police-woman, sitting in the kitchen at home discussing the detail of the discovery, was a cop-out. Abigail deserved better than that. She deserved the full story.

So . . . it was late afternoon on a Sunday in November. Ten years ago. Emma was fighting against the wind towards the slight dip in the land where the converted chapel which was the Mantel family home lay. She was already upset and angry. Angry enough to storm out of the house on a foul afternoon, although it would soon be dark. As she walked she raged in her mind about her parents, about the injustice of having a father who was unreasonable, tyrannical, or who had seemed to have become so as she grew up. Why couldn't he be like other girls' fathers? Like Abigail's, for example? Why did he talk like a character from a Bible story, so when you questioned him it was like questioning the authority of the Bible itself? Why did he make her feel guilty when she couldn't see she'd done anything wrong?

She caught her foot on a sharp piece of flint and stumbled. Tears and snot covered her face. She remained for a moment where she was, on her hands and knees. She'd grazed the palms of her hands when she'd tried to save herself, but at least here, closer to the ground, it was easier to breathe. Then she'd thought how ridiculous she must look, though there could be no one out on an afternoon like this to see her. The fall had brought her to her senses. Eventually she would have to go home and apologize for making a scene. Better sooner than later. A drainage ditch ran along the side of the field. Getting to her feet the wind struck her with full force again and she turned her back to it. That was when she looked into the ditch and saw Abigail. She recognized the jacket first – a blue quilted jacket. Emma had wanted one like it but her mother had been horrified when she'd seen the price in the shops. Emma didn't recognize Abigail, though. She thought it must be someone else, that Abigail had lent the jacket to a cousin or a friend, someone else who had coveted it. Someone Emma hadn't known. This girl had an ugly face and Abigail had never been ugly. Neither had she been so quiet; Abigail was always talking. This girl had a swollen tongue, blue lips and would never talk again. Never flirt or tease or sneer. The whites of her eyes were spotted red.

Emma wasn't able to move. She looked around her and saw a piece of black polythene, tossed by the wind so it looked like an enormous crow, flapping over the bean field. And then, miraculously, her mother appeared. Emma could believe, looking as far as the horizon, that her mother was the only other person alive in the whole village. She was battling her way along the footpath towards her daughter, her greying hair tucked into the hood of her old anorak, wellington boots under her Sunday-best skirt. The last thing Robert had said when Emma flounced out of the kitchen was, 'Just let her go. She has to learn.' He hadn't shouted. He'd spoken patiently, kindly even. Mary always did as Robert told her, and the sight of her silhouette against the grey sky, fatter than normal because she was bundled against the cold, was almost as shocking as the sight of Abigail Mantel lying in the ditch. Because after a few seconds Emma had accepted that this *was* Abigail. No one else had the same colour hair. She waited, with the tears running down her face, for her mother to reach her.

A few yards from her, her mother opened her arms and stood waiting for Emma to run into them. Emma began to sob, choking so it was impossible for her to speak. Mary held her and began to stroke her hair away from her face, as she had when they'd been living in York, when Emma had still been a child and prone to occasional nightmares.

'Nothing is worth getting that upset for,' Mary said. 'Whatever's the matter, we can sort it out.' She meant, *You know your father only does what he thinks is right. If we explain to him he will soon come round.*

Then Emma pulled her to the ditch and made her look down on Abigail Mantel's body. She knew that not even her mother could sort that out and make it better.

There was a horrified silence. It was as if Mary too had needed time to take in the sight, then her mother's voice came again, suddenly brisk, demanding a reply. 'Did you touch her?'

Emma was shocked out of the hysteria.

'No.'

'There's nothing more we can do for her now. Do you hear me, Emma? We're going home and we're going to tell the police and for a while everything will seem like a dreadful dream. But it wasn't your fault and there was nothing you could have done.'

And Emma thought, *At least she hasn't mentioned Jesus. At least she doesn't expect me to take comfort from that.*

*

In the Captain's House, the wind continued to shake the loose sash window in the bedroom. Emma spoke in her head to Abigail. *See, I faced it, remembered it just as it happened. Now, can I go to sleep?* But though she wrapped herself around James and sucked the warmth from him, she still felt cold. She tried to conjure up her favourite fantasy about Dan Greenwood, imagined his dark skin lying against hers, but even that failed to work its magic.

Chapter Three

Emma couldn't tell the aftermath of her discovery of Abigail as a story. It didn't have a strong enough narrative line. It was too muddled in her head. Details were missing. At the time it had been hard to follow what was happening. Perhaps shock had made it difficult to concentrate. Even these days, ten years on, the image of the cold, silent Abigail flashed into her mind when she least expected it. That evening, the evening after the discovery of the body, when they had all sat in the kitchen at Springhead House, it had lodged in her brain, blocking her vision and making all the questions seem as if they were coming from very far away. And now it made the memories jerky and unreliable.

She couldn't remember the walk back to the house with her mother, but could see herself, hesitating by the back door, reluctant still to face her father. She always hated to disappoint him. But even if he'd been preparing a lecture when he heard them approach, he soon forgot about it. Mary took him into a corner, her arm round his shoulder, and gave a whispered explanation. He stood for a moment still as a stone, as if it was too hard for him to accept. 'Not here,' he said. 'Not in Elvet.' He turned and took Emma in his arms, so she could smell the soap he shaved with. 'No one should have to see that,' he said. 'Not my little girl. I'm so sorry.' As if he, somehow, was to blame, as if he should have been strong enough to protect her from it. Then they wrapped her up in the scratchy blanket which they used as a rug on picnics and there were urgent phone calls to the police. Shocked as she was, she sensed that once he'd come to terms with what had happened, Robert was rather enjoying the drama.

But when the policewoman arrived to speak to Emma, he must have realized that his presence might make things more difficult and he left the three women on their own in the kitchen. That would have been difficult for him. Robert always felt he had a contribution to make at a time of crisis. He was used to dealing with emergencies: clients who slit their wrists in his waiting room, or had psychotic episodes, or jumped bail. Emma wondered if that was why he enjoyed his work so much.

Perhaps someone else came to Springhead with the detective and talked to Robert in a different room, because occasionally in the lull in the conversation, while Emma struggled to answer the policewoman's questions, she thought she could hear muffled voices. Above the wind it was difficult to tell. It was possible that her father was talking to Christopher and she was imagining the third voice. Christopher must have been in the house that day too.

Mary made tea in the big brown earthenware pot, and they sat at the kitchen table. Mary apologized.

'It's so cold in the rest of the house. At least here there's the Aga . . .' And for once the Aga behaved itself and gave off some heat. Condensation had been running down the windows all day and had formed lakes on the sills. Mary hated the Aga then, before she got more used to its ways. She faced it every morning as if preparing for battle, muttering under her breath, a prayer, *Please get hot today. Don't die on me. Please stay warm long enough to cook a meal.*

The policewoman, though, still seemed cold. She kept on her coat and clasped her hands round her mug of tea. Emma must have been introduced to her though that bit escaped her memory, escaped as soon as it had been spoken. She could remember thinking that the woman must have been a policewoman although she was wearing her own clothes, clothes which had seemed so smart to Emma that she noticed them as soon as she walked in. Under the coat there was a skirt, softly fitted, almost full length and a pair of brown leather boots. Throughout the enquiry Emma would struggle to remember this woman's name, although she would become the family's only contact with the police, returning whenever there was a development in the case, so they wouldn't have to find out from the press.

As soon as she sat down the policewoman – Kate? Cathy? – asked that question, 'What were you doing there, out on your own in the storm?'

It was so hard to explain. Emma could hardly just say, *Well, it's Sunday afternoon.* Although in her mind that was all the explanation needed. Sundays were often tense, all of them in together, trying to be a model family. Nothing much to do after church.

That Sunday had been worse than usual. Emma had some good memories of family meals at Springhead, occasions when Robert was expansive, telling silly jokes that had them doubled up with laughter, when her mother waxed passionate about some book she was reading. Then it almost seemed that the good times they had enjoyed in York had returned. But those had all been before Abigail died. That Sunday lunch had marked a watershed, a change in atmosphere. Or so it would seem to Emma later. She remembered the meal with unusual clarity: the four of them sitting at the table, Christopher uncommunicative, caught up as usual with some project of his own, Mary dishing out the food with a sort of desperate energy, talking all the time, Robert unusually silent. Emma had taken the silence as a good sign and slipped her request into the conversation, hoping almost that he wouldn't notice.

'It is OK if I go round to Abigail's later?'

'I'd rather you didn't.' He'd spoken quite calmly, but she had been furious.

'Why not?'

'I don't think it's too much to ask you to spend one afternoon with your family, do you?'

She'd thought that was so unfair! She spent every Sunday cramped in the horrible damp house while her friends were off enjoying themselves. Never before had she made a fuss.

She'd helped him wash the dishes as usual but all the time her fury had been growing, building like a flooded river behind a dam. Later, when her mother had come in to see how they were getting on, she'd said, 'I'm going out now, to see Abigail. I won't be late.' Speaking to Mary, not to him. And she'd rushed past them, deaf to her mother's frantic requests.

All that seemed stupid and trivial once she knew Abigail was dead. The temper tantrum of a two-year-old. And with her mother, sitting beside her, and the smart woman looking at her, waiting, it was even harder to explain her frustration, her need to escape.

'I was bored,' she said in the end. 'You know, Sunday afternoons.'

The policewoman had nodded, seeming to understand.

'Abigail was the only person I know. It's miles by the road. There's a short-cut across the fields.'

'Did you know Abigail would be in?' the policewoman asked.

'I saw her at youth club on Friday night. She said she was going to cook her father a special Sunday tea. To say thank you.'

'What did she want to thank her father for?' Though Emma had the impression that the policewoman already knew the answer, or at least had guessed at it. How could she? Had she had time to find out? Perhaps it was just that she carried round with her an aura of omnipotence.

'For asking Jeanie Long to leave, so they could have the house to themselves again.'

And at that the policewoman nodded once more, satisfied, as if she was a teacher and Emma had answered a test question correctly.

'Who is Jeanie Long?' she asked and once more Emma had the impression that she already knew the answer.

'She was Mr Mantel's girlfriend. She used to live with them.'

21

The policewoman made notes in a book but she made no comment.

'Tell me all you can about Abigail.'

Emma, no longer the rebellious teenager – that had been shocked out of her – was eager to please and started talking at once. Once she started there was so much to say.

'Abigail was my best friend. When we moved here it was hard, different, you know. We were used to the city. Abigail had lived here most of her life but she didn't really fit in either.'

It had been something they'd talked about at sleepovers, how much they had in common. How they were soulmates. But even at the time Emma had known that wasn't true. They'd both been misfits that was all. Abigail because she had no mother and her father gave her everything she asked for. Emma because she'd moved from the city and her parents said grace before meals.

'Abigail lived on her own with her dad. Until Jeanie came to stay, at least, and Abigail couldn't stand her. There's someone to do the cleaning and the cooking, but she lives in a flat over the garage and that doesn't really count, does it? Abigail's dad's a businessman.'

Those words still conjured up for Emma the same glamour as when she'd first heard them. They made her think of the big smart car, with the leather seats, which had collected them sometimes from school, of Abigail all dressed up to go out to dinner with her father because he was entertaining clients, of the champagne Keith Mantel had opened when it was her fifteenth birthday. Of the man himself, suave and charming and attentive. She couldn't explain that to the woman, though. To her *'businessman'* would just be the description of an occupation. Like *'probation officer'* or *'priest'*.

'Does Abigail's father know?' Emma asked suddenly, feeling sick.

'Yes,' the policewoman said. She looked very serious as she spoke and Emma wondered if she'd been the one to tell him.

'They were *so* close,' Emma murmured, but she felt those words to be inadequate. She pictured father and daughter cuddled on the sofa in the immaculate house, laughing at a comedy on the television.

She must have told the policewoman more about Jeanie Long at that first meeting, about why Abigail disliked her, but lying in the bed next to James, the details of that part of the conversation eluded her. Neither could she recall seeing Christopher in the house between lunch and much later in the evening. Now Christopher was a scientist, a postgraduate student, studying the breeding behaviour of puffins and spending part of every year on Shetland. Then he had been her little brother, self-contained and annoyingly brainy.

Had he always been like that, so distant and closed off from the rest of them? Or had that only happened after Abigail's death? Perhaps he'd changed then too, although he'd only witnessed the drama second hand, and it was her memory which was faulty. Had it been the move to Elvet that had changed him and made him so focused and intense, or Abigail's murder? At this distance she couldn't decide. She wondered how much of that day he remembered and whether he'd be prepared to discuss it with her.

Certainly in York he'd been more open, more . . . in her mind she paused, hesitating to use the word, even to herself, more . . . normal. She remembered a rowdy little boy, chasing round the house with his friends, waving a plastic sword in the air, then at another time sitting in the back seat of the car on a long journey, giggling at a joke he'd brought back from school until tears had run down his cheeks.

She was now certain that he was in the house on the day Abigail died. He hadn't been away on one of his solitary walks. Later, once the policewoman had gone, they sat together in his bedroom which was in the roof, and which looked out over the fields. The wind blew a gap in the clouds and there was a full moon. They watched the activity in the bean field, the flashlights throwing strange shadows, the men below them looking very small. Christopher pointed to two of them struggling through the mud, carrying a stretcher between them.

'I suppose that's her.'

Then one of the stretcher bearers tripped and fell onto one knee, and the stretcher tilted alarmingly. Emma and Christopher looked at each other and both gave an awkward and embarrassed giggle.

The church clock struck two. The baby cried out in his sleep as if he were having a nightmare. Emma began to doze, and remembered, as if *she* were already dreaming, that the policewoman's name had been Caroline. Caroline Fletcher.

Chapter Four

In the beginning was the word. Even as a teenager Emma hadn't believed that literally. How could you have a word without someone to speak it? Impossible for the word to come first. She'd never had it properly explained though. Not in the sermons she'd sat through during the family service on Sunday mornings. Not during the dreary evenings of the confirmation classes.

What she'd thought it meant was: *In the beginning was the story.* The Bible was all stories. What else was there to it? The only way she could make sense of her own life was to turn it into a story.

As she grew older the fiction – was it fiction? – grew more elaborate.

Once upon a time there was a family. An ordinary family. The Winters. A mother and father and a son and daughter. They lived in a pleasant house on the outskirts of York in a street with trees on the pavement. In spring the trees were pink with blossom and in autumn the leaves were gold. Robert, the father, was an architect. Mary, the mother, worked part time in the university library. Emma and Christopher went to the school at the end of the street. They wore a uniform with a maroon blazer and a grey tie.

And repeating the story in her head now, Emma saw the garden in the York house. A red brick wall with sunflowers in a row against it, the colours so vivid that they almost hurt her eyes. Christopher was squatting next to a terracotta pot with lavender growing in it, a butterfly trapped between his cupped hands. She could smell the lavender and there was sound too, the bubbling notes of a flute from an open window, played by the teenage girl who came occasionally to babysit.

I'll never be so happy again. The thought came unbidden into her head, but she couldn't allow that to be part of the narrative. It was too painful. So she continued the story as it was always told . . .

Then Robert discovered Jesus and everything changed. He said he couldn't be an architect any more. He left his old office with the long windows and went to university to become a probation officer.

'Why not a vicar?' Emma had asked. By now they had started going regularly to church. She'd thought he'd be a good vicar.

'Because I don't feel the calling,' Robert had said.

He couldn't be a probation officer in York. He wasn't called to stay and anyway there wasn't enough money to keep the big house in the quiet street. Instead they'd moved east to Elvet, where the land was flat and they needed probation officers. Mary had left the university and took a job in a tiny public library. If she'd missed the students she hadn't said. She'd gone to the church in the village with Robert every Sunday and sang the hymns as loudly as he did. What she'd thought about their new life in the draughty house, the bean fields and the mud, Emma hadn't been able to tell.

But of course that wasn't the complete story. Even aged fifteen Emma had known it couldn't be. Robert wouldn't just have discovered Jesus in a flash of lightning and a crashing of cymbals. Something had led up to it. Something had made him change. In the books she read, every action had a cause. How unsatisfactory if events came out of the blue, at random, unexplained. There had been some trauma in Robert's life, some depression. He had never discussed it, so she was free to create her own explanation, her own fiction.

It was Sunday, and on Sunday the whole family went together to family Communion in the church on the other side of the square. After Matthew had been born Emma had been allowed a few weeks off, but a month after the birth Robert had called at the house. It had been mid morning, a week day, and she'd been surprised to see him.

'Shouldn't you be at work?' she'd said.

'I'm on my way to Spinney Fen. Plenty of time for a coffee and a look at my new grandson.'

Spinney Fen was the women's prison with the high concrete walls on the cliff next to the gas terminal. He had clients there, offenders he'd been supervising in the community and others about to be released on licence. Emma hated driving past Spinney Fen. Often it seemed shrouded in sea mist, so the concrete walls seemed to go up for ever into the clouds. When they'd first moved to Elvet she'd had nightmares about his going in through the narrow metal gate and never being allowed out.

She had made him coffee and let him hold

Matthew, but all the time she'd wondered what he was really doing in her home. On his way out he'd paused on the doorstep.

'Will we be seeing you at church on Sunday? Don't worry about the baby. You can always take him out if he cries.'

And of course on the following Sunday she'd been there, because since the death of Abigail Mantel, she hadn't had the will to stand up to him. To stand up to anyone. And he still had a way of making her feel guilty. Part of her felt that if she hadn't disobeyed him that Sunday, ten years before, history might have been different. If she hadn't been there to find the body, Abigail might not have died.

Robert and Mary always arrived at the church, St Mary Magdalene, before Emma and James. Robert was churchwarden and dressed up in a white robe himself, when it was time, and served wine from the big silver chalice. Emma was not quite sure what he did in the half hour before the service began. He disappeared into the vestry. Perhaps there were practical tasks; perhaps he was praying. Mary always went into the small kitchen in the hall to switch on the urn and set out the cups for coffee afterwards. Then she went back into church and stood by the door to hand out hymn books and service sheets. When Emma had still been living at home she had been expected to help.

James hadn't been at all religious when Emma first met him. She had brought the matter up on their first date just to check. Even now, she thought, he didn't actually *believe* in God, or in fact in any of the things he claimed to believe, when he was reciting the creed. He was the most rational man she had ever met. He laughed at the superstitions of the foreign sailors he met at work. He liked going to church for the same reason that he liked living in the Captain's House. It represented tradition, a solid respectability. He had no family of his own and that too had been a major attraction. Often Emma felt he was closer to Robert and Mary than she was, certainly he was more comfortable in their company.

They were late arriving at church. The story of Jeanie's suicide had been on the front page of the newspaper, which was always delivered on Sunday. Her staring face had looked up from the doormat at Emma, stopping her in her tracks. Then there had been a last-minute flap because Matthew threw up over his clothes just as they were leaving the house. In the end they scuttled over the square like fractious children late for school. There was a sudden squall and Emma tucked the baby under her coat to protect him from the rain. She realized it made her look pregnant again. A group of reporters who were standing, smoking outside the church, ran for their cars.

The first hymn had already begun and they followed the vicar and the three old ladies who made up the choir up the aisle, forming an undignified tail to an already shambling procession. Mary moved up to let them into their usual places near the front. Emma tripped over the fat patchwork bag that her mother always carried and which had been left on the floor.

Only after she'd knelt for a moment of breath-catching, which passed as prayer, and was on her feet to sing the last verse, did she notice that the church was busier than normal. The pews were usually only this full for a baptism, when, as her father scathingly put it, 'the pagans' were in. But today there was no baptism and, besides, most of the faces were familiar. It was not that the church was full of strangers, rather, it seemed everyone had made the effort to turn out. In Elvet bad news always generated excitement. If Jeanie Long's suicide could be considered bad news.

The arthritic organist was coming to a close with a trembling chord when the door opened again. The wind must have got behind it because it closed with a bang and the congregation turned in disapproval. Dan Greenwood was standing at the back of the church next to a large, formidably ugly woman. Although Emma felt the usual thrill of excitement at his presence, she was disappointed to find Dan there. She had never seen him in church and thought he despised it. He'd made no concession in his dress, however, and was still wearing the jeans and smock from the night before. The woman was in a shapeless Crimplene dress covered with small purple flowers and a fluffy purple cardigan. Despite the cold, on her feet she wore flat leather sandals. There was something portentous about the way they stood there and for a moment Emma expected an announcement, a demand that the church be cleared because of a fire in the vicinity or a bomb threat. Even the vicar hesitated for a moment and looked at them.

The woman, however, seemed perfectly composed, even to be enjoying the attention. She took Dan by the arm and pulled him into a seat. The familiarity of the gesture disturbed Emma. What was her relationship with him? She was too young to be a mother, not ten years older than he was. But her ugliness surely made it impossible that they could be romantically attached.

31

Emma had many insecurities but was always confident that she was physically attractive. She took it for granted that James would never have asked her to marry him if she'd been fat or had acne. During the remainder of the service Emma heard the woman's voice above the others in the hymns and responses. It was clear and loud and quite out of tune.

There was no mention of Jeanie Long in the sermon and Emma thought perhaps the vicar had not heard about the suicide, but her name was there, along with Elsie Hepworth and Albert Smith, in the prayers for the deceased. Sitting with Matthew on her lap, looking down on the bent heads of the congregation who were kneeling, she tried to conjure up an image of Jeanie. She could only remember meeting her once at the Mantel home. Jeanie had been playing the piano which Keith had bought for Abigail when she showed a fleeting interest in having lessons. A tall, dark young woman, rather intense and earnest, bent over the keyboard. Then Keith had come in and she'd turned and her face had relaxed into a smile. It was hard to realize that Jeanie had been younger then than Emma was now, hardly more than a student.

The service moved on towards the Communion. Robert in his white robe was standing at the altar next to the vicar. Mary was first to take the bread and wine, then rushed to the kitchen to spoon instant coffee into vacuum jugs. The arthritic organist struggled back to her place and began to play something gentle and melancholy. A queue had formed in the aisle. Emma handed Matthew to James, who had never been confirmed, despite Robert's best efforts, and stood to take her place. Ahead of her was a tall, stooped man in a shiny grey suit which was too big for him. He wasn't a regular worshipper although she thought she might have seen him in the village. He had been sitting on his own, and no one had approached him, which was unusual. The parish ladies prided themselves on making strangers welcome.

The line moved slowly forward. The man knelt awkwardly and she took her place next to him, aware suddenly of the over-powering smell of mothballs. It had been a long time since the suit had been worn. He held out his cupped hands to take the wafer. They were hard and brown like carved wood, strong although he must have been at least sixty. The vicar caught his eye and gave a small smile of acknowledgement. Then Robert approached with the chalice, wiping the lip with a white cloth. Automatically the man reached out his hand to steady it, before raising it to his mouth. Then he looked up into Robert's face and there was a shock of recognition. As Robert moved on towards her, the man spat out the mouthful of wine in his direction. The white robe was splashed with red from the thick, sweet wine. It could, Emma thought, have been blood seeping from a wound. There was a gasp of excitement masquerading as horror from the woman on the other side of Emma. The vicar hadn't seen what had happened and Robert took no notice. The man got to his feet, and instead of returning to his pew, continued down the aisle and left the church.

The incident had happened very quickly and, hidden by the backs of the Communicants, it wouldn't have been visible from the nave. But as the man passed her, Dan Greenwood's companion got to her feet and followed him out.

Chapter Five

Every week after church they went back to Robert and Mary's house for lunch. It was an immutable part of the ritual, like the reading of the Epistle and the collect of the day. Emma thought it unfair that her mother, who spent an hour after the service pouring coffee and washing dishes, should immediately throw herself into domestic activity at home. Mary claimed to enjoy it, but the Mary she remembered from York hadn't been at all domestic. There'd been a cleaning lady then, and they'd eaten out a lot. Emma had memories of a family-run Italian restaurant, long Sunday afternoons of pasta and ice cream, and of her parents leading them tipsily home just as it was getting dark.

James always brought a couple of decent bottles of wine with him to the lunch. Emma thought he needed the alcohol to ward off the cold and numb the tedium. But when she'd suggested that they should make an excuse and stay away he wouldn't hear of it.

'I like your parents. Your father is interesting and intelligent and your mother is charming. You are fortunate that they're so supportive.'

After that implied rebuke she didn't bring up the subject again.

Springhead was a square, grey house just out of the

village. Once it had been a farmhouse, but the land had been sold off. This was the house the family had come to when they'd moved out of York. Robert had been triumphant to find it. All their savings had been used up during his social work training, and he'd never believed it would be possible to find somewhere so spacious within his budget. He'd dismissed the surveyor's report, which highlighted rising damp and woodworm in the roof joists, insisting this was the place the family were meant to be. Emma thought it had probably been for the best. She couldn't imagine him in a semi on a new estate. She told herself his ego wouldn't survive in a cramped space, though knew that was probably unfair. She was desperate, really, for his approval.

From Christopher's old room in the attic, it was still possible to see the field where Abigail's body had lain. The view hadn't changed. The land here was so flat and near to the coast that development wasn't allowed. A recent report from the Environment Agency predicted not only flooding, but the possibility that the whole peninsula could be washed away.

It was raining hard as they drove out to Springhead, so dark that they needed headlights. The ditches were full and surface water ran down the middle of the road. They were in James's Volvo. Robert and Mary had gone on ahead.

'Who was that dreadful woman with Dan?' James asked. He liked beautiful objects. Emma believed that was why he put up with her moodiness now.

'I haven't a clue. I hadn't seen her before.'

'I wondered if she could be a business contact. You

could imagine her running a craft shop. Harrogate perhaps, or Whitby.'

'Oh yes!' Sometimes she was surprised by how perceptive he could be. That was when she liked him best – when he surprised her. 'But Whitby, surely. Not classy enough for Harrogate.' She paused. 'Do you think that was why Dan was in church? To please her? In the hope of securing a sale? It seems an odd thing to do. And not like him. He always seems so straight. I can't imagine him manipulating a situation for his own ends.'

'No.' James slowed the car to a crawl. A ditch had burst its bank and formed a peaty stream across the road. 'I think he must have known Jeanie Long. He seemed very upset last night when he talked about her suicide. Church seems the right place to be sometimes, even if you have no belief.'

'I suppose he *could* have known Jeanie.' Emma was doubtful but she didn't want to dismiss the idea. It had been a long time since they had spoken like this, so easily. 'He didn't move to Elvet until later, but she was away too, at university. She'd only recently graduated when she moved in with Keith Mantel. Dan could have met her when she was still a student but I can't see how.'

James ignored the speculation. 'Dan thought the suicide might distress you.'

'I didn't know her. I was trying to think in church. I only met her once.' She hesitated. 'Do you realize it's almost exactly ten years since Abigail Mantel died? The suicide seems a horrible coincidence. Or do you think she realized and planned it? A dramatic gesture to celebrate the anniversary?'

'Perhaps,' James said after a pause. Then, 'I've always thought of suicide as a very selfish act. It's the people left behind who suffer.'

Because they were being so companionable, she was tempted to tell him about the tall man who had spat out his Communion wine at Robert, but the event still seemed so shocking that she couldn't bring herself to speak of it. James turned into the straight, bumpy track which led between two enormous fields to the house and she sat beside him in silence.

In the kitchen Robert was standing in front of the Aga. His trousers were steaming. Emma looked for some sign that the incident at the Communion rail had shocked him as much as it had her, but he said with a little smile, 'We took Miss Sanderson home. I only helped her out of the car but I'm soaked.'

'Go and change, dear. You'll catch cold.' Mary was fretting about the vegetables and he was in her way. Despite the position of authority he held at church and at work, sometimes she treated him like a child.

Robert seemed not to hear her and only moved away from the range to pour them each a glass of sherry. Emma put the baby in his seat on the floor and tucked a blanket around him. Mary lifted the chipped cast-iron lid of the stove to reveal the hotplate. The room seemed suddenly warmer. She stooped to heave a casserole from the oven and slid it onto the plate. It began to bubble. Her face was flushed from the heat and the exertion. Her fine grey hair was tied back and Emma thought she should get it cut, coloured even. A ponytail looked ridiculous on a woman of her age. Mary wrapped a tea towel around the casserole lid and took it off to stir the contents. There was a smell of lamb, garlic and tomatoes, and Emma was suddenly certain that this was the same meal they'd eaten the day Abigail was strangled. She looked sharply at her mother expecting her to remember it too, but Mary only smiled with relief that the Aga had stayed sufficiently hot to cook the meat, and Emma felt foolish. She wondered if her mind was playing tricks. Her fantasies always seemed so real.

At this time of year they ate in the kitchen. The dining room had no grate and although there were storage heaters they were barely tepid when the family got up, and cold by the evening. Emma laid the table, slipping into the familiar routine, her hands moving to the cutlery and glasses without thought. It was as if she'd never gone away. Hard to believe that, like Jeanie Long, she'd spent years at university. If she hadn't met and married James she would never have come back. Was that at the heart of her dissatisfaction with him?

Robert had finally gone upstairs to change and returned wearing jeans and a thick navy sweater. James opened one of the bottles of red wine. They took their places and waited for Robert to say grace. He always said grace even when only he and Mary were present. But today he seemed not to realize that they expected it of him, took the ladle and began to serve himself. Emma looked at her mother who only shook her head, humouring him again, and passed around a bowl of potatoes.

Mary never washed-up after Sunday lunch. Robert would put a match to the fire he'd already laid in the living room and she'd sit there, drinking coffee and reading the Sunday papers until they joined her. By then the room would be almost warm. She was always grateful for this time to herself and never forgot to thank them.

Robert and Emma were alone in the kitchen. James had taken the baby upstairs to change him.

'Who was the man who spat at you?'

He answered without turning away from the sink. 'Michael Long, Jeanie's father.'

He'd changed, she thought. The Michael Long she remembered had been strong, broad shouldered, loud.

'Why did he do it?'

'People often need someone to blame at a time like this.'

'But why you?'

'I had to submit a report to the parole board. I couldn't recommend her as suitable for parole.'

'Jeanie Long was your *client*?'

Now he did turn round. He dried his hands deliberately on the threadbare towel hanging from the Aga, then sat next to her at the table.

'Only for the past twelve months.'

'Didn't anyone think that was wrong? That it might be considered, I don't know, some sort of conflict of interest?'

'Of course we discussed the suitability of my taking over the case, but the problem wasn't one of a conflict of interest. You never appeared as a witness for the prosecution. It was a matter of whether I could develop a relationship with Jeanie, whether I could deal with her in a fair and open-minded way, and we decided that I could. The question of her guilt or innocence never came up. Not at that point. That was decided at the original trial and at a later appeal. I didn't know Jeanie before she was sentenced. And I didn't know Abigail, even though the two of you were friends.'

And now she thought about it, she supposed he was right. There had only been six months between the Winter family's move to Elvet and Abigail's death. During that time Springhead had been even more inhospitable than it was now. The elderly couple who'd lived in it before had only used two rooms, the rest of the house had been full of rubbish. There had been disasters with the plumbing, embarrassing smells, sudden blackouts. It hadn't been a place to bring a new friend. All the sleepovers, the giggly nights of videos, chocolate cake and illicit bottles of wine, had taken place at the Mantel home. Mary had met Abigail on a couple of occasions, at school events, the brief encounters on the doorstep when she dropped Emma off at the Old Chapel. Robert, eager to make an impression in his first post as probation officer had worked long hours, and was seldom around.

'Is it true that the case was to be reopened?'

'I presume it still will be. If Jeanie was innocent, someone else must have killed Abigail Mantel.'

They sat for a moment looking at each other. Emma thought it had been a day for unusual conversations. Her father had never spoken so simply or so frankly to her. By now it was quite dark outside. The wind blew through gaps in the window and moved the heavy curtain which covered it. From upstairs came the sound of the baby chortling.

'Did *you* think she was innocent?'

'It wasn't my place to make that sort of judgement.

I'm an officer of the court. I have to accept the court's decision. She always claimed she was innocent, but so do many of the offenders I work with.'

'What was she like?'

He paused again and his hesitation made him almost unrecognizable to her. He had always been a man of certainties.

'She was quiet, intelligent . . .' There was another break in his speech, almost a stutter. 'Most of all she was angry, the most angry person I've ever met. She felt betrayed.'

'Who did she feel had betrayed her?'

'Her parents, I think. Her father, at least. But most of all Keith Mantel. She couldn't understand why he never visited her. Even after he'd asked her to move out of the house she still believed he loved her.'

'But she'd killed his daughter! What could she expect?'

'Certainly he thought she had. And according to Jeanie that was the worst betrayal of all. That he could think her capable of murder.'

'Why didn't you recommend her for parole?'

Emma thought he would refuse to tell her. He never talked about the details of his work. It was confidential, he'd say. He had the same responsibility as a priest to keep secrets. But today he seemed eager to talk. It was as if he needed to justify his decision to her.

'Partly it was her anger. I couldn't be sure she could control it. At the trial the prosecution claimed that she strangled Abigail in a moment of rage and jealousy. I couldn't take the risk that she might lose control again, strike out at someone who'd hurt her. It might have been different if she'd shown a willingness to cooperate with the prison authorities. I asked her to attend one of the anger management courses which we run at Spinney Fen but she refused. She said that if she attended it would be like admitting her guilt, admitting that her behaviour needed to change.'

James appeared at the door with Matthew in his arms. She caught his eye. 'Can you give us a few minutes?' she said. He was surprised – usually she was only too happy to be rescued from her family – but he backed away.

Robert, still engrossed in his own thoughts, seemed not to notice the interruption. He continued, 'Then there was the home circumstances report. I went to see Michael Long to discuss it. Jeanie's mother used to visit her in prison but Michael never did. Since Mrs Long died, Jeanie had no visits at all. I wanted to find out if there was a possibility of a reconciliation. If Michael had agreed that she could stay with him on release, even for a short period, that might have made a difference to the board.'

'But he wouldn't?'

'He said he couldn't face having her in the house.' Robert looked up from the table. 'So you can see why he felt so guilty, why he needed to blame me. He had believed his own daughter to be a murderer.'

Chapter Six

Michael slipped out through the church door and
paused to catch his breath. He was shaking. The rain
was blowing straight into the open porch. It stung
his face and hit the grey fabric of his suit, each drop
spreading as the Communion wine had spread through
the fibres of Robert Winter's white surplice. Michael
struggled into the waterproof jacket he still carried
over his arm, and although the storm showed no sign
of abating he started off for the road. The service would
soon be over. The old crones inside would be coming
through on their way to the hall for coffee and he
couldn't bear the thought of them gawping.

The sweet taste of the Communion wine remained
in his mouth and on his lips, and suddenly he was desperate for a real drink to wash it away. He hesitated
outside the Anchor. He hadn't been inside for years,
but still he was tempted. Then he realized the place
would be busy with men waiting for their Sunday din-
ners to be cooked, and he didn't want to meet anyone
he knew. He didn't think he'd manage to be polite. The
fury which had overcome him when he'd seen Winter,
coming towards him with the chalice, still roared
around his head. He wasn't proud of the scene he'd

made, but if he hadn't spat at him, he'd have had to hit him. He still wanted to hit someone.

It had been a crazy idea to come to the service in the first place. He saw that now. Whatever he'd hoped to get out of the ritual, he'd been disappointed. Peg had been the one for the church, not him. He'd always thought it a daft do. Grown men dressing up in frocks. What had he expected anyway? Jeanie's voice sailing out of the rafters, 'It's all right, dad. I forgive you.'

He lived in a small row of council bungalows, just behind the church, had done since he moved from the Point after Peg had died. The reporters who'd been there when he'd left, still stood on the corner, shouting their stupid questions and waving their microphones. He ignored them and opened the door just enough so he could slide in. He didn't want them looking inside. He thought, as he always did coming in, how small and cramped it was. How dark. That was one of the reasons he didn't like going out much. Coming back each time was like being locked up in a prison cell. He hated it.

He hadn't thought Jeanie had hated prison. Of course no one would enjoy it, but he hadn't thought being shut in would send her into a panic. She'd never liked the outdoors much. She'd been terrified in a small boat, even when it was flat calm and she had a lifejacket on. She preferred being inside with her music, and she'd had that in prison. They'd taken her a cassette player and a load of tapes. Her music was all she'd really needed. That was how it had seemed to him and Peg when she was a youngster. She'd shut them out, excluded them. They'd brought her up and that didn't seem fair. Like she'd dumped them when they stopped being useful to her. Then she'd hanged herself and he wondered if he'd got it wrong about her not hating the prison. That and other things.

He tried not to think that he might have been wrong. If Jeanie had hated the prison even as much as he hated this place, it must have been a nightmare for her. He couldn't contemplate that, whatever she'd done, and grasped around for someone else to blame, knowing it was unreasonable even as he was doing it. He settled on Winter, the do-gooder, the pretend vicar. *He* was an easy target.

In the cupboard in the kitchen there was a litre bottle of cheap whisky he'd had delivered from the Co-op with the last lot of groceries. He half filled a tumbler and drank it down in burning gulps, then ran his tongue around his lips. He still fancied he could taste the wine and poured himself another glass, carried it with him.

He walked through to the bedroom and began to change out of his suit. He took the trousers off first and folded them over the back of the chair. Some change fell out of the pocket but he left it where it dropped. He thought of the bedroom in the house on the Point, the window so close to the water that its reflection bounced off the ceiling. It had been as near to being on a boat as you could get on dry land. There had been a continuous watery soundtrack – the call of seabirds and waders, the drag of the tide on the shingle, the breaking of waves. He had taken it for granted until he'd moved here and had been almost suffocated by the bungalow's dense and dreadful silence. Here, the rooms were so small that he could stand with his arms outstretched and almost touch the walls on each side.

He should never have retired as coxswain of the pilot launch.

That was what Michael told himself, standing in his underpants, struggling to get the fold in his trousers in the right place. But to tell the truth he hadn't had much choice when it came down to it. If he hadn't resigned from the launch they'd have had him out anyway, using the drinking as an excuse. As if all the pilots didn't like a drink. At least this way there'd been a bit of dignity in his going. Peg would have approved of that. But he missed it with the same ache as he missed Peg. He missed the crack with the pilots and the girls in the data centre. He missed the satisfaction of bringing the launch into the lee of a big ship, holding it steady, while the pilot climbed down the ladder and jumped aboard. It hadn't been like him to go without a fight and it still rankled. He'd felt the same humiliation as when Winter had turned up on the doorstep of the bungalow wanting to talk about Jeanie.

It had been a while ago now, but Michael still remembered the encounter with great clarity. He had gone over it many times in his mind. It was like one of those fairy tales about giants and monsters that children return to: frightening, but comforting in its familiarity. And it stopped him from thinking of worse things. Jeanie hanging in her cell by a bit of torn sheet. Him being wrong about his only daughter.

So, Winter had turned up on his doorstep. It would have been January or February almost a year ago. Michael had only gone to answer it because he'd thought it would be the lad from the Co-op with his groceries. Normally he didn't bother answering the door. He had no time for people selling things or collecting for charities. But there was this man. Winter. Michael hadn't recognized him. He'd been dressed in a brown duffel coat, the sort naval officers used to wear in the war, but Winter had had the hood up, pulled right down over his forehead, so Michael had been reminded more of a monk.

'Mr Long,' he'd said. 'I wonder if I might come in for a minute.'

Michael had been about to slam the door on him, to mutter something about it not being convenient, but the man had put his face very close, so Michael felt he couldn't breathe, and he'd said in a quiet, preachy voice, 'It's about Jeanie.'

And it was the last thing he'd been expecting, so he'd stepped back in surprise, and Winter had taken that as an invitation to come in.

'Perhaps I could make us both some tea,' he'd said. And Michael had been so affronted by the cheek of the man that he couldn't speak. And again Winter had taken the shocked silence as an invitation. He'd walked into the kitchen as if it were his own and filled the kettle right to the top with no thought for the extra electricity that might use.

They'd sat in the little front room. It was filled with the few bits of furniture Michael had brought with him from the house on the Point and they'd had to sit almost knee to knee in the big armchairs.

'What's Jeanie to you?' Michael had demanded. He still remembered that. He'd thrust his face towards Winter's hoping to cause the same panic *he'd* felt on the doorstep. 'What's Jeanie to you?'

'I'm her probation officer,' Winter had said. 'I have to prepare a report.'

'She didn't get probation. She got life. And there were reports enough done at the time.'

Too many reports. All of them prying. All of them wanting to find someone else to blame for what Jeanie had done. Him and Peg had never been given copies of the reports of course. They'd been excluded in that process too. But he guessed that they'd featured. It was always the parents' fault, wasn't it? The reports would have said that they'd never understood Jeanie, never given her what she'd needed. He could figure out that much from what had been said in court.

'This is different,' Winter had said. He'd had one of those voices stuck-up teachers use with daft children. Patient, but as if it's a real strain being patient. As if he was a saint to be able to manage it. 'Jeanie will soon be eligible for parole. If she's released back into the community, it'll be my job to supervise her on licence.'

'They're not thinking of letting her out?'

'Don't you think she should be?'

'It just seems like she's been in no time. And after what she did to that lass . . .'

'She still says she's innocent, you know . . .' He'd paused as if he expected a response from Michael. Michael had been staring at the little window which was shrouded in net so he couldn't see out, unable to take in the notion that his daughter might soon be released. 'It won't help her case for parole, I'm afraid, insisting she didn't commit the murder. Prisoners are supposed to confront their offending behaviour and show remorse for their actions. I've tried to persuade her.'

'I wouldn't think she'd be much good at remorse.'

'I'm new to the case, Mr Long.' Winter had leaned

forward, so Michael had been able to smell his breath, peppermint masking something spicy from the night before. Not booze, of course. Winter wouldn't be a drinker. There wasn't the life in him for that. 'But there's no record of you having visited your daughter.'

'Peg went, before she got too poorly.' The words had come out before Michael could stop them, though he'd sworn to himself that he'd tell Winter nothing. He'd driven his wife on visiting days, dropped her right outside the prison gate, because there always seemed to be a wind when they went and rain blown almost horizontal. Then he'd taken the car to the visitors' car park and sat with his paper lying unread on the steering wheel until all the people streamed out. He'd been surprised by how ordinary they'd looked, the parents and the husbands of the women locked up. From a distance he'd not been able to pick Peg out from the rest.

'But not you?' Winter had kept the patient voice but his eyes had been full of judgement and distaste.

'Nor Mantel,' Michael had said. 'He never visited her either.'

'Hardly the same thing, Mr Long. He believed she'd killed his only daughter.'

And Michael had turned away at that, acknowledging the justice of the words, but hating the contempt in them.

'And he told Jeanie that he loved her,' he'd said quietly. A futile attempt at defiance. Then, on firmer ground, 'Have you got a daughter, Winter?'

'That's hardly relevant.'

'Aye, you do have a daughter.' He'd been able to tell by something in Winter's face. 'Imagine how you'd feel if your lass did something like that. Strangling a child

just because she'd come between her and her lover.
You'd feel able to support her, would you? You'd not
mind visiting her in that place?'

Winter had hesitated for a moment and Michael
had felt a stab of triumph. Then the probation officer
had resumed in the saintly voice which made Michael
want to slap him, 'I might hate the crime, Mr Long, but
I'd not hate the girl who'd committed it.' He'd set down
his cup and continued briskly, 'Now about the parole.'

'What about it?'

'The parole board would need to know she had
somewhere to come back to. Support.'

'You're asking if she can move in with me?'

'I know you've found it difficult, but it need only be
for a short time until she sorted out somewhere more
suitable.'

'Have you been listening to a word I've said, man?'
Michael had discovered that he was screaming. 'She
killed that lass and that killed my wife. How can I have
her under the same roof as me?'

Only now it seemed she hadn't killed Abigail Mantel. Sitting here on a wet Sunday after church, with
nothing to cling on to but the remains of the whisky,
he kept coming up against the fact and sliding away
from it. It was too much for him to accept all at once.
If Jeanie hadn't been a murderer, what sort of monster
was he? He'd turned her away. Outside the sky dark-
ened but he still didn't move. Only when the taped
bells in the church tower started up again, scratchy and
raucous, for the evening service, so that he knew
people would be walking past, did he get up and draw
the curtains and switch on the light.

Chapter Seven

The next morning Michael was awake before six as usual. It was a habit he'd never get out of now. Activity was an addiction. He'd worked twelve-hour shifts as coxswain of the pilot launch, and even after being on call all night, he'd not been able to sleep during the day. The enforced idleness of retirement made him panic. Jeanie had been lazy. Some days she'd spent hours in her room, and when he'd asked her what she was doing, she'd say she was working. It hadn't seemed much like work to him. Occasionally she'd left her door open a crack and he'd peered in. She'd be lying on her bed, not always even dressed, and there'd be music playing and she'd have her eyes closed. He liked some music – a brass band or a march, a tune with a beat, the songs from the old musicals – but she never played anything like that. This would be strings usually, or a piano, something high-pitched which made him want to piss. 'Wee-wee music' he'd called it to her, sneering, when she was being stony and blank. He didn't know why her stillness had irritated him so much, but it had. He'd felt like screaming and lashing out at her. He never had but the anger and resentment had bubbled away. Only Peg knew it was there.

Maybe they should never have had a child. They'd

been happy enough as they were. He had been, at least. He'd never really known what Peg had thought about it. Or perhaps by the time Jeanie arrived he'd been too old, too set in his ways. But he thought he'd done right by his daughter. He couldn't see what he could have done differently. He'd paid up for the music lessons, hadn't he? He'd driven her every week into the town, listened to the scratchy violin, the repeated scales on the upright piano which had belonged to Peg's mum. Peg had played the piano too. After a couple of brandies when they'd had a few friends round, she'd played for them. It had always been songs which belonged to their parents' generation, old music hall turns, but they'd all joined in, making up the words as they went, collapsing in laughter before they'd finished. He couldn't remember ever having seen Jeanie laugh like that, even as a kid.

At least that daughter of Mantel's had had a bit of life about her, a bit of spirit. He'd seen it during the Sunday dinner when they'd all come to the Point. You could tell by the way she'd tossed her head; she'd wanted you to look at her. If Jeanie had been a bit more like that perhaps they wouldn't have fought so much. Except, he thought, there had never been much real argument. More a bad-tempered silence, with Peg acting as a buffer between them, squashed between Jeanie's surly resentment and his anger. The Sunday dinner had been Peg's idea. 'Jeanie's obviously mad about the man. He's older than her but that's no reason to disapprove, is it? You're older than me. It's not like he's still married.' He'd tried to explain to her that there was more to it than that, but she hadn't been able to see it.

At seven o'clock Michael allowed himself to get out of bed and make some tea. Still all he could think about was Jeanie and how he might have got her wrong. The anger had become a habit like waking up too early, only now he had no one to turn it against except himself. Even conjuring up images of the probation officer didn't work any more. While the kettle was boiling he thought of the whisky in the cupboard under the sink and it was a real effort not to reach down and fetch it out. Then he heard Peg's voice. Had to stop himself from turning round because he could almost believe she was in the room with him. *Drinking before breakfast, Michael Long? I'd not put up with that.* As he squeezed out the tea bag against the side of his cup it occurred to him that he might be going mad. What he was going through would send anyone crazy. How could he stand the same thoughts and memories rolling around in his head until he died? That was why he'd gone to church of course. He'd thought there might be magic, that when he put the round cardboard wafer on his tongue, they'd all disappear. It was nothing to do with repentance or forgiveness at all. But it hadn't worked. Nothing would.

He took the tea to the bedroom but he didn't get back into the crumpled sheets. He sat on the edge, holding the cup in one hand and the saucer in the other. He heard himself slurping the hot liquid and imagined Jeanie's horrified face whenever he'd done that in public. Mantel's daughter had only laughed. It had been at the same lunch, the only time Mantel had stepped foot inside the house on the Point as far as he knew. Peg had made a pot of tea after the meal, and he'd drunk it as he always did, only perhaps he was even noisier because he had been drinking before they arrived to give himself a bit of courage. There'd been a silence, the look of disgust on Jeanie's face, then Abigail Mantel had thrown back her head and laughed. Somehow that had broken the ice and they'd all joined in; even Jeanie had eventually managed a thin smile.

The prison governor had come to tell him about the suicide. It had been about this time of day, maybe a little later. Michael had opened the door to fetch in the milk and he'd been standing there, a tall grey man in a suit and a black overcoat. He must have been planning in his mind what he intended to say, because his lips had been moving. The sight of Michael, still in his dressing gown, had surprised him. He'd recovered himself quickly though. You had to think on your feet if you were a prison governor.

'Mr Long,' he'd said. 'I'm from Spinney Fen . . .'

Michael had interrupted. 'You're wasting your time. I told the other one. I can't have her here.'

'Jeanie's dead, Mr Long. I think you'd best let me in.'

And he'd sat in the small front room for more than an hour telling Michael what had happened. How an officer had come to unlock Jeanie for the morning and had found her. How she'd already been dead for a long time, probably soon after lock-up the night before. How there'd been nothing anybody could do. 'We're all dreadfully sorry, Mr Long.' Sounding as if he meant it. The bombshell had been dropped when he'd been about to leave. 'It's possible that Jeanie was innocent, Mr Long. I understand the police intend to reopen the Abigail Mantel case. Jeanie hadn't been informed. There was nothing official, you understand. Nothing we could do at this point. But I thought you should know.' He'd paused in the hall. 'Would you like to see your daughter, Mr Long? I can arrange that if you'd like it.'

For a moment Michael had been tempted. Then he'd thought, *I don't have the right. I wouldn't see her when she was alive. What right do I have to intrude on her now?*

He'd shaken his head without speaking.

The man had walked out of the front door, stooping as he went, because he was so tall that he was afraid of hitting his head on the lintel. Michael had watched him go to his car, which was bright red and rather sporty, and had decided that he could kill himself too. There'd been one indulgent day when he'd fantasized how best to go about it – hanging like Jeanie herself, or pills, or drowning. He'd fancied drowning. This time of year when the water was cold it didn't take long to lose consciousness and there was something fitting about a boatman sliding to rest under the waves. He hadn't done it, of course. He'd seen it as cheating. He'd stay around long enough for Abigail Mantel's killer to be brought to justice. He owed Jeanie that much.

Michael went to the bathroom and washed and shaved. The last few days he hadn't bothered, except yesterday just before church, but if he were going to stay alive he supposed he'd have to do it properly. Play by the rules to the end. For the same reason he put some bread under the grill for breakfast and forced himself to eat it.

He was drying up the plate and the cup when the doorbell rang. It was just after eight thirty. It wasn't the day for the woman who came once a week to clean for him, so he ignored it. It would be the press again, some reporter offering a fortune for a picture of Jeanie, promising to tell his side of the story. The bell continued, a sharp continuous ring, as if someone was leaning against the button. He went into the hall. Through the frosted glass of the front door he saw a shape, a bulky shadow.

'Go away,' he shouted. 'Leave me alone. I'll call the police.'

The noise of the bell stopped and the letter box flap was pushed open from outside. He saw an open mouth, a throat, moving lips.

'I *am* the police, pet, and if you don't fancy a little jaunt in a jam-sandwich to the police station you'd best let me in.'

He opened the door. A woman stood on the doorstep. Something about the way she stood there reminded him of Peg, and he changed his attitude and felt well disposed towards her for no other reason than that. Perhaps it was her size which triggered the memory, the thick legs and heavy, comforting bust. But there was something else. The way she smiled, knowing he was a grouchy old git, but miraculously seeming to like him anyway. She walked into the hall.

'Bit poky in here,' she said.

He didn't mind. Not like he minded the probation officer Winter pushing his way in, presuming to know something of what he was feeling. She was the sort of woman who said what she thought as soon as she thought it. There was no putting on a show for the rest of the world.

'I saw you in church yesterday,' she went on, 'followed you out. But you seemed a bit upset and I thought it would best wait a day.'

'Probably just as well.'

'Have you had breakfast?' she asked.

He nodded.

'Must be coffee time then.'

'I don't have coffee,' he said. 'Will tea do?'

'It will if it's strong. I can't bear weak tea.'

She was still standing when he came into the lounge with the tray. He'd made tea in a pot, and covered it with a cosy Peg had knitted using up old scraps of wool. There were mugs. He thought she might sneer at a small cup. She was looking at the photographs on a shelf in the alcove next to the gas fire. One of him standing next to the boat that day they'd given him the award, a big grin on his face which had more to do with the ale he'd supped, than with the medal. And another of him and Peg on their wedding day, him as skinny as those Africans they showed on telly whenever there was a famine, her all soft and round with a circle of silk flowers in her hair and roses in her hand.

'No picture of Jeanie?' the woman asked. 'You didn't sell them to the press?'

'I wouldn't have done that!' He was horrified she could think him capable of it.

'No,' she said calmly. 'Of course you wouldn't. Why no photos then?'

'I thought she was guilty. All the way through I thought she was guilty.'

'Only natural. All the evidence pointed that way.'

'So you think she was guilty too?' He couldn't tell if it was hope he felt, or dread.

'Nah.' She paused. 'You know she said she'd gone to London, the day Abigail was killed?'

'Aye. No one saw her.'

'A witness has come forward. A student who knew her. He swears she was in King's Cross that day. I've talked to the lad. If he's lying I could get a job modelling nude for the cover of *Vogue*.'

'It wasn't just that I thought she killed that schoolgirl.' Michael felt a need to explain. 'It was that I blamed her for Peg dying too.'

'Did Peg think she'd committed the murder?'

He shook his head. 'Not for a minute. She fought all the way through for Jeanie, talked to the press, the police, the lawyers. The effort wore her out.'

'I don't suppose your attitude helped, you stubborn bugger.'

He didn't have any answer to that so he poured out the tea, swirling the pot first to make sure it was strong enough. She sat heavily on an armchair. He put the mug carefully on the small table in front of her, waited anxiously while she tasted it.

'Perfect,' she said. 'Just as I like it.'

He took his own place then and waited for her to explain.

'I'm Vera Stanhope. Inspector. Northumbria police. A case like this they send an outsider in. Fresh eyes. You know. Check they did everything right first time round.'

'There was a woman in charge before.' It had been strange to him at first. A woman leading a team of men. But when he'd met her a couple of times he could understand how she managed it.

'So there was.' Vera was noncommittal.

'What was she called?' His memory was a sludge as he grasped for a name. All he could see was a woman in silhouette, sat in the kitchen at the house on the Point. Light from a low winter sun was pouring through the window behind her. She was very smart in a black suit, short skirt, fitted jacket. He'd noticed the legs in sheer, black tights. Even then, when they'd thought Jeanie was a murderer, he'd found himself looking at the legs and wondering what it would be like to stroke them.

'Fletcher,' Vera said. 'Caroline Fletcher.'

'She thought Jeanie was guilty. Right from the start. Not that she wasn't polite with us. Perhaps that was how I could tell. The sympathy, you know. The pity. She knew what we'd have to go through when it came to court.'

'She left the service a while back,' Vera said. 'You'll have to make do with me this time. Not so nice to look at, huh?'

'Easier to talk to though.' He hadn't found it easy to talk to Inspector Fletcher. She asked a lot of questions but he had the feeling that she wasn't really listening, that behind the polite smile and the glossy eyes her mind was already racing ahead to form conclusions that had nothing to do with the words he was speaking.

'That's why I'm here,' Vera said. 'I want you to talk to me.'

'I could have got her parole,' he said suddenly. 'If I'd said she could come here, that I'd support her when she came out. She'd still be alive if I'd believed her story.'

There was an angry set to her mouth as she put down her mug and faced up to him. He thought she was going to let fly at him, tell him what she thought of his lack of faith in his daughter.

'You didn't put her there.' She spoke very slowly and deliberately, an emphasis on every syllable as if she was marking the beat in a piece of music. 'We did that. Us. The police and the Crown Prosecution Service and the judge and the jury. Not you. You're not to blame.'

He didn't believe her but he was grateful to her for saying it.

'What do you want to know?'

'Everything,' she said. 'Everything about that time.'

'I'm not sure I'm up to remembering. I might get things wrong. Details.'

'Nah,' she said. 'It's the details we get right. That's what we remember best.'

Chapter Eight

Peg had been the only other person Michael could have talked to like this, and when he broke off his story occasionally to look at Vera's face – to check that she was listening or judge her reaction to something he'd said – he was shocked because he half expected to see his wife's features. Vera always *was* listening.

He started right from the beginning. 'I was never bothered about kiddies. I thought we were happy as we were, but it mattered to Peg. She'd have liked a big family, I think – she was one of five girls. Her father farmed up Hornsea way. When she found out she was pregnant she was thrilled. She'd pretty well given up hope of it happening. I was pleased for her, like, but not so much for myself. I couldn't see how things could get any better.

'And then Jeanie was born on the night of a big spring tide. She was long and skinny, even as a baby, with thick, black hair.'

'You were living on the Point then?'

'Aye, it was a part of the job. And we didn't think it'd be a bad place for a child to grow up. There was space to run around. Good fresh air. It's not a lonely place. There were other kids in the lifeboat houses and when she was bigger, Peg brought her into Elvet for the

61

playgroup. But she never needed company much, even when she was little. It was always books and music with her. Right from the start.'

He looked up. 'Peg always said she took after me, but I could never see it myself. I'm not one for books. "Jeanie's proud and she's stubborn," she'd say. "Who do you think she gets that from?"'

'I've been trying to trace her friends,' Vera said. 'I'd like to talk to other people who knew her. There must have been girls at school . . .'

'There were friends, I suppose. Lasses from school like you said. She'd go to their birthday parties and Peg'd invite them back to the Point for tea.' He remembered those days. The house had seemed full of them – pretty little girls in party dresses who giggled and chattered and chased each other around the garden. 'But I could tell Jeanie was never close to them. There was something solemn about her. She took life too seriously. I don't know where she got that from. Peg and I always enjoyed a laugh.'

'What about boyfriends?'

'There was no one while she was at school. She said she was too busy with exams. Peg would tease her about it sometimes, tell her she couldn't spend all her time working. And she'd say – dead serious, "But I like work, Mum." There might have been lads at the university but we wouldn't know about that. She went away to Leeds. She kept in touch – phoned her mother every week and came home every now and again for her Sunday lunch – but she never mentioned a boyfriend.' He paused. 'There might have been someone. She might have told Peg and asked her to keep it a secret from me. She thought I was always criticizing and perhaps I was. I should have made more effort to get on with her.'

'And she should have made more effort to get on with you,' Vera said gently.

'No. I thought so at the time. But I was too full of myself.'

'What do you mean?'

He struggled to explain. It was hard without boasting and this wasn't the time for blowing his own trumpet. 'I was someone in this village then. Parish councillor. Coxswain of the launch which takes the pilots out to the ships in the river. You'll have seen the launches if you've been down to the Point. Moored by the long jetty.'

She nodded.

'There's a buzz about that. An excitement. That's why you do it, but all the same it's a worthwhile job and you think you deserve some respect.' He hesitated again. 'Peg thought children have no obligation to their parents. She said they don't ask to be born. The obligation all goes one way. I didn't see it then but now I think she was right.'

Vera didn't express an opinion on the question. 'I've never had any kids myself,' she said.

He would have liked to ask if she'd ever wanted children. He'd assumed that all women got broody as they got older. But although he felt close to the fat woman whose presence seemed to take up half his lounge, he thought the question was a bit personal.

'How did Jeanie meet Keith Mantel?' Vera asked suddenly, and he was glad the interview had moved on to surer ground. He was better with facts.

'Here in Elvet. In the Anchor. She'd worked there

part-time since she was at school. Washing up, waitressing, a bit of bar work when she got older. They thought the world of her. The most reliable student they'd ever employed, Veronica the landlady said.'

'You must have been proud of her.'

'Aye,' he said reluctantly. 'I was. And not just about her work at the pub. About the exams and the music and everything. I was too stubborn to tell her. Most people liked me then. Mike Long, life and soul of the party, holding the village together. She didn't. I couldn't understand it, couldn't forgive her for not being taken in by me.' He shot her another look. 'Sorry. Just talking daft.'

'Wasn't Jeanie still at the university when she met Mantel? I don't understand what she was doing here. She'd hardly have come back to Elvet from Leeds for a Saturday job.'

'She was on study leave before her finals. Home for a couple of weeks before the exams. Peg had persuaded her to come back. She said it would be quieter for her to revise. Really, of course, she wanted to pamper her a bit. Feed her up. Veronica must have heard she was here because she phoned up in a panic. Would Jeanie mind helping out in the Anchor for a couple of evenings? One of the barmaids was off sick and she was rushed off her feet. So Jeanie went in as a favour.'

'And that's where she met Keith Mantel?'

'So it seems. Not that she told us at the time, of course.'

'How did she come to move in with him?'

There was a silence. 'That was my fault,' he said at last. 'Speaking my mind without thinking. As usual.'

Vera didn't say anything. She wasn't going to help him out on this one.

'She came home as soon as the exams were finished. We weren't expecting it. She'd talked about spending the summer travelling. She wanted to go to Italy.'

'On her own?'

'Aye. That was how she preferred to be. Until then at least. Any road, she came back. The story was that she needed to be around in case there were any auditions. It made sense. She'd always wanted to be a professional musician and it's a competitive business. She said she couldn't afford to be out of touch all summer. Peg was delighted. And Veronica took her back on in the pub.'

'How did you get on with her when she came home?'

'Better. I thought it was because she'd been away. She didn't seem so touchy. And maybe I was getting a bit more mellow in my old age.'

'But really it was because she was in love.'

He shot a furious look at her but she wasn't mocking him. There was nothing amused about her face. She looked very sad.

'I saw them together,' Michael said. 'Her and that Mantel. He must have given her a lift home from work after the lunch-time shift. She'd have thought I'd be out. They were sitting in that flash car of his. The roof was down. They were all over each other like a rash. He had his hand up her shirt.' He felt himself blush like a girl. 'It was broad daylight.'

'Why did you disapprove so much?' Vera asked. 'I mean he was older than her but he wasn't married.

And you'd wanted her to lighten up a bit. She must have been twenty-one then. Not a child any more.' He didn't answer and she persisted. 'You did recognize him when you saw them in the car together? If he was a regular in the Anchor, you must have known who he was.'

'I knew him all right. He had a reputation, did Keith Mantel. Still does, come to that.'

'What as?' she asked innocently.

'As a crook,' he said. 'That's what.'

'I've checked his record. He's never been charged with anything. There've been a couple of motoring offences – speeding mostly – but nothing serious.'

'He's never been caught, that's all. Like I say, he's a crook.'

'And why do you say that, Mr Long?' She grinned at him and he sensed a challenge in her words, but sympathy too. She had her own ideas about Keith Mantel. 'What do you know about our Keith?'

The cramped little room seemed more airless than before. He felt his chest tighten and his breathing was shallow and fast. What was going on here? This woman was bringing him painfully back to life. She was the first real human contact he'd had since Peg had died. The first person to take him seriously.

'He's a charmer,' Long said. 'He had everyone fooled when he first moved here.'

'But not you. You'd have seen through him.'

'I had my suspicions.' He paused, teasing her, making her wait. 'There was that house for a start. He wasn't the first to apply for planning permission to convert the old chapel, but it had always been turned down before. Not just because of the risk of flooding and erosion. There was no access road, see, and this area's not zoned for housing. Only building for agricultural purpose is allowed. There's nothing agricultural about that mansion Mantel put up for himself. He must have greased a few palms to get that through the planning committee.'

'There'd have been bad feeling in the village about that . . .' She was playing straight man to him. Stooge. He knew and he didn't mind.

'At first maybe. Then there he was in the Anchor, buying drinks all round. A donation to the cricket club to mend the pavilion roof. Another to the village school to buy a couple of computers. He had them eating out of his hand. And he got the sympathy vote for bringing up the little girl on his own. It was soon forgotten he was here under false pretences.'

'But not by you. You didn't forget.'

Michael knew what she was doing. Making him feel clever. Special. But all the same he loved it. 'I never took to him. He got himself elected onto the parish council. We didn't see eye to eye.'

She let that go for the moment. 'You must have had more reason to dislike him than that. He'd not be the first to pull a few strings to get a new house built. Not major league crime.'

'I made a few enquiries.'

'That's the sort of thing I'd say. Maybe you should have been a detective.'

'I'd have been a good one,' he said seriously. 'Not boasting, like.' Then they grinned at each other.

'What did you come up with, then?' She leaned forward so her elbows were resting on her broad knees.

The dress, which his Peg'd not have had in the house as a dish rag, was stretched between them.

Michael leaned back in his chair and half closed his eyes. All this he knew by heart. He'd just never had the chance to share it. 'Mantel grew up locally, in Crill, the town up the coast. Father was a schoolmaster. Mother worked in the post office. A nice family by all accounts. But it was never enough for Mantel. He had expensive tastes, even when he was a lad. He was still at school when he started working for an elderly widow who lived close by – a bit of gardening, odd jobs, shopping. A companion he called himself.'

'Kind.'

'Aye, you could call it that. When she died she left him all her money in her will.'

'She had no family?'

'A nephew in Surrey. He tried to contest it, but it seemed above board.'

'Mantel had her charmed, then?'

'Or scared her witless.'

They sat for a moment in silence. They could hear the ticking from the fat, round clock on the mantelpiece.

'That's when he started investing in property. Still not twenty, and he bought a couple of terraced houses in the town. Let them out to students. Bought a few more. One of them burnt down. Probably faulty electrics, but no proof and he collected the insurance anyway. He was lucky no one was trapped inside. The college authorities weren't happy, though, and by then he'd decided the students weren't ideal tenants. Too lippy. Too ready to complain. They knew their rights. So, he started taking in families on housing benefit.'

'Lots of scope there for a scam. Especially when the benefit's paid straight to the landlord.'

'Right. And if money was tight he'd offer his families a bit to tide them over.'

'Like I said,' Vera's eyes were shining. He could see she was enjoying herself, 'kind.'

'Not at the rate of interest he was charging.'

They stared at each other.

'I knew some of that,' she said at last. 'I'd heard he was into benefit fraud, loans. Not for years of course. Now he's a respectable businessman. Urban regeneration's his thing. Working with the community. He has lunch every other week with the Prince of Wales. Almost a saint.' She paused for breath before continuing, 'I never knew where he got his money in the first place. It must have taken a bit of digging around to get at that.'

'I'm a stubborn bugger. I don't give up.'

'It must have been personal though. You must have started checking up on Mantel before he took up with your Jeanie.'

'I'd found out some of it before then. Took it more seriously later.'

'What made you start?'

'He challenged my authority in the village. Made me look a fool. I couldn't have that. I thought if I told the others where his money had come from, the sort of man he really was, they'd drop him.'

'Did you tell them?'

'I didn't get the chance. In the beginning I didn't have the proof. And when Jeanie moved in with him, they'd have thought that that was what it was about. A grudge because he was screwing my daughter. Then his little girl died and it didn't seem so important any more.'

'But you did try to tell Jeanie?'

He nodded. 'That afternoon when I'd seen them together in his car outside my house. I was angry. It all came out wrong. She didn't believe me. She packed up all her things and stormed out.'

'That was when she moved in with Mantel?'

'Yes. So it *was* all my fault. The girl's death. Jeanie's imprisonment. If I'd kept my temper none of that would have happened.'

'We don't know that. Not yet. When Mantel asked Jeanie to leave, she came back to you?'

'She didn't like it, but she had nowhere else to go. She was still infatuated with Mantel. She wouldn't move away. And we'd mended things a bit between us. That was Peg's doing. "I know you don't like it, but we'll lose her altogether if we don't make the effort." Peg invited them round for Sunday lunch – Mantel, Jeanie and the daughter. You'd have thought we'd had royalty in the house the effort that went into that meal. It was one of the hardest things I've ever done, sitting down at the table with that man. Watching him smiling. Knowing damn well he knew exactly what I was going through.' Michael paused. 'I've wondered over the years if that was why he took up with Jeanie. Why he stayed with her so long, at least. If he did it just to spite me.'

Chapter Nine

After the Sunday lunch at Springhead House, James was surprised to see Emma huddled in conversation with Robert in the kitchen. He knew he enjoyed these family occasions better than she did and she wasn't usually easy in Robert's company. James had never been able to work out what objection she could have to her parents. They were perfectly reasonable and civilized. They made few demands. He knew better than to say so, but when Emma complained about Robert and Mary, he thought she was acting like a spoilt child. He didn't mind too much. It had been her youth which had attracted him in the first place; she'd seemed untarnished by experience.

They were sitting in the living room at Springhead, drinking tea and eating fruit cake, when the subject of families came up. James had known it would happen sometime, but now he was unprepared. The conversation began safely enough.

'It's Mary's fiftieth birthday next month,' Robert said. 'We were thinking of having a party.'

'Were we?' Mary was crouched by the fire, trying to poke life into it. They were burning elder which was still green and gave off no heat, but her face was red because she'd been blowing into the embers.

'Well, I thought we should. We didn't do much for our silver wedding and I'd like to make a fuss of you.'

'I don't know . . .' The prospect seemed to terrify her, though Robert didn't notice. 'Who would we invite?'

'I thought we could make it open house. Ask our friends from the church, the youth club even. I miss having young people in the place.'

'Oh, no, really, I don't think that would be a good idea at all. I'd rather something smaller. Just the family.'

That was when the unexpected happened.

'If that's what you'd prefer,' Robert said. 'I did think it would be a good opportunity to get to know James's family at last. You won't mind them, I'm sure.'

James felt the stab of panic, hoped he was concealing it better than Mary had hidden hers. 'That's very kind. But there's no one really. No one close.'

'I always found that hard to believe. It was so sad that there were no relatives to help you celebrate your wedding. If it's a question of a family feud, surely this is the time to make up. There's a new generation to consider now.'

'No,' James said, more sharply than he'd intended. 'There's nothing like that.'

'Think about it,' Robert said. 'If you remember anyone, ask them along. We all have ancient aunts, second cousins. We'd like to meet them.'

'Honestly.' James kept the irritation from his voice. 'I'm quite alone. That's why I'm so grateful to be an honorary Winter.' He knew at once that had been the right thing to say. Robert beamed.

In the car on the way home Emma apologized for

her father's behaviour. 'Really,' she said. 'He's so rude. He can never stop prying. He's just the sort of person who gives social workers a bad name.' She was always in a better mood after a Springhead Sunday. The ordeal was over for another week. James, in contrast, felt unusually jittery. Though he'd satisfied Robert this time, he suspected there'd be more questions.

Once they were in the house he relaxed, thought his panic had been ridiculous. The baby had been fractious in the car and Emma took him immediately upstairs to bath. James changed out of his suit then stood leaning against the bathroom door to watch. This was all he had ever dreamt of. This house. This family.

They went to bed early because he was still on call, and by now he must be near the head of the turn list. He worked twelve days on and eight days off. He fell immediately into a deep sleep, untroubled by worries about Robert.

Emma had married him because she had a romantic notion about the sea. And him. And he hadn't lived up to the fantasy.

The thought came to him, unbidden, in a flash, between the second when the phone woke him and the moment of answering the call. Then it disappeared from his mind, like the remnants of a dream once you are properly awake.

It was a summons to work as he had known it would be. Two women worked in the data centre, collecting calls from ships' agents, then contacting the next pilot on the turn list to join the vessel, which was either approaching the mouth of the Humber or preparing to leave port. He recognized the voice at once. Marcia. He preferred her to Jo. Marcia was efficient and always respectful. He switched on the bedside light and jotted down the few details he needed.

'It's a ship out of Goole, Mr Bennett.' Her voice was calm. She made him think of a hospital sister in charge of a ward at night. 'Russian. A cargo of wood.'

Goole was always a long job – at least eight hours from door to door – but today he didn't mind that. He dressed quickly, though at this time of night with no traffic, there was less pressure. Daytime could be a nightmare. All it took was a hold-up on the road into Hull and you could miss the tide. There was no slack in the system. These days it was all stress, even the drive to the office. Emma didn't realize that. She thought he had no emotions. That he felt nothing.

She had stirred when the phone rang, but now she was asleep again, deeply asleep, lying on her back. He had waited to find the right wife and had known as soon as he'd walked into the classroom where she'd been preparing her first lesson, that he had found her. She had been writing the Russian alphabet on the board, frowning in her concentration to keep the line straight. He'd been first to arrive and she'd ticked his name off on the register, a little girl playing at teachers. When the evening class was over, he'd hovered in the corridor, and asked if he might buy her a drink. To thank her for making the first lesson so painless. He'd said he hated school as a child and had been nervous about enrolling in adult education.

Of course there had been other women before her but he had promised them nothing, made it clear that commitment wasn't an option. He had planned his life. He was in every sense a self-made man. The right wife had been as important as becoming the youngest first-class pilot on the Humber. He stuck rigidly to the structure, would consider no flexibility. He was ambitious, but there was more to it than that. The plan was all that held his life together. And it had worked out. Emma had been everything he had hoped for.

Outside it was still raining, but a persistent drizzle. He thought this part of the country had more shades of grey than anywhere he had ever visited. And he had travelled the world to get his master's ticket. Grey sea mist in the summer, slatey storm clouds, a sea that was almost black. Tonight it was a dense, pale grey, like thick smoke, which bounced back the car's headlights.

The windscreen wipers had a soporific effect and the car journey to the pilot office was so familiar that it took no concentration. Occasionally James came to a junction, saw a pub sign or a church lurk out of the gloom and became aware with a jerk of where he was. Otherwise he drove automatically, in a daze. It would have been easy to lapse into thoughts of the past in this state. Robert's probing about his relatives had disturbed him – *There must be someone . . . We all have ancient aunts, second cousins.* And then there was Keith Mantel. His face was everywhere. Staring out of the television, the front page of newspapers. It would be easy to allow himself to dwell on that. But James had trained himself to avoid unpleasant thoughts. He had too much to lose by giving in to panic. He breathed slowly and thought of Emma, the perfect pilot's wife, gentle and undemanding, lying dreaming in his bed.

He had come to the outskirts of the city. Everywhere, along the river, there were scars of development. Half-built new roads, sleeping cranes, the skeletons of demolished buildings. Until a year before, the pilots had been based in an eighteenth-century house which stood on the corner of a pleasant street and looked out towards the waterfront. James had loved working from there. He'd sensed the men who'd gone before him when he walked through the door, imagined he could smell them, their tobacco and the salt on their clothes. It had been his way of making himself part of the tradition. For many of the men that came naturally. Their fathers and grandfathers had been pilots and they'd been boys together in the Trinity House School. Whenever he came to work, he planned his route so he still passed the old pilot office. It was empty, waiting for refurbishment, too valuable an asset to be used for the purpose for which it had been built. He slowed the car as he drove past, enjoying the lines of the building, allowing himself the memory of his first day there. Then he saw that the house had been sold. A huge notice with a familiar logo had been fastened to the front wall, between the two lines of long windows. *Property acquired by Mantel Development for conversion to luxury apartments. All enquiries to our Kingston upon Hull office.*

For a moment the reaction to this notice confused him. He didn't recognize the emotion. It had been so long. Anger, of course. There was a moment of liberation when he felt he could give into it. Then there was only disgust. As if someone had ground dog muck onto a valuable carpet. And by the time he walked into the shabby prefab which had become the pilot office, he was all smiles, all quiet charm.

'What is the name of the ship? I didn't catch it on

the phone. Oh yes. The skipper's an old friend. There'll be no problem tonight.'

He picked up the keys to the pool car and went on his way. The M62 was almost empty and he drove too fast.

Goole is a small town, dominated by the docks. The river seems to cut right into the heart of the web of narrow streets. It must be strange to look out of a bedroom window and see a huge container vessel sliding past, so close that you feel you could reach out and touch the hull, that the seaman drinking from a mug in the cockpit might offer you a drink too. When James drove through the town it was empty. Two in the morning, and still raining. He could believe that everyone was sleeping except for him and the crew who waited for him.

But as he walked from his car to board the ship, out of the corner of his eye he saw a man standing next to a pile of containers. The figure was familiar. Hair so short it looked as if it had been shaved. The navy donkey jacket. James had to stop himself from calling out. Only later he told himself it would be impossible to have seen colour in this light. That it had been a mistake or a hallucination. He didn't believe in ghosts.

Chapter Ten

Some men hated the night tides, the lack of sleep, the effort of making conversation with a captain who wanted to practise his English in the early hours of the morning. But James had practised the art of being pleasant until it came naturally. He could be almost asleep on his feet, but still he would look at the photos of the skipper's wife and children back home, discuss the relative merits of the goods displayed in the Argos catalogue with a seaman who was astounded by the variety reproduced on the cheap, shiny paper, gratefully accept a mug of tea although the milk was sweet and thick and came out of a tin.

Tonight he spoke Russian. The skipper's English wasn't bad, but James's Russian was better, and he was glad of the necessity to concentrate. It stopped him thinking of the glossy sign outside the pilot office. The shadowy figure on the dock. Drowned men returned to life. James had enlisted in Emma's evening class to learn a few basic phrases: *ten degrees port, Captain, twenty degrees starboard*. So there would be no misunderstanding when he gave directions and he wouldn't be dependent on someone else to translate. He'd done Spanish the term before for the same reason. But then he'd seen Emma and he'd stayed in the class all year, working harder than he'd ever done at school, eager to impress. He had an A level to show for it. And a wife and child.

There was no room for error bringing a ship out of Goole. The River Ouse was narrow there, with concrete sides like a canal. It was tight for a boat of this size. For a containership it seemed impossible on the approach and seamen who'd never visited the port before were horrified. *What is this place you bring me to? This is not possible. No, there is some mistake.* James enjoyed the delicacy of the work. It was a challenge, a test of his skill.

The ship moved slowly away from the dock, which was spotlit like a movie set. Black and white. The silhouettes of the cranes and warehouses two dimensional as if they'd been built from hardboard. The river widened and the wind became fresher. The rain stopped and the visibility improved suddenly, so he could make out each bank, marked by pinpricks of light: street lamps, headlights, the lit-up windows of insomniacs and feeding mothers.

A boy with a mouthful of decaying teeth brought him more tea and a meal, a greasy stew with livid orange carrots and grey potatoes, which tasted better than it looked. He would have eaten it anyway. It seemed a long time since lunch with his in-laws at Springhead, and it would have been bad manners to turn the food away.

At the mouth of the estuary the wind increased again into sudden gusts which whipped the river into little pointed waves and sent spray over the deck. In the daylight it would be possible from here to see the spire of St Mary Magdalene church in Elvet, the track along the shore, where sometimes James took the baby in his pram. To walk and remember. It was six o'clock. Morning. Matthew would soon be waking. The coxswain on duty at the Point would have been warned that James would need collecting in the launch.

That thought, or rather the coincidence of thoughts – Mary Magdalene and the coxswain of the launch – forced a connection of memory, and James realized that the man who'd been sitting in front of them in church the day before had been Michael Long. James hadn't recognized him at the time. He'd been a bluff, rather aggressive man when James had worked with him, impervious, it had seemed, to James's charm. Of course he'd been in the church to mourn his daughter. Suicide. A terrible accusation. James shivered although where he stood at the helm he was protected from the weather and the small room was warm, almost stuffy. He wasn't given to fancies but suddenly he was aware of the depth of water below the hold of the ship, wondered what it must be like to drown.

They were rounding the Point. James could see the jetty all lit up, the fretwork of black metal, and the VTS tower where the pilot master would be sitting. The waves were longer and deeper here and the ship was starting to roll. Soon they would be in open water.

'Make a lee, Captain,' James said calmly. His work was almost over.

The ship swung slowly, so the long side of the hull faced into the wind. The launch was on its way. The crackling voice of the coxswain reported its progress. James went onto deck to watch its approach – at first it was a flicker of light which disappeared with each wave. The Russian captain stood beside him and slapped his back as if they were best friends.

'Good work, sir,' he said in English. 'It is always a pleasure to work with you, Pilot.'

He slipped a bottle of vodka into James's bag and waved the latest Argos catalogue in salute. James smiled his thanks, as if vodka was his favourite drink in the world. The launch was circling the Russian boat, so it came alongside sheltered from the wind. James climbed down the pilot ladder with his bag over one shoulder, checked that the launch was in position and jumped aboard.

The coxswain was a woman called Wendy, slight and dark and determined to do well. Michael Long hadn't liked that, James remembered. Being replaced by a woman had been the final straw. She turned to see that he was safely in his seat, opened the throttle and they started back to the Point.

'Good passage down, Mr Bennett?' she shouted above the engine noise.

'A bit murky over the Whittons,' he said. 'All right once the ebb got away.'

It was eight o'clock and light now. Faint sunshine penetrated the cloud. On the south bank of the river refineries and chimneys glowed silver through the mist, looking in outline like a great city. Venice perhaps, or St Petersburg. James had the cold, empty feeling which comes from having too little sleep. After the swaying of the ship, his first couple of steps along the jetty seemed unnatural, as if the boards had lifted and hit the soles of his feet a beat too soon. He saw there was no pool car waiting for him to drive back to Hull, thought that if he had to get a taxi, at least there'd be a chance of sleep.

Wendy seemed to guess what was going through his mind.

'Bert will be here soon. There's a tanker due for Immingham. He says if you hang on you can take his car back. Go on in. You look as if you could use a coffee.'

'I could use a couple of hours' sleep.' But it wasn't a real complaint.

The steward in the pilot office made him a hot drink and a bacon sandwich. There was a Calor gas stove which hissed and smelled and immediately after eating James must have dozed, because when Bert did arrive it was light outside.

James emerged into a day-time world of children's voices and a woman in one of the lifeboat houses hanging washing on the line. It was an odd community here on the Point. Half a dozen families, cut off from the mainland, only attached by a thin strip of sand, mud and concrete which could be breached by the next high tide. And most of their life was spent waiting. The coxswains of the pilot launches waited for the tide and the crew of the sole permanently manned lifeboat station in the country waited for a collision, for someone stranded on a sandbank. Their only activity would come out of someone else's tragedy.

Still dazed from the Calor fumes and fuzzy with sleep, James stood for a moment to clear his head. His muscles felt stiff and clumsy. He walked past the VTS tower to the rise in the land where he'd get a view of the open sea. On this side of the Point there was a thicket of bramble and sea buckthorn, overrun by rabbits. A long beach ran north towards the mainland coast. The mist had cleared suddenly while he'd been sleeping and the light had the clear, sharp quality which comes before rain. The tanker waiting offshore seemed ridiculously close and the launch which was already circling towards it had the bright detail of a plastic toy.

Two people were walking along the beach, close to the tideline. A man and a woman. Not birdwatchers. Birdwatchers were regular visitors to the Point, but they all dressed the same and they carried binoculars and telescopes. Besides, they didn't wander much onto the beach. They stood where he was standing now to get a panoramic view of the passing seabirds, or they pushed their way through the paths cut in the undergrowth. James wasn't sure what had first attracted his attention to the walkers. Perhaps it was the man, something about the way he was walking was familiar. He was wearing a long gabardine coat, too smart for a stroll on the beach and his hands were thrust deep into his pockets. And then there were his shoes. Most people would put on wellingtons or boots, but he wore polished leather shoes. The salt would stain them. James crouched so he couldn't be seen and continued watching. The man stopped suddenly, but he was still talking. The abrupt halt had only added emphasis to the words, demanding that the woman stop too and give him her full attention.

It was Keith Mantel. Since he and Emma had moved back to Elvet, James had managed to avoid him, and he looked older than when James had last seen him. His hair was grey, cut very short. Perhaps he'd put on a bit of weight. James wasn't sure but he thought the face was fatter. Then the man turned and the couple continued on their walk and immediately James thought he must have been mistaken. He'd been thinking too much of Mantel recently and in his tiredness had dreamed him up. This was a respectable couple, taking the air before going into the city to resume their stressful lives. Or a not-so-respectable businessman snatching a few illicit moments with his mistress. Though there seemed to be nothing romantic about this encounter. Rather, it was confrontational. The woman deliberately allowed a space to grow between them, stooped and picked up a pebble and threw it into the water with a violence which suggested anger.

James turned away and walked back to the road where the company car was parked. Emma had enough stories and fancies for both of them. In the car, the heater was full on, blasting hot, stale air. James switched it off and backed away from the river. He drove slowly up the narrow track past the small group of houses and the cafe which provided mugs of tea and piles of chips to visitors in the summer. He was about to speed up a little, when he braked and pulled into the public car park. He was too curious, after all, to let it go. There were only two vehicles there, standing side by side, facing out into the estuary. One was a smart, black saloon, the other a boxy four by four. On the side of the latter was painted the logo which James had seen on the notice at the pilot office in Hull. And the words *Mantel Development*. Not his imagination then. Not a dream. On this occasion at least he wasn't hallucinating.

Who was the woman? She was more mature than

the usual lovers. When James had known him Mantel always went for young women. Inexperienced. Had he hoped some of their innocence would rub off on him? And more recently James had heard rumours in the village. The women in church loved to be shocked. Another young lover, he'd understood, had moved into the smart house where Mantel still lived. The woman on the beach had been well preserved, well groomed in an efficient, businesswoman sort of way, but she had been middle aged. In her forties at least. James switched off the engine and got out of his car. He walked slowly round the black saloon, not touching it, but peering in through the windows. It was a top of the range model with leather seats, all the latest gadgets on the dashboard. There was none of the mess which Emma gathered in her car – baby clothes, sweet wrappers, Coke cans. Not even a brief case. But on the passenger seat was a pile of letters. The woman had picked up her mail before setting off, though she hadn't had time to open it. The top envelope was face up and was an advertising circular from a credit card company. James recognized the printing. At least now he had a name for the woman. The letter was addressed to Caroline Fletcher.

When he finally reached home it had gone ten o'clock. The house was quiet. Matthew would be in his cot, just settled for his morning nap. Emma was in the living room. She'd lit a fire; he could smell the pine logs as soon as he came into the house. She was sitting in a big armchair, her legs tucked under her, and there was a book lying in her lap. Flaubert's *Emma Bovary* in French. Her eyes were shut and her breathing was regular. When he approached her she stirred.

'Oh God,' she said. 'I'm so sorry. I had a dreadful night with the baby. I must have dozed off. And you must be exhausted.'

'Not too bad,' he said. 'Second wind.' He nodded at the book. 'What's this?'

The question seemed to make her uncomfortable. 'You know what they say about languages – use them or lose them. I might want to go back to teaching. I don't want to get rusty.'

'Good idea. Coffee?'

'I'd love some. But let me get it.'

'No really,' he said. 'I meant what I said. Second wind.'

When he came back, carrying mugs and the biscuit tin, she was fast asleep.

Chapter Eleven

In her sleep, Emma was fifteen and it was summer.

The house where Abigail lived with her father was bigger even than the house in York which Emma's father had designed. Once, it had been a chapel belonging to a grand house with a formal garden and a park. There was still a long leaded window in the entrance hall though all the stained glass had been removed to allow in more light. The big house had burned to the ground a hundred years ago leaving the chapel stranded and useless, until it was developed by Abigail's father.

Now, only that long window and the steep roof gave an indication of its original purpose. The ground had been landscaped and the house extended. There was a new garage and a flat above it for a housekeeper. Stone from the ruin had been used to build the living room where Jeanie Long was playing the piano. Glass sliding doors led from there into a conservatory. The living room was furnished in a style which Emma knew her father would despise – reproduction sideboards in dark wood, over-stuffed sofas, mirrors with gilt frames. He *would* approve, she felt, of the conservatory. There, the table and chairs were plain and functional. Big plants stood in terracotta pots, which reminded Emma immediately of the garden in York. A striped hammock swung from the roof.

Jeanie Long was practising. Since she moved to the house to be Keith Mantel's lover, it seemed she hadn't stopped playing. Often the same piece was repeated over and over. This seemed to drive Abigail to fury. It provoked a continuous battle, or rather maintained the hostilities which had begun with Jeanie's arrival. Abigail refused to speak to the woman. She banged doors, had stopped eating, burst into tears whenever her father was around to see. Jeanie fought back with the only weapon she had – her music. She would begin as soon as he left in the morning and continue until his return. There were other rooms of course. Abigail could avoid the sound if she wanted. There were rooms in the old part of the chapel which had televisions, a sound system, a computer, and because the piano was in an extension separated from the rest of the house by thick walls, the sound of the playing was barely audible from those. But that didn't matter to Abigail. She threatened to take an axe to the piano late at night and Emma believed that she might do it. She imagined the splintered wood and the twanging strings.

Emma and Abigail were in the conservatory. Abigail was swinging on the hammock, one leg hanging over the edge. It was the last day of the school summer holidays and Emma wanted to enjoy it. The sun was shining. She could have been on the beach, topping up her suntan so she wouldn't seem so different from the girls who'd been to a Greek island or Tenerife. Keith had flown Abigail to Florida before Jeanie had taken up residence but she didn't have the sort of complexion which tanned. Her skin was as white and smooth as wax. Abigail had refused the beach and to take the bus to Hull to look at the shops. Instead she'd insisted on staying in to stoke up her fury. She pushed against the one stone wall of the conservatory with her foot, making the hammock swing violently. The ropes creaked where they were mounted on the ceiling. The noise was loud and regular like the braying of a donkey, but still Jeanie bent over the piano keys. Either she was so absorbed that she didn't hear or she was determined not to react.

Then the door opened and Keith Mantel was standing there. He was nearly twice Jeanie's age but even Emma could understand the attraction. His hair was a sandy blond and his face *did* show the effect of the Florida sun. He was dressed in a grey suit and white shirt and he carried a briefcase, but somehow managed to look neither stuffy nor respectable. For a moment Jeanie didn't realize he was there, then perhaps he moved or there was a breeze through the open door, because she stopped playing in the middle of a phrase and looked round. The girls' whispered giggles hadn't disturbed her, but his entrance had penetrated her concentration immediately.

She swivelled on the embroidered top of the stool so her back was to the piano. She was caught in the full sunlight which flooded through the glass doors. Her face was lit up not just by the sunshine but at her pleasure at seeing him.

'Wonderful,' she said. 'You're home early.'

He set down his briefcase and walked up to her. He put his hands on her shoulders which were bare, because she was wearing a thin, strappy top, and he kissed the top of her head. Beside Emma, Abigail was making noises like someone being violently sick. Emma felt a violent stab of envy. She didn't believe anyone would kiss her in that way.

Emma had been trying to remember more of her encounter with Jeanie Long since that one flash of recollection in the church. When she woke it was almost lunch-time and her book had slid to the floor so the place was lost. Upstairs Matthew was lying awake in his cot, reaching out occasionally towards a bare branch moving just outside his window. James had gone to bed. His uniform cap lay on the dressing table. His breathing was soft and regular. He claimed never to dream and looking at him there so calm and still, she could believe that was true. Emma changed Matthew then took him into the living room to feed him. She zapped on the television for the local news, and caught a piece on the reopening of the Mantel case.

'A witness has come forward who can place Jeanie Long in London on the day attractive teenager Abigail Mantel was killed. Miss Long always claimed she was in the capital on the day the crime was committed, but until now there has been no evidence to support her. Officers from a neighbouring force have been brought in to reassess the case. The Chief Constable of Yorkshire and Humberside Police denies that this shows a lack of confidence in the original investigation. "Often," he says, "it's useful to look at a case with fresh eyes".'

There followed a piece of old news footage showing witnesses leaving the court after Jeanie Long's trial.

Emma buttoned up her shirt and pulled down her sweater. She put the baby in the pram which lived in the hall and went upstairs to prepare to go out. She opened her wardrobe door very quietly so as not to disturb James and saw all the clothes she used to wear before she was pregnant, the jackets and skirts and smart little blouses she dressed in for the classroom. None of these seemed suitable today and she chose instead a pair of black trousers and a lambswool sweater with a big collar, and her long black coat which she lay on her side of the bed. She sat in front of the dressing table, wondering about make-up, compromising finally with a splash of red lipstick but nothing more. She wrote a note for James. *Needed some fresh air. Taken Matthew for a walk.*

In the pram the baby looked out at her. He was wearing a bright red hat and red mittens. She pulled up the hood, forcing the hinges into place. She didn't want the wind to blow it down as soon as she stepped outside. Matthew chortled when she opened the door and bounced the pram by its back wheels down the steps to the square. She knew Dan Greenwood was in the pottery. The doors weren't padlocked and anyway she'd seen him arrive at nine o'clock. She knew the best time to look out for him. She'd watched him arrive and leave most days since she'd stopped work. In the summer he left the big double doors open and then she'd seen inside. But this would be the first time she would fulfil her fantasy and go in.

At the far end of the building there was a corner which he seemed to use as an office. Behind an old desk was a filing cabinet and a computer table. And today Dan was there too, sitting at the desk, lit by an anglepoise lamp. He was looking at some papers and frowning and she could tell the contents irritated or annoyed him. He wasn't a man who hid his feelings easily. Once, in the summer when the big door had stood open, she'd seen him take hold of a pot he was painting and hurl it against the far wall of the building, frustrated, she supposed, because he hadn't managed to achieve quite the effect he'd wanted. The scene had shocked and fascinated her. James would never have given way to such a spontaneous show of feeling.

Now the lamp gave the scene a contrived, staged look. Little natural light came through the dusty windows in the roof and the strip tubes fastened to the rafters had been switched off. Emma, the audience, was in shadow. She closed the door behind her and Dan looked up.

'Emma.' He half rose, then sat back in the chair which looked as if it had been rescued from a village school. His movements were always sudden. His hands were so big that she wondered they were capable of holding the small brushes, the more delicate pieces. There was the tension she'd always sensed between them. She'd thought it was the frisson of mutual attraction. Now she wasn't so sure.

She'd met him first when he'd thrown a party to celebrate the opening of the pottery. He'd held it in the pub and they'd all been invited, everyone who lived on the square. She'd been newly married, realizing even then perhaps that it wouldn't be the escape she'd hoped, but not looking for adventures. She'd had adventures enough in her life already and she had her work then to satisfy her. Dan Greenwood had been at the door to greet them all, and she still remembered the first encounter. She'd lifted her face so he could kiss her cheek and had seen the shock in his eyes, felt it in the brief press of lips and the brush of his hair like a feather on her skin. It had been as if he were meeting an old lover, although she had been sure they had never met. And all evening, as the locals grew more rowdy on the free beer, she had been aware of his gaze on her, flattered but not surprised. She had known the effect she could have on lonely men.

He must have approached everyone else in the room to introduce himself, enquire about his neighbours. His manner was reserved, but overhearing the conversation, she'd thought there was something very blunt about his questions. Direct, like a child. He wasn't much good at flattering small talk. Certainly he had talked to James that evening. She had watched them laugh together. But he had made no effort to come up to her. It was as if he'd sensed that there would be a danger in their being physically too close. That was what she'd thought then. Now she wondered if she'd been deluding herself. He and James had become friends in that easy, casual way that men do. They often met up for a pint on Friday nights. They both played cricket for the village team. She didn't know what they talked about – their work, she supposed, sport, gossip.

Now, she felt awkward, tongue-tied. She had often dreamed about coming here, confronting him with how she felt, but this would be a different confrontation.

'Emma.' This time he did stand up, and he walked

round to the front of the desk. He was frowning, anxious. 'Is anything the matter?'

She ignored the question. 'You never told me you used to be a policeman.'

'It was a long time ago. Something I try to forget.'

'You worked on the Mantel case. I've just seen you on the television.'

He seemed to be forming an explanation but she didn't allow him a chance to speak. 'You recognized me when we first met. Did you come to Springhead the day I found Abigail? I don't remember.'

'I spoke to your father.'

'But you saw me?'

'Through the kitchen door. Briefly. And then later James confirmed who you were.'

'Does he know you're an ex-cop?'

'It's not something I feel I have to hide. It came up recently in conversation.'

How? she wondered. Does James use that incident in my past as an excuse for my behaviour? *We'd have you round to dinner, but Em's not very good in company. She found the body of her murdered best friend* . . . As if one had any relevance to the other.

'Didn't you think I'd be interested to know that you'd worked on the case?'

'I didn't think you'd want reminding of it.'

'It's hard to forget,' she said. 'Now, with all that's going on.'

'Have you been bothered by the press?'

'No.'

'They'll track you down. I know you use your married name but it might be worth changing your phone number.'

'We're ex-directory.'

'That won't stop them.'

The exchange seemed unnaturally loud and fast. The words seemed to ricochet off the walls. They looked at each other for a moment in silence.

'Look,' he said. 'I can make you a coffee.' He wiped the seat of the chair with his sleeve. 'Why don't you sit down?'

'I want to know what's going on,' she cried. 'No one's been to see me. It's not fair. I'm involved.'

She had the argument clear in her head. The grievance had been growing all night. She hadn't thought it would be directed towards Dan Greenwood. *That Inspector Fletcher, Caroline, made the effort then. She kept us sweet while the police were preparing the case for court, while I could still be of use. She came every day to see what I could remember. Now I have to hear about developments on the news.*

Though that wasn't true. Dan had warned her, through James, of Jeanie's suicide and that the case might be reopened.

While she hesitated, wondering what tone to take, her thoughts were interrupted by a voice behind her.

'That seems fair enough to me, pet.' The voice was very close. It seemed to rasp in Emma's ear. She turned. The woman from the church was leaning on the wall behind her. 'But that's the police all over for you. They keep you in the dark and they feed you shit. That's why Danny got out. Or so he says.'

She had emerged through a door. Emma could see a small room cluttered with boxes. There was a rickety armchair, a kettle, a tray of grubby mugs on the floor in one corner. The woman had been sitting there and had overheard everything they'd said.

'Who are you?' Emma demanded. Then, before the woman could answer, remembering Dan's earlier warning, 'Are you a reporter?'

The woman gave a wheezy laugh. Her enormous bosoms shook.

'Not me, pet. I'm on the side of the angels.' She held out a hand the size of a shovel. 'Vera Stanhope. Detective Inspector Vera Stanhope. Northumbria Police. I've been brought in to clear up this particular pile of crap.'

Chapter Twelve

Emma thought Vera Stanhope was the most thick-skinned person she'd ever met. It was not only in that she was impervious to embarrassment or offence. She was literally thick-skinned. Her face was scaly and uneven, covered in places by crusted blotches, her hands were hard and worn. Some sort of allergy or disease, Emma thought, but couldn't bring herself to pity. She wasn't the sort of woman you could feel sorry for. Vera stood, looking at them both, narrowing her eyes.

'Did you say something about coffee, Danny? But not here, eh, pet. Let's go somewhere a bit more comfy.' She directed her gaze towards Emma. 'Don't you live just over the square?'

Emma knew what was expected. She was supposed to invite them in, sit them in the best room, brew coffee, set out fancy biscuits. Then answer this extra-ordinary woman's questions. Go over the old ground. And all the time Vera's reptile eyes would be taking in the surroundings, probing, as curious as the old ladies from the church who'd invited themselves in to see the baby when she'd first come home from hospital. She couldn't bear it.

'We can't go to my house,' she said quickly. 'My husband's asleep. He's been working all night.'

Dan Greenwood rescued her. Perhaps he sensed her panic, though she could no longer persuade herself that they had a special understanding.

'Why don't you come back to my place. I'd be breaking for lunch about now anyway.'

Vera turned a wide smile on him, as if that was what she'd been hoping for all the time.

Outside the rain had stopped and there were jagged splashes of sunlight reflected in the puddles and the wet pavements. Emma waited for Dan to lock up. Even now, she found herself watching him. He had dark hair on the back of his hands. His sleeve fell back from his wrist as he clamped together the padlock and she imagined what it would feel like to touch his arm.

'I'll drive round,' she said. 'Matthew always falls asleep in the car. It'll mean we can talk in peace.'

It wasn't far to Dan's house but she didn't want to be seen traipsing after them along the narrow pavements, part of a strange procession, a circus freak show. He lived in a crescent of 1930s semis on the edge of the village. Once they'd been council houses and there were still one or two belonging to the local authority, identifiable by the uniform green paint. The rest had been bought by their owners or sold on to incomers like Dan. They had long, thin gardens at the back, fanning out towards farmland.

Emma took her time. She let herself into her own home and watched them set off before carrying Matthew to the car and strapping him in. She didn't want to arrive ahead of them, and thought if she passed them on the way she might feel obliged to offer them a lift. The thought of Vera Stanhope in her car gave her the same threat of violation, as if she'd been forced to ask her into her home.

When she arrived at the Crescent Dan's door was open, and she went in without knocking, lifting the car seat with Matthew into the narrow hall. She had never been inside the house, though she knew James had. It was one of his excuses for lateness during the cricket season. *I just called into Dan's for a beer after the match.* Hovering outside the kitchen it occurred to her that James had probably known all along about Dan Greenwood's role in the Abigail Mantel murder. The subject of Dan's previous career must have come up during those boozy Friday night discussions. It wasn't something to be ashamed of, as he'd said.

There was a tiny living room and a kitchen of a similar size with a door leading into the garden. The kitchen wall had been painted a deep green and there was one of Dan's jugs with some chrysanths on the window sill, but everything else could have belonged to the previous owners. You wouldn't have guessed an artist lived here. There was none of the mess or clutter she'd have expected. They all sat at the kitchen table and Vera seemed to take up most of the room. Emma was reminded of train journeys, strangers cramped around a table, trying to make sure their knees and feet don't touch. Dan had changed from his work boots and was wearing the sandals climbers wear. His feet were brown. He'd made filter coffee and set out chocolate biscuits on a plate. Emma couldn't tell what he made of this invasion. Had Vera Stanhope been foisted onto him or were they allies, old friends? His attitude towards her was affectionate but cautious. It was as if she were a large dog, generally well behaved but given to lashing out at strangers. He seemed to be trying very hard to sit still.

Vera leant back in her chair, her eyes covered with thick, inflexible lids.

'Well, pet, what is it you'd like to know? Just fire away. Dan and me'll do our best to help.'

'Are you sure Jeanie was innocent?'

'Positive.'

'What makes you so certain?'

Vera slowly sat forward, reached out for a biscuit. 'She always claimed she went to London that day. An impulse, she said. She wanted to get away from the area, hide in a big city, be anonymous. Keith had asked her to leave the Old Chapel and she was devastated. She'd thought she was in love.' Vera munched the biscuit, wiped the crumbs from her chin, continued to speak though she'd not finished chewing. 'She got the train from Hull. So she said. Wandered round the South Bank and listened to the free lunch-time music, went to the Tate Gallery, then got the train home. But no one saw her. She told Danny's colleagues she'd left her car in the long-stay car park, but they couldn't find the sticker she'd have had to put on her windscreen. The guy who sold her the rail ticket was shown her photograph but didn't recognize her. No one travelling on the train came forward to identify her. And it was the same in London. You can't believe anyone can be *that* invisible. It was a Sunday, not such a busy day for travelling, but nobody had noticed her. Even more strange, she never mentioned her trip to her parents. Not before she went or when she got back. Her car was gone from outside her parents' house on the Point from eight in the morning until seven in the evening. That was all they could be sure of.'

She eyed the remaining biscuit but left it where it was. 'Perhaps they could have done more. Gone national. Appealed for witnesses. But they thought she'd killed the girl. It wasn't their responsibility to make the case for the defence.' She gave a wide, dolphin's smile. 'That's right, isn't it, Danny? You all thought you'd got your murderer. What is it they call it? Noble cause corruption. And who could blame you for being corrupted? The motive was clear from the beginning. Jeanie hated Abigail Mantel because she could persuade her father to do anything, and she'd persuaded him that the two of them were happier on their own.'

Dan didn't reply, seemed not even to hear. He was looking out of the window so Emma couldn't tell what he made of Vera's words, what he'd thought at the time.

'So, it's precisely ten years on and there's a small piece in the *Guardian* about Jeanie Long. Not claiming she's innocent. Not exactly that. But claiming she was turned down for parole because she refused to admit her guilt. And that she would have been moved to an open prison years before if she hadn't stuck to her story. The article gave a bit of background to the case and mentioned that she'd never found an alibi to support her story. The next thing that happens is that a witness comes forward. You wouldn't believe it could happen, would you? Not after ten years. But this is for real . . .' She paused. 'What's his name, Danny?'

Emma knew that Vera remembered the man's name quite well. The pause was for dramatic effect.

'Stringer,' Dan said. 'Clive Stringer.'

'Clive was at university with Jeanie. It seems he had a bit of a crush on her, even went out with her once or twice during their first year. He saw her at King's Cross on the day of the murder.'

'How can he remember after all this time?' Emma heard the desperation in her voice. The story which had been constructed ten years earlier, the story which had made some sort of sense, was starting to crumble.

'The date meant a lot to him. He was on his way to Heathrow. He'd been offered a postgraduate research post at a university in the States, and that was the day he flew. Even if there had been an appeal for witnesses, he wouldn't have been around to hear it. He didn't even know that Jeanie had been charged with murder until he read the *Guardian* piece.'

'Couldn't he have made a mistake? You see someone in a crowd, it's easy to convince yourself . . .'

'I've spoken to him,' Vera said. 'He's down-to-earth. Not given to flights of the imagination.'

They looked at each other across the table. Emma didn't know what to say.

'I did think at first he might be an attention seker,' Vera went on gently. 'We come across plenty of those in our line of work. But he keeps a diary. Has done since he was a bairn. It's a bit sad, I think, summing up your life in a few lines scribbled at night. There must be more to it than that. In this case, though, it's a blessing. I've seen the entry for November fifteenth 1994. Do you know what it says? "*Saw Jeanie at King's Cross Station, looking lovely in a bright red sweater. Red always suited her.*" We checked. Jeanie was wearing a red jersey when she returned to her parents' house that night. Forensic took it. Of course they didn't find anything to link her with the murder. But it didn't really matter. She was charged anyway.' For the first time Emma realized that Vera was angry, volcanically, terrifyingly angry.

Vera must have seen that Emma sensed her fury. She shifted in her chair and smiled again to prove she wasn't dangerous, became confiding and folksy.

'I'm from up country,' she said. 'Nothing to do with Yorkshire and Humberside Police. I'm impartial, that's the theory. It's my job to look at the Mantel case again, see what went wrong. And the sooner I can get it done and go home the better, as far as I'm concerned. I'm used to the hills. There's nowhere to hide here, is there? You can see some bugger's washing on a line in the next county. It gives me the creeps.'

'What do you want from me?'

'Your memories,' Vera said immediately.

'I'm not sure how reliable they are after all this time.'

'Don't worry. It's what I'm best at. Working out what's real and what's fantasy. Joe Ashworth, my sergeant, thinks I'm a witch.'

Emma looked up sharply but couldn't tell from Vera's face whether she was mocking herself or her audience. Because that was what Dan and Emma had become. Vera was playing them as if she was the best stand-up in the business. And already she'd moved on, taking them with her.

'Suppose today, we just start with a few questions. Things that have been troubling me, and no one else has been able to answer. Not even Danny here. Like, why did Keith Mantel ask Jeanie to move out?'

'Because Abigail asked him to.' If she can't

understand that, Emma thought, she might as well piss off back to her hills now.

'But he must have realized there'd be a problem before he moved Jeanie in. I mean he and Abigail had lived in that place on their own since her mam died. Everyone says he treated her like a princess, spoilt her rotten. If they were that close he wouldn't have brought his lover into the home without mentioning it to the girl. *What would you say if Jeanie came to live with us?* They say men aren't the most sensitive beasts in the universe but he'd have managed that. And if she hated the idea, Abigail would have said, wouldn't she? She doesn't strike me as the shy type. *No way, Dad. It won't work.* Something like that. And he'd have listened to her and made some excuse to Jeanie, even if only to spare himself the hassle. *Sorry, love, but Abigail needs more time.*'

Listening to the detective Emma thought she was some sort of witch, because even if those precise words hadn't been used, it was just what each of them might have said. But Vera was continuing. 'So that's my problem. I don't see how he got himself into that mess.'

'I don't think he had a lot of choice.'

'What do you mean?'

Emma hesitated. 'This is what Abigail told me. I don't know if she was telling the truth.' Because Emma knew now better than anyone that Abigail could be the biggest liar in the world.

Vera nodded encouragingly. 'Like I said, you can leave that for me to decide.'

'According to Abigail, Keith hadn't really wanted Jeanie there in the first place. She'd had a row with her parents and just stormed out of her home. She turned up on the doorstep of the Chapel with a ruck-sack of clothes and her violin. He couldn't turn her away.'

'Too kind-hearted for his own good, I daresay,' Vera said, and Emma could tell she'd already formed an opinion of the man and disapproved of him.

'The first thing Abigail knew about it was when she found Jeanie in the kitchen cooking supper.'

Abigail had recounted the story the next day. It had been another hot afternoon, sultry, airless. There must have been rain that summer, sea fog, but Emma couldn't remember it. That day Abigail *had* agreed to go with her to the beach and they'd walked there together down the path between the sandy fields. Already most of the harvest had been in but in the distance she'd heard the churning of a baler and there'd still been a patch of barley left to cut. The feathery fronds had brushed their legs as they walked. There had been a row of swallows on the wire, and clouds of insects, and Abigail, striding in front along the narrow path, had shouted to Emma, following behind. She hadn't stopped talking all the way. Her voice had been incredulous and she'd repeated herself often to show that she still couldn't believe the cheek.

'I mean she was just standing there, rooting through the cupboards. And then she started on the freezer. "I thought I'd do risotto. Is that OK with you, Abby?" I mean, no one, but no one calls me Abby. You don't call me Abby and you're my best mate. And still I didn't get it. I thought it was a one-off, one night. Then I went up to dad's room and there were the things she'd already unpacked. Like, she'd been there an hour, and already her clothes were hanging in his wardrobe and her knickers were in his drawer. Well, I know he won't stand for it. She'll be out by the end of the week. Dad likes his space. Even I'm not allowed into his room without asking.'

'Why *did* he stand for it?' Vera asked. 'That's the question. More relevant than why he asked her to leave in the end. Jeanie was there for three months. Why didn't he boot her out sooner?'

'He loved her,' Emma said. 'Didn't he?'

'Oh, no,' Vera replied, quite certain. 'Love didn't come into it. Not on his part.'

'Abigail was certainly surprised that she didn't get her own way immediately.' Emma smiled, remembering her friend's frustration, the strategies which all seemed to fail. There had seemed some justice in the fact that Abigail had been forced to suffer an upset in her life. Emma had looked on at the rows with the same mixture of sympathy and pleasure as if Abigail had sprouted an enormous pimple on the end of her nose.

'Why did Keith suddenly give in?' Vera demanded. 'After three months?'

'Perhaps she just wore him down with her persistence.'

'Aye. Maybe.'

'Why don't you ask the inspector who worked on the case at the time? She must have spoken to people, come to a conclusion.'

'Caroline Fletcher doesn't work for the service any more,' Vera said briskly. 'Like Danny here.' She paused. 'Strange, isn't it, that the two officers most actively involved in the investigation retired from the police soon after Jeanie Long went to court?'

She turned her wide smile on Dan, inviting him not to take offence.

Chapter Thirteen

Outside the sun was still shining. A gusty westerly promised more rain. Cloud-shaped shadows were blown across the fields where the green shoots of winter wheat were already showing. In the little house Vera was still holding forth and Dan was still listening. Emma made her excuses and left them to it. She drove to the end of the Crescent, then, instead of turning towards the village, she took the opposite direction towards the coast. Wendy, the coxswain of the pilot launch, was the nearest thing she had to a friend here, and liked it when she dropped in with Matthew. Emma felt she needed an excuse to be out of the house, away from the television and the local news. She couldn't face seeing Dan again on the screen. He'd been thinner then, his hair shorter. But the way he'd been glowering at the camera, you could still imagine him letting his temper get the better of him. She couldn't imagine him taking orders easily and wondered if that was why he'd left the police.

Every year in the autumn there were predictions that the Point would be washed away by the tides of the equinox. One big gale, people said. That was all it would take. And certainly it was skinnier than it had been, a spit of land, shaped like a drooping, wasted phallus, hanging into the mouth of the river from the north bank. In places the old road disappeared into the sea and a new track had been made through the sand, the sea holly and the buckthorn. The Point bulged slightly at the tip, where the jetty was and the houses belonging to the lifeboat station had been built. These houses were incongruously modern, all the same, as if they'd been made from a kit. Easy to leave behind, Emma supposed, if that one big gale did come. Only the cottages where the coxswains lived had any substance.

She parked opposite the houses, next to the mobile cafe which sold coffee and fry-ups to the birdwatchers and fishermen. Matthew was awake and began grumbling as soon as the car stopped. She fed him there, sitting in the front passenger seat, looking out over the water, with her coat draped around them both. There was no one to see but she didn't even like going without a bra. Wendy, who claimed never to have been broody in her life, loved to watch the baby feeding, but Emma didn't want an audience. Not today. James said the baby was as regular as the tide in his habits and it was true. Her life was punctuated by six hourly interruptions. She was getting used to it.

Mathew settled and she allowed her mind to wander. These quiet times of waiting were when she would usually conjure up dreams of Dan Greenwood. There would be nothing exotic about her fantasies. At night she would wander into the pottery and he would kiss her and touch her. She seldom imagined herself making love. Hers were the fantasies of an immature teenager, comforting and harmless. The fantasies she might have had when she was fifteen, before Abigail

ANN CLEEVES

had died. She told herself she should leave them
behind. She was grown up and they had no meaning
now. But it was harder than she had imagined to let
them go.

As she pulled down her jumper two teenage lads
raced from one of the houses and began to kick a ball
against the sea wall. Still carrying Matthew she got out
of the car and looked down the river. The smell of mud
and seaweed mixed with the frying bacon and chip fat
from the cafe.

The cafe was a relatively new arrival on the Point.
Before it, there had been an ice-cream van, but only on
fine days and at the weekends. And, thinking of the
ice-cream van, Emma suddenly remembered that this
was where she had first met Abigail Mantel. She hadn't
thought of the encounter for more than ten years.
Even relating the history of their friendship to Caroline
Fletcher, it had slid somehow out of the story. Perhaps
it had been too trivial. Now it came back in jagged
flashes, like the sunlight on the pavements. She
thought, *This is what it is like to be old. This is how old
people remember their childhood.*

It was June, the end of their first week in Springhead
House. Robert was still elated by the new purpose in
his life, optimistic about the house, his work, the whole
deal of living in the country. 'A new start,' he'd say,
over and over again. 'Really, we are so blessed.' Though
Emma didn't feel blessed. She felt uprooted. Literally.
As if someone had yanked her out of hard-packed soil
and dumped her to rot. She'd tried to talk about it to
Christopher, but he'd only shrugged. 'It's done,' he'd

said. 'They won't move back. Not now. Best make the most of it.' She'd thought then it was the sort of thing an adult might say and had considered him almost a traitor.

In contrast, Robert had bounced around the place, wearing them out. And now it was Saturday and although their belongings were still in boxes and Mary looked exhausted, he insisted that they take a trip out to explore their new surroundings. Perhaps they were carried along by his enthusiasm or perhaps they didn't have the energy to put up a fight, but it was agreed very quickly without argument. A bike ride, he said. Obvious. Ideal because the country's so flat. And he climbed over the packing cases in the garage to pull out their bikes.

They rode in line with Robert at the front. He was dressed in big khaki shorts which flapped at the leg and a T-shirt with the Christian symbol of the fish on the front. Emma enjoyed the sensation of riding, the pull on her legs, the smell of salt and seaweed and mud. But all the time she was thinking, *Please don't let anyone from my new school see me. Not with my parents and my nerdy brother, all of us looking like something out of Enid Blyton.*

Then they were at the Point, and that must have been where Robert was aiming for all the time though he never said. And suddenly it was like riding over the sea, with water on both sides and gulls flying alongside them. At the ice-cream van they stopped. They flopped onto the grass, with the bikes on their sides next to them, while Robert went to buy the ice creams. Christopher rolled onto his stomach and trapped a ladybird under his cupped hands. He'd always captured insects that way. He was looking at it through a hole he'd formed between his thumbs and first fingers, then there was the roar of an engine. He sat up to look and the ladybird flew away.

Arriving back with the ice creams, Robert glowered at the noise. His perfect family afternoon had been disturbed. He muttered about hooligans. The car was black and shiny, a convertible with the roof down, and it pulled up beside them. Loud music, which Emma failed to recognize, continued even after the engine had been turned off. In the passenger seat was Abigail Mantel, her red hair in effective disarray. At first, Emma thought the car must belong to a boyfriend. Abigail seemed much older than she was. Even at that first glimpse you could tell she was the sort of girl who would attract a boyfriend with a powerful car.

Abigail slid out of her seat. She was wearing a denim skirt with a slit down the side and a tight red vest top. They presumed she intended to buy ice cream and made a point of not staring, though Christopher didn't manage too well. Emma was surprised. She'd never seen him take any notice of girls before. But to everyone's astonishment Abigail approached them. The ice cream dripped down soggy cones. She lowered herself onto the grass beside Emma. Christopher's mouth was slightly open, but he was too far away for Emma to kick him.

'Hi,' Abigail said. Her voice was slightly drawling, but not unfriendly. 'Aren't you the new girl? I've seen you on the bus. I thought it was you. I asked dad to stop.'

Emma hated the school bus. It was crowded and noisy and no one had made an effort to be friendly.

Each morning she made sure she sat in a corner and stared out of the window. Certainly she had never noticed Abigail.

'Yes,' she said. 'Of course. Hi.'

Had Keith got out of the car to join them too? Although she strained to think, Emma couldn't form a picture of him sitting on the grass beside them. She couldn't hear his voice in her head. Robert certainly had spoken to Abigail. There'd been quite a conversation and he'd been impressed by her politeness. He'd asked her name, then introduced the family. They'd discussed where she lived and the subjects she was taking at school. When at last she'd returned to the car with a wave, he'd said, 'She seems a pleasant girl, Em. There, I said it would be easy to make friends in the country.'

Mary hadn't said a word. She'd seemed frozen. It had been as if she were holding her breath. Perhaps she'd been less certain than Robert that they'd be readily accepted by the natives.

It occurred then to Emma that the meeting with Abigail on the Point must have slipped from Robert's mind too. He'd told his manager that it would be appropriate for him to supervise Jeanie Long because there was no conflict of interest. He hadn't known Abigail Mantel, hadn't even met her. Emma supposed that such a fleeting conversation would hardly count as a meeting.

Wendy, always immaculately turned out for work, always precise and meticulous in anything concerning the launch, lived in domestic chaos. Emma loved the disarray in the whitewashed cottage. Perhaps that was the basis for her affection for the coxswain. They had little else in common. In this house of overflowing waste bins and mountainous laundry baskets she felt liberated, and at the same time superior. She envied Wendy's confidence. How sure of herself she must be! To allow people into a kitchen with unwashed dishes, the foil containers from last night's takeaway piled on the table, knickers, still slightly stained despite having been through the wash, draped on a radiator. But despite the envy Emma felt she was a better person because her house was more ordered. She was proud of the clean windows, the boiled dish cloths, the washed curtains.

'I'm really not sure how Wendy would cope with a baby,' she'd once said to James, knowing as she spoke how smug she must sound.

Today Wendy had finished her twelve-hour shift at midday, but Emma had known she'd still be about. She seemed not to need sleep. Cigarettes and caffeine kept her going, she said, and today there was a cigarette drooping from the corner of her mouth, as she used both hands to rewire the plug of an iron. She always kept busy despite the mess. When Emma brought in the baby she stubbed out the cigarette and opened a window, but the smell of smoke lingered, hiding something more unpleasant which Emma couldn't quite identify. Rotting vegetables perhaps, or sour milk. It appeared to come from the larder. Wendy seemed not to notice. She moved her bag of tools from a kitchen chair so Emma could sit down.

'Did you hear the news about Michael's daughter?'

Her first words, with her back to Emma, as she poured boiling water over instant coffee. Then she turned to judge Emma's reaction, to share the shock. Throughout the village, Emma thought, people are talking like this. Enjoying the excitement. Feeling that geography has given them an unexpected role in the drama.

'Yes,' Emma said. 'I saw it on the television.' Then, offering up the information as a gift, as you might bring chocolates and wine to a dinner party, 'Michael was in church yesterday.'

'Was he? I can't say I liked the old bugger, but you can't help feeling sorry . . .'

'He walked out,' Emma said. 'I suppose he didn't want to face people after.' She couldn't bring herself to mention the scene he'd made, spitting wine at her father.

'You realize what this means, don't you?' Wendy leaned forward. She'd changed from her uniform into jeans and a big, hand-knitted sweater. Her eyes were bright with exhaustion and something else, which made Emma wonder about her, wonder what was really going on in her head. What was it? Desperation? Exhilaration? Wendy wasn't always alone. There'd been men friends, lovers. Occasionally they'd moved in, but they'd never stayed long. Wendy had made out she didn't mind, and at the time Emma had been taken in.

'What does it mean?' she asked gently.

'That the murderer's still out there, of course,' Wendy said. 'And I can't see that it could have been a stranger. The police must have asked, ten years ago, if anyone had seen a stranger around. It would have been noticed, wouldn't it? A Sunday afternoon in November, you don't get many trippers. And if you were the sort who liked young girls, you'd not expect to find one lurking on the edge of a bean field. Besides, she weren't raped, were she?'

She stopped abruptly, her hand over her mouth, a gesture too stagy, surely, to be sincere.

'I forgot. She were a friend of yours. I am sorry, love.'

'No,' Emma said. 'She wasn't raped.' She looked across her coffee mug to Wendy. 'Were you living round here then?' Wendy must be in her thirties. She'd have been about the same age Emma was now.

'In Elvet. In one of the council houses. Married to a bastard. Just before I saw sense and started work on the ferries.'

'Did you know Jeanie Long?'

'I went to school with her. Not that we mixed much. She weren't my type.' The eyes flashed. 'All I'm saying is watch yourself. Don't take chances. I'm surprised James let you out today on your own with the baby.'

'He's asleep. He doesn't know.' She looked at her watch. It was nearly four o'clock, already getting gloomy outside. 'Perhaps we should get back.'

'Aye,' Wendy said. 'You get on before it gets right dark. And take care now.'

But when Emma left she didn't lock the door behind her guests. She lit the cigarette and returned to the iron, as if she sensed that *she* was in no danger.

Chapter Fourteen

When they returned from the Point it was dark and the doors of the pottery were padlocked shut. The square was deserted. It could have been midnight. Inside the house, Emma felt suddenly safe. There was that relief of coming in and slipping off her shoes and making tea, which she remembered from when she'd been working. Perhaps that's all that's wrong with me, she thought. I've been spending too much time in this house. I can't appreciate it. Perhaps it's time to think about going back to work.

James was up. He'd drawn the curtains in the living room and banked up the fire. The walls in this room were dark red and hung with large pictures in gilt frames which he said he'd inherited from ancient relatives. He loved it. When they came in he was sitting on the leather sofa reading a newspaper, but he stood up and took Matthew from her, held him in the air above his head.

'That was a long walk,' he said. He didn't sound anxious and she felt resentful. There was a murderer on the loose and he wasn't even concerned. Instead he stood leaning against the window sill looking around the room, beaming.

'We went to see Wendy.'

'She'll have liked that.'

'She thinks the person who murdered Abigail Mantel could still be living round here.'

He frowned. 'I suppose it's possible. Does it bring that all back? Like a nightmare? Of course, I can't possibly understand what it can be like.'

She was surprised and moved, went up to him and kissed his forehead.

'I won't let anything happen to you,' he said. 'Not to either of you.'

'I know.'

'Why don't I cook? You get the baby ready for bed, then put your feet up.'

She thought this was how it could be. She could give up her dreams of Dan, who after all was edgy and unpredictable, not even likeable if she thought about it seriously. They could be content, the two of them. She could make small concessions, like going willingly to church with him, and taking more interest in his work, like initiating regular if unimaginative sex, and he would take care of them. For some reason she knew she could trust him to do that. He would agree to her returning to teaching, even if he didn't much like the idea. Their marriage would survive without argument or disturbance; it would be at least as happy as that of most of their friends. Was that what she wanted? And anyway, did she deserve it?

When she came downstairs from settling Matthew to sleep, James was in the kitchen. He was standing at the workbench chopping onions and garlic, concentrating so hard that he didn't hear her approach. He'd changed into jeans and a thin woollen jersey. There was nothing between the jersey and his skin and

Emma found herself thinking, with an odd excitement, about the faint irritation this must cause. She stood behind him and slid her hand beneath the jumper, moved her fingers down the knots of his spine, inside the waist of his jeans. He turned, still with the knife in one hand, a bulb of garlic in the other, disarmed. He bent and kissed her forehead, ran the tip of his tongue over her eyelids.

'Why don't you leave that?' she said. 'We can have it later.' It was an experiment. Could she forget her fantasies of Dan Greenwood and learn to make do with reality? A quiet domestic life?

James reached behind him to replace the garlic and knife on the bench. It was as if he had his hands tied behind his back. All the time he was kissing her, and just for a moment she felt herself relaxing.

Then there was a banging on the door. The heavy knocker was rammed down three times. In the quiet house the sound seemed to echo. Emma immediately imagined Vera Stanhope standing there. She was certain it was her, could picture her, legs apart, putting all her weight behind the knocking.

'We could ignore it,' James said. Emma thought the suggestion was half-hearted. It would be too daring for him, and already he was feeling slightly embarrassed by his abandon.

She came to his rescue. 'No.' If it was Vera Stanhope she wouldn't go away. She would stand there all night if necessary, get a warrant and smash in the door.

Emma had been so convinced that the inspector would be standing there that she almost felt cheated. She'd been planning an angry outburst. *Do you realize my baby's asleep? I've already told you everything I know.*

The figure on the doorstep was taller than Vera Stanhope, better proportioned, almost athletic. He'd turned away and was looking out at the square. His long hair was tangled. He wore a thin waterproof anorak and there was a small rucksack at his feet. It was the last person she would have expected.

'Chris. What are you doing here?'

He turned to face her. His face still had the brooding quality he'd developed as an undergraduate. She'd thought it was a pose, a way of attracting women, but now it seemed to have become a habit. There were dark shadows under his eyes, emphasized by the light over the door, which also made his features more angular than she remembered.

'I've come to see my sister,' he said. 'Of course.' He bent and pecked her abruptly on her cheek. His lips were icy. 'I hope you've got some beer in there. Otherwise we'll have to send James out to find some. I've been travelling all day. I'm desperate.'

'How did you get here?'

'Last bus from Hull. It took bloody hours.'

'You should have phoned. I'd have come to get you.'

'I don't believe in cars.' He laughed. She couldn't work out if it were a joke at his expense for having such uncomfortable principles, or if he were mocking her for taking him seriously. She'd never known how to react to him. Although she'd been the older one, she'd always been intimidated by his intelligence. The gap between them had grown wider since Abigail's death. Neither of them had made the effort to bridge it.

She realized she was still standing in the doorway, blocking his way into the house. She moved aside.

'Come in. James is cooking supper. I'm sure there's beer.'

The kitchen was at the back of the house and she led Chris through. During the day it seemed dark and rather gloomy, but now, after the chill of standing on the step, it was warm, even welcoming. James had returned to chopping onions. He sliced them into fine, almost translucent semicircles.

'Will there be enough food for three? Look who's come to supper.' Her voice sounded unnaturally bright. She wasn't really sure how well the two men got on. They seemed pleasant enough to each other, though once, in an unguarded moment, James had told her he thought her brother arrogant. It was true, she thought. Sometimes Chris gave the impression that he despised the whole world, apart perhaps from a couple of Nobel scientists.

James looked up from the chopping board. He must have heard Chris's voice at the door and had his response already prepared.

'Sure,' he said. 'It's great to see you.' He paused for a beat. 'Do Robert and Mary know you're here? We could invite them round too.'

'God, no.' Chris was horrified. 'I need a good night's sleep before I can face that.'

James slid the onion from the board into a frying pan.

'There's beer in the fridge,' he said. 'You can get me one too.'

When Chris had his back to them James rolled his eyes and pulled a face. What was that about? Chris's attitude to his parents, or his own disappointment that they would no longer have the evening to themselves? Emma couldn't tell.

They would eat in the small narrow room which led immediately from the kitchen. Emma lit candles and set the table, while Christopher went upstairs for a shower. James moaned gently at her through the open door while he prepared a salad.

'Really,' he said. 'Chris could have given us some warning. We might have been busy. Who else would just turn up on the doorstep like that?'

'He's very focused,' she said. 'He decided he wanted to visit and that was it. He wouldn't think much of anything other than how he'd get here, once the decision was made.'

Christopher had always been like that, even when he was quite young. He would become obsessed with an object of study or a project. All his energy would be taken up with that. Other school subjects would be dealt with in a cursory, detached way, but his teachers would know that his mind was elsewhere. The fixation would end as suddenly as it had begun and he would move on to something else – dinosaurs or gravity or an obscure composer. He had stuck with seabirds for a surprisingly long time. Perhaps the puffins had come to bore him and that was why he was here.

At the time the family had put his sudden passions down to the eccentricity of an academic. Now Emma wondered again when the fixations had begun. With the move to Elvet or Abigail's murder? And were they as harmless as they had seemed at the time or the indication of a deeper disturbance? She wished she'd made more effort to understand him when they'd both been living at home, decided that his appearance was a good sign. It wasn't too late to understand him better.

They ate at first in silence. The wind had dropped to a murmur, but Emma was aware of it still in the background. She made a few attempts at conversation, asking about Christopher's work, the flat in Aberdeen, but soon realized that he was exhausted. He sat with his left elbow on the table, resting his head on his palm, holding his fork in his right hand, pushing pasta into his mouth. She could tell James disapproved. He had an obsession about table manners. Occasionally Chris's eyelids would droop, then something would jerk him awake and he would stare wildly at them for a moment as if he'd forgotten who they were. He had drunk the beer and most of a bottle of Australian red. Emma considered what problem might have brought him home. Could he have become addicted to drugs? Is this how someone who was suffering withdrawal might behave? She had no idea. Perhaps his depression – she thought he probably *was* depressed – was the result of the end of a love affair. It didn't occur to her that Chris's arrival in Elvet could have anything to do with Abigail Mantel.

They had moved on to the cheese and fruit. James said to him, quite gently, 'Look, you're obviously tired. Go to bed whenever you like. We won't mind.'

'No!' Christopher's head jerked back in spasm again. 'It's no good. I won't sleep yet.'

'Well, I think I'll go. I've got an early start in the morning.' He gave Emma a meaningful look. Perhaps he thought they could carry on where they'd left off when Chris interrupted them.

'I won't be long.' But she was careful to keep any

hint of promise from her voice. And she knew him. Once James was in bed he would go straight to sleep.

She waited until he'd gone upstairs then fetched more wine from the kitchen, opened it and poured each of them a glass. It was the most she'd drunk since she'd found out she was pregnant. She'd never had to play big sister before. As a child she'd been the needy one. Chris had been independent, self-contained.

'What is it, Chris?' she asked. 'What's the matter?'

He sat upright for the first time, looked directly at her.

'Don't you know?' Brutal, cruel. 'Really, are you so thick that you never realized?'

She felt her eyes prick with tears.

'I'm sorry,' he said. 'I'm a mess. I haven't slept since it all started again.'

'What?' she demanded. 'What started?'

'Abigail Mantel. All that.'

'Jeanie's suicide was only in the paper yesterday.' She couldn't make sense of it.

'That was what made me come, of course,' he said. 'But it started long before that. There was that piece in the *Guardian*. It seems as if people have been talking about her for weeks.'

'I didn't realize she meant anything to you.'

She thought of the evening after she had found Abigail's body, the two of them looking out of his bedroom window at the moonlit image of the stretcher bearers. He hadn't seemed upset then, had he? Or had she been so absorbed by her own place in the drama that she hadn't noticed?

'She meant everything,' he said. 'At the time.'

'But you were young.'

'Fourteen,' he said. 'Given to obsessions.'

'You can't have gone out with her?' Abigail had considered herself too sophisticated for the lads in their own year. Certainly she would never have deigned to go out with someone like Chris.

'No,' he said. 'Nothing like that.'

'Well then?'

'I followed her. Everywhere she went. All that summer.' He stared into his glass. 'It started when we met up on the Point. The first time you spoke to her. We'd just moved. Dad had dragged us out for a bike ride. You remember?'

'We were eating ice creams.'

'Yes!' he was almost shouting. 'Yes!'

'And Abigail arrived in her father's car and got out to introduce herself.'

'That was the start of it. After that I couldn't stop thinking about her. Literally. I'd wake up thinking about her, she was there, lurking at the back of my mind all day, and at night I'd dream about her.'

'She was your project for the summer.' She was frightened by his intensity and hoped to tease him out of it, but he answered her seriously.

'No. Projects are intellectual. Abigail was more than that. I can't explain it even now. I don't expect you to understand. Look at you. Married, a mother, too sensible to have dreams.'

'Marriage doesn't stop you dreaming,' she said, but very quietly and anyway, he wasn't listening. She thought suddenly, *If Abigail had heard me say that she'd have pretended to be sick. So predictable. So cheesy.* For the first time in years she missed the girl who had been a real friend despite all the later misgivings.

He went on. 'It's never gone away, you know. If she hadn't died I expect I'd have moved on, got over her. As it is I'm stuck with it. A passion I'll never satisfy. A fantasy I can never make real.' He tried to smile. 'Crazy, huh?'

He reached for the wine bottle. She saw that his hand was shaking. 'Do you know I've never had a girlfriend,' he said. 'Not a real one. The occasional fumbled one-night stand. Usually when I'm drunk. Usually with a girl with red hair. But nothing more than that.'

For a moment Emma said nothing to him. She looked at him across the table, not sure what to make of it. Christopher had never spoken to her like this before. He had never spoken to her about anything important. She wasn't even sure she believed him.

'I never realized,' she said in the end. 'Why are you telling me now?'

'Because I had to talk to somebody. I think I'm going mad. I'm not sure what's true any more.'

'It is crazy,' Emma said. 'You have to let go.'

'And did you?'

'What do you mean?'

'You're holding onto stuff. What is it? Guilt? You never liked Abigail much, did you? It must have been a shock but I doubt if you felt much grief.'

'She was my best friend.'

'No,' he said. 'She was your only friend. All you had. And she never let you forget it, did she? She never let you forget how much you owed her.' He held her eyes for a moment. 'I always thought,' he paused, 'that deep down you hated her.'

'No,' she said, but the image she'd had a moment before, of Abigail pulling faces, of them laughing together, had already faded.

Chapter Fifteen

Emma left Chris sitting at the table, staring moodily into his wine glass. He had become silent and unresponsive, and when she said goodnight he seemed not to hear. She climbed the stairs slowly, not prepared to make more effort on her brother, but not yet ready for bed.

The day before, they'd moved Matthew into his own bedroom. James had prepared it when she was pregnant. A labour of love, because the colours she'd chosen hadn't been to his taste at all. Under her instruction he'd painted the grubby wallpaper yellow and stuck up a frieze of waves and boats and fish. A mobile of silver stars hung from the ceiling. At the open door she paused to look in. The baby was lying on his back in his cot, his arms flung out, relaxed and floppy as a rag doll.

As she'd expected, James was already asleep. She stared down at him trying to recreate something of the excitement she'd felt when she'd touched him earlier, but it had quite gone. He didn't stir when she moved around the room. She began to undress, but still felt too restless for sleep. The wooden floorboards were uncarpeted, stained and varnished and the feel of them on her bare feet always reminded her of PE lessons in the gym at school. One of the teachers had been keen on contemporary dance, and dressed in black leotards, they'd leapt and writhed around the hall to weird electronic music. Expressing themselves. Abigail had thought the exercise ridiculous and made her feelings clear. Emma had been torn. Secretly she'd enjoyed the freedom of the movement. It was like running across a beach towards the sea. The same exhilaration. But because of Abigail, she'd had to sneer too.

Chris had been right in one sense. After Abigail's death, school had become more bearable. In the few weeks before the summer holidays and in the first half of the Christmas term she was known only as *Abigail's mate*. Afterwards, she had become an object of interest in her own right; the pupils had been curious about the murder investigation, the teachers sympathetic. Under their attention she had flourished.

Was it that autumn term she'd discovered her facility for languages? It had been a piece of translation, German into English, and when it had come to her turn she'd rattled it off, understanding immediately what the writer had been trying to say.

'Very good, Emma,' the teacher had said automatically. Emma had come in for a lot of praise since Abigail's death. As if that was some compensation for the shock of finding a strangled body. Then the teacher had repeated, meaning it, surprised. 'Really, that was very good.'

So language had become her thing. French and German to A level and Spanish as an extra GCSE in the sixth form, then Russian for her degree. She hadn't been brilliant. She'd just scraped a 2.1. But it had been more than her teachers would have predicted when she was fifteen. Her parents too had been surprised by her success, though they'd tried not to show it. How could she explain it? *Well, it's much easier to speak in other people's voices. It's more comfortable.* How would they understand that?

That had led to her meeting James. After university she'd taken a job with a small shipping company based in Hull. Why had she come back? After being in Exeter for three years and Frankfurt for one, she'd thought herself free of the influence of Robert and Mary. She could have found work anywhere in the country, anywhere in the world. Yet, almost without making a conscious decision, she'd found herself back here. She had felt some responsibility for her mother of course. She couldn't imagine what it could be like for Mary, with just the two of them rattling round that big house. Even now her parents' marriage was a mystery to her. What was it about Robert which inspired such devotion? Not just from her mother but from all the women in the parish. But that hadn't been the only reason for her return. She'd been scared all the time she'd been away. Of the strange places and the jostling cities and of people she didn't know. Of the unexpected. Perhaps that had been the legacy of discovering Abigail's body. She was terrified of stumbling across another horror. She knew she wouldn't cope with it on her own. Here, her parents drove her to distraction, but they'd be there to support her, as they had the first time.

There'd been some translation work in the Hull office, but she'd felt her grasp of the languages slipping away through lack of use. When she'd been approached to teach an adult education class she'd taken it on reluctantly, just as a way of keeping Russian at least real in her mind. And at the first class James had walked in, straight from work, still in his uniform. Her dreams about him had been just as vivid as those about Dan Greenwood. Hadn't they?

She moved across to the window, had to fight against the compulsion to relive her favourite day dream: *Emma sees herself slipping out into the square and, keeping to the shadows, walking across to the forge. She pushes open one of the big doors which form an arch, like the door of a church, and steps inside.* It would be so hard to let this go. But how could she continue now she knew there was no attraction, just an embarrassed recognition of a schoolgirl who had once been on the edge of one of his cases? She would miss those languid afternoons when she lost herself in daydreams, the nights when she looked out to see if he was there.

A light was on in the pottery and the door was not padlocked. Dan was working late. Emma supposed Vera Stanhope had demanded his time all day and he had to catch up. Or perhaps the night shifts with the police had given him a taste for working late. The light went off. Dan emerged from the pottery and stood for a moment, looking up and down the square. He locked the door and fixed the padlock, but still he stood where he was. Emma had a sudden and irrational certainty that he was waiting for her. She stared down at him, willing him to look up. But as there was no light in the bedroom how would he notice her? The orange street lamp would be reflected in the glass forming a barrier he'd not be able to see through. She considered pushing up the sash window as she had on the night when he and James had discussed Jeanie's suicide, wondered if she could do it without waking her husband.

A car drove into the square. It was black and long. It pulled up smoothly besides Dan and he climbed in. Emma couldn't see who was driving. She supposed it could be Vera Stanhope with more questions, though there had been something furtive about the way Dan looked all around him before getting in. Perhaps it was a woman, a lover he'd managed to keep secret from the rest of the village. The car revved its engine and drove off very fast. Emma climbed into bed and lay with her back to James.

She woke to light, in a panic.

'Where's Matthew?'

James was dressed. The light came from the lamp on the dressing table. He was stooped in front of the mirror, knotting his tie.

'Asleep,' he said. 'It's still early.'

'Are you sure? He never sleeps through.' Her heart was thudding. She felt clear headed, wide awake.

'I checked.' He pulled a face to confess that he'd panicked too.

As if on cue there was a grizzle from the monitor they'd bought, then a small cry.

'You stay there,' James said. 'I'll get him.'

She propped herself against all the pillows on the bed and wondered why she couldn't be happy with this: a good husband and a baby to feed.

She kept Matthew with her and read until the light came through the window and the traffic started moving. James had long gone. She changed the baby and put him back in his cot, then went downstairs to make tea. She half expected to find Chris where she'd left him, slumped over the table amidst the remains of the meal, but there was only the debris. He must have roused himself sufficiently to drag himself to the spare room. It would have been late though. She hadn't heard him. She filled the kettle then stacked the dishwasher and switched it on.

When the tea was made she decided to share it with Chris. She pictured herself sitting at the end of his bed, the duvet tucked around her feet, continuing the conversation of the night before. It wasn't too late for them to become close. She had to set the tray on the table on the landing so she could knock at the door. There was no reply. She wasn't surprised. He must be practically unconscious after all that booze and so many nights without sleep. Still she persisted. She knocked louder, then opened the door.

The bed was empty and still made, though it was slightly crumpled, as if Chris had lain on top of it. The rumpled cover was the only sign that he had ever been there. His bag was gone and he hadn't left a note.

Downstairs, Emma sat in the warm kitchen. She drank the tea while it was still hot. After two cups she telephoned her parents' house. There was no reply.

Chapter Sixteen

Michael was coming back to life, thawing out. And it was painful. Like when a numb foot gives way to pins and needles or cramp. It had started in the church: the stab of fury, which had caused him to spit the wine at Robert Winter, had cut through the dead iciness. Then Vera Stanhope, big and warm and generous, had continued the process. Now he was restless, fidgety. He couldn't sit in the bungalow waiting for things to happen.

'What can I do?' he'd said when he stood up to let the inspector out of the house. 'I want to help.'

She'd hesitated and he'd held his breath, dreading a patronizing response. *Leave it to us. I'll let you know if I think of anything.* The silence had gone on for so long that he'd thought she never would answer. She'd walk out into the street, leaving him still waiting.

'Mantel,' she'd said at last. 'Is he still involved in village life?'

'As far as I know. I haven't mixed much since Peg . . .' He'd been ashamed to admit how isolated he'd become. He never went out. Before the escapade in the church and Jeanie's funeral, his only trip out was once a month to the barber, and then he'd go early on a week day when he knew the shop would be empty.

'It'd be useful to find out what he's up to. Not just work. Has he got a woman, for example, in that fancy house of his? People will talk to you when they won't to me.'

'Haven't you spoken to him?'

'Not yet. I will do, of course, but I want to know what I'm dealing with first.'

'You don't think he killed his daughter?' Michael had felt dizzy at the thought. Was that where Vera's enquiries might be leading?

She hadn't answered. She had stood for a moment, just inside the door, then she'd said very formally, 'Goodbye, Mr Long,' given him a big wink and walked out into the street.

At lunch-time he got ready to go out. He didn't dress up in the suit he'd worn to church, but he chose his clothes carefully, an actor intent on giving the right impression through his costume. Comfortable was what he was after. Comfortable and relaxed, as he'd been in the old days before Abigail Mantel had died and Jeanie had been locked up. He chose a pair of corduroy trousers which still had a splash of varnish on one knee and a fawn ribbed jumper, then a waterproof, because there were still flecks of rain against the window. Outside, he fumbled a bit with his keys when he locked up but there was none of the usual panic. He walked past the knot of reporters on the square with his back straight and his head high.

At the door of the Anchor he stopped and marvelled at the change that had come over him. Then he opened the door and the smell was the same as it had always been. Hops and cigar smoke – Veronica's husband, Barry, smoked fat stubby cigars – wood polish and a hint of fried food from the kitchen at the back, even though no one was eating today. Veronica was behind the bar and Barry, a slight, sandy man with fishy eyes, was sitting on the punters' side, on one of the tall stools. He was the laziest man Michael had ever known. Rumour had it that he was dying of some rare illness, but Michael had heard that rumour fifteen years ago and Barry was still alive. Still propping up the bar and listening to gossip like a woman. His name was over the bar but everyone knew it was Veronica who ran the place.

It was Veronica who saw Michael first. She looked up from the glass she was polishing and gave him a quick, polite smile as if he were a stranger, a tourist who'd wandered in for a bar meal. Then she registered who he was. There was a moment of wonder as if she could hardly believe her eyes.

'Hello, love,' she said. 'The usual?'

All those years and she remembered. That was a landlady for you. She was wearing a white blouse of some silky material and he could see the more dense white of her bra through it. He remembered suddenly that he'd fancied her, even when Peg was still alive. Just as in a very different way he'd fancied Abigail Mantel. But all men would be the same, wouldn't they? There was no need for the sinking sense of shame in the pit of his stomach.

Veronica was staring at him. 'It *is* Theakston's, isn't it, love?'

'Please,' he said.

Barry swivelled on the plastic seat of the bar stool as if the effort was too much for him. He was always curious and usually sat half-turned to face the door, so

he could see who was coming in. He almost fell off
when he saw Michael.

Michael walked slowly towards them. What did this
remind him of? One of those Westerns he'd liked as a
kid. He was the old deputy returning to his home town
for the last time to see off the villain. Swaggering into
the saloon. Letting the townsfolk know he was back,
still alive.

Veronica set the pint on the bar for him. 'On the
house,' she said. 'Welcome back, love.'

'When's the funeral?' Barry asked, the wide pebble
eyes unblinking. 'Your Jeanie's, I mean.'

He'd never be a *great* gossip, Michael thought. No
tact. No subtlety.

'It's come and gone. I didn't want a fuss.' He was
looking at Veronica. If Barry carried on like that, he'd
be tempted to give him a slap. Better ignore him, try to
shut him out. The funeral had been arranged by the
prison chaplain, a young woman so short it had been
hard not to think of her as a child. They'd decided on
the crematorium. He couldn't stand the thought of
being buried and at the last minute had decided it
wouldn't be right for Jeanie either. She must have
hated cramped, suffocating places too. The chaplain
had sat beside him. The governor who'd come to the
house had read from the Bible. There'd been a couple
of women he hadn't recognized. He supposed they
were prison staff, teachers, maybe. Smart anyway, in
suits. At the end of the service the chaplain had put her
hand on his and he'd had a jolt of surprise. It hadn't
just been the physical contact – though that had been
a shock in itself after all this time. But her hand had
looked just like Jeanie's, the fingers tapering and

strong, although she was such a short woman. She had even worn a silver ring very similar to one that Jeanie had possessed. At that moment, for the first time, he'd come close to tears.

'I wish you'd let me know,' Veronica said. 'I'd have liked to be there. You know I thought the world of Jeanie.'

'Aye, well,' Michael felt close to tears again now. 'I wasn't thinking straight.'

'They said she never committed that murder . . .' Barry fed on information. Perhaps that was what had kept him alive for so long. A determination not to miss out on anything. The joy of sicking it up to the gang of cronies who gathered round the bar every night. Now his mouth was slightly open and he was breathing hard. Michael wondered what Veronica had ever seen in him.

She spoke before Michael had a chance to think up an answer. 'Of course Jeanie never killed that lass,' she said firmly. 'None of us ever thought for a moment that she had.'

Michael met her eyes. He hoped she couldn't tell what he was thinking.

'I thought I'd better make an effort to get out more. I couldn't sit wallowing in the bungalow for ever.' Again he was speaking just to her.

'Quite right, love. Another pint?'

He saw with surprise that his glass was already empty. He nodded and slid a ten-pound note across the bar.

'Get something for yourself,' he said. 'Barry too.'

The pub was quiet. Outside the rain was stopping and the sky was lighter. There was a cobweb, which had been invisible in the gloom, stretched across a corner on the ceiling above the bar. Barry lit a cigar. He puffed out his cheeks to blow away the smoke.

'So,' Michael said, 'what's been going on, then?' He hardly recognized his own voice. It sounded jolly. Not the voice of someone who'd buried his only daughter the week before. 'What have I missed? I heard the lifeboat was out last month in that gale.'

'A trawler from Grimsby,' Barry said. 'Engine failure.'

'Casualties?'

'None. They got everyone off safe.'

'Nice work in that weather.'

Michael tried not to think too closely about the rescue. If he imagined himself there, if he could hear the straining engine and the wind and the creaking wood, taste the salt and the diesel, he'd only realize how much he missed his work on the launches.

Barry returned the cigar to his mouth, sucked so his cheeks were hollow and his eyes more prominent than ever. Michael waited in silence. 'Keith Mantel's trying to raise money for an inflatable,' Barry said at last. 'For inshore work. Anglers stranded on the mud banks. Kids who get out of their depth swimming.' The mention of Mantel was mischievous. On top of everything else the landlord was a stirrer. He wanted to see what sort of reaction he could provoke.

Michael sipped his pint, seemed to consider before replying. 'Makes sense. It'd be quicker to launch. Cheaper to run. More use in the shallows. Keith's still a leading light on the committee then?' *Keith*. As if they were mates. Bosom pals.

'They'd never survive without his fundraising.'

They managed before he turned up here, Michael thought, but he only nodded in agreement. 'You need someone to look after the money side.'

'You've changed your tune,' Barry said sharply, stung by the lack of response. 'I thought you couldn't stand the man.'

'Aye, well. Maybe I've learned a bit of sense in my old age.'

'He's having a fundraiser at his house.' Barry was getting desperate. 'I can sell you a ticket if you like.'

'I tell you what, Barry, let me have two. I think I'll bring a friend.'

'You're joking!'

'Not at all. It's a good cause.'

Barry didn't know what to say to that and plugged his mouth again with his cigar.

'Is Keith still living in the Old Chapel?' Michael asked.

'Yes,' Veronica said cautiously. 'He's still there.'

'Everyone thought he'd move out after that tragedy with his daughter.' Barry tried another tack. Michael thought he was like one of those snidey kids there'd been in every class, the sort who'd pick away with jibes and insults until they got thumped. Then they'd burst into tears until the teacher came. 'But he stayed on in the end. He said he needed the memories.'

'Aye, well,' Michael said. 'I can understand that.' But his memories of Jeanie in their old house on the shore were unpleasant – fights, sulky silences, shut doors with music like sobbing seeping out from under them. He envied Mantel his memories. 'Does he live there on his own, or is there a woman?'

'Of course there's a woman.' Barry chortled unpleasantly. Veronica gave him a warning look, which he ignored. 'You'd not expect Keith to do without for long. This one's called Deborah. Debs. An actress. Or so he says. Blonde. Nice tits. Young enough to be his daughter.'

Michael couldn't help himself this time. 'He always did like them young.'

Barry weighed this up seriously. 'Not always,' he said. 'He likes them tall, skinny. And he likes the lookers. But there have been a couple of older ones over the years.'

'You sound as if you're talking about beasts at a market.' Veronica was unusually tetchy. She wasn't given to feminism. The conversation had made her uncomfortable for other reasons. Michael thought she wasn't as easily taken in by his conversion to the Keith Mantel fan club as Barry.

'How long has he been knocking around with this Debs?' Michael asked.

Barry looked at his wife for confirmation. 'Six months? Something like that. She's been hanging round the village all summer anyway. She must have been bored when Keith was at work. She spent a lot of time in here.'

'Is he in the same line of business?'

'I never knew what line of business that was. It's not something you can pin him down on. Property. Leisure. That's what he tells you. Could mean anything. We own the Anchor. So we're in property and leisure too, when you come to think about it.' It seemed to be a point he'd made before. He thought it was clever, expected that to be acknowledged.

'You're right.' Michael gave a little smile. 'So you are.'

'Can I get you another pint?' Veronica asked. She had her back to him, returning some glasses, and spoke over her shoulder. The bra strap at the back was very thin. Only one catch, he reckoned. When he was young he'd have had that undone in seconds.

The third pint was tempting, but he shook his head. He had things to do. It struck him again how things had changed. He was walking away from a drink, and for the first time since Peg had died he had things to do.

'Best get back,' he said. 'Don't want to overdo things first time out.' He grinned to show he was joking, that there was nothing of the invalid about him. He pulled out his wallet from his jacket pocket. 'Now, how much are these tickets for the lifeboat going to set me back?'

Barry slid off his stool and mooched into the back room to find the tickets. Veronica leaned right across the bar so he could smell the shampoo on her hair. She whispered, 'You know what you're doing, don't you, love? You won't make a scene?'

Before he could stop himself he reached out and patted the back of her hand, just as the little chaplain had done in the crematorium.

'Don't worry about me. I know just what I'm doing.'

Chapter Seventeen

The next morning Michael woke very early again. The darkness was still thick and there was no traffic moving on the road outside. Today, he realized, he didn't have to force himself to stay in bed. He could get up. He repeated the comforting mantra which he'd started in the pub. He had things to do. The things he had to do were still vague in his head, but that didn't matter.

The clothes he'd taken off the night before were still folded on a chair at the end of his bed. Peg hadn't been a house-proud woman, but she'd liked him neatly turned out. Her last couple of months, when she'd not been able to get out of bed, she'd worried about that. She'd pulled him close to her, made him listen to the rasping whisper. He'd thought it would be something important, significant, a declaration of love, and perhaps it had been in a way. *Are you managing? With the washing and ironing?* He'd taught himself to do it so she'd have less to fret about.

Now the memory made him think he might be running short of underpants. He gathered up the dirty washing from the basket in the bathroom and stuck it in the washing machine. A week ago the laundry would have been a full day's occupation. He'd plan it in advance, sit in the kitchen watching his Y-fronts tumble around in the suddy water, feeling he was doing something useful. Today it was a chore to get out of the way. He had things to do.

He was hungry. Had he eaten the day before when he'd arrived back from the Anchor? He couldn't remember. His head had been full of plans, his excitement fuelled by the whisky he'd finished off. Now he raided the fridge like a kid ravenous after a day at school, and fried up eggs, bacon, a few leftover cooked potatoes. He left the plate in the sink, already fidgety to be out, with no real idea of where he'd go. As he left the bungalow the church clock struck the three quarter hour. Seven forty-five. Still too early for all the things he'd planned the night before, but he couldn't face going back inside.

The rain had stopped. He took the lane which led towards the estuary. The path was lit by widely spaced street lamps and the wet road underneath looked black and shiny like melted tar. On one side there was a row of brick cottages. Lights were on now and an occasional sound – a door slamming, a burst of the radio – escaped to be tossed away by the wind. On the other side were fields with rough grazing and a few sheep. He couldn't see the sheep but he knew they were there. He could hear them moving. The fields were separated from the lane by a stone wall and he walked briskly against the wind until he came to a break in it. There were no more houses now. He'd reached the edge of the village.

The gap in the wall was blocked by a gate and he thought for a moment that it might be locked and that he'd be forced to scramble over it. He'd been here before but only in daylight. Late afternoon, usually, when the sun slanted through the big sycamores. Not recently though. Recently he'd neglected even to get here. Sycamores always held their leaves well into the autumn and some of the trees were still in leaf even now. The wind made a sound in them, so he was fooled briefly into thinking he could hear the tide ebbing in the estuary.

The gate was on a latch and opened easily. He was inside. Surrounded on four sides by the trees. He didn't stop to read the notice on the gate. He knew it read *Elvet parish cemetery. Established 1853.* In the east the sky was starting to lighten and he could make out the pale slabs of the headstones. He could have found Peg's even if it had still been pitch dark. She had wanted to be buried. It had been one of the instructions she'd given him, forced it out through dry lips in the same way as she'd told him how to use the washing machine.

He'd come to make his peace with Peg. He'd been putting together the words as he walked along the lane. *I went to pieces after you died. You know what I'm like. No good without you. Things'll be different now.*

But instead of talking to her he found himself remembering the first time he'd realized she was ill. It had been a couple of weeks after the Mantel girl had died. The murder had upset her. *Really* upset her, as if she'd been Abigail's mother. She'd said that was what it felt like, like she'd lost a daughter. It had been a dreadful time. Jeanie mooning around the house, trying to phone Mantel though he'd made it clear he didn't want to speak to her. Peg grieving for a girl she'd hardly known. That morning the two of them had been in the kitchen. Peg had been baking for some do at the church. The autumn fayre? She'd rolled out the dough for scones and had started cutting them out with an upturned wine glass. Suddenly she'd seemed to crumple and the glass had rolled out of her hand. She'd stood there, bent double with the pain. He'd just come in from a shift and was drinking tea at the table. He'd caught the glass just before it rolled onto the floor, but when he'd got up to help her she'd waved him away as if she knew what to do, and he knew that this hadn't been the first time it had happened. Then the doorbell had rung and Peg had said, 'Go and get it, will you?' All impatient. He'd understood that the pain had made her fractious, but also that she'd needed time to pull herself together.

Two police officers had been standing on the doorstep. Not in uniform, but he'd recognized them. One was the woman, the inspector, the other her sergeant, the big bloke. Greenwood. Michael could picture them now, standing there. It had been snowing and the big soft flakes were sticking to their coats, melting slowly, keeping the shape of the crystal. The woman had smiled. It hadn't been a false smile. It had been as if she'd been really pleased to see Michael, and he'd loved that feeling. He'd always been a fool around women. Always taken in by their flattery.

'Mind if we come in for a few minutes?' she'd said. She'd stamped her boots on the step to shake off the snow. The boots had narrow heels, almost pointed, and although she'd been otherwise soberly dressed, he'd thought there'd been something frivolous about them, tarty even. The man, Dan Greenwood, had seemed uncomfortable, edgy. Later, when he moved to the village, he'd been followed by rumours. Michael had heard he'd had a breakdown. Perhaps he'd been on the verge of illness even then. Michael had felt it had taken an effort of will for him to follow his boss into the house.

'Is Jeanie around?' Fletcher had asked, not as if she were desperate to speak to the girl. More as if she'd been passing anyway so she might as well have a word. Through the open kitchen door Peg had caught Michael's eye. He'd thought she was trying to tell him something, but he hadn't worked out what it could be. He hadn't sensed the danger.

'She's upstairs,' he'd said and had yelled up at Jeanie to come down. Peg had turned away in despair. She'd always been smarter than him. She must have known, even then, what the police were there for.

Jeanie hadn't come out of her room immediately, and they'd stood in the hall looking up to the landing, necks cricked in anticipation. There had been no response to Michael's shout of command, no sound or movement and he had felt the tension stretch, saw it like a piece of elastic about to snap. Had he realized even then what the police were really there for? Or had he still been too dumb?

There had been the soft click of the door being opened and Jeanie had appeared at the top of the stairs. She'd been wearing blue jeans and a green sweater with a big cowl neck. No shoes but thick woollen socks which made no sound when she walked. It had been the socks they'd seen first through the banisters as she'd approached them down the stairs. She'd lost weight since Abigail's murder. Michael had noticed that looking up at her from the unusual angle. He'd thought uncharitably that she'd not stopped eating through grief for the girl. It had been a pathetic love sickness. She'd wasted away because Mantel had refused to have anything more to do with her.

At that point Peg had come out of the kitchen, her body held rigid as if she'd been scared the pain would return, but fighting all the same.

'What do you want with her now?' Spitting out the words towards the inspector.

Fletcher had turned towards Peg. Her hair had swung like the hair in shampoo advertisements, polished, falling obediently back into place. She'd looked at Peg for a moment, considering if an answer was necessary.

'We'd like to ask Jeanie a few more questions. At the police station. We need her to help us with our enquiries.'

'You'll not talk to her without a solicitor!'

'Yes,' the inspector had said, giving a quick nod of approval, as if Peg had been the only other person present bright enough to realize the gravity of the situation. 'I think you should arrange for her lawyer to be there as soon as possible.' She'd paused and then added, 'And you might like to pack a small bag for Jeanie. Essentials. It's very likely that we'll be charging her.' Her voice had been measured, melodious, but looking back Michael understood that this had been her moment of triumph.

She'd looked at them both in turn. 'You do understand what I'm saying? If we arrest your daughter, she'll be held in custody until we can get her to court. She won't get bail. No chance of that when the charge is murder. It's only fair that you understand that's a possibility.' She'd smiled at them as if she was doing a favour by taking them into her confidence.

'What happens if she refuses to go with you?' Peg had demanded.

'Then we'll arrest her now.'

Peg had looked as if she'd been punched, but Michael hadn't taken in the implication of the scene which was being played out in front of him. He'd seen the inspector's mouth move, but his attention had been held by the man, by Dan Greenwood standing just behind her. Greenwood had stepped forward, had even, Michael thought now, remembering the event for the first time in years, spoken to intervene. 'Ma'am—' A hand upraised. A mouth open. A single word. 'Ma'am.' The snow had all melted on his jacket now. Water like dewdrops had clung to the fibres.

Inspector Fletcher had glanced over her shoulder at him.

'Yes, Greenwood?' As glacial as the weather outside. And Michael had thought there must be something personal between these two, something more than professional rivalry. A failed love affair? Perhaps that had been it. There'd been that sort of tension. Michael had been thinking all that, while Peg had been coming to terms with the fact that her only child might be arrested for murder. And what had Jeanie been thinking? At the time he hadn't considered Jeanie's feelings at all.

The sergeant hadn't answered immediately and the inspector had sensed her advantage and demanded more sharply, 'Well, Greenwood? What is it?'

And for some reason the sergeant's courage had suddenly left him. He'd crumbled. 'Nothing, ma'am.' And then had hated himself for his cowardice. Michael had recognized how he was feeling. Hadn't *he* once sat down for a meal with Keith Mantel? That had been a betrayal too.

At that point Michael had realized that something more was expected of him. The focus had shifted and he'd seen the whole picture instead of the detail: Peg in tears, Jeanie as pale as a corpse. He'd had a part to play as head of the household and he'd played it in the only way he knew, blustering and raging.

'What right do you have to come into my house and accuse my daughter of murder?'

But his heart hadn't been in it and they'd been able to tell. Jeanie had walked out to the car between the two officers, looking back once with that blank and empty stare which had always shut them out. She'd seemed to wince as a snowflake fell on her cheek.

Now, staring down at Peg's grave, Michael shivered. From the corner of his eye he caught a movement on the other side of the cemetery. Another mourner. He realized how strange he must look, standing in the half light, bedraggled and tearful. Some lunatic let loose from the madhouse. But the figure who had just come in through the wrought-iron gate seemed equally distraught and it was clear that he hadn't noticed Michael. They were two of a kind. Though the newcomer was younger, tall and stringy, it seemed that he too was passing through an emotional crisis. He was wearing a long anorak, unfastened. He had his hands thrust deep in the pockets and walked jerkily, moving his arms at the same time, so the front of the coat flapped like wings. He stopped once with his back to Michael and stood with one hand to his ear. He seemed to be muttering to himself. Then he moved on past the line of graves. Any respectable passer-by would conclude,

Michael thought, that there'd been a mass break out from the asylum.

Michael didn't move. He had no wish to disturb the stranger, who seemed so preoccupied by his own thoughts that he was unaware of anything outside his direct line of vision. The young man found the headstone for which he'd been searching and stopped. Tentatively he reached out and touched it with a gentle stroking motion as if he were stroking hair from a loved one's forehead. Then he turned abruptly and marched away.

Michael roused himself to follow, but curiosity overcame him. He walked to the grave where the young man had been standing. When he saw the name there was no surprise. It had been inevitable. *Abigail Mantel.*

By the time Michael reached the lane there was no sign of the disturbed young man. Perhaps he had taken the other direction, towards the river, though there was no shelter there, at this stage of the tide, nothing but an expanse of mud, a couple of stranded boats, marauding herring gulls.

Back in the middle of Elvet, a gaggle of teenagers was waiting by the church gate for the school bus. They were a scruffy and unruly lot. His Jeanie had never behaved like that. You wouldn't have caught her wearing a skirt which showed her backside and more make-up than a pantomime dame. That was what Michael told himself as he approached. That he disapproved and their parents should know better. He specially disapproved of two girls who were standing apart from the others. One of them was smoking a cigarette and the other was talking into a mobile phone.

The way she stood, holding the phone to her ear triggered a memory and he was back in the cemetery by Peg's grave, lost again in the past. The girl gave a shrill laugh and he was brought back to the present. He knew then he was deluding himself. He didn't disapprove of them at all. He admired them. They had the same sort of spirit as Abigail Mantel. And they excited him too with their curly hair scrunched up to the top of their heads, their defiant eyes and their silky legs. He'd have liked to say something to them, nothing important, just a word of greeting to make a connection, but at that moment the bus came along the road, wheezing and grinding. The girls hoisted their bags onto their shoulders. One threw the cigarette end onto the pavement and stamped on it with her clumpy shoe. Just as well, Michael thought. He'd only have made a fool of himself.

As the bus pulled away he saw that he wasn't the only person watching. Outside the Old Forge, preparing perhaps to open up the pottery, stood the ex-policeman, the one who had come with Fletcher to arrest Jeanie. Caught under the street light, the man had the same wistful expression on his face as Michael realized he probably had. What was he regretting? Sex or age. It had to be one or the other. Michael hurried on to phone Vera Stanhope.

Chapter Eighteen

When James arrived home the house was quiet. He had been working, delivering a tanker from the mouth of the river to the docks at Hull. A short shift. No complications. No visions of ghosts. He'd worked with the skipper a few times before and they got on well. As he'd waited on the Point for the launch to take him to the ship, James had looked at Wendy's house and seen that the curtains had been drawn. There'd been a light behind them and he'd thought he'd noticed movement. Not one shadow. Two. But then Stan, the other coxswain, had called him to the launch and he couldn't be sure. Not his business anyway.

So everything had been normal until he approached the front door of his house, his keys ready in his hand. Then he found himself shaking. He had to steady himself against the door frame. There was a sudden, irrational fear that something terrifying had happened in the house. Suddenly he was a young man again, returning home to bad news. He fumbled to unlock the door and pushed it open.

'Emma. Emma. Are you there?'

She came out into the hall to greet him.

'Of course. Whatever is the matter?'

He didn't answer immediately. He could hear a

strange woman's voice, then realized it was coming from the radio. He tried to recover his calm.

'Nothing. I didn't know what I'd find here. I mean what chaos Christopher might have caused.'

Emma frowned. 'You don't have to worry about him any more. He's gone. He didn't even bother to say goodbye.'

He followed her back into the kitchen and saw she'd been baking. A pile of buns were balanced on a wire tray to cool. She switched off the radio and screwed up her face critically.

'Not brilliant, are they? I don't know why they didn't rise.'

'I'm sure they'll taste OK. They smell delicious.' He knew the cakes were for him. Not to eat specially. More a symbol. *Look, I'm making the effort to be what you want.* He wondered why she had felt the need to make the effort today. Something to do with Chris?

She smiled and he thought she was like a little girl playing house, with the tea towel tied round her waist as an apron and the smudge of flour on her cheek. That was just what he liked.

'It's true,' she said. 'Chris has disappeared.'

'What do you mean?'

'He'd already gone when I got up. Did you see him this morning?'

James shook his head. He was concentrating on making tea. He liked leaf tea, the ritual of the strainer and the warmed pot. 'I expect he's at Springhead.'

'He hasn't even spoken to Mum and Dad. They didn't know he was coming.'

'I suppose that's it, then. He ran away before he had to face them.'

'There are times,' Emma said, 'when I know just how he feels.' She pulled off the tea towel and wiped her face with it. He thought at first she was just cleaning away the flour, then saw there were tears too. Not grief, he thought. Anger. Frustration. 'Dad called in today. He brought some tickets for the fireworks at the Old Chapel tonight. He thinks I should go. It would do me good. Help me come to terms with Abigail's death, Jeanie's suicide. He's fixed everything up, even arranged for an old biddy from the church to babysit, so you can come too. I said you were on duty, but he realized if you were working this morning you were unlikely to get called out again. I mean, the nerve of it. He didn't even ask. Just assumed that he knew best, that all I need is a jolly family party and I'll forget all about it.'

She had run out of breath, inhaled in a sort of sob.

James's first reaction was one of panic. He had spent his time in Elvet avoiding Keith Mantel, not making a big show of it, just keeping away from the places Mantel liked to be seen. More a superstition than a real feeling of danger. After all this time and all this planning, he had thought Mantel couldn't touch him.

'What exactly is going on at Mantel's?'

'A fundraiser for the RNLI. They want to get a new inflatable for the river.'

'A good cause.' James poured out the tea. The cups were porcelain, so delicate you could see the line of liquid rise through the china, as if it was opaque glass. He'd bought the tea service from an antiques fair before he'd married. Another of the possessions which defined him.

'You don't want to go!'

He thought about that. Perhaps Robert's assessment

of Emma's situation applied equally to him. He had blown Mantel up in his mind as a monster, an agent of destruction with the power to wreck everything he had created here. It was probably time to face the nightmare, banish the ghosts.

'I'd like to spend an evening with you without worrying about the baby.'

'But I would worry about him. What if he woke, needed feeding.'

'He won't. You know him. Regular as the tide.'

'But an event like this . . . All the village there . . . Everyone talking about Abigail . . . Just snooping around so they can see the house where she lived . . .'

'If it's dreadful we can always come home. Or go into the pub for a drink. At least it'll be quiet in there.'

He wondered why he was making so much effort to persuade her and realized that he was desperate now to see Mantel again. He was overcome with curiosity, and he wanted to see if the tragedy of his daughter's death had changed the developer at all. Now, on the anniversary of her death, how could he throw open his house for a celebration, however good the cause?

'You think Dad's right then? You see this evening as therapy?' Her voice was bitter. 'In that case it's a pity Chris didn't stick around to benefit from it too.'

James pulled her to him. He sensed he would get his way. 'I don't want you to do anything you wouldn't be comfortable with. I'm not trying to manipulate you.'

'It happened,' she said. 'It was horrible, but it happened. Reality. Perhaps my father's right and it's time to come to terms with it.'

*

Robert picked them up and drove them to the Old Chapel, though James said that as he was on call he wouldn't be able to have much to drink anyway. It seemed to him that Robert was treating Emma as an invalid. He asked her if she had a warm enough coat, opened the car door for her, waited until she'd slid into the back besides Mary before shutting it. The tickets he'd given them said *Open House* but when they arrived they found very little of the Old Chapel open. They parked behind a line of cars in the lane, then a boy James recognized as the son of one of the lifeboat crew directed them to the back of the property. He had loomed out of the mist grinning at them, dressed in yellow oilskins and waving a torch, like something out of a teenage horror movie. It was colder, the low cloud pierced in places so stars showed through. The trees were still dripping but the rain had stopped. James thought later it might freeze. He'd listened to the shipping forecast which had mentioned high pressure, a cold front coming in from the east.

'I thought the press might be here,' Robert said. 'Wherever I went yesterday there was a gang of them. Very intimidating. Perhaps it's not the weather for door-stepping. Or by now the Mantel case is already old news. It's a relief anyway.'

James thought it more likely that Mantel had warned the reporters off. He had that sort of power.

A bonfire had been built in a paddock which was separated from the garden by a low fence. It had not yet been lit but a group of shadowy figures stood looking at it, as if debating whether the moment was right.

Emma followed his gaze. 'Abigail kept a pony there,' she said. She was standing close beside him. Mary and

157

Robert had already been accosted by people from the church. 'But that was before we moved to Elvet. By the time I knew her she thought she'd grown out of ponies. She still talked about the horse though. It was called Magic. That was the stable.'

And the stable, open on one side now, with the stalls removed, had been turned into a cookhouse. A couple of barbecues had been built from stacked breeze blocks and long metal grills. The charcoals smouldered and spat as sausage fat dripped onto them. The sparks lit up the faces of the big, beer-drinking men who flipped burgers.

'Are you OK?' James asked.

She took his hand and in the darkness he smiled.

The bar was in the large conservatory which ran along the back of the house and they could see beyond that into a room with tables arranged around the walls. A few elderly people had escaped there from the cold. The rest of the Old Chapel was in darkness.

'The piano's gone,' Emma said.

'Sorry?' James had just glimpsed Mantel. His thoughts were elsewhere.

'In that room there was a grand piano. Jeanie used to play it. Abigail's father must have got rid of it . . .'

James thought she had said something more but her words were drowned by a surge of rock music from a sound system outside, then the cheers of the crowd as the bonfire went up in flames. The music was switched to a less painful level but by then she had stopped talking.

Mantel was standing just inside the conservatory welcoming people as they came in. He had a politician's knack of greeting them as if they were old friends, though he spent so little time in the village that it was impossible that he could know them all. A tall blonde who was dressed in jeans and a white linen shirt stood at his side. Her boots had heels and made her taller than him. *Very nice, Keith. Much classier than the women you used to knock around with. But then you always had taste* . . . James thought for a moment that he must have spoken the words out loud because Emma clutched suddenly at his arm. There was a shot of anxiety when he thought Mantel might have heard, then he saw that the scene was playing out quite normally around him, and then all that remained was a mixture of exhilaration and fear. It had always been like that with Keith. The couple ahead of them in the short queue moved on and he was face to face with Mantel. He took a quick breath, but it was Emma whom Mantel recognized and turned to. He pulled her towards him in a hug. James sensed her awkwardness but there was little he could do.

'Emma, my dear. How brave of you to come here at a time like this! I've been thinking of you. All this dreadful publicity.' His voice was quiet.

'It's a good cause.' James thought he heard the irony in his repeated words but Mantel accepted them straight.

'Oh, I do agree. I've always been a supporter. Even when I lived in the town.'

'This is James,' she said. 'My husband.'

Mantel, with his eyes still on Emma, still clasping her hand in his, hardly looked up.

'You're back in Elvet, I hear. In the Captain's House.'

'James is one of the Humber pilots. It's very convenient.'

Then Mantel did turn to James with a small frown. James didn't think it was a frown of recognition but a gesture he had seen before: Mantel was fixing the bit of information in his mind because one day it might become useful. It disappeared almost immediately.

'Now what would you like to drink? Debs will get you something. This is Debs, the new woman in my life.' Another frown to show he wasn't oblivious to the sensitivities of the situation. It had only been a matter of days since a former young lover had hanged herself after all. A certain tact was called for. 'Are your parents still at Springhead, Emma? And didn't you have a brother? A clever lad who went away to university. He was sweet on Abigail at one time I remember.'

It was the first time he'd mentioned his daughter. He paused and James thought he was like an actor waiting for applause. He expected some acknowledgement of his courage. And Debs, well trained, squeezed his shoulders sympathetically. Emma had been more moved by the words, but Mantel did not wait to see their effect on her. He turned away quickly and had already passed on to greet the next person in the queue.

Chapter Nineteen

Emma wasn't taken in by Keith Mantel. He was putting on a good show but she thought he was still desolate about Abigail's murder. That was why he had turned away from her so quickly after talking about his daughter. He hadn't wanted Emma to see how upset he still felt. And how had he known about Christopher? Abigail must have realized that Christopher was infatuated and mentioned it to her father. Emma hoped they hadn't laughed at him. She had a horrible picture of Abigail sniggering, of father and daughter mocking Chris for being so soppy, sitting together on the fat, pink sofa where now an old lady was clutching a sweet sherry.

Throughout the evening, she found herself looking out for Dan Greenwood. It was what she had always done at these gatherings when most of the village were present. Even while she talked to James or exchanged horror stories with a young mum she'd met at antenatal classes, she was alert for his presence. Secretly watching and listening. Hoping he'd turn up. Then she'd be rewarded by the sound of his voice across the room, his bulky shape in the distance. And she'd try to catch his eye.

And still, tonight, she looked out for him. Because

after all this time it was hard to stop. It had become a habit, like staring out of her bedroom window on windy nights when James was working. When she heard him exchange a few words with Mantel, she forced herself not to turn, but there was the same excitement. She tried immediately to damp it down. I'm not a teenager, she said to herself. I'm not fifteen any more. I was flattered by his response to me and even that was a mistake. But she couldn't stop. The excitement was addictive.

Standing by the bar, though, she strained to listen. Mantel must have asked Dan about the case. *Is there any news? Can you tell me what's going on?* He must have spoken quietly and discreetly. Certainly there had been no attempt to make a fuss. Emma hadn't heard him speak, but she did make out Dan's response.

'You know I can't help you with that. I'm not on the case any more. I'm a civilian. I know no more than you.'

The words were bland, conciliatory even, but she was used to pulling meaning from what he said and it seemed to her suddenly that he disliked Keith Mantel. She had thought everyone in the village liked Abigail's father, felt nothing but sympathy for him. First Vera had been dismissive. Now Dan's response was a surprise and disconcerting.

She wandered outside, passing so close to Dan Greenwood that she could smell the wax on his Barbour jacket. The sky had cleared overhead completely. There was a thin moon and sharp pinpricks of stars. It must still be misty out to sea, because below the voices she could hear the fog horn on the Point. A deep rumble like thunder. The evening had begun in a rather decorous and subdued way, but now there was a pile of empty beer cans in the corner by the barbecue and the lifeboat crew cooks were laughing and shouting.

The brief lull in sound was unexpected. The music had stopped for some reason and the loudest cook was scooping a sausage into a bun, concentrating, his fat tongue showing through the vice of his teeth. In the silence, falling into it, not realizing it was coming, someone said, 'Bloody hell, there's old Mike Long. I haven't seen him for years.' Then the noise started again, but by then everyone had stared at the tall, thin man and at the woman who was walking beside him.

Emma recognized the name and then the man in the light of the flames which the frost seemed to have tinged blue. She wondered if Robert had noticed him, if there would be another scene. But Michael Long no longer seemed angry. He was moving hesitantly among the crowd, meeting old friends. If he recognized Robert he didn't show it.

The woman with him was Vera Stanhope. She saw Emma looking and came up to her, waving a can of lager as greeting. She had changed from the usual shapeless dress into crumpled baggy trousers and a huge navy sweater with a roll neck. She was still wearing the sandals.

'What are you doing here?' Emma asked. It was illogical but she blamed Vera for interrupting her meal with James the night before. The image of the detective standing on the step, battering at the door had been so strong that she couldn't lose it, even though it had been Christopher standing there.

'Everyone has a night off, pet.'

Oh no, not you. You pretend to be a clown, but you're the most intelligent woman I've ever met.

'Besides, it's a good cause, isn't it?' Vera beamed. 'Lifeboats and that. Saving folks.' She looked back to the house. The fire was reflected in the long chapel window. 'So this is where you and Abigail spent that summer. Sharing your secrets. Best friends.'

Emma looked at her sharply wondering how the detective could have guessed that best friends hardly described the relationship they'd had. Because the tone of her voice echoed Christopher's when he'd said the night before, 'She was your only friend. I always thought you hated her.' Had it been hatred? Emma wondered. Abigail had been the mistress and she the paid companion, flattering, laughing at the jokes, sympathizing when Jeanie Long came along to spoil it all. There had been resentment, certainly. But hatred? Why had she stuck it out for so long? Because there had been moments of real affection. And because in the Mantel household there had been a glamour missing in the rest of her life.

Vera was looking at her as if she expected an answer.

'We'd not long moved here,' Emma said. 'I was lonely and Abigail was the first person I met who was friendly. Yes, we spent most of that summer together.'

'She was a bonny lass.' Vera emptied the can, squashed it in her fist and threw it onto the pile by the cookhouse. 'I've seen photos. I can't believe there weren't any admirers.'

'There were lots of them.'

Lads who offered to do her homework and came into school clutching cassettes of the music they'd taped specially for her. Lads who turned blotchy and tongue-tied when she gave them any encouragement.

'But no one special?'

'Not that I know of. She said she wasn't interested in kids.'

'Someone older then? A lad from college maybe. Home for the summer.'

'She didn't mention anyone.'

'Would she have done?'

At one time Emma would have answered immediately. *Sure. Of course. We told each other everything.* Now she hesitated and chose her words carefully.

'I don't know. Thinking about it again, recently, I probably didn't know her as well as I thought I did. I mean, kids can be devious too, can't they? And sometimes you don't want to share your secrets with anyone. Not even your friend.'

Vera raised her caterpillar eyebrows and seemed about to speak, but then her attention was caught elsewhere. A woman was standing in front of the fire. She was side on, in silhouette, alone. She held a glass of red wine, which, with the fierce light behind it, looked black.

'Well, well, well . . .' Vera sounded pleased with herself. It was as if she'd been given an unexpected treat. 'What's she doing here, do you suppose?' Then to Emma, 'You'll recognize her, won't you, pet? She's not changed that much. Obviously kept in trim. The sort to go to the gym a couple of times a week, I'd say. And you can do a lot with make-up. Or so they tell me.'

The woman turned. She was slim, dark, well groomed. Her nails were the same colour as the wine.

'If I was a bitchy cow,' Vera said, 'I'd have said she'd had a nose job. What do you think?'

Emma was about to say that she'd never seen the woman before in her life, then the way the sleek, black hair swung when she moved, reminded her. 'It's Caroline Fletcher, the detective in charge of the Mantel case the first time round.'

'Full marks for observation.'

'You'd have thought she'd want to keep a low profile,' Emma said. 'After all that comment in the press.'

'From what I hear, our Caroline's never done low profile in her life. But she's got nerve. I'll give her that. Rattling a few cages, I'd say. Putting on the pressure. They tell me she was a decent little detective in her time. She'll not have lost the knack. Or it'll be a fishing expedition, maybe. Everyone friendly and informal, more likely to gab. She'll want to know which way the wind's blowing.'

Vera was muttering almost to herself. If she'd bumped into her in town, Emma thought, she'd have put her down as a bag lady, one of those smelly women of indeterminate age, who sit on park benches talking to the trees. She looked around for James, thought he might be amused that this was the detective who had been sent to sort out the case, but he seemed to have disappeared.

'You must already have talked to Caroline about what happened back then,' Emma said.

'Must I? Na, pet. That's not the way I work. I make up my own mind first. Look at the notes, talk to the people who count. And the police don't count for much in most cases. I'll talk to Caroline when I'm good and ready.'

'Perhaps that's why she's here. To talk to you.'

'You think?' Vera gave a little laugh and walked away, helping herself to someone else's lager as she went. When Emma saw her next she was still muttering, but now into Dan Greenwood's ear. Dan had been a cop, Emma thought. And he seemed to count. When she looked for Caroline Fletcher, the dark woman had disappeared too.

The screaming started at about the same time as the fireworks, so for a short time Emma missed it, because it was hidden by the screech and wail of exploding rockets. She heard it first because she was standing furthest away from the fire. She didn't like to admit it, but fireworks scared her. It was the breathless moment between their lighting and the rush of sound. In that beat of silence she felt her heart pound and she became faint. She would have liked James's arm around her so they could cover the silence with conversation, but he was talking to Dan Greenwood and Robert. They were standing, all blokes together, laughing. A rocket shot into the darkness, exploded in a shower of gaudy stars and she heard screaming.

She walked around the side of the house towards the road because that was where the sound seemed to come from. The lane was lit with sparse street lights and the skinny moon. A woman was standing and screaming. It was like when she had found Abigail Mantel's body, but in negative, a reverse image, a parallel universe. Because this time it was her mother who screamed and she who ran. And her mother pulled her arm and pointed into the ditch by the side of the road. And again there was a body.

But Abigail Mantel had looked ugly in death, much uglier than when she'd lived. Christopher, lying on his back in the ditch, was lit by the moon so his skin had a frosty blue sheen, which reminded her of the fabric of a bridesmaid's dress she'd worn once to a cousin's wedding. A densely woven satin with a matt finish and silver threads. All this was going through her mind as she took Mary into her arms and whispered the same reassurances she'd been given ten years before, 'It'll be all right. Everything's going to be all right.' Not believing what she was saying, but feeling her mother's sobs subside and her breathing grow calmer.

Then Vera Stanhope appeared, solid and brusque.

'Who's this, then?'

'It's my brother, Christopher.'

There was a horrified pause then, 'Oh, pet,' she said, and briefly cupped Emma's face in her huge hands, so for a moment, in her confusion, Emma thought she intended to kiss her. Instead she put her arm round each of the women's shoulders and led them away from the scene. Then she stood in the middle of the road so no cars could pass and spoke urgently into her phone.

Part Two

Chapter Twenty

The eczema on Vera Stanhope's legs distracted her. Her limbs felt alive, as if small burrowing animals had penetrated the surface, were living off the fat and the blood. She imagined she could sense the snuffling and digging. It was always the same when she wore trousers. She longed to let the air to the skin, but there wasn't much she could do about that now. It wouldn't be seemly for a senior investigating officer to drop her pants in front of the hoopla of a crime scene. Whatever would the pathologist, the examiners in their white paper suits and the local detectives make of it? If she *was* to be the senior investigating officer, which had still to be established.

Her doctor had said that stress made her skin condition worse, but it wasn't stress she was experiencing now. It was exhilaration and guilt. She didn't believe police officers who denied being excited by murder. Who would fail to be turned on by the drama, the costume and the show? Why else had they joined the service? It was different for the relatives, of course, and that was where the guilt came in. She had a responsibility. She'd been playing this slowly, nosing around like the mythical creatures under her skin, feeling her way into the complexities of the situation, picking up on hostilities and lies. She worried that if she'd adopted a more orthodox approach, this other death might not have occurred.

Aye, and you'd still be in the dark, pet. If you'd had them into the station, taken them through their original statements, word for word, you'd be none the wiser than the day you arrived. This way at least you understand the people. You have a feeling for what went on.

She'd never been lacking in confidence and usually didn't see the point of regret.

They'd rigged up spotlights and a tent over the ditch. There was the rumble of a generator, four-wheel-drive vehicles reversing at the bottom of the narrow lane, earnest conversation. She thought there was nothing to be gained here now. She'd been liaising on the Mantel case with a local DI called Paul Holness. He was a middle-aged man, bluff and cheerful, and he'd joined the force from Lancashire since Abigail's murder. Ambitious in theory, he was too idle on the ground to be any threat. No way would he want to be Senior Investigating Officer. Too much responsibility in this particular case. Too much shit flying around. He was talking to the pathologist in the gateway to the Old Chapel. She made her way to join them.

'Definitely murder,' Holness said. 'You can't see with him lying on his back, but his head's bashed in.'

'Any sign of the murder weapon?'

'Not yet, but they've not had a chance for a proper search. We're organizing that now.' He stamped his feet and wrapped his arms across his chest. He was wearing sheepskin gloves but he still seemed to be feeling the cold. Vera thought they were a soft lot, these

Yorkies. 'What was the mother doing out here anyway?' he asked. 'Has anyone said?'

'She was feeling the cold and came to get an extra jacket from the car, according to the husband.' She hadn't been able to get any sense out of Mary. 'Any idea of the time of death? I mean could he have been here for hours, only nobody noticed him on their way in?'

Holness shook his head. 'You know pathologists. They never like to commit themselves. But highly unlikely, she said. She thinks he was dead for less than an hour when Mrs Winter found him.'

'Can you take over here?' Vera asked. 'I want to talk to the witnesses before they have time to embroider. You know what it's like. Everyone wants a consistent story and they fill in the gaps, without realizing what they're about.' She saw with some satisfaction that she'd lost him. 'I'll be at Springhead House if anyone needs me.' It wasn't a bad thing to stamp her authority, she thought. Make sure everyone realized she saw this death as part of the Mantel case. That she was still in charge.

She'd arranged for someone to take the Winters home. The woman wouldn't stop sobbing and the noise had got to them all. Robert had wanted to take his own car.

'This is a crime scene,' she'd said. 'There could be a trace, you know, someone knocking against your vehicle. We have to check.'

He'd accepted that and gone quietly enough in the end.

Above her the sky was still clear, but pools of mist had collected over the ditches and in dips in the fields.

The track to Springhead House was pitted and her tyres crunched through the frozen puddles. The people inside must have heard the engine, but they didn't move when she went in. A uniformed police woman opened the door and showed her into the kitchen where they were all sitting, facing towards a big brown teapot on a tray, not speaking. Robert Winter sat at the head of the table with his wife slumped beside him. James clasped a mug of tea between both hands. Emma was holding a sleeping child on her knee.

Vera nodded gently towards the baby. 'You collected the bairn, then?'

It had been Emma's main concern when Vera had asked them all to leave the lane and wait for her. Robert had wanted them back at Springhead. Mary was hysterical, he said. She needed to be in her own home. Emma had been worried about Matthew and had insisted on going to the Captain's House first. Vera had been surprised by that. The woman's brother had been killed and her only response had been a calm insistence that they go back to Elvet to collect her child. But then Vera couldn't imagine what it must be like to be a mother and anyway people expressed their grief in different ways.

Vera hadn't expected Mary still to be with them. That grief had been raw and obvious, especially shocking because the woman seemed so reserved. Later Vera would tell her sergeant that it was like a vicar's wife getting up on the church hall stage and doing a striptease. It made you uncomfortable. She had told the policewoman, detailed to stay with the family, to get a doctor, had imagined Christopher's mother would be in bed, sedated.

Though they all sat wrapped up in thick sweaters, the kitchen was warmer than it had been outside. The sudden increase in temperature set off Vera's eczema again. She resisted the urge to scratch the back of her knees and joined them at the table.

'Tea, ma'am? It's not long been made.'

The constable was hovering. Vera waved her away impatiently. The others sat, looking at Vera with fixed, dazed expressions, waiting for her to speak. Despite herself, Vera savoured the moment. She'd always liked an audience.

'We believe that Christopher was murdered,' she said carefully. She knew they'd find it hard to take in the facts. It was a kindness to be straight with them. 'He has a wound to his skull.'

'Could he have slipped?' James asked. 'The road was very icy.'

'He could have slipped and knocked his head on the road, perhaps. But that wouldn't explain his lying in the ditch. There was nothing there which could have caused that sort of injury. I'm sorry.'

Mary gave a deep intake of breath which was released as a sob.

'Are you ready for this?' Vera asked. 'I can speak to you tomorrow, if you'd prefer. Should we call a doctor?'

The last question was directed towards Robert but before he could answer Mary said sharply, 'No. No doctor.'

'It would help me to know what Christopher might have been doing at Mr Mantel's house.'

'He could have been there to look for us.' Vera thought Emma spoke reluctantly, but perhaps she was just being quiet, worried about waking the baby.

'Of course. That must be it!' Mary seemed feverish. Her eyes were bright and there was a flush to her face. 'He came to Mantel's to find us. There were posters all over the village about the open evening for the lifeboat. I told you, Robert! I told you he wouldn't go back to the university without coming to see us.'

'Christopher was a student?'

'He held a postgraduate research position at Aberdeen,' Robert said. There was a pause. 'He was an extremely gifted scientist. A zoologist.' He looked at Vera apologetically as if he'd realized that this wasn't the moment for parental boasting.

'Was there any special reason for the visit? Was it planned?'

'No,' Emma said. 'But nothing much he did *was* planned. Except his work. He was always completely wrapped up in that.'

'Had he warned Mr and Mrs Winter of his visit?'

'No,' Robert said. 'We didn't know anything about it. We didn't know he was in Elvet until Emma phoned me at work at lunchtime.'

'You work as a probation officer, Mr Winter?'

'That's right.'

'You worked with Jeanie Long?'

'I prepared the home circumstance report for the parole board. That was all.'

Vera made no comment. There was a moment of silence, which Emma filled. 'I phoned Mum and Dad here as soon as I realized Chris had gone, but by then they'd both already left. I didn't like to bother them until lunchtime. I didn't see him this morning, you see. He'd gone by the time I got up.'

'An early riser, was he?'

'Not usually, no. I was surprised, a bit worried, I suppose.'

'Worried? Why was that? It seems a bit strange to be worried about a grown man.' There was a pause. 'How did he seem last night?'

Emma and James looked at each other. Vera suspected an unspoken request from Emma, which James ignored.

'He was behaving oddly,' James said. 'He was drunk but there was more to it than that. He'd always come across as intense about his work, pretty self-obsessed, but last night he seemed completely absorbed by some problem of his own. I wondered if he was having a sort of minor breakdown. It sounds callous but I was too tired to deal with it and I was still on call. In the end I left Em to cope with him. I don't know if she got any sense out of him.'

'Did you, Emma?' Robert asked. He had been sitting, quite calmly, following the conversation. Vera couldn't make him out. His son had been murdered but she had no sense that he was grieving. There was a terrible self-control. Perhaps it had something to do with his faith. Dan Greenwood had told her Winter was an evangelical. She'd always thought they were the showy bunch who waved their hands in the air, though there'd been no sign of that at the church service she'd attended. Did he think it would be wrong to grieve for a son who was now with his maker? Is that why he sat, rigid and frozen, so only his eyes moved?

'We talked,' Emma said at last. 'Like James has told you, he was very drunk. He didn't make a lot of sense.'

Vera nodded sympathetically, but there was the flash of excitement, which was why she'd come into this job, what it was really about. *You're lying, pet. You know more than you're saying. Why's that then? What did your brother tell you? Skeletons in his cupboard, maybe. Are you trying to protect your mum and dad? Or is something more sinister going on here?*

'How old would Christopher have been when Abigail Mantel died?' she asked.

'Fourteen,' Emma said. 'He was a year younger than me.'

'Did he know her?'

'He'd seen her around with me. And at school.'

'Go back to that Sunday, the day you found her body. Was Christopher at home that day?'

'He came to church with us,' Robert said. 'Then we all had lunch. He was still here when Emma went out. It wasn't the weather for being outdoors.'

'The original investigating team would have spoken to him?'

'I can't remember.' Robert frowned. 'They were here, of course, that afternoon, talking to Emma. I presume they interviewed Christopher but I can't remember it.'

'There'll be a record, at any rate,' Vera said, though she wasn't convinced. There were more gaps in the Mantel file than a trawl net drying at North Shields Fish Quay. And the smell was much the same too. 'But if he was in all day he couldn't have seen anything which would have been a threat to the murderer. You see the way my mind's working?'

'I've said he was a quiet boy, but he wasn't lacking in confidence,' Robert said impatiently. 'If he'd seen something suspicious he'd have said so at the time.'

'You know, I don't think that's necessarily true.' Vera sat with her forearms flat on the table. 'It didn't take the police long to arrest Jeanie. He'd have no reason to question their judgement. It's not only bairns who believe we're infallible. He'd have dismissed any evidence which pointed elsewhere, wouldn't he?'

'Until now,' James said quietly. 'Until it's become clear that there was a miscarriage of justice. Then he'd remember. Did he mention anything like that last night, Em?'

Emma shook her head. 'He wasn't very coherent, but no, we didn't discuss Abigail's murder. Not specifically.'

'Besides,' Robert said. 'We've already established that Christopher was with us all that Sunday. He couldn't have seen or heard anything significant.' Vera thought he had the tone of an irritable schoolteacher trying to drum the obvious into a stupid pupil's head.

'You could see the field where I found Abigail from his bedroom,' Emma said slowly. She turned to Vera. 'His bedroom was right at the top of the house. Afterwards, that night, we watched from the window. The spotlights and the scientists in those white paper suits. Just like tonight. We watched them carry Abigail's body back.' She seemed lost in the memory.

'Did he spend a lot of time in his bedroom?'

'Hours,' Robert said, more irritable than ever. 'I've explained. He wasn't the sort of boy who needed company.'

Vera thought Emma was about to comment, but seemed to think better of it, so she stood up suddenly, scraping her chair on the tile floor.

'That's enough for tonight,' she said. 'We'll talk

again tomorrow.' She touched Emma's arm. 'Before we go would you show me where the lad used to sleep?'

Emma handed the baby to James and led the way upstairs. As they reached the second landing they could hear the baby screaming. Emma paused for a moment, then the noise faded and she continued.

The room was on the third floor and much as it had been when Christopher had been sleeping there. It was long and narrow, with one long side making up the outside wall. In that there were two windows. The opposite wall was covered with book shelves. The books were mostly non fiction and looked as if they'd been collected from charity shops and jumble sales. There was a single bed with a striped quilt, and a wardrobe which had been painted white. Ice like fine lace spread up the windows from the sill and the rest of the glass was covered in a mist of condensation. The window sills were low and thick enough to sit on. Emma leaned against one and wiped a hole in the mist with her hand. Vera took the same position at the other.

'This is where we sat,' Emma said. 'The two of us. You can't see much now. You'll need to come back in daylight.'

Vera stared out at the scene. The moonlight was pale and none of the details of the landscape were clear. 'Where was the body?'

'About three fields in.'

There were no houses visible, no street lamps or car headlights. The Mantel house was hidden by a clump of trees and a slight dip in the land.

'Flat as a witch's tit,' Vera said. 'You could see for miles, couldn't you? Anyone coming and going along that path. Do you remember your brother being interviewed?' She knew the answer before Emma had shaken her head.

Chapter Twenty-One

Vera drove slowly away from Springhead House towards Elvet. It was late, but she felt more awake than she had done since arriving in East Yorkshire. Her thoughts were clear and sharp and focused on Caroline Fletcher. They came fully formed and beautiful like the crystals of ice on Christopher Winter's bedroom window.

Caroline would have been waiting for a phone call since the case against Abigail Mantel had fallen to pieces. She must have been. She'd have been expecting a phone call or a letter, a formal summons to the station for interview. She'd have run the questions in her head. *Can you explain your reasons for charging the suspect at that point? Why did you restrict your lines of enquiry in this way?* And she'd have rehearsed the answers. Over and over.

Caroline must have heard that Vera and her team had been called in. She'd still have friends at head-quarters. Maybe she'd done a bit of research, asked about Vera's style, looked at old cases. She'd have been wired up and ready. But the days had passed and nothing had happened. Her nerve would have been starting to crack. Perhaps that was why she had turned up at the bonfire. It took guts to sit and do nothing but wait.

And now she'd be more strung up than ever. Another murder and her at the scene.

Vera was planning her approach. She'd turn up on Caroline's doorstep. No warning. Nothing official. *I thought it would be a good idea if we had a chat, pet. No need for a solicitor, is there? Put on the kettle and we'll see if we can get it sorted between us.* She'd play on their sisterhood, the struggle they'd both had to be taken seriously by male colleagues. She imagined reeling Caroline in, disarming her. Beautiful women never see fat, ugly ones as a threat. She longed to take on Caroline now, was almost too excited to wait, but she knew that wouldn't do. It was already midnight and if the woman *did* get hold of a competent solicitor Vera didn't want accusations of harassment flying around. She'd go back to her hotel, get a couple of whiskies and a few hours' sleep and hit Caroline Fletcher first thing in the morning.

Her phone went. She pulled onto the verge. The road was greasy with ice and she couldn't do two things at once at the best of times. The signal wasn't brilliant and she got out. The cold took her breath away. Her feet snapped the frozen blades of grass.

'Ma'am.' Faint and familiar, slightly ironic. She grinned slowly.

'Joe Ashworth. Where the hell have you been?'

'You said to leave it a few days. Then when the news of the Winter lad's murder came through I thought you'd like me there immediately.'

'Taken to mind reading now, have you, lad?'

'Not really. It was the boss's idea.'

But your suggestion, she thought. *You'd not want to miss out on anything.* 'Where are you?'

'The services on the M62. About half an hour from Hull. They've booked me into the same hotel as you.'

'Have they, though! It's a decent sort of place. I hope their budget will run to it.'

She stood there for a moment before driving off. Ashworth was her sergeant. Not perfect by any stretch of the imagination. Too gullible for one thing and born a city boy for another. Too wrapped up in his wife and baby. But he'd be an ally against all these bloody Yorkies. And he was the closest thing to a son she'd ever have.

They arrived at Caroline Fletcher's house early the next morning. The quiet spell of weather was over. There was a piercing east wind and rain with shards of ice in it, sharp and grey as flint. It was seven o'clock and the street was waking. Caroline lived a couple of villages inland from Elvet and the estate was new and smart. There were double garages and fancy cornices, and a fat conservatory bulged behind every house. It was the sort of place Ashworth would like to live one day, when he got promotion. Vera would have been hounded out for an untidy garden and unruly friends.

She stood on the drive and looked around her, challenging the neighbours to notice. 'I think we've been very discreet,' she said. 'We could have come in a panda.'

Ashworth could tell she was enjoying herself and knew better than to spoil her fun. A small child was peering through the curtains of the house next door. It was a girl in a pink dressing gown with curly hair, about the same age as his son. He waved at her and she disappeared. Vera was already banging on the front door. There was a light in an upstairs window. They heard footsteps.

The door opened. A tall man with a newt's face and a long neck looked out at them. He was wearing a sober suit and a dark tie. *Undertaker or accountant,* Vera thought. His hair was still wet from the shower.

'Can you tell Caroline we'd like a word?' Vera gave a wide, easy smile.

A paperboy in a black anorak slouched up. Like a woman in a burqa, the hood hid everything but his eyes. He thrust a copy of the *Financial Times* into the newt's hand. Accountant then. The newt seemed distracted by the headline and didn't answer immediately.

'We've not got all day.'

'I'm not sure . . .'

Vera breathed in deeply, then spoke loudly, with an exaggerated clarity. 'I'm Vera Stanhope. Northumbria Police. I want to see Caroline Fletcher.'

The paperboy stopped at the gate and turned to stare. It would be all round the estate before he got home from school. The man's face turned scarlet, the colour of the curtain which covered the small window beside him. *Very fetching,* Vera thought. *Maybe he's not a newt after all. More like a chameleon.* 'Go in,' he said quickly. 'Caroline's inside.' Then with an attempt at dignity, 'You'll have to excuse me. I'm just on my way to work.' He grabbed car keys from the hall table, a briefcase from the bottom of the stairs and pushed past them.

Caroline was standing in the middle of the living room. She must have heard the exchange, but she waited until they'd stepped in and closed the door behind them before she spoke.

'Can I help you?' As if she was one of those icy women who sell perfume in high-class department stores. The ones who usually let Vera walk past unhindered. It was still not seven thirty but she was dressed and made up. It was as if she'd known that Vera would turn up, though she couldn't have had inside information. Vera had told no one at HQ of her plans. But of course Caroline had worked in CID for six years. She'd been promoted quickly, had been good at her job. Vera had underestimated her. This would be how she'd have played it too.

'Who was that?' Vera asked. 'Your hubby?' They were all still standing.

'You know I'm not married. You'll have checked. Alex and I have lived together for four years.' She looked severe, dressed in a black skirt over black boots, a roll-necked top the colour of ripe plums. No bulges or sags, everything trim and in its place.

'Very nice,' Vera said vaguely. She sat on an easy chair next to the gas fire, pulled a notebook and biro out of her bag. 'How old are you now?'

'You'll have checked that too. Forty-six.'

'You're wearing well,' Vera said with admiration. She meant it. There wasn't much difference in their ages but Caroline looked ten years younger. 'What are you doing with yourself now?'

'I'm an estate agent.'

'Any good at it?'

'I shift more property than anyone else in the company.'

You'll have to be best at whatever you set your

mind to, Vera thought. *Where does that come from, then? And is that why you left the police? Nothing more sinister than a fear of getting it wrong. Because in this job failure's inevitable. Not every time. But most of it.*

'Coffee?' Caroline asked.

'Aye, why not? White, one sugar. Joe here takes his black.'

While the coffee was being made Vera doodled on her pad. Spiders and interlocking webs. Joe Ashworth, looking at it from across the room, thought a psychiatrist would have a field day. Caroline must have had everything prepared in the kitchen, the tray laid, the kettle boiled, because she returned almost immediately, preceded by the smell of the coffee. She set the items on the table – a large cafetière, three matching mugs, sugar bowl, milk jug, an arrangement of shortbread biscuits on a brown plate. Vera looked up.

'Were you still at Mantel's when they found the lad's body last night?'

'No.' Caroline focused her full attention on pouring coffee. 'I only bought a ticket because it was such a good cause. I didn't stay.'

'You'll have heard who was killed though?'

'It was on the radio this morning.' *And someone will have phoned you,* Vera thought. *Bound to have.*

'Christopher Winter, the brother of the lass who found Abigail Mantel's body.'

'A strange coincidence,' Caroline said calmly. She handed a mug to Ashworth.

'Aye. Maybe.'

'You think his death is relevant to the original enquiry?'

Vera didn't consider that worthy of an answer. 'You must have talked to the boy first time round. What did you make of him?'

There was a brief pause as Caroline sipped at the coffee. She left a smear of lipstick on the white porcelain. 'I don't remember,' she said. 'I mean I don't remember even talking to him. He was just a kid. Younger than Abigail. Not in the same year at school.'

'But he could have been a witness.' Vera kept her voice even, reasonable.

'He was with his family all day. Church at ten thirty, then home for lunch. He didn't go out. Dan Greenwood had a chat with him the day of the murder.'

So you do remember. Or you've looked at your records. Prepared your story at least. Looking more closely at Caroline, Vera saw how tired she was. Had she slept? Been to bed, even? Had she been up all night trawling through her memory for facts to use in her defence? Vera tried to ward off a wave of sympathy. 'Did you ever see his bedroom?'

There was a pause. No immediate response. She was good, Vera thought. She'd have been brilliant in court. Unshakeable. The Crown Prosecution Service would have loved her.

'I don't remember,' she said. 'I'd have to check my notes.'

Vera leaned forward. 'Look,' she said. 'I don't understand why there's a problem here. I mean, what have you got to lose by playing it straight with me? You've already left the service. No one's going to find you negligent. What would be the point? Or if they do, it'll be in an internal report that'll never hit the press.'

'I'm an ideal scapegoat, then, aren't I?'

'I'm writing the report. You'll not end up carrying all the crap. Not unless you muck me about. I know what it's like to be a woman working with this lot.' She paused. 'So, I'm going to ask you again. Did you look in the boy's bedroom?'

'No,' Caroline said. Then, interested despite herself. 'Why should I have done that?'

'From his bedroom he had a view of the field where Abigail's body was found. He was there all afternoon. He could have been a witness to her murder.'

She crumpled as if she'd been thumped in the stomach and winded. 'Shit,' she said. 'Oh, shit. How could I have missed that?'

'You were blinkered. Convinced from the beginning that Jeanie Long was the murderer.'

'Everything pointed to it. She had motive, opportunity, the alibi she gave didn't check out.'

'But no forensics. And no confession, even after ten years.'

'It was the murder of a young girl. A pretty young girl. You know what it's like. Her picture on the news every night. The press, the politicians all after a result. There's a pressure to clear it up quickly.'

'Aye,' Vera said. 'That's true enough.'

They sat in silence. The rain spat against the window.

'So it wasn't personal, then?' Vera asked.

'What do you mean?' Caroline's head shot up. She was ready for a fight again.

'Maybe you took against Jeanie Long.'

'I'd never met her before the murder.'

'That's not what I meant. Some suspects . . . It's hard to stay detached . . . They get under your skin . . .'

'Perhaps there was something like that,' Caroline conceded. 'She wasn't easy. Arrogant, I suppose. Superior. As if a degree and a knowledge of posh music made her better than the rest of us.'

'I know the type.'

'And she hated Abigail. OK, I accept now that she couldn't have killed the girl. But she was pleased she was dead.'

'Was there ever anyone else in the frame? Before you pulled in Long, I mean.'

'Not really. Keith Mantel put us onto her very quickly. He said Jeanie had always been jealous of Abigail and then when he asked her to leave it was the girl that she blamed.'

'You checked out the local loonies and sex offenders?'

'Of course, though I never had it down as an attack by a pervert. There'd been no sexual assault. Her clothes hadn't even been disturbed. And if not that, who else, besides Jeanie Long could have had a motive? Abigail was only fifteen, for Christ's sake. A schoolgirl. No money to leave. She'd hardly lived long enough to upset people.'

'Was she a virgin?' Though Vera knew, of course. She'd read every report there'd been.

'No, but that isn't unusual for a fifteen-year-old, even ten years ago.'

'Did you trace any boyfriends?'

'No one who admitted sleeping with her. But they wouldn't, would they? She was under age.'

'What did her father make of that?'

'He wasn't shocked that she'd had sex. He told me

he never played the heavy-handed father. It wasn't his style. He just warned her to take precautions.'

'Did she ask his advice? Talk to him about the lads she was going with?'

'He said not, and I believed him. Why would he lie?'

'Emma, the lass who found the body . . .'

'Yes?'

'You'd have thought she'd have known who Abigail was sleeping with.'

'Perhaps.' Caroline hesitated. 'I didn't ask her. Once we had Long in custody it didn't seem relevant. I didn't see the point in raking through a young girl's past.'

Vera considered this without speaking. Ashworth, too, seemed lost in thought. Outside the window a cat was crying, but despite the rain, no one got up to let it in.

'Why did you leave the job?' Vera asked.

It was a question Caroline hadn't planned for. A crazy oversight like not interviewing Christopher. Was *that* all her failure came down to? Vera thought. A lack of thoroughness in her approach to her cases.

'It was personal,' Caroline said in the end. 'Nothing to do with the work.'

'You know better than that,' Vera snapped. 'Nothing's personal in my enquiry.'

'I was engaged. I thought that was what I wanted. Marriage, kids, the whole package. I didn't see how the job would fit in with that.'

'What happened?'

'It didn't work out. I mean, I couldn't go through with it. Maybe I'm not the marrying kind.'

'But you didn't come back?'

'I got used to regular hours, a full night's sleep, bloody big commissions.'

'You enjoy what you do now?'

'I told you, I'm good at it. Selling. Sometimes I think that was what I was born for.'

What was I born for? Vera wondered. *Seeing through people who lie to me? Then why can't I make out exactly what's going on here?* She knew there were more questions but couldn't find the right words to ask them. She stood up. Joe Ashworth followed, surprised the interview was over so quickly. Caroline Fletcher didn't show any relief at their leaving. Vera thought she understood they'd be back.

Chapter Twenty-Two

When they arrived at the Captain's House, Emma was sitting at the kitchen table surrounded by the remains of breakfast. James was on his way out and dressed for work. Vera looked him up and down admiringly as he let them in. The uniform suited him, though he looked very tired and pale.

'I'm glad you're here,' he said, keeping his voice low. They were in the high-ceilinged hall but the door to the dining room was open and they could see through into the kitchen beyond. 'I don't really like leaving Emma on her own and she doesn't want me to call in her parents. She says they've got their own grief to cope with.'

'Do *you* have any family who could keep her company?' asked Ashworth. He came from a close family and so did his wife. He couldn't imagine an important event in their lives without an audience of relatives. On those occasions his parents' small terrace would be crammed, people knee to knee on chairs pulled from all over the house, kids running wild upstairs, his mam in the kitchen preparing catering quantities of sandwiches and tea, his dad handing out beer to the men. Looking back, the events which had brought them together – bereavements, engagements, christenings – all blurred together.

James, however, seemed to regard the question with suspicion. 'No one local,' he said. He shouted goodbye to Emma and left the house.

Emma apologized for the mess but didn't make any move to clear it. 'Who are you?' she asked Ashworth, then immediately she put her hand to her mouth, 'Sorry. I didn't mean to be rude. I suppose I'm used to Dan.'

'This is my sergeant, Joe Ashworth.' Vera ignored the reference to Greenwood. She didn't know what to make of it. Was there something going on there that she didn't know about? Dan Greenwood playing silly beggars? She could see him as the sentimental type, falling for someone unattainable like the pilot's wife. 'Joe works with me in Northumberland. He's here to help. Why don't you chat to him while I make some coffee.'

Ashworth took a seat opposite Emma. He pushed aside a cereal box so there was nothing between them. Vera put the kettle on and stood by the sink, watching the conversation, keeping her mouth shut even when she was tempted to interrupt with a question of her own.

'Did Christopher have a girlfriend?' Ashworth asked gently. 'Someone who should be informed of his death.'

'I don't think so. No one regular.' Emma looked up sharply. Vera saw that she'd been crying. She'd prob-ably been awake and crying for most of the night. The skin around her eyes was tender and swollen as if she'd been thumped. It looked as if you could rub it off with your thumb, like the skin of an over-cooked beet-root. 'Christopher blamed Abigail for that. When we were talking that night he was here, he said he'd been obsessed by her. That summer and ever since. No one else could live up to her. That wasn't true of course. If he was obsessed with her at all it was only the fantasy his girlfriends couldn't live up to. How can you com-pete with make believe?'

'Are you saying he went out with Abigail the sum-mer before she died?'

'No. Of course not. In his dreams.'

'Are you sure?'

'She wouldn't have looked at him twice. Except to mock. He was younger than she was, geeky, a bit weird. I thought he'd grown out of that, but maybe not. He seemed weird enough when he was here.'

'Abigail *did* have a boyfriend, though.'

No, Vera screamed in her head. *Don't move on. Not yet. Follow up on the weirdness. Was he different from the other times he visited? Why?*

But Emma was already answering Ashworth. 'I didn't know about a boyfriend. It seems unlikely. I mean, we spent a lot of that summer together and she never mentioned it.'

'She wasn't a virgin. Did you know that?'

'No!' Emma seemed astonished, shocked. There was a pause while she seemed to assimilate the infor-mation. 'But I was very innocent, very naïve. I'd led a sheltered life. When I thought about boys I imagined them kissing me, putting their arms round me. Noth-ing more than that. I knew about the biology, but it wouldn't have crossed my mind . . .'

'And Abigail was more worldly-wise?'

'In every way, but that wouldn't have been difficult. I thought of her as sophisticated. She knew so much more about everything.'

'Like what?'

'Music. I'd never heard of half the bands everyone was talking about at school. We didn't have a television. Do you know what a handicap that is? I went to her house to watch *Top of the Pops*, and they had satellite even then . . . Make-up. I didn't even know how to use cleanser and moisturizer. It wasn't that I wasn't allowed any of that stuff. Just that it would have been considered frivolous, a waste of time and money . . . Fashion . . . The names of film stars . . . She made me realize I was ignorant about everything.'

Ashworth smiled. 'You must have known things that she didn't.'

'Yeah, right. Latin verbs. Equations. The Bible. Just the stuff you want to boast about in front of your mates when you're fifteen.' She paused. 'Look, mostly it was her talking and me listening. I didn't realize at the time, but that was what I was there for. To show her how clever she was in comparison.'

'Sounds like she was insecure, maybe? Always needing to be right.'

'You think so? I never saw it like that.'

There was a moment of silence. From the baby monitor on the dresser they could hear Matthew snuffling in his sleep. He began to whimper.

'Did she talk to you about sex at all?'

'All the time in general terms. At that age you don't think about much else. But it was stuff like who we fancied. Which pop stars, which teachers, which of the lads at school. She certainly didn't tell me she was sleeping with anyone.'

'Why do you think that was? Was she worried about shocking you?'

Again there was a silence. At last Emma said, 'It's so hard after all this time to know what she was thinking. I had one memory of her and then Christopher gave me another. I'm not sure any more what was going on in her head. I don't think she'd worry about shocking me. She enjoyed making me out to be stuffy and old-fashioned. Perhaps her boyfriend wasn't as impressive or cool as she'd want him to be. A bit of a loser. She'd keep that to herself. Otherwise I can't see why she'd want it to be a secret.'

'Not even from her father?'

'No. I always thought she and Keith got on really well. I mean they never rowed. He never shouted. She could do what she liked. I thought he trusted her. But he can't actually have spent much time with her. He had Jeanie to keep sweet and work took up most of his time. Abigail could have anything she wanted but I'm not sure he listened to her. His mind was on other things.'

'Poor little rich girl?'

'Yeah, something like that. I suppose she was lonely and that was why she took up with me.'

'Can you give me the names of her other friends?'

'It's odd but there really wasn't anyone else. Not once I turned up. Not girls, at least. It was as if she didn't consider anyone else worth making an effort for. I found that flattering at the time.'

'Lads then?'

'There was one boy. Nick Lineham. His father was

deputy head of our school. He was a couple of years older than us and she fancied him like crazy.'

'Could he have been the lover?'

'I can't see why she wouldn't have told me.'

'Does he still live round here?'

'He teaches English at the FE college in town. We kept in touch after school. The odd phone call, you know. He never bothered with me when Abigail was alive, but perhaps he felt sorry for me. Or felt we had something in common. He got me a job at the college. Adult education. I taught languages.'

Vera caught something wistful in the voice and wondered what had caused it. The man or the work? She poured water onto instant coffee, took it to them. She'd restrained herself for long enough. 'Last night your husband said Christopher was drunk when he was here. Drunk and upset. Going through some sort of crisis. What do you think that was all about?' She pulled out a chair and sat down heavily. It was one of those bent wood affairs, old and stripped down. It creaked when she moved.

'I think Christopher was being overdramatic, blowing the whole thing out of proportion. Maybe he did have a crush on Abigail when he was fourteen. So what? He told me the other night that he followed her around like a juvenile stalker but I can't see it was the big deal he made it out to be. We'd have noticed if he'd been lurking in the bean fields every day. Like you said, it's pretty flat round here. There's nowhere much to hide. And I don't remember him changing that summer. He was still into the things he'd always been passionate about – natural history, astronomy. If he was pining away he was discreet about it.'

'What had upset Christopher so much now, then?' Vera demanded. 'Could it have been Jeanie Long's suicide?'

'Perhaps. Though I don't think he ever knew her. How could he?' Emma hesitated. 'I think the publicity around the anniversary of Abigail's death provided him with a convenient excuse. He was miserable. Perhaps some woman had dumped him. Perhaps things hadn't been going well at work. So he resurrected his adolescent fantasies about Abigail and convinced himself that she was the cause of his depression.'

The baby's whimper had turned into a high-pitched whine which shredded Vera's nerves. 'Look,' Emma said. 'He'll need changing. I'll have to fetch him. Is there anything else?'

'Not for the present, pet.' Vera was glad of the excuse to leave.

'Do you think the brother was mad?' They were sitting in the car, cut off from the rest of the village by the horizontal slashes of rain. Ashworth was in the driver's seat, waiting for instructions. The question seemed to come from nowhere. There was no thought behind it. He opened his mouth and it came out.

'I don't know,' Vera said. 'Depressed maybe.'

'You don't suppose . . .' he hesitated.

'Go on, pet. Spit it out.'

'He couldn't have killed the girl? If he *was* obsessed with her, despite what the sister says. Obsessed and keeping it to himself like a guilty secret. Perhaps she teased him, taunted him, like, and he snapped.'

'Then went home and pretended that nothing had happened?'

When they'd first started working together Ashworth would have left it at that. But he had more confidence these days. 'Pretended so well that he convinced himself too. Hid it away somewhere at the back of his mind, told himself when Jeanie was found guilty that it was all a bad dream. Until she committed suicide and the case was reopened. That would explain why he was behaving so oddly. Imagine waking up one morning and remembering you strangled a lass. You'd need a few drinks to come to terms with that.'

'You've been watching too much day-time telly,' Vera said. 'Tame psychologists spouting off. I don't believe in that sort of amnesia. Too convenient. Besides, he didn't leave the house the Sunday Abigail died. Everyone said so.'

'Would they remember? After ten years? Would they know? He could have gone out while they thought he was in his bedroom.'

She pictured the layout of Springhead House. There was one door into the kitchen from the yard which the Winters usually used, but another at the foot of the stairs leading out into a small walled garden. It was an old house and the walls were thick. They wouldn't have heard his leaving.

She saw the boy, slight and skinny, as he'd been in the photo there'd been of him in the hall at Springhead, running against the wind along the path between the fields towards the Mantel house. Had he been hoping to spy on Abigail? See her in her bedroom through an uncurtained window, trying on new clothes, brushing her hair? But perhaps the girl had been bored, left alone again by her father. Perhaps she'd set out for the Winters in search of an audience. And they'd met on the path.

He'd been a strange boy. They'd all said that. Self-contained. Obsessed. Vera pictured him blocking the girl's way, insistent.

I have to talk to you.

What do you want?

I can't stop thinking about you.

What? As if the thought had disgusted her. Though deep down she'd have been flattered, he wouldn't have realized that.

Perhaps she'd tried to push past him and he'd held onto her shoulder, desperate now that he had her to himself to make her understand. And, excited by the touch of her, he hadn't let her go.

Fuck off, you little prick.

But he'd twisted her towards him, stronger than he looked, and put his other hand on her neck, almost a caress. She'd shouted at him to let her go, told him what she thought of him in language which would have shocked a well-brought-up lad. He'd pulled her scarf tight around her neck, thinking only to cut off the words she was spitting out at him, but not able to stop, even when he realized what he was doing.

The rumble of an East Riding bin lorry, blurred by the rain into an unrecognizable shape, brought her back to the present. She shook her head to clear the nightmare from it.

'I can see Christopher killing her,' she said. 'Being driven to it in the way that you said. But forgetting all about it afterwards. Nah, I don't buy that.'

Chapter Twenty-Three

They drove in silence to Springhead House. Vera had her head full of the Winters and what it must have been like for Emma and Christopher growing up there. It was too close to making fiction, she thought, this attempt to recreate the past. But how else could she do it? She couldn't depend on the memories of the family. Even if they believed they were giving her the truth, after all this time there'd be gaps, bits that had changed with the telling over the years.

When they arrived they stood for a moment outside the house. The old farmyard was empty. There wasn't even Robert's car to provide shelter from the weather.

'A gloomy sort of place,' Ashworth said. 'You can see why the lad wouldn't want to come home much. What are they like, the parents?'

'Decent. Hard working. On the surface at least. You can never tell with families, can you, lad?' She slid him a sly, teasing look. He was a great one for families.

She knocked on the kitchen door and was surprised when Mary answered. The woman was wearing a grey tracksuit and a worn fleece, bobbled by too many washes. She'd aged overnight, shrunk inside her skin.

'What is it? Is there any news?' Vera couldn't tell if

she was grasping at the possibility or if she was scared that there might be something worse for her to cope with.

'Not yet, pet.' She paused. 'Where's Linda?' Linda was the officer who'd stayed overnight.

'I sent her away. She was very kind, but sometimes you need to be on your own.'

'And Robert?' Vera asked gently.

'He's in church.' Mary stood aside to let them in. 'I told him to go. He couldn't settle. I heard him all night, moving around the house. I thought he might find some peace there. But he's been longer than I expected. That was why I was so jumpy when you knocked at the door.'

Vera said nothing. She'd been brought up by her father to believe that atheism was the only rational standpoint, at a time when all her friends were sent to Sunday school. She'd watched the others straggle back from the parish hall clutching their coloured pictures of the disciples fishing and Jesus walking on the water and wished she could be allowed to join in. Church had been a forbidden attraction, the only social centre in their small village. Besides the pub. She'd crept in once to a harvest festival and had loved the noise of the organ and the singing, the colour of the stained-glass windows and the piles of fruit. But she couldn't see what Robert would get out of being in church at a time like this. Wasn't one gloomy building much like another? Wouldn't he be better off here, comforting his wife?

Perhaps Mary sensed her disapproval and felt the need to explain. 'He's confused, angry. It's a testing time.'

'For you both.'

'Faith has always been more important to him than it has to me.' She hesitated, then went on in a rush, 'He does so much good here. In the village. With his work. It would be a dreadful thing if that was lost. My role has always been to support him in that.'

Vera would have liked to follow this up but she didn't know what questions to ask. She was out of her depth. She wanted to say, *You're an intelligent woman and he's a grown man. Why can't he support the work you do?* But she didn't want to offend her. She looked towards Ashworth. He too seemed uncomfortable with the idea of faith.

'Was he specially close to Christopher?' she asked at last. 'His only son?'

The last phrase had a vague resonance, but she didn't pick it up and wondered why Mary looked at her so oddly.

'Robert was proud of Christopher, of course.' Her voice was clear and considered. Words mattered to her. 'He was a brilliant child, one of those who can pass examinations without really trying. But I don't think you could call them close. No. Not like some fathers and sons.' She paused to gather her thoughts and when she continued her voice was wistful. 'I work in a library. Most of the staff are women and they gossip about their relatives. I hear them talk about husbands who take their boys to football matches, fishing, and when they're older, to the pub. We aren't that sort of family. Not social in that sort of easy way. Do you understand? Perhaps it was a sacrifice we all had to make. For Robert's work. That had to come first. It was hard on the children.'

'But you see James and Emma, your grandchild?' Vera felt the need to reassure her.

'Oh yes, and that's wonderful! Such a blessing! We always have Sunday lunch together.' She paused and then added sadly, 'But that's more formal, planned. We're not very good about spontaneity. We're all very careful about how we treat each other. Perhaps it was a result of Abigail's death. Knowing that tragedy can strike at any time, it seems important not to argue. We'd been arguing that afternoon . . .' She came to a stop but Vera waited. This was what she needed. A picture of the household Christopher had grown up in.

And soon Mary continued. 'I'm not blaming Robert for the formality. No, I'm not saying that at all. In fact, Robert is somewhat more gregarious than I am. He suggested only last week that we should have a party for my fiftieth birthday. Invite all the family, friends. That's the sort of thing normal people do, isn't it? *We* used to have parties when we lived in York, go out to dinner, have meals with friends. The city is very different, of course. Perhaps I have become antisocial, but the idea of a gathering like that here terrified me.' A thought flashed into her mind. 'I suppose now I've an excuse to cancel it.' Immediately after the words were spoken she looked up, her face tight with shock. 'That was a dreadful thing to say. How could I? I'd suffer a thousand parties to have Christopher back alive.'

'I know,' Vera said. 'I know.'

Absent-mindedly Mary moved to the range. She lifted the lid and slid a wide-bottomed kettle onto the hot plate. 'I'll make some tea, shall I? I expect you'd like tea.'

'Can we talk to you about yesterday?' Vera asked.

205

'Of course. I feel so helpless. It's something I can do, at least. Answer your questions.'

'Did you know that Christopher was planning to visit Elvet?'

'No. But that wouldn't have been unusual. He did turn up occasionally, out of the blue. He hadn't lost the knack of being spontaneous, perhaps. It was always lovely to see him, but I wouldn't have wanted him to feel it was a duty, an obligation.'

Vera remembered that Michael Long had said something similar. *Children owe nothing to their parents.* So once Christopher had left home Mary had been forced to be patient, to say nothing, to wait for her son to drop in on a whim.

'You must have missed him. It wasn't like Emma living just up the road.'

'I did,' Mary said. 'Very much.'

'Whose idea was it to go to the lifeboat fundraiser?'

'Robert's. A last-minute decision. He felt, I think, that we all needed cheering up. This weather is so depressing. It gets you down in the end. And Emma has been tied to the house since Matthew was born.'

'Were you friends with Mr Mantel?'

'Friends? No!' The idea seemed impossible to her.

'Your daughters were once close friends. I wondered if you'd got to know each other socially at that time.'

'No, he's very busy, isn't he? And rather grand in that smart house with his shiny car. I'm not sure we'd have had very much in common. I mean, we knew him to say hello to. We bumped into him at village events. But there was always an awkwardness. It was ridiculous, I know, but I always felt guilty when we met.'

'Because your daughter was alive and his wasn't?'

She looked up gratefully. 'Yes, exactly that.' There was a moment of silence then she added, 'Now, I suppose we have both suffered the loss of a child and perhaps I'll feel differently.'

The kettle suddenly whistled. Vera found the noise unbearable and had to force herself not to leap to her feet and move it from the heat. For a moment Mary seemed not to hear it. At last she got up to make tea.

'Can you talk us through yesterday evening?' Vera asked when Mary settled at the table again. 'From arriving at the Old Chapel, if you wouldn't mind.'

'We parked in the lane with everyone else and walked round to the back of the house. There was a queue of people waiting to meet Keith and his young girlfriend. As if we were at one of those weddings, where the bride and groom stand at the door of the reception to greet their guests. Or as if they were royalty.'

'You sound as if you don't like Mr Mantel very much.'

'Do I?' Mary frowned. 'I don't mean to.'

'How did you feel about Emma and Abigail becoming friends?'

'We were relieved that Emma had found a friend at all. We'd underestimated, I think, how much the move from York would upset her.' She paused for a moment. 'It effected both the children in different ways. Emma had become rather withdrawn before she met Abigail.'

'But was Abigail the sort of girl you would have chosen as a suitable companion?'

'Why not? She was different in temperament from our daughter. More confident. More flamboyant, perhaps. But we knew nothing against her. I was more worried, I think, that she would suddenly become bored by Emma and drop her for someone else. I don't think Emma could have coped with that.'

Vera let that line of questioning go and returned to the evening before. 'So you greeted Keith and his girlfriend? What happened then?'

'We helped ourselves to drinks and tried to join in. There were lots of old friends. People from the church. Robert's quite a public figure because he's a warden. He's well known in the village. I stayed indoors for a while. Most of the older people were sitting in there. Outside it was cold and rather rowdy. Noisy music. I chatted to a couple of women from the Mothers' Union, then I went to find Robert.'

'Are you sure Christopher wasn't there?'

'I can't be. There was quite a crowd by the time I went out. And it was dark of course. The people in the field by the fire were just shadows.'

'Did you notice Caroline Fletcher?'

'I'm sorry. That name doesn't mean anything to me.'

'She was the police inspector who investigated Abigail Mantel's murder.'

'Of course. I'd forgotten the name. I should have remembered. She was supportive at the time of the trial. Was she there? I'm not sure I'd have recognized her. Not after all this time. Does that mean she'd kept in touch with Mr Mantel? How thoughtful!'

'Aye,' Vera muttered. 'That's one way of putting it.'

'Why did you go out into the lane, Mrs Winter?'

Ashworth spoke for the first time and Mary seemed thrown. She looked towards Vera as if she needed permission to answer.

Vera smiled encouragingly.

'I wasn't really enjoying myself,' Mary said. 'I never do, these days, in crowded places. It's strange how things change, isn't it? When we were younger, I'd have loved it . . . I asked Robert if we could leave. I was sure someone else would give Emma and James a lift back to the village. I said I was cold, which was true, but an excuse too, I'm afraid. Robert took me at my word. He said there was a thicker jacket in the car. He offered to fetch it but I took the keys and went myself. I was glad of a few moments alone.'

'What made you look in the ditch?' Ashworth asked.

'I'm sorry?'

'It was dark in the lane. No street lights to speak of. Only one just outside the house. Moonlight apparently, but you'd have to look where you were putting your feet. It was icy. So, I'm trying to understand how you came to see your son's body. If you were concentrating on not slipping. I'm sorry to make you go through it again, but it's the details which can help sometimes. Was there something in the hedge which caught your eye?'

'No,' she said. 'Nothing like that. The car was parked right on the verge so other vehicles could pass. The grass is rough and the car wasn't level. It was Robert's. He uses it for work and I never drive it. I knew there was a lever on the dashboard which opened the boot but I couldn't find it immediately. While I was fumbling I turned on the headlights by mistake. The beam shone down into the ditch. That was when I saw Christopher.'

She stared blankly out at them.

'Could he have been there when you arrived?' Ashworth asked. 'Or would you have seen him when you parked?'

'I was sitting in the back with Emma. Chatting. Trying to pretend that I didn't mind Christopher going back to the university without making the effort of visiting us. But James and Robert would have seen if he'd been there. No, Christopher must have died while we were at the Mantel house. He was so close. But we could do nothing at all to help him.'

Chapter Twenty-Four

'What did you make of her?' Vera asked. 'Was she telling the truth?'

'She didn't seem the sort to me who'd lie.'

They'd taken time out for tea and buns. Vera's decision. She wanted to talk to Robert Winter but he was still in the church – at least his car was parked in the square – and she thought she couldn't face him with low-blood sugar. She'd need to be on top of her game for that conversation. Besides she was embarrassed about breaking in on him. Suppose he was praying. She couldn't imagine herself sitting on a pew next to him, while he was on his knees. Just along the street from the Bennetts' house there was a bakery. She'd smelled the yeast and the sugar from the forge once and Dan had taken her in. Next to it there was a small, dark room, with a couple of tables where they served weak instant coffee and bacon sandwiches. And sticky cakes from the shop. From the narrow window they could see the church and Winter's car in the street. There was no one to overhear. The other table was empty and the waitress was in the shop gassing to the woman behind the counter.

'Maybe not,' Vera said. 'But there's a difference

between lying and telling the whole truth. She was very careful in the words she chose, wasn't she?'

'I can't see it. I thought she was a decent woman.'

'Not a lot of fun in her life, is there? Work and church. Do you think that's all there is?'

'Maybe that's all she wants.' Ashworth shrugged. 'Someone of her age . . .'

'Listen, lad. She's about the same age as me and I can still manage a few laughs. But it strikes me there's not much to laugh about in Springhead House.' She spooned sugar into her tea. The way she was feeling she needed the energy. 'Do you think the husband slaps her around?'

'No!' Ashworth was shocked. But then he was easily shocked. Some days that was the only entertainment Vera had, provoking a response from him.

'You didn't think she was frightened of him, then?'

'No,' Ashworth said slowly. 'Frightened *for* him perhaps. Worried that he was taking so long in the church. More protective I'd say. Like she was the mother and he was a kid.'

'A spoiled kid,' Vera said. 'As I heard it, he joined the God Squad, decided to give up his business in York and move out here and she just went along with it, dragging the family along with her.'

She broke off. Her attention was caught by Dan Greenwood, who emerged from the pottery and blinked as the cold air hit his face. Without bothering to lock the door behind him he ran across the street into the bakery. Vera watched him, wondered what it was about him that stopped her looking away. He disappeared from view, but they could hear him in the shop next door ordering a roast ham and mustard barm cake and a vanilla slice to take away. He returned to the Old Forge without seeing them.

'What *is* the story with Dan Greenwood?' Ashworth asked.

'He worked on the Mantel case first time round,' she said. 'Fletcher was his boss.'

'Like you and me then,' Ashworth said. He looked about six, Vera thought. A gob of red jam from a dough-nut on his chin. Not fit, really, to be let out alone.

'Oh, aye, I look a lot like Caroline Fletcher.'

'Was there something going on there, like? Did he fancy her?'

'No. They never got on.' Though that wouldn't have stopped Dan fancying her, then despising himself for it, Vera thought.

'Oh?'

'You could see what Fletcher's like. Hard as nails. On the surface at least. And Dan was too sensitive for his own good. One of those people who don't like the sort of games you have to play to get on. He's simple. Not dumb, I don't mean that. But straightforward. No pretence. No small talk.' *Intense*, she thought. *That's why you can't take your eyes off him.* Too much emo-tional energy. Then wondered if she was being daft.

'Is that why he left? Personality clash? You'd think he'd manage a transfer.'

'He had a breakdown,' she said. 'Stress related. He'd always struck me as a bit nervy. One of those people who can never sit still. He left on medical grounds soon after Jeanie Long was put away. Later he moved to Elvet and set up the pottery over the square.'

'Was it the Mantel case which made him ill? I'd not have thought there'd be that much pressure. The press would be pushing all the way, of course, but they cleared it up canny quickly, didn't they?'

She could tell he was thinking of some of the cases *he'd* worked on. Cases which had gone on for months, days without sleep, without seeing his family, and then no result at the end of it.

'He never believed Jeanie was guilty,' Vera said. 'But he didn't have the guts to make a fuss at the time.'

'So now he blames himself for her suicide?'

'Maybe.'

'How do you know him?'

'We'd met a couple of times, courses, training days. Then a lad from Wooler jumped bail and ended up down here. I came down for a few days. I liked Dan. He was one of those people you take to straight away. Like I said, no side to him. No agenda. He phoned me before he left the service. They'd offered him this deal and he asked my advice.'

'What did you tell him?'

'That we needed people who cared about the job, but that if it was making him ill he should take the money and run.'

'Why did he think Jeanie Long was innocent?'

'He was in on the interviews. He believed her.'

'And that was it?'

'There was no forensic evidence. And Dan said it all happened really quickly. Easily. As if it had been set-up. As if someone was pulling the strings.'

'You think that was Mantel?'

'You get a grieving father pointing the finger, saying he knows who killed his daughter, that's hard to ignore. Especially when he says it in public. And when he's a big figure locally. With friends who are magistrates and on the police committee.'

'In everyone's interest to clear it up quickly, then.'

'Everyone's except Jeanie Long's.'

'Whose strings exactly was Mantel pulling?'

Vera pushed half a curd tart into her mouth. 'We'll have to ask him, won't we? But that'll have to wait. There's Robert Winter coming out of the church.'

Winter was still standing in the church porch when they met up with him. He was poised as if to set off down the path towards the gate, restrained, it seemed by an invisible barrier. The path was slippery with wet leaves and at one point Ashworth almost tripped, but Winter gave no sign that he had seen them approach. He stared out at the bare trees which lined the churchyard.

'Your wife will be worried about you,' Vera said.

Only then did Robert acknowledge them with a courteous nod. He didn't respond, though, to the words.

'We've only just come from your house. Mary wasn't expecting you to be so long. Here, give her a ring.' Vera groped for a mobile phone in her bag. 'Tell her we want a quick word with you first, but you'll not be long.'

'Yes,' Robert said. 'Of course. I've been very thoughtless.' He took the phone and at last made the effort to leave the porch, walking a few paces away from them, turning his back so they couldn't hear what was said.

'Is there somewhere we can talk?' Vera asked when he'd finished.

'Here? In the church?' As if, she'd say to Ashworth

later, she'd suggested an interview in a brothel or a gents' lav.

'If we wouldn't be intruding.'

'I'd prefer not to.'

So they ended up in the little room by the bakery again, with more tea. On the way they passed the newsagent's and the headlines in the local papers screamed Christopher's name. But Vera couldn't feel sorry for Robert Winter and all the time they were talking she wished she'd been more forceful, stood her ground. What was it about the man that he always seemed to get his own way?

She began with a question he wouldn't be expecting, hoping to throw him.

'Why the probation service? A bit different from architecture.'

'More challenging.' He smiled politely. She thought he'd played these word games before.

'What do you get out of it?'

'Not money, certainly,' he said. 'Architecture was more lucrative. Most professions would be.'

Beside her, she could sense Ashworth willing her to change tack. She knew what he was thinking. Robert Winter was a bereaved relative who should be handled with a bit more sensitivity.

'So, what then?' she demanded.

'Occasionally we can make a difference,' Robert said. 'Change lives. When that happens there's no more rewarding job in the world.'

'Did you make a difference to Jeanie Long?'

'Obviously not.' Still he kept calm, didn't even show a trace of irritation. 'I accepted the judgement of the court that she was a murderer. I failed her because I didn't believe her story.'

'You must feel bad about that.'

'Of course I do, but I can't let it affect my work with other prisoners. I don't think I can blame myself. Many of the people I work with are manipulative and plausible. Many of them claim to be innocent. Sometimes we get it wrong—'

'You see,' Vera interrupted, 'I think it must be a bit like joining the police. The same motivation, I mean. It gives a licence to meddle. It's a way into all that muck and corruption we respectable folk wouldn't normally come across. There's a glamour about crime, isn't there? An excitement. Everyone's curious about it, but *we're* paid to stick our noses in. And so are you.'

'That's one interpretation, Inspector. But not one I'd subscribe to.'

'Did Christopher have any girlfriends while he was living at home?' Vera asked.

'Not that I knew of.'

'Would you have known? Is that the sort of thing you'd have talked about?'

'Possibly not. Christopher was a very private young man.'

'Ironic, isn't it?' She smiled to show that she intended no offence at all. 'You probably knew more about the lives of the offenders in your care than you did about your own son.'

She moved on quickly before Robert could respond. 'Why were you so keen to take your family to the bonfire last night?'

'It had been a difficult time for us all. Jeanie's suicide, the Mantel case all over the newspapers again, it had brought back the unpleasant memories. I thought it would be good for us to get out for the evening. Stop brooding.'

'Didn't you think that meeting Keith Mantel might have the opposite effect. On Emma, at least?'

'No,' he said. And Vera saw that it was possible he was telling the truth. He hadn't realized Emma might find it hard to return to the house where her best friend had lived at the time she was murdered. And Ashworth thought *she* was insensitive. 'No. It happened a long time ago. Emma has moved on. We all have. I thought it would be a pleasant evening for everyone.'

'You hadn't expected to meet Christopher there?'

'Not at all. I was sure he'd gone straight back to Aberdeen. It was inconsiderate – he knows his mother looks forward to his visits – but quite in character.'

Quite suddenly he seemed to lose patience with the questions. 'Is there anything urgent, Inspector? Anything which won't keep? Only my wife's been alone for a long time. As you said. Really, I think I should go back to her.' Without waiting for a reply he stood up and walked out. Through the window they watched him stride along the pavement. An elderly woman, obviously distressed, scurried up to him to offer her condolence. He stopped, bent towards her and took her hand in both of his. Then he continued towards his car.

'I wonder,' Vera said slowly, 'why I dislike him so much.'

'The religion?' Ashworth suggested. 'It was never your thing.'

'Maybe. But I want you to get a list of the people who were at Mantel's last night and talk to them all.

Did any of them notice Robert Winter leave the bonfire? Did anyone see him out in the lane?'

'And what will you be up to?'

'Me?' she answered. 'I'm going to the prison. Where Jeanie Long spent the last ten years. There's another victim in all this. And I don't feel I know anything about her.'

Chapter Twenty-Five

Vera parked where it said *Visitors*. The place was nearly empty. The staff car park was nearer, but there was a barrier operated from the gatehouse. Some days she'd have enjoyed pushing the buzzer and demanding to be let in, but today she wasn't in the mood for a fight.

She'd phoned ahead and they were ready for her. She'd asked to speak to anyone who'd known Jeanie well and was surprised when she was shown straight to the governor's office. She thought she could work out what that was about. Suicide in custody was a sensitive business. There were probably league tables. He'd want to make it clear that his institution wasn't responsible, that they'd followed the guidelines to the letter. But as soon as she saw him she realized she'd misjudged him. He was standing at the window, looking down at a square of concrete, which was already dark because of the high walls surrounding it. A group of women was being escorted across it. They stood waiting, stamping their feet and shouting, while an officer locked the door of one building and walked round them to unlock the door of another.

'That's the education block,' the governor said. 'Jeanie spent a lot of time in there. I thought it might help, that she'd see it as a constructive way to pass the time. Obviously I was wrong.'

'You didn't consider her a suicide risk, then?'

He turned back into the room. 'No. But I wasn't surprised when it happened. I feel responsible. I should have seen it coming.'

'You have a lot of women in your charge.' She said it as a fact, not an excuse, but he dismissed the idea, shaking his head.

'None of them had been here as long as Jeanie. It was a terrible waste. She was never a security risk. If she'd said the right things, she could have moved to an open prison years ago.'

'But she refused to play the game?'

'I think she was incapable of lying,' he said. 'I've worked for the prison service for twenty years and I'd never met anyone like her.'

'You believed her defence at the trial, then?'

'Jeanie Long didn't kill anyone,' he said firmly. 'I was quite sure of that as soon as I met her.'

Vera thought that he'd been a little bit in love with her, and that he was too easily moved to be in charge of a women's prison.

'How did she fit in here?'

'She didn't. Not with the other women. Lifers often achieve the status of celebrities. It's not that everyone here is a ghoul. It has more to do with the publicity surrounding the case than the nature of the crime. For the lifers themselves, it's easy to be flattered by the attention and it can make life inside easier. Jeanie refused to play the role. She only talked about the offence to protest her innocence.'

'Was she close to anyone?'

'As I said, to none of the women. We appointed a new chaplain a year ago and Jeanie seemed to respect her.'

'What about the officers? The teachers?'

'No. Prison works on the principle of consent. Offenders recognize their guilt and the right of the authorities to order their lives. Jeanie never did. She questioned, challenged. It made her unpopular. The standard of teaching in prison, especially a prison like this, which doesn't hold many long-term inmates, has to be pretty basic. Jeanie could be dismissive, almost rude. She'd had a better education than most of the teachers and didn't hide it.'

'How did she get on with her probation officer?'

'There wasn't much contact. Probation officers are supposed to maintain a link with offenders in custody, but there are often more pressing demands on their time. I looked at the welfare report after Jeanie died and Robert Winter seemed to have been very fair. He tried to encourage her to say and do all the right things. He visited her father in the hope of finding her a supportive home after her release. I'm afraid Mr Long wasn't very helpful.'

'Long thought she'd killed the girl and deserved to be here.'

The governor seemed unable to speak. Vera wanted to slap some life into him. 'Did you know that Mr Winter was indirectly involved in the Mantel case? His daughter found the girl's body.'

'No.' The governor seemed shocked. 'But then I never met him. I had no reason to. I have regular contact with the welfare officers who are based here, of course, but not with those who come in from outside.'

'When did he last visit Jeanie?'

The governor reached over and pulled a file from a tidy pile on the table under the window, but Vera had the impression he knew the answer already.

'Three days before she died.'

The chaplain had a small office behind the chapel. Usually she would have left by now, the governor said, but she'd hung on specially to see Vera. He called an officer to take her, a friendly young woman, who shouted to the women on the wing by name. It was teatime and they'd formed a disorderly queue along the corridor to collect food from a hatch. A very thin girl with unkempt hair and slashes on her wrists was singing to herself. Something loud and aggressive. No one took any notice. *Jeanie would have stood here too*, Vera thought. Aloof and friendless.

'Did you know Jeanie Long?' she asked the officer.

'Yes.'

'What did you make of her?'

The woman shrugged. 'Not much to tell the truth. She thought she was better than the rest of them. And she'd managed to twist the number one governor round her little finger. Not that it's hard to do that. He's taken in by all their sob stories.'

She realized that she'd been indiscreet and they walked on through the jostling, curious women in silence.

The chaplain was small. She wore a white nylon roll neck sweater, under a brightly coloured cardigan, to represent the dog collar, and red cord trousers. She made Vera tea.

'That's all some of them come for,' she said. 'Tea in a china cup and biscuits. I don't mind. It doesn't seem a lot to ask occasionally, does it?'

'What did Jeanie Long come for?'

'She said it was for some intelligent conversation and a break from the noise on the wing.'

'That sounds reasonable.'

'Perhaps. And rather arrogant. I didn't find her an easy person to like, Inspector. She believed she was different from the other women. She wasn't prepared to give them a chance.'

'She was innocent,' Vera said, trying to contain her anger. 'That made her different. How often did you see her?'

'Once a week, on Friday mornings. The governor asked me to talk to her when I first arrived here. He said she was having a hard time. She wasn't getting on with her named officer. We fell into the habit of weekly meetings. I'm not sure what she really got out of them.'

'What did you talk about?'

'Not religion,' the chaplain said quickly. 'She made it clear from the beginning that that was a no-go area. "My mother believed in all that crap and look what it did for her." She was always on her guard against anything which might seduce her away from the fight. As if she had to stay angry to keep faith with herself. "It would be *so* easy to give in," she said once. "To let it go." The only times I ever did see her let it go was when she talked about music. She became a different person then, gentler and more relaxed.'

'Did you discuss the Mantel case?'

'She did certainly. At every opportunity. I was uncomfortable. I didn't know how to react. I didn't want to encourage false hopes. The case went to appeal once, soon after she was sentenced, but it was thrown out. There was no new evidence. I couldn't see that it would ever be reopened. And of course all my training and belief, and the ethos of the prison, is about acceptance of wrongdoing. That has to come before the possibility of rehabilitation.'

'You believed she killed the girl, then?' Vera thought this was a load of sanctimonious nonsense.

'I'm naïve. I didn't think the court could get it that wrong. I thought perhaps she'd convinced herself that she was innocent because she couldn't face the horror of what she'd done. And I couldn't dismiss the possibility that she was very manipulative, that I was being conned.'

'Did she take any practical steps to clear her name?'

'I think she did in the beginning. She wrote letters to the newspapers, and anyone else she could think of, protesting her innocence. Though soon she wasn't news any more and the press lost interest, until *The Guardian* picked up on the ten year anniversary of the trial. Soon after her conviction her mother took out an advert in one of the London papers with a photo, asking anyone who'd seen Jeanie on the day the girl was killed to come forward. Then her mother died, and I suppose she gave up hope. All she could do was to go over and over the facts.'

'And that's what she did at your meetings?'

'For much of the time. I didn't think it was healthy, repeating the same stories, week after week. She said she had to remember. Everyone else would forget what had happened. Some day, she said, she might have to stand up in court and give her version of events again. She'd need to know what to say.'

'Can you remember what she told you?'

'Oh, I think so,' the chaplain said. 'I heard it often enough.' She turned slightly in her chair, so she wasn't looking directly at Vera. Outside there was a brief commotion, raised voices, the shout of an officer, but she took no notice. 'Jeanie was passionate about music. Ambitious. She wanted to make a career of it. Not teaching, she said. She'd never have managed that. She knew it would be tough to get into the profession, so at university she stayed focused, concentrated on her work. She went out with a couple of lads, but there was nothing serious. They'd have got in the way. Then she met Keith Mantel and she was in love. The way most kids are when they're fifteen and fall for some popstar. But Keith Mantel was real and available and he seemed to reciprocate her feelings.'

'What did she feel about Mantel when she was inside?'

'She said she had no regrets. That summer was the most wonderful time of her life. Remembering it was all that kept her going. I think she still had the fantasy that when her name was cleared they'd get back together.'

'Did she talk about Abigail?'

'Yes, and it was almost as if she blamed the girl for her own murder. I hated the way she spoke about her. She said the power Abigail had over her father was unnatural, strange. "If I was religious, I'd have said she was evil. I tried to understand her, but it's hard to understand someone who's that screwed up and self-obsessed. Of course, I could see how it had happened

– her mother dying when she was young, her father spoiling her. But she'd turned into a monster and there's no excuse for that." She blamed Abigail, of course, for Keith's decision to throw her out. I could tell that still hurt. She was still making excuses for it, trying to find an explanation which didn't have her playing the role of spurned lover.'

'Did she describe the day of the murder?'

'Yes, and it was much as she told it in court. She phoned the Old Chapel early in the morning. There was only the answer machine. That didn't mean Keith wasn't in. She said he wouldn't talk to her, that he knew if they spoke together he'd have to let her back. She was tempted to go to see him, but it was a weekend and she knew he wouldn't be himself if Abigail was there. On a whim she decided to go away for the day. She drove to Hull and took the first train to London. She got a train back in the late afternoon. No one saw her or spoke to her. When she arrived back at her parents' house she learned that Abigail was dead. She tried to phone Keith to offer her sympathy, but again there was no reply. Her parents persuaded her not to go to the house. Later she was told that he'd moved in with a friend so he could grieve in peace. Only a few days later she was arrested.'

'Did she have any theories about who had killed Abigail?'

'Usually she spoke vaguely about Abigail asking for trouble. The way she dressed and led men on. Posing and giggling and flirting. Some sad, sick old man, Jeanie said. I did wonder . . .'

'Yes?'

'I did wonder if Jeanie might have been talking

about her father. If that was why she hated him so much. Not because he'd killed Abigail. She'd have forgiven him for that. But for letting her take the blame. For leaving her to rot in here. I didn't believe that, though. Not for more than a moment. I thought she was guilty.'

Chapter Twenty-Six

When Vera arrived back at her hotel it was almost dinnertime and she was spoiling for a fight. From the prison she'd gone into Crill, into the police station, where the incident room had been set up. She'd expected to be treated as she was at home. Not quite as a female deity, but as someone whose word counted for something. It hadn't been like that. Paul Holness had been there, lording it over the incident room, shouting his orders, handing out scraps of praise to his adoring team. He'd treated her requests first with a patronizing amusement then with downright hostility. She'd misjudged him. Holness might not be bright but he didn't want her playing an active role in the Christopher Winter murder enquiry.

In the hotel, she went straight to the bar. It was furnished like a gentleman's club with dim lighting and music so low it was impossible to make out what it was. It seemed more like a vibration in the background than music, the irritating hum of an insect. She could have done with a shower but she needed a drink more. And she didn't feel like drinking on her own. She phoned Ashworth's mobile.

'Where are you?'

'Just got in.' He sensed her mood and added

'ma'am'. An insurance policy. It didn't do any harm and sometimes it mollified her. Not tonight.

'Get down here. I'm buying.'

She sat, taking up most of a leather Chesterfield with her bags and her coat, fuming, until he arrived.

'How was the visit to the prison?' he asked, mildly.

'Interesting, but we'll talk about that later.'

'And your meeting with the local plods?'

She didn't answer directly. 'What did you make of them, anyway? Did they give up the list of witnesses who were at Mantel's? Without a fight?'

'No bother. But it saved them a bit of work, didn't it? An extra body to check through the statements and do the follow-up visits. They weren't going to turn that down.'

'I found them bloody obstructive.'

He said nothing, thought, *You didn't get your own way, then.*

'They want to treat the two cases as separate investigations. There's no evidence to link the two enquiries at this point. So they say. So Holness says. It's madness. And even if there were, it's not my role to find out who killed Abigail, only to reach a decision about how the original team got it wrong.'

'It'll be political,' he said. 'They'd not want an outsider taking over a live murder case. It'd make them all look incompetent. You never thought you'd get away with that? I can't imagine you agreeing to it on our patch.'

'Maybe not,' she said.

'Holness could have asked you to put the Mantel enquiry on hold, while the current investigation is underway.'

'I'd like to see him try!' She hated Ashworth when he was being reasonable. 'Besides, the press would see it as a cover-up.'

'Are any of the officers who worked on the Mantel case part of the team looking into Christopher Winter's murder?' he asked.

'No.'

'I can't see that you can object, then. It's a fresh team. Not likely the same mistakes will be made this time. And they'll keep you informed of developments . . .'

'They *say* they will. Especially if they turn up anything which relates to the Mantel investigation.'

'Well, then.'

She drank her Scotch and suddenly grinned at him. 'Don't mind me, pet. I just want to be home. You know.'

He nodded.

'How did you get on?' she asked.

'I don't think we'll get much from the witness statements. It seems the Winter family were among the last people to arrive at the party. Caroline Fletcher arrived later but she told the locals last night that she didn't meet anyone in the lane on her way in.'

'So if anyone at the bonfire killed Christopher, she was the most likely?'

'Nah,' he said. 'Any one of them could have slipped out to meet the lad without the rest of the crowd noticing. No one saw Robert Winter leave, but then they didn't miss Mrs Winter either when she went out to fetch her coat.'

'Have they found the murder weapon yet?'

'No. They're going to continue the search at first light.'

'They're not much further forward then,' she said, unable to keep the satisfaction from her voice.

'What's the plan for tomorrow?'

'We need to talk to Mantel. They can't object to that. He was our victim's father. It's only right.'

When they approached the Old Chapel the next morning it was only just light. The rain had stopped, though there was still the wind, which blew a paper fertilizer sack into the road in front of them, and dead twigs from the bent trees, and eddies of sand and straw. It was the wind which Mantel mentioned first when he opened the door. 'Blowing into a storm,' he said, looking up into the grey, racing clouds, as if he'd lived in the country all his life, as if he knew about boats and tides and the weather.

Vera introduced herself.

'You're leading the new enquiry into my daughter's death?'

'That's right. This is my sergeant.'

'I thought you might have been here to see me earlier. It would have been courteous. I only heard they were reopening the case from the press.'

Vera muttered something about only having made preliminary enquiries, but she knew he was right and anyway he hadn't made the point aggressively. Whatever his past record, whatever Michael Long had thought, seeing him now, she felt sorry for him.

'You're lucky to catch me in. I decided to work at home today, cancelled all my meetings. I couldn't face it. That business with the lad the other night, it brought it all back.'

They were still standing at the arched wooden door and could see the crime scene. A bit of blue and white tape had come loose and was blowing crazily, like the tail of a big, flash kite, the sort controlled by two strings. A line of officers in overalls and navy anoraks walked slowly, eyes to the ground, across a neighbouring field.

'Two young people dead,' Mantel said. 'What a terrible waste.'

'Three,' said Ashworth. Mantel didn't respond, but Ashworth had spoken quietly and perhaps he hadn't heard.

They followed him through to the room where the old ladies had sat two nights before. No evidence remained of the gathering. The extra chairs had been removed, the carpet hoovered. In the conservatory beyond, a plastic crate stood by the outside door. It contained empty wine bottles, some jammed, neck down, into the layer below. Through the glass they saw the remains of the bonfire and dead fireworks strewn on the grass.

Mantel nodded at them to sit down. 'Do you think they were killed by the same person?' he demanded. Then, when there wasn't an immediate response, 'I mean Abigail and the Winter boy.'

'There's no evidence either way yet.'

'I was convinced Jeanie was guilty. It was all that kept me going. The anger. The court case. Seeing her sent down. I went to court every day, sat in the gallery after I'd given evidence, waited the four days it took them to come up with a verdict. I'd have hanged her myself then, if it had been possible.' He stopped abruptly. 'You *are* sure she was innocent. It's not just the press after a story, her lawyers playing the system.'

'Quite sure.'

He sat very still. 'I didn't believe it until last night,' he said. 'I thought it was the do-gooders and liberals out to clear her name. Then when there was another body . . . Even I could tell it was too much of a coincidence.' He looked up sharply. 'What do you think? Some mad man on the loose?'

'It's too early to come to any conclusions. They're treating it as two separate cases until there's more evidence either way.'

He seemed about to argue, but thought better of it. 'What do you want from me?'

'Tell me about the months leading up to Abigail's death.'

'What good will that do after all this time? You must have access to the statements.'

'It's not the same as hearing it from you.'

He shut his eyes, scrunched them up tight like a child trying to fight off tears, but when he opened them again and started speaking, his voice was calm.

'Her mother died when Abigail was six. Breast cancer. She was only thirty-three. Still lovely. If you've been doing your job properly you'll know I played a bit dirty when I was younger, but by the time she became ill I'd settled down. I didn't think I deserved it, losing her, I mean. I pushed the rules to the limits perhaps, but I stayed within them. Then at least. I was successful. Lucky. Tragedies like that didn't happen to me.

'When Liz died I wanted to run away, pretend it had never happened. But I couldn't because of Abigail. I suppose I spoilt her but that's what fathers do, isn't it?

They spoil their little girls. And then I spent so much time at work. When I *was* around, I wanted to make it special for her.' He paused. 'There'd been other women before Jeanie. I'd brought some of them home. But they all knew that Abigail came first.'

'Jeanie must have been special, then.'

'Not particularly, no. She was young, pretty enough. A talented musician. But there have been others prettier, sexier.'

'Yet she was the first one you moved in.'

'I didn't move her in. She turned up, uninvited, with all her bags, after a row with her father. When I came in from work she'd unpacked. A fait accompli.'

'Why did you let her stay?'

'Apathy. Devilment. Her father had never liked me and it was amusing to wind him up. And there was something about her. Something innocent, I suppose. She reminded me a bit of Liz when she was a girl. She made me feel young again. That first night she was so grateful to be here, so eager to please. She'd have done anything for me. It was flattering. I took the easy way out. It wasn't as if I was home much. I told myself it would be good for Abigail to have the company of someone nearer her own age.'

'But Abigail didn't like her?'

'Couldn't stand her,' he said simply. 'Too used to getting her own way, I suppose. Always being the centre of attention.'

'So you told Jeanie she'd have to leave?'

'Eventually. In the autumn. I could tell by then it wasn't going to work. I was too old after all. She was so intense and it became clear that she wanted more from the relationship than I did.'

'Marriage?'

'Maybe. She never mentioned it but I wouldn't have been surprised.' He hesitated. 'Besides, there was someone else. I was looking for an excuse to get rid of Jeanie. The situation was messy, a distraction.'

'What happened when you asked Jeanie to leave?'

'It was horrible. I knew she could be moody, unpredictable, but that day she lost it completely. She blamed it all on Abigail. I'd always thought of her as rather prim, but she let fly with a stream of filth.'

'What did she say about Abigail?' Vera asked. 'Precisely.'

'She called her a dirty little slut. Amongst other things.'

'You didn't mention that in your statement.' Vera waited but Mantel didn't respond and she continued slowly, 'I can understand why you were so angry. What do you think made Jeanie so abusive?'

'Because she knew it would hurt me. She was jealous.'

'Why slut though? Why that particularly?'

'If you want to know about Abigail's sexual history, you could ask,' Mantel said and that made Vera feel like a worm again, as she had when they'd first arrived.

'Yes,' she said. 'I'm sorry. You do see why it could be important.'

'They asked about boyfriends first time round. Sexual partners, they said. It hadn't occurred to me that she might have been sleeping with someone.'

'You were shocked.'

'I had no right to be shocked. I slept with women, many of them not much older than Abigail. I was surprised. I had thought she would talk to me about something like that. I'd known it would happen, of course. I'd prepared myself for it. Imagined her bringing some boy home. I knew I wouldn't take to him, however decent and respectable he might be, but thought I could pretend. Welcome him in. Then I wouldn't lose her. I hadn't thought she'd keep it a secret.'

'She was under age. The boy would have been committing an offence.'

'Perhaps that was it.'

'You had no idea at all who she was seeing?'

'None at all. She had a party for her fifteenth birthday. There were boys here for that. I could probably remember the names of some of them. But I was around for most of the evening and there didn't seem to be anyone special.'

'Nick Lineham? Does that ring a bell?'

'The teacher's lad. Yes, he was one of them.'

'And Christopher Winter?'

'Emma was here, of course. She and Abigail were best friends. But I don't remember seeing the boy. Abigail had laughed about him, talked about a crush, but I don't think he'd have been invited. Wasn't he quite a lot younger?'

'Only a year,' Vera said. 'That was all.'

He was staring out into the garden, distracted for a moment by the cloud of rooks which scattered from an old sycamore and he seemed not to hear.

'Let me take you back to the night of the bonfire.' In her mind she saw him, standing there, welcoming his guests with his trophy girlfriend by his side. Middle-aged of course but fit and charming. This person seemed older. She liked him better. 'Did you see Christopher Winter during the evening?'

'I don't think I would have recognized him. Ten years makes a lot of difference to someone that age and I only saw him a few times while Abigail was alive. Sitting in the back of his mother's car when she came to collect Emma. Once on the Point, I think. His parents were here last night. They'd have seen him, surely, if he'd been one of the guests?'

'Probably. Were there many strangers here?'

'People I didn't know, certainly. The tickets were on sale in the pub and the post office. The lifeboat crew brought their friends.'

'You recognized Caroline Fletcher?'

'Yes. She was the officer in charge of the original enquiry.'

'Did you invite her?'

'No.'

'Why was she here?'

She could see him framing a noncommittal reply in his head, then give up on it, too exhausted perhaps to make the effort to lie. 'To check up on me. To remind me that we could both face problems if I spoke to the authorities.' Then, flippant, 'Because she can't keep away.'

'I'm not sure I follow you.' Though she was beginning to. Understanding was seeping into her brain like water into an estuary.

'Look. I said that I'd met someone else before Jeanie moved in here and it made things messy, complicated.' He paused.

'Go on.' She was sitting very still, staring into his face.

He returned her gaze. Again she thought he would refuse to answer.

'The woman was Caroline.'

'You were going out with Caroline Fletcher while she was investigating your daughter's murder?' Vera was apoplectic, scarlet, marble-eyed. Only just holding it together.

'We were close, yes.'

'And it never occurred to her to declare an interest? She could have wrecked the whole case.'

'We'd been discreet. We didn't think anyone would find out.'

Dan Greenwood had guessed, Vera thought, but he'd been too daft and too loyal to say anything. No wonder Fletcher had taken against Jeanie from the beginning.

'What did you promise her to get a conviction?' Vera demanded.

'Nothing. There was no need. She wanted it as much as I did.'

She was besotted, Vera thought. What is wrong with all these women? She was a strong, clever woman and she threw her career away for a prat like you. That was why she left the service. So she'd be free to marry you when you asked her. Is that what you promised? But you never did. She was even more of a mug than Jeanie Long.

Mantel walked with them to their car, and stood shivering while Ashworth patted his pockets for the keys.

'One thing,' he said.

'Yes?'

'Emma's husband. The one who calls himself Bennett. The pilot on the river.'

'What about him?'

239

'I recognized him last night. He didn't realize. You should check him out. That wasn't his name when I first met him.'

'What was his name?'

He shrugged and Vera couldn't tell whether he didn't remember or he thought he'd told them enough.

Before they could ask him more he turned and walked quickly back to the house.

Chapter Twenty-Seven

Vera was stranded in the deep armchair. It was too low for her to climb out with any sort of dignity. She ate the last chip, licked her finger and collected the last scraps of batter, then screwed the greasy paper into a ball and hurled it overarm towards the waste bin in the corner. Dan Greenwood retrieved it from the floor. They were in the Old Forge, in the room next to his office. Just her and Greenwood. She'd sent Ashworth to the FE college where Emma had worked, to talk to Nicholas Lineham who, when he was a lad, might once have had sex with Abigail Mantel. So many connections, she thought. People waltzing in and out of each other's lives. She felt her eyes glaze as she pictured the patterns, the lines of connection. Her lids began to droop. At her age she deserved a nap in the afternoon.

'Did you make that coffee?' she said. Some temptations you couldn't give into.

He nodded to the tray on the upturned crate beside him.

'Well, it's no good to me there.'

He lifted the mug to within her reach.

'How did you know Mantel was screwing Fletcher?'

'I didn't.' Defensive, touchy.

'You're not surprised though.'

'She was never happy without a man in her life. She doesn't come across as the needy sort, but it was like she couldn't believe in herself without a man to admire her.'

'Oh, God.' She leaned back in her chair, legs stretched ahead of her, heels on the floor, and stared at the ceiling. 'Not another one.'

'What?'

'I've had Ashworth spouting psychobabble ever since he arrived.' She pulled herself more upright so she could look Greenwood in the face. 'Did she ever have a go at you?'

'What do you mean?' He took out a tin of tobacco and began to roll a cigarette. His hands were shaking.

'Don't go all coy on me, Danny. You know what I'm getting at.'

His neck, underneath the beard was flushed. 'Nah,' he said. 'I wasn't important enough. She never took me that seriously.'

'Did you ever see them together – Fletcher and Mantel?'

He shook his head slowly. 'I heard a phone call. She didn't know I was there. I mean, it could have been to anyone. By that time my judgement was shot and my paranoia was sky high, but I thought it was to him.'

'What did she say?'

'It was just after we'd taken Jeanie into custody. She was telling him that she'd be charged by the end of the day. That was all. But it was the way she was saying it. Like she was a little girl. A good little girl who'd done as she was told.'

'Christ,' Vera said. 'You'd want to puke.'

'I felt sorry for her really.' Greenwood nipped the

end off the cigarette. 'Like I said, my judgement was shot. I should have stood up to her. I knew we were cutting corners.'

Vera drank her coffee as if she couldn't trust herself to say anything.

He rolled the cigarette in his fingers but still he didn't light up. 'I met her last week.'

'You met Fletcher?'

'She phoned me, asked if we could go out for a drink. I told her I was too busy. Just a quick one before closing time, she said. She picked me up from here . . .' He looked at Vera, but she refused to help him out. 'By then the pubs were closed so we went back to my place.' He blushed. 'Nothing happened. Nothing like that. Just a drink and a chat.'

'What did she want then?'

'To know if I'd heard anything, if you'd been in touch. She couldn't understand why she'd not been contacted.'

'And you told her. Of course.'

'I felt sorry for her. I explained. She's not as tough as she makes out.'

'You do realize she's a suspect in a murder enquiry? Probably the prime suspect as things have turned out.'

'No.' A rejection of the whole notion.

'She certainly had a motive for killing Abigail Mantel and arresting Jeanie Long. We've only her word for it that she didn't speak to Christopher Winter at the time of the original enquiry. It's possible that he saw her with Abigail that afternoon and she persuaded him it was of no importance. You can see she could be persuasive. Especially with a young lad. Perhaps that was why he turned up in Elvet now. He wanted to set things straight.'

'No,' Greenwood said again. She thought he would like to put his hands over his ears and shut out her words.

'She was there the night he died,' Vera went on relentlessly. 'She had possible motive, opportunity. And she disappeared just before the body was found. There's a stronger case against her than against anyone else involved.'

He'd been looking at the cracked and dusty tiles on the floor. Now he looked straight at her. 'You don't really believe she's a double murderer?'

'Probably not,' she said. 'But she's bad news. If she gets in touch with you again let me know.'

They sat for a long time, staring at each other in silence.

'What do you know about James Bennett?' Vera said at last.

'He's a pilot on the Humber.'

'I know that, man. It's all anyone says about him.'

'You can't have him down as a suspect. He wasn't living round here when Abigail Mantel was killed.'

'How do you know?'

'He only moved into the village when he married Emma and they bought the house over the square.'

'When was that?'

'Not long. Two years at the most.'

'You're mates, aren't you?'

'I suppose so.' The concept seemed to embarrass him. 'We both play cricket for the village team. Have a few pints together after a game.'

'So he'll have talked about his background, his family. You know where he grew up.'

'Not really,' Greenwood said. 'Mostly it's talk about the mid-order collapse or where we can find a decent bowler.'

'You're winding me up.'

'He likes talking about his work. Pilotage.'

'Safe ground,' she said. 'He won't be caught out on that.'

'What do you mean?'

'According to Mantel, he's not who he says he is.'

'How would he know?'

'He recognized him apparently.'

'And you believe Mantel?'

'Yes,' Vera said. 'I think I do.'

She stood up. She'd arranged to meet Ashworth in the teashop over the road. It would do as an office for the time being. Better than the station in the town which had turned out to be enemy territory. Eventually, she supposed, she'd have to put in another appearance there, show her face round the door of the incident room, smile to show they were all on the same side, working together, but at the moment it suited her to keep her position ambiguous and detached. Better all round if no one knew where she was and what she was up to. Caroline Fletcher, it seemed, still had a way of inspiring loyalty among her former colleagues. She looked down at Greenwood. He was hunched forwards, his shoulders tense.

'Will you be all right?' Trying not to fuss.

He looked up and forced a smile. 'Sure. It's about time I did some work here. There's a trade fair at the end of the week. I should be preparing for that.'

'You should find yourself a good woman.'

He paused before speaking and she waited, expecting some confidence, but obviously he thought better of it. 'Yeah, well. Easier said than done. I've never had much luck in that line.'

He looked straight up at her. Those dark eyes that made you think like something out of a soppy magazine.

I'd be your woman. Good or bad. Only no man has ever wanted me. The words came suddenly into her head and she was shocked by their bitterness. She turned away. Outside the light had almost gone and the street was quiet. There was a smell of wood smoke. Not from a bonfire. There'd be wood-burning stoves in the big houses on the other side of the square. It was a wealthy village this, she thought. It wasn't showy like the estate where Fletcher lived, but there was plenty of money around. As she waited to cross the road Ashworth pulled up. While he was parking she watched a group of girls in school uniform come out of the post office with cans of Coke and bars of chocolate. She wondered what they'd do in a place like this for a good night out. All kids liked to take risks, but until the murders you'd have put this down as one of the safest places on earth. So what would they do? Hang around each other's houses looking for porn sites on the Internet? Drink too much? Have sex with unsuitable lads? A girl like Abigail Mantel must have been bored silly here. What games had she been playing to bring a bit of excitement to her life?

'We'll be closing in five minutes,' the woman in the bakery said as soon as they opened the door.

'Eh, lass, what about this wonderful Yorkshire hospitality we hear so much about. A pot of tea and a couple of currant tea cakes and we'll be no trouble. You can leave us to ourselves and finish up in here.'

The woman shrugged but she nodded them through to the back room before changing the sign on the door to *Closed*. She'd know who they were by now. It would be something to talk to her friends about. Vera thought again Elvet was that sort of place. You had to find your excitement where you could.

The chairs had all been put upside down on the tables. She chose a place furthest away from the shop and made herself comfortable. 'Well?'

Ashworth sat opposite her. 'Lineham's a really nice bloke . . .'

Vera sighed theatrically. Ashworth thought well of everyone. He made most of the social workers she'd come across seem flint-hearted.

'He is! He was wondering if he should come to speak to us. Then he thought it might not be relevant and that we'd see him as some sort of ghoul wanting to get mixed up in a murder investigation.' Ashworth stopped speaking as the woman from the shop came in with a heavy tea tray and continued once she'd left. 'He was older than her, in his last year of the sixth form when she died.'

'Did he sleep with her?'

'Only once, he says. One afternoon. Soon after her fifteenth birthday party. They both bunked off school, drank a couple of bottles of wine that had been left over from the party, and ended up in bed together.'

'Where?'

'Her house.'

'I thought there was some sort of housekeeper who was there to keep an eye on her.'

'There'd been a succession, apparently. None of them stayed long. According to Lineham it was the woman's day off.'

'So it was planned in advance?'

'By Abigail, at least. It was all her idea.'

'According to him.'

'He sounded genuine to me,' Ashworth said. 'His dad was a teacher at the school and it was hard for him to get away with much. The way he tells it, it was a sort of a dare. She taunted him into skipping a class and going back with her. Afterwards he threw up. More nerves than the drink, he said.'

'Was she experienced?'

'More experienced than him, but that's not saying much.'

Vera tried to picture the scene, get it clear in her head. She wished she'd been there at the interview. She'd like to have known what the weather was like, where they'd sat to drink the wine, what music they'd listened to. 'How did they get from the school to her house?'

'The lunchtime bus to the village and then they walked.'

'Was it a regular thing for her, sagging off school?'

'He said he had the impression that it had happened before. But she could have been showing off.'

'How could Emma Bennett not have known about this?' Vera was speaking almost to herself. 'She must have realized Abigail was playing truant. Unless Abigail lied to her, came up with a plausible explanation for the absences. Or perhaps Emma has been lying to us'. She shared the last of the tea from the pot between them. 'What do you think?'

But Ashworth hadn't been listening. 'There's more,' he said.

Something in his voice made her look up sharply. 'Spit it out, man.'

'Afterwards Lineham got cold feet. Maybe the . . .' he struggled for an appropriate word '. . . encounter didn't live up to expectations. Maybe he was so scared of his father that he wasn't prepared to risk another dirty afternoon with the girl, however good it was. Anyway, he told her that was it. He didn't want it to happen again. Not until she was sixteen, at least, and he'd finished his A levels.'

'Oh, she wouldn't like that,' Vera said. 'Not a spoilt little girl like Abigail.'

'But Lineham said she *did* like it in a strange kind of way. She saw it as a challenge, a game.'

So, Vera thought. That was how she got her kicks.

Ashworth was continuing, 'If he'd gone along with her she'd probably have lost interest, but it gave her the excuse to play nasty.'

'In what way?'

'She said he had no right to treat her like that. If he didn't agree to spend more time with her, she'd go to his dad and tell him what had happened. But she'd say it had all been Lineham's fault. That he'd got her drunk and seduced her.'

'Innocent little darling,' Vera said. 'Wasn't that what one of the headlines called her at the time?'

'You can't really blame the lass,' Ashworth said. 'Only fifteen and no mam to keep her straight. The lad didn't have to jump into bed with her.'

Vera said nothing. Perhaps Ashworth was right. And perhaps Caroline was misunderstood too and as vulnerable as Greenwood had made out. But she thought the men's brains had turned to jelly. They couldn't see straight. Faced with a pretty woman they all seemed to lose their reason. Then she brought herself up with a start. What was she thinking? That the girl had deserved to die horribly at the edge of a windswept field one cold November afternoon? That she'd asked for it? That made her as bad as Jeanie, brooding in her cell, calling the girl evil.

'What happened?' she asked. 'Did Lineham call her bluff?'

'He didn't need to. The following week she was killed.'

'Oh, God,' Vera said. 'Another bloody suspect.'

'No. He was in Sunderland all weekend with his family. His grandma's funeral. I'll check, of course, but I'm sure he's telling the truth.'

'Abigail used blackmail to bring a bit of excitement into her life,' Vera said. She saw the woman from the shop standing in the doorway with a mop and bucket and stood up to show they were ready to go. 'What else turned her on, do you suppose?'

Chapter Twenty-Eight

Vera was having problems seeing Jeanie and Mantel as a couple. Michael Long had described how they'd met, but he'd put his own spin on it. He'd disapproved from the beginning and hadn't bothered trying to understand. The prison governor thought Jeanie had been a saint and the chaplain hadn't got on with her. Vera wanted to understand what had brought the two of them together. She thought she owed Jeanie that. Ashworth went off to check Nick Lineham's alibi for the day that Abigail was strangled, but Vera stood in the street, pondering the matter, not ready yet to go back to the hotel.

The pub had just opened for the evening and was still empty. Vera pushed her way in. She was an expert on pubs and thought she wouldn't mind this as her local. There was a jukebox, but no background music and none of those machines that beeped and flashed lights. The ashtrays were clean and the tables were polished. She'd guess the beer would be well kept. Not that she was a snob about such things.

She sat at the bar for a moment before a woman came from the back to serve her, apologizing for keeping her waiting. She was in her fifties, smart and if she'd seen her in the street, Vera would have put her down as one of those efficient businesswomen who can hold a company together. Vera ordered beer. Too early for whisky, she decided.

'And whatever you're having . . .'

The landlady pulled the beer, then took a small bottle of orange juice, opened it expertly, checked the glass was spotless and poured it.

'You must be Veronica,' Vera said. 'Michael told me about you. You'll know who I am. A place like this, word gets about.'

'You're the inspector come to find out why an innocent woman spent ten years in jail, then killed herself because she could see no way out.'

Vera was surprised by the anger. It was the first unambiguous support she'd heard for Jeanie in Elvet. She liked the woman.

She lifted the glass to her lips. She'd been right about the beer. 'Aye,' she said. 'It was a tragedy.'

'It was a crime.'

'Did you tell them first time round you'd thought they'd got it wrong?'

'I tried,' Veronica said. 'I made an appointment to see that other woman. Fletcher.'

'What did she say?'

'That if I didn't have any evidence, or couldn't provide Jeanie with an alibi, I was wasting my time. But as I saw it, they didn't have the evidence to convict her. I worked as secretary to a solicitor before Barry and I took this place on. I've never seen a case handled like this one. As I saw it there was no one really to fight on Jeanie's behalf. Michael had never understood her and Peg was ill by the time it came to court.'

'You knew them all? Mantel and Jeanie and the girl?'

'Mantel and Jeanie certainly. My son went to school with Abigail, but he was a bit younger so I didn't really know her. She came in here once with a couple of lads, dressed up so I hardly recognized her, hoping to get served. Stupid to think she'd get away with it, but they all try it on at one time or another.'

Vera had a thought. 'Did you know Christopher Winter? He must have been the same age as your son.'

'Not then, not at the time of the murder. He'd only just moved to the village, and though he was in the same year as my boy, he was a different type of lad. Academic. Later I got to know him a bit better.'

'How?'

'He came in here a few times when he was home from university. Looked like he could use someone to talk to. If it was quiet I'd chat.'

'Was he always on his own?'

'Aye, always.'

'And what did you talk about?'

'Nothing important. Anything that took his fancy. World news. Village gossip. I had the impression he just wanted an excuse to be out the house for a bit. Glad to escape his father, maybe. I don't think they got on.'

Vera sat for a moment, thinking about a boy whose only entertainment on his break from university was to sit in a quiet pub making small talk with a middle-aged woman.

'Did he drink too much?'

'Sometimes. No more than other lads his age. But he never got fighting drunk, never made a nuisance of himself. I saw him come over a bit sentimental a couple of times and that's when he talked about his father. "Sometimes I don't think I'm his son, at all. I can't believe he's anything to do with me."'

An elderly man came in. Veronica had his pint pulled before he reached the bar. He put a couple of coins on the counter and carried the drink to a corner without speaking. Vera waited until he was out of earshot then continued.

'You must have known Jeanie well, though. She worked for you.'

'Aye, in the restaurant first, then when she was eighteen in the bar too. I liked her very much, though Barry said she was too quiet to be a barmaid. Not outgoing enough. I didn't care about that. She was interesting. I looked forward to the days she was working. We talked about music and books. You don't get much of that conversation in here.'

Or with Barry was the implication.

'Not everyone seemed to have liked her,' Vera said. 'I've talked to a few people. Arrogant, they called her. Cocky.'

Veronica thought about that. 'Maybe she could seem that way if you didn't know her well. She was different from the other girls in the village. She couldn't talk to them. But it was more shyness than anything else. And later, after she'd been through the court case, I suppose she had to be hard to survive.'

'Did you ever go to visit her in prison?'

'I told Peg that I'd go if she wanted me to. I asked her to get Jeanie to send me a visiting order. But she never did. Perhaps she couldn't bear anyone else to see her in that place.' There was another pause. 'She was proud. Even when she was a youngster. Sometimes you get some comments in here. Lads when they've had too much to drink, sneering, acting all macho. She'd never show that they'd got to her.'

'Did her father get to her?'

'Oh, aye. I don't know what it was with Michael. He could never let her be. Always criticizing and passing comment. About her clothes or her hair or how she spent her time. But she'd not let on that he bothered her either. Like I said. Proud.'

'Tell me about how she met Keith Mantel. Was that while she was working here?'

Veronica stared towards the door, as if she hoped someone would come in, so she could avoid answering. 'I worry about that sometimes. The way things happen. If I hadn't taken her on here, perhaps she'd still be alive.'

'You can't think like that, pet. It would drive you crazy.'

'I know, but maybe I should have done more to warn her off Mantel. She might have listened to me. But he charmed her. Keith can be irresistible when he turns on the charm. I've seen him in action in here.'

'What was the attraction for him? I mean, why Jeanie? I can't see her as his type.'

'She was beautiful,' Veronica said simply. 'In the way some models are. The ones that make all the money. Not pretty. Abigail was pretty. Jeanie was stunning. And it happened very quickly. One day, it seemed, she was this gawky teenager given to spots, then this interesting young woman. Not everyone saw it. They remembered the old Jeanie, even when the new one was standing right in front of them. Even

Michael didn't realize. Mantel saw it though. I could see him watching her. Jeanie didn't realize herself how she'd changed, until he pointed it out.'

'That's why she fell for him, then?' Vera said.

'Aye, he was older, a bit of a crook, but he made her feel attractive for the first time . . .' Veronica paused. 'It helped of course that her father couldn't stand him.'

'What *was* all that about? Why did Michael take against him?'

'Michael had pretty well run the village before then. His family's lived here for generations. His father was cox of the lifeboat. He kept a fishing boat down on the shore. And Michael had worked for the pilots since he was a young man. Then Keith Mantel turned up, throwing money around, and folk started taking notice of him instead. Stupid really. Like little boys in a playground. It made you want to bang their heads together.'

'Did Jeanie carry on working here after she moved in with Mantel?'

'No. He wouldn't have liked that. He likes his women dependent on him. And I know what he said in court, about Jeanie turning up on his doorstep and him not being able to turn her way. As if he didn't really care about her one way or the other, but I'm not sure that was true. Not at the beginning. At the beginning, she really got under his skin.'

Vera considered this for a moment. Perhaps she'd been wrong about Mantel. Perhaps he'd been capable of love after all. Perhaps if the couple had been left alone, if Abigail and Michael and everyone else in Elvet had left them alone they could have been happy. No, she thought then. This was never going to be a fairy-tale romance. He'd still been seeing Caroline Fletcher all the time. It would never have worked out.

She emptied her glass and set it on the bar.

'Another?' Veronica asked.

Vera thought about that seriously. 'Best not.' She slid from her stool.

'I saw Jeanie,' Veronica said suddenly, and Vera hoisted herself back onto the seat. 'The week before Abigail was killed. I never said at the time. If the police had asked me about it, they'd have got the wrong impression.'

'In what way?'

'She turned up here just before opening time and I made her a coffee. She just wanted to let off steam. About the girl – Abigail. About what a little madam she was. "I don't know what to do. If I tell Keith what she's getting up to, he won't believe me. But I can't just let her get away with it."'

'Away with what?' Vera asked.

Veronica shook her head. 'I don't know. If I'd pushed her maybe she'd have told me. But it was nearly opening time and one of the reps came in. She said she could see I was really busy and she'd come back. Ten days later the police had her in custody for murder.'

Chapter Twenty-Nine

The next day Vera drove to the Point. There was a car park in the dunes. She left her car facing the river and walked down the track towards the jetty. It was nine o'clock, and there was a bright, morning light. Sharp shadows and a glittering reflection from the water. She was pleased to be away from the village, from the suspicious glares of the locals and the persistent probing of the journos who seemed to lurk on every corner. They'd seen her in the bakery and some of them had taken up permanent residence there.

She'd sent Ashworth to check Bennett was who he said he was. Birth register, national insurance number, passport details. It would take time, but he'd do it well. He'd already found out that Nick Lineham had been sobbing his heart out in a crematorium in Sunderland when Abigail had died. She'd suggested that he work from police headquarters. She wanted to know what was happening with the Winter investigation and Holness wasn't going to volunteer information to her. Not after the way she'd spoken to him when they last met. People liked Ashworth. Wherever he went they trusted him, talked to him. She knew she rubbed people up the wrong way. She hoped Ashworth would come back with a feel for how the Winter enquiry was progressing.

If she asked for specific details the local team would probably tell her, but she wanted more than that. She needed the wild theories, the gossip in the pub at the end of the day. Besides, she had too much pride to ask.

She was glad to be outside to clear her head. Each night she promised herself she'd have a night off the drink but she never quite managed it. She never got drunk, not stupid, student drunk, but some evenings she knew it was the only way she'd sleep. She had to reach just that point when her thoughts got mellow and blurry, and the details of the investigation didn't matter quite so much. Then in the morning she'd wake up with a distant, heady feeling. And that was how she'd felt this morning. She'd carried on drinking when she'd got back to the hotel.

The smell of frying bacon came out of one of the lifeboat houses, and she walked past quickly, because the way she was feeling she'd rather have salt and sea-weed in her nostrils. Beyond the modern lifeboat houses there were two square white cottages, which had once housed the coastguards, but where the coxswains now lived. In one of these Jeanie Long had grown up, and Michael had nursed his wife until she died.

A woman came out of the cottage nearest to the sea. She was dressed in the coxswain's uniform but her shirt was unbuttoned at the neck and she didn't make her way to the jetty where the launch was moored. She was carrying a white enamel bowl. She walked round the house to a whitewashed shed in the back garden and returned with the bowl half full of sandy potatoes.

'A bit early for your dinner,' Vera said.

The woman stopped. It seemed she didn't mind

chatting. 'I'll be working most of the day. Might as well get them peeled now.' With a bit of a wink. 'I've got a friend coming for supper.' Then, 'My dad's got an allotment. He keeps me in veg.'

'Nothing like home-grown.'

'So he's always telling me.'

Vera took out her warrant card. 'I'm looking into the Abigail Mantel murder. Have you got time for a word? You can do the spuds while we're talking.'

'Nah,' she said. 'I'll be glad of an excuse for a coffee. Come in. I'll stick the kettle on.'

Her name was Wendy Jowell. The first female coxswain on the Humber, she said. It wasn't like being a proper pilot. All she did was take the launch out to collect the pilot from the ship once he'd got it out of the river. Or take him out.

'The pilots,' Vera asked. 'They're all men, are they?'

'Of course. That's where the money is, isn't it?'

They laughed. 'One time,' Vera said, 'you never got female detectives. Not above the rank of sergeant. Things change.'

'I'm not sure I'd want it, anyway. Too much responsibility. Too much pressure. I'm all right where I am.'

'Do you know Michael Long?'

'He took me out a few times when I was training. Not that he liked doing it, miserable sod. He couldn't understand how they could appoint a woman. Then I took over from him when he retired. I've not seen him lately. He hid himself away after Peg died.'

'Were you living round here at the time of Abigail's murder?'

'In Elvet, in one of the council houses. I was still married then. It was just before I saw sense.'

'Did you know Jeanie?'

'A place this size, you know most people. To say hello to at least. She worked in the Anchor sometimes. We might even have been at school together though I don't remember that. She'd have been younger than me.'

'What did you make of her?'

'I liked her. Some people said she was a bit arsy just because she got all her exams and went off to university. I think she was shy, that's all. You'd see her in the pub, blokes making smutty jokes, pervy Barry eyeing her up and she hated it. She put on a good front. I admired her for that. But she wasn't used to it. She'd been away to college yet you'd think she was just a kid. And it can't have been much fun having Michael Long as your dad.'

'Why not?'

'Not exactly sensitive, our Michael. Typical bluff Yorkshireman and proud of it. Bit of a bully on the quiet too.'

'Violent?'

'Not that I've heard, but aggressive. Especially when he's had a few drinks. The way he talks now, you'd think him and Peg had never had a cross word, but it wasn't always like that. Before she got ill he didn't mind having a go at her. In public sometimes. Once in the Anchor, when she was trying to persuade him to go home, he started yelling at her, calling her all sorts. I wouldn't have put up with it, myself.'

'It's humiliating,' Vera said, 'when it happens in public.'

'Too right.' There a moment of silence when they both seemed lost in memory.

'What about Emma Bennett?' Vera asked. 'Emma Winter she'd have been then. Did you know her around the time of the murder?'

'She'd be the exception that proved the rule. I wouldn't even have known her if I'd bumped into her in the street. She was a lot younger than me and they'd only just moved into Springhead then. After it had happened people pointed her out. You know how people gossip – "See that lass, that's the one who found the Mantel girl's body." But until then I had no idea.'

'And now she's married to one of the pilots.'

'Aye, to James.' She lingered just long enough over the words to give a sense of appreciation. Vera said nothing, hoped she'd continue. 'Now, James Bennett,' Wendy said at last. 'There's a man who's too good to be true.'

'What do you mean?' Vera kept her voice even, barely interested.

'Well, he's something else, isn't he? Good looking, considerate. And a bloody good pilot.'

'So everyone tells me.'

'Some of the pilots hardly acknowledge you. I mean, it's like they've called a minicab on a Friday night to get them home from town. You get a grunt if you're lucky. James is different. Even when you can tell he's knackered, he's polite.'

'Does Emma know how lucky she is?'

'James is besotted, I know that.'

'And Emma?'

'You can't tell, can you? She's a bit like Jeanie Long. All restrained and tongue-tied. Repressed. Another one with an overbearing father.'

'How do you know Robert Winter?' Vera was surprised. She wouldn't have thought they moved in the same circles. But maybe, as Wendy had said, in a place the size of Elvet everyone knew everyone else. Or thought they did.

Wendy paused and for a moment Vera thought she would avoid answering. 'I married a loser,' Wendy said in the end. 'He was a flash bastard, full of schemes and dreams and promises that we'd be rich, but it was all make believe. All that happened was that he ended up in court charged with fraud and nicking credit cards.'

'He got probation,' Vera said.

'Aye, and he always had something better to do than keep his appointments in the office, so we'd have Robert Winter sniffing about the place looking for him.'

'You didn't like Mr Winter?'

'He was so patronizing. Like he was perfect or something and the rest of us were too dumb to organize our own lives. Jed, my bloke, was no angel. He was into all sorts of stuff that I didn't know about. Didn't want to know about. And he could get nasty when he'd had a few drinks. Like Michael Long. I could recognize the type. But I didn't need Robert Winter to tell me that. And I'd have left him a hell of a lot sooner if Winter hadn't kept telling me to.' She smiled. 'I always was a stubborn cow. Never liked being told what to do.'

'No,' Vera said. 'Nor do I. That's why I got myself up the ladder a bit. So I could do the telling. I wouldn't have thought that'd have been Mr Winter's style, though. I'd have thought he'd have been into the sanctity of marriage. He's religious, isn't he?'

'He's a creep.' But Wendy seemed to have lost interest. 'Anyway, I didn't have to see him much after that. Jed got nicked again and was sent away. By the time he got out of prison I'd got a job on the ferries. That gave me the bug and I ended up here.'

'How did James end up here?' Vera asked, as if it was the most natural question in the world, as if, really, she couldn't care less. 'I mean what's his background?'

'I don't know,' Wendy said. 'That's one of the great things about him. He doesn't talk much about himself. With most blokes it's all *me, me, me*, isn't it? Not James. He just seems interested in other people.'

Outside in the glaring sunlight, Vera thought that did sound a bit too good to be true. She sat on one of the wooden benches outside the cafe and drank milky coffee, not really sure what she was waiting for. A couple of birdwatchers in ridiculous hats munched their way through sausage sandwiches. They spoke with their mouths full about birds they'd seen and missed. Vera, whose father had been a birdwatcher of a kind, felt a strange nostalgia. Grease from the sandwich dribbled down one of the men's chin but he wiped it away before it hit the lens of the binoculars which were strung round his neck. Wendy Jowell came out of her cottage and walked along the jetty to the launch. Vera watched it slide from the shelter of the river into open water, then bounce against the incoming waves, until it disappeared round the Point. The birdwatchers wandered away and she was starting to feel cold, but still she couldn't bring herself to move off.

Her phone rang just as the launch came back into view. It was Ashworth.

'I thought you'd like to know what we've got so far.'

We. So he'd already started to work his magic, making allies, building bridges. The local team would feel sorry for him, being managed by a fat cow like her.

'Go on.'

'I've checked with the DVLC and the passport office. According to them everything seems OK. James Richard Bennett. Date of birth the sixteenth of June 1966. Place of birth was Crill, East Yorkshire.'

'Local then. And Mantel must have got it wrong when he said Bennett wasn't his real name. Or be making mischief. According to Michael Long they grew up in the same town. Maybe it was a case of settling old scores.' She was disappointed. She'd felt in her water that James Bennett wasn't real. He wasn't a man she could believe in. Like Wendy had said, too good to be true.

'Not necessarily.'

'Oh?'

'His birth wasn't registered in that name. No national insurance number, no record of his existence until 1987.'

'When he'd have been twenty-one. So if Mantel knew him as someone different he'd have been very young. But they could have met. They both lived in Crill. I wouldn't have put it past Mantel to involve young people in his dodgy businesses. They come cheap, after all.'

'I checked with the Public Record Office. He changed his name by deed poll in 1987. Did everything right. Got an old teacher to support the application. It has to be someone who's known you for at least ten years. Advertised in the *London Gazette* like you're supposed to. Signed the deed poll in his old and new name.'

'What was his old name?'

'Shaw. James Richard Shaw.'

'Not a name that you could take exception to,' Vera said. 'I mean some names, you can see why someone would want to change them. But not Shaw. So why go through all that effort? Who did he want to hide from?'

'Mantel?' Ashworth suggested.

'Maybe. Bennett went away to sea. That suggests running away to me. Then perhaps he came back when he thought he was safe.'

'To a village where Mantel was living? That doesn't make much sense.'

'Perhaps the situation had changed. Perhaps he was prepared to risk it for Emma to live close to her parents. People can look a lot different after fifteen years. Do you think the wife knows about the name change?'

'She wouldn't have to. If you're already married, you have to notify your spouse of a name change, but banns of marriage can be called in the new name.'

'All the same,' Vera said, 'it's a big secret to keep. You'd need a good reason not to tell your new wife that you grew up with another name. And wouldn't she find out when she met all the relatives?'

'Perhaps she hasn't.'

'I don't suppose James Richard Shaw has a criminal record. That he was in a Young Offender Institute until 1987 and he changed his name to put that behind him?'

'I did check,' Ashworth said. 'First thing I thought of.'

Smart-arse, she thought. 'Well?'

'Nothing. Hasn't been in trouble in either name. Not even a speeding ticket.'

She didn't speak again immediately. The launch

was pulling back into the jetty. She saw two dark silhouettes on the deck, sharp against the sparkling
water. They began to climb the ladder from the boat.

'What would you like me to do now?' Ashworth
asked.

The figures reached the top of the jetty and she
could see them more clearly. One was James Bennett.

'Nothing,' she said with regret. 'A bit more digging.
If there's something odd about Bennett we don't want
to let him know we're onto him. Not until we've a bit
more of an idea what it's about.'

She was still sitting outside the cafe when the pilot
drove past. She didn't think he noticed her.

Chapter Thirty

When Michael Long opened his door to her, she was surprised by the response – a mixture of irritation and relief.

'I've been trying to get hold of you,' he said, as if she'd been deliberately trying to avoid him.

'Well, you've got me now so you'd best let me in.'

He stood aside and she went ahead of him into the small front room where they'd sat and talked the week before.

'Every time I phoned there'd be someone different to talk to. Sometimes no one at all, just a recorded message. And none of them would put me onto you.'

'They're busy,' Vera snapped. 'A case like this, do you know how many calls they get to the incident room?'

He looked at her as if she'd bitten him, but he stopped complaining. She thought there'd been no need to be so sharp with him. Was she less sympathetic because of what Wendy Jowell had said about him being a bully? She was trying to think of something to say to make him believe she was still on his side, but he spoke first.

'I'll put the kettle on, shall I? Daresay you're ready for a brew.'

God, she thought, any more tea and I'll float away up the Humber like one of those bloated container ships. 'Aye,' she said. 'Why not?'

When he came back, carrying the tray, he was so eager to please, to pour the tea strong as she liked it, that it was easy to appear understanding.

'Why did you want the pleasure of my company, anyway?' she said. 'What was it that wouldn't wait?'

'I saw the lad, Christopher Winter, the day he died. I didn't know it was him when I saw him. But they had his picture in the paper, asking if anyone had seen him. I recognized him from that.'

'You should have told the officers in the incident room,' she said carefully, not telling him off exactly, just making the point. 'It could be important.' But even as she was speaking she couldn't help feeling a childish satisfaction because she'd got hold of the information before the local team.

'Aye, well. I might have done if they'd been less rude.'

She let that go.

'Where did you see him?'

'In the cemetery at the edge of the village. I'd gone to visit Peg's grave. It'd been a while since I'd been there and I wanted to pay my respects. Show her I was on my feet again, like.' He looked up. 'Daft, I know.'

'Not daft at all,' she said. 'What time was this?'

'Early in the morning. Around eight o'clock.'

'What was Christopher Winter doing?'

'Same as me, I think. Mourning. He was standing next to the grave of the lass our Jeanie was supposed to have killed.'

'Did you speak?'

Michael Long shook his head. 'He was too upset to notice me. I mean, there still wasn't much light, but even if there had been, I don't think he'd have seen. Besides, I wasn't in the mood for a conversation myself.'

'What was he wearing?'

'One of those long waterproofs with a jumper underneath. Jeans, I think.'

She nodded. Those were the clothes he'd been wearing when Mary had found the body.

'Did you see where he went after? Or was he still there when you left?'

'He went before me,' Michael said, 'but he seemed to vanish into thin air. I walked back to the village soon after he'd left but I didn't see him ahead of me.'

'Maybe he just walked faster than you.'

'Aye, maybe. But I don't move badly for my age. It wasn't the weather to hang about. And if he'd gone back to Elvet someone would have seen him. He'd have had to pass the bus stop and there were a load of kids waiting there.' He seemed to lose his concentration for a moment. Vera waited for him to continue. 'At the time I wondered if he'd gone in the opposite direction, towards the river, but I can't think what would have taken him there at that time of day.'

'Is there anything else?'

'I'm not sure,' he said. 'I might have got it wrong and I know how important it is, not jumping to conclusions . . .'

'You know how important it is people speaking up. If that lad who saw Jeanie at King's Cross had said so at the time . . .'

'I heard him talking,' Michael said. 'At the time I

thought he was just raving. I mean, that's what it looked like. Some madman. You could believe he was talking to himself. Later I wondered if he had a mobile phone. The way he was standing, he could have been using a mobile. I saw a couple of lasses at the bus stop later gabbing into one and that made me think.'

'Did you hear what he said?'

'He sounded angry, frustrated. But I couldn't hear the words.'

'Thanks,' she said. 'That could make all the difference.'

She sat quite still for a moment before she remembered what she'd come for.

'You must have worked with James Bennett.'

'Aye, he started a year or so before I retired.'

'What did you make of him?'

'All right. A competent pilot.'

'Did you realize he'd married the lass who found Abigail Mantel's body?'

'Someone must have told me. A place like this you get to know things without realizing how.'

'When you were playing detective, digging up the dirt on Keith Mantel, did you ever come across mention of Bennett?'

Michael looked at her as if she was crazy. 'Of course not. Why?'

'Don't know,' she said. 'A stupid idea probably. Did Bennett ever talk about his past to you, his family, what he did when he was a kid?'

'We weren't on those sort of terms.'

No, she thought. James Bennett wasn't on those sort of terms with anyone. She ferreted in her bag for her phone. 'I need to make a call,' she said. 'Do you mind?'

'I'll make myself scarce. Wash these pots.'

He was on his way to the kitchen when she called him back. 'Would you show me after where you saw the lad? The cemetery first, then we could take a walk to the river. Show me the path you think he might have taken. If it's no bother.'

'No.' He smiled, glad to be in her good books again. 'It's no bother at all.'

Ashworth must have been in the canteen because she heard a background clatter of crockery and chat.

'Are you OK to talk?' She meant was he on his own.

'Go ahead.'

'Did Winter have a mobile phone on him?'

'No one's said. Do you want me to find out?'

'I've got a witness who saw him early that morning. He thinks Winter was talking into a mobile. Could have been, at least. If the lad did have a mobile on him, they'll probably already have checked the calls, but this makes it a priority, doesn't it? And before you give me a lecture I'll bring my witness in to make a statement this afternoon. You hang on for me there.'

She switched off the phone before he could ask for more details and called to Michael who was making a show of waiting tactfully in the kitchen, 'Ready when you are, pet. Let's take a constitutional. I could do with some air.'

Vera could tell people were taking notice of them walking down the street together. There was nothing obvious, no staring or twitching of curtains. But it was there in the studied way the old ladies in front of the post office continued their conversation, only breaking off later to follow them with their eyes. And the vicar, who seemed about to cross the road to talk to Michael, stopped when he saw Vera and contented himself with a wave. Only a lone reporter approached them, but she flapped her hand at him, and without his colleagues he seemed to lack the courage to pursue them. Vera wondered if the locals were all just curious or if they believed she had a professional interest in Michael. Could they think she was arresting him? Was that the cause of their awkwardness?

She knew about small places, villages where people had grown up together and knew each other's secrets, but Elvet depressed her. It was something to do with the flat countryside, everything the colour of mud, the unrelenting wind. No wonder Christopher Winter had been reluctant to return once he had escaped. What had dragged him back? He hadn't been summoned for a special family occasion. He could have kept away.

There was a pile of dog muck on the pavement, and Michael took her arm briefly to steer her round it. She thought people who didn't know them could take them as a married couple. Shambling and dysfunctional, dependent on each other for survival. She moved away from him and they walked down the lane several feet apart, not speaking.

There were no ancient graves in the cemetery; it must have been established once the churchyard was full. The sun had gone and the breeze was cooler than ever, tearing at the remaining dead leaves on the sycamore, shredding them so only the stalks and the veins were left.

'Was Christopher here before you?' Vera asked.

'Can't have been. I'd have had to walk right past him to get to my Peg.'

'Did you see which way he came from?'

Michael only shook his head. The place seemed to have knocked all the spirit out of him. Vera stood looking about her for a moment. Beyond the drystone wall there was open country on three sides, tussocky grass grazed by sheep. In a field there was something dead. It was too small for a sheep, probably a rabbit. It had been picked over by crows, and only bones and a scrap of fur remained. The wall was too high to be scrambled over without a fuss. Christopher Winter must have come through the gate.

'Show me where this road goes, then,' she said, opening it to let him out. 'Can you drive all the way down?'

'Aye, some people keep boats there in the summer, and there's a bit of a car park for folks who want a stroll along the riverbank. Do you want to go back for your car?'

'Is it far?'

'Half a mile at most.'

'We'll walk it, then, shall we?' She was thinking she should warn Joe Ashworth that they'd be a while getting in to the station, but when she looked at her mobile there was no signal. The lane was straight, with a sparse hawthorn hedge on one side and a full ditch fringed with blackened reeds on the other. The hawthorn bushes had knotted trunks, smeared with green lichen and a scattering of berries. A small flock of redwing chased along the hedge, flipping occasionally into the field beyond. In the distance was a farmhouse surrounded by a graveyard of rotting machinery.

'Who lives there?' she asked.

'No one now. Cyril Moore died a month or so ago. Someone said it's been sold. They're going to turn it into a riding school. No money in farming these days.'

The tide was out when they arrived at the river. There were acres of ridged sand and mud, which seemed to stretch almost all the way to the Lincolnshire coast. A cloud of small wading birds, gathered like insects into a swarm, rose in a cyclone above them then settled back onto the mud. The hull of a clinker-built boat rotted upturned on the shore. There was a rough car park containing a red telephone box, a notice board, which might once have given details of how to contact the coastguard but which had faded into illegibility and a white wooden post with a lifebelt attached.

'Is this it?' Vera demanded. She was hungry and cold and thought she'd come on a wild goose chase.

'I did say I couldn't think what could have brought him here.'

'So you did.' She tried her phone again. Still it refused to work.

They were back at the edge of the village when she realized how stupid she'd been. She recreated that morning in the cemetery in her head, trying to bring it to life. Christopher Winter had been at Emma's. He'd sat up all night getting maudlin drunk, decided before it was even light that he needed to visit Abigail's grave. Then what? He'd phoned someone. To accuse them of her murder? To demand an explanation? Support? Help? If he'd tried his mobile, it would probably be a number he'd kept in his head, or that he'd already saved on his phone. So it would be someone he knew well, or a number he'd checked in advance. But what if the phone hadn't worked? Perhaps this was one of those black holes which swallowed mobile signals. It was possible that the angry words Michael had heard were the lad venting his frustration on the limitations of technology. What would he have done then? Surely he'd have found a phone box, used that. The nearest public phone was at the river car park. He'd have known it was there. He'd have played all round the shore when he was a boy.

Vera stopped abruptly and Michael considered her anxiously. 'Are you all right?'

'Go back to your house and ring this number. It's my sergeant Joe Ashworth. Direct him to the car park on the bank and tell him to meet me there immediately. Say it's urgent.'

'What are you going to do?'

'None of your business,' she said, giving him a wink to soften the blow. What would she say even if she trusted him absolutely? *I'm going to freeze my butt off standing guard over a stinking phone box in case a member of the public thinks to cover any fingerprints of Winter's which might still be there.* 'Was that lad wearing gloves when you saw him in the cemetery?'

'No,' Michael said. 'I thought at the time he'd be feeling the cold.'

When Ashworth arrived, Vera took his car and left him to wait for the crime scene examiner. She was sitting in the caff next to the bakery, full of sausage sandwich and chocolate eclair, when he arrived. The resident reporters must be following some other lead because she had the place to herself. It was warm in there and she could feel herself nodding off. She knew she'd be more use taking Michael into the station and getting his statement, but she was curious.

'Well?'

Ashworth waited until he'd sat opposite her, leaned forward so the staff couldn't hear. 'He got a couple of decent prints. One from the handset and one off the interior door handle. They'll test for a match.'

'Could be anyone's, though, couldn't they? I mean, I can't imagine people queuing to use the phone, but it could have been used once in the last couple of days. It'll be worth seeing if there was a call from it the morning Winter died, though.'

'Not really,' he said.

'What do you mean?'

'It's bust. Has been for at least a fortnight according to BT, but because it's so little used this time of year the repair wasn't a priority.'

'Bugger,' she said. Not angry. Resigned. It had been that sort of day.

'We'll know from the prints if he tried to make a call. He didn't have a mobile on him, by the way.'

She looked up at that. 'Did he own one?'

'They're trying to find out.'

'You'd better tell Mr Holness,' she said, 'that trying's not good enough.'

Chapter Thirty-One

She caught up with Caroline Fletcher at an ugly house in Crill, the seaside town further up the coast where Keith Mantel had first made his money. The estate agency had given a list of addresses of the properties on her books and Vera had chased from one to another always just missing her.

To reach the town she had to drive past Spinney Fen, the prison. A ragged line of people were hurrying out of the gate. The end of afternoon visits. After the death of her mother Jeanie had received no visitors. She'd had to listen to the other inmates relive their conversations with loved ones, knowing that if she admitted her guilt she'd be moved to a less secure prison with more humane conditions, where there would be more contact with the outside world. Vera briefly stopped the car outside and thought about that, wondered if she'd be so principled or so stubborn. Maybe she would. She was known for her stubbornness after all. But she'd have promised anything to avoid the ministrations of Robert Winter, the preaching and the pity.

The house Caroline was trying to sell was a mock Tudor monstrosity in a road which ran along.the edge of the cliff just outside the town. Another twenty years of erosion, Vera reckoned, and the garden would be crumbling into the sea. The prospective buyers didn't seem impressed either. It was dark by then. They must have come straight from work and she could tell all they wanted was a strong drink and something mindless on the telly. Vera sat in her car and watched them make their escape, in too much of a hurry even to shake hands with the agent on the doorstep.

Caroline was still locking the door when Vera caught up with her. Vera could move quietly when she wanted. It was one of the skills she'd learned from her father. But Caroline didn't seem startled by her approach. Maybe she thought it was the purchasers returning. Maybe she had a clear conscience.

'Inspector,' she said. 'I hope you know what you're doing.'

'Probably not. But what do you mean?'

'I'd hate you to jeopardize your position in the service. There are too few successful women as it is. Not exactly orthodox, is it? Bothering me at home. And now at work. Especially when you're on your own. Or is your little friend waiting in the car?'

'Nah,' Vera said easily. 'Joe's mam wouldn't let him out to play today. It's you I'm thinking of, pet. We can go back to the station if you like, but I thought it might be embarrassing for you. Having one of your old mates sitting in on the interview, I mean. Or did they all know about you and Keith?'

Caroline's hand was still for a moment, poised with the key not yet in the lock, but there was no other reaction.

'He told you, I suppose,' she said.

'Did you really think he'd keep it quiet?'

'I thought, as things are, he had as much to lose as me.'

'Shall we go back in and talk about it? Like I said, more discreet than the station.' Behind her back, Vera crossed her fingers. She no more wanted to make this official than Fletcher did.

Caroline shrugged, as if to say she didn't care either way, but she opened the door and led Vera inside. The house had been cleared of furniture but the owners must have left the heating on, because there wasn't that chill you get in an unused house. There were no light shades and the naked bulbs showed the patch of damp on the ceiling and the peeling wallpaper in the hall. Caroline threw open the door to the living room and allowed Vera to go ahead of her, as she must have done with the prospective buyers earlier. It was a big room, with a bay window looking out to sea. For the first time Vera thought it might not be a bad place to live. In the distance there was a constellation of tiny lights – ships, presumably waiting for the tide at the mouth of the river – and somewhere down the coast, the mesmerizing flash of a lighthouse. In the bay window stood a card table and three folding chairs, on the table a pile of estate agent brochures, a floor plan of the house, mortgage information. There was no other furniture. Here Caroline must sit her customers, positioning them so they looked out at the view and had their backs to the scuffed skirting boards and snot green paint. Vera took a seat and nodded for Caroline to join her. She stretched out her legs and the chair creaked. Opposite, the estate agent regarded her with distaste.

'What has Keith Mantel got to lose, then?' Vera asked.

'It looks like corruption, doesn't it? He wanted a result and he got it. He's a pillar of society now, sits on committees, talks to ministers about neighbourhood renewal. Being a bit wild when he was a kid is one thing. Colourful. They can forgive him that. But pulling strings in a murder case which only happened ten years ago and won't go away, that's something quite different.'

'So why did he tell me?'

Caroline seemed hypnotized by the irregular beat of the lighthouse. 'Who knows? Perhaps he's been living the good citizen for so long that he actually believes it. Perhaps he's got so many powerful friends he thinks nobody can touch him. Perhaps he hates me so much he doesn't care.'

Vera was surprised by the bitterness and hurt in the woman's voice. 'When did it start between you and him?'

'Before Jeanie Long moved in, ages before that.'

'How did he explain that one away?'

Caroline turned away from the window and shrugged again. 'He didn't need to. I could tell Jeanie wouldn't survive. She was only a distraction, not really his type.'

'You weren't bothered about sharing him?'

'I was more bothered about losing him altogether.' She sat very upright in her chair, constrained by her suit, by the short neat skirt and black tights, waiting for another question. But none came. 'There hasn't been a day since we met when I've not thought about him. I keep telling myself I'm behaving like a crazy teenager and that it'll pass but it doesn't. I moved in with Alex because I thought that would make a difference, but it hasn't.' She looked up at Vera. 'You must think I'm mental.'

Vera didn't reply directly. 'How *did* you meet?'

'At a party. He was a friend of a friend. I presume Keith had been told I worked for the police, thought it would be useful. I'd just started as a DC. Maybe he even got me invited. All I knew at the time was that he was a businessman, a widower with a little girl. I don't know what he did that night or what he said that was different from all the other men who've chatted me up at parties. But something happened. He got inside my head and under my skin. An addiction. It's still there. That night Christopher Winter died, I didn't go to the Old Chapel to find out if you'd talked to Keith. I told myself that was why I was there, but it wasn't true. I wanted him to touch me. I wanted a fix. No self-respect, you see. That's what addiction does to you.'

'What happened?'

'Nothing. He told me to get out. To leave him alone . . .' She paused for a moment. 'I'd met him a couple of days earlier at the Point. I said we should get our stories straight before you interviewed us. He'd told me then to stay away from him. Only I couldn't do it.'

Vera didn't know what to say. Mantel had lost patience. That was why he'd told her about his relationship with Caroline. She'd become a nuisance and he'd wanted the police to do his dirty work. Vera couldn't bring herself to rub the woman's nose in it. She picked a question at random. 'Did you ever meet Abigail?'

'A couple of times.'

'What did you make of her?'

'Honestly? I suppose I resented her. Keith was besotted. I tried to make friends with her because I knew that was what he wanted, but she never took to me. She could probably tell what I was after. She was a bright little thing. A shame because I thought we had a lot in common. Both obsessive personalities perhaps and you could tell she was lonely. If I'd had her on my side things might have been different. I mean really different.'

'Marriage? Happy families? A white meringue dress and a kid of your own?'

'Yeah,' she said defensively. 'Why not? Other people have it.'

'Aye,' Vera said. 'But we're not other people, are we, pet?'

They looked at each other across the wobbly table.

'Who do you think killed her?' Vera demanded, suddenly businesslike. 'We know it can't have been Jeanie Long, so who was it?'

'I really thought it was her. Maybe I took a few short cuts, missed things, but it wasn't because it was convenient to have her out of the way.' She looked up at Vera and repeated more forcefully, 'I really thought it was her.'

Vera couldn't let that go. 'And so did Keith. No doubt he was pleased when it all got cleared up so quickly. Grateful, was he? I bet he was. Not grateful enough to marry you, though. Is that what he'd promised?'

'Something like that.'

'Where were *you* the afternoon she died? You'll have thought about it. You'd know I'd be asking.'

'On my own,' she said. 'In my flat in town. A day

off.' She paused. 'Crying my eyes out because Keith had said he'd take me out and he'd phoned up at the last minute to cancel. Abigail had said she'd cook him supper so he had to stay at home. I was so pissed off I went into work. That's why I was there when the call first came through.'

'Was Keith at home when she was found?' Turning the knife. Not proud of it.

'No. They finally tracked him down in his office. Something urgent which turned up at the last moment. So he claimed. Like I said Abigail and I had a lot in common. He let her down too.'

'You haven't said who you think killed her now you know it's not Jeanie.'

'You'll think I'm really crazy . . .'

'Go on.'

'The girl that found her, Emma Winter . . .'

'Emma Bennett now.'

'There was something about her, that first day I turned up to do the interview. Something weird. I thought it was the shock. Stumbling across her best friend like that, I mean you'd be expecting her to be acting strangely. But it was as if none of it was real. Like she was telling a story she'd already made up, that she'd rehearsed somehow, over and over again, though how could she? It didn't take us long to get there that afternoon.'

Vera sat for a moment taking that in. 'Could she have done it? Would the timing have worked out?'

'The pathologist said Abigail couldn't have been dead long when Emma found her. You know they can't be precise about these things. I'd say it was possible that they met up on the path, had a row and Emma killed her then. I'm not saying that's what did happen. But you were pushing me for an opinion.'

'Aye, maybe I was. Was there anything else which pointed in that direction? Besides Emma's behaviour when you interviewed her.'

'The way I'd heard Abigail talk about her. She was really patronizing. As if Emma was the most stupid person she'd ever met. She once said to her father while I was there, "Emma doesn't know *anything*." If I'd been Emma, I'd have felt like killing her.'

'Was Abigail bullying her?'

'Probably not. Just pretending to be her best friend and undermining her every chance she got. And Emma was the sort who'd let that get to her. A natural victim. They can be dangerous when they let go.'

'Emma was hardly likely to do away with her brother, though.' Vera seemed to be talking to herself. 'And I might not have realized that his bedroom had a view of the field if she'd not pointed it out.' *But she's a strange woman, you're right about that. Full of fancies. And where does the husband fit in?*

'What do you know about James Bennett?'

'Nothing. He wasn't living there when Abigail was murdered.'

'Keith never mentioned him?'

'Why would he?'

'I had the impression they were friends once. In the old days.'

'Oh, Keith had a lot of friends in the old days. He never introduced many of them to me.'

'Did he ever ask you to do anything else for him?'

'What do you mean?'

Vera banged her fist on the table. The noise echoed

round the empty room. 'Don't play games with me, lady. You know exactly what I mean. Did he ask for information? Tell you to turn a blind eye? Influence any other investigation in any way?'

'Only once.' The words seemed like a whisper after Vera's dramatics. 'And it was information which he'd probably have been able to get hold of anyway.'

'Well?'

'He wanted to see a copy of the sex offenders register.'

'Why would he want to do that?'

There was a pause. 'Keith's work is all about influence. He needs people on his side. Councillors. Planners. Maybe he felt he could exert a tad more influence if he knew something about the people he was working with.'

'Was he interested in anyone specific?'

'Maybe. He never said.'

Blackmail, Vera thought. *That's what he was after.* So it ran in the family. She kept her voice even. 'When was this?'

'Not long before Abigail was killed.'

Chapter Thirty-Two

Vera had decided it was time to speak to James Bennett. She could have gone back to Keith Mantel, but no way was he going to give up more information than he wanted. Joe Ashworth had been digging, but he wasn't local, he didn't have the contacts and she didn't want to wait any longer. She found out that James was working and took Ashworth with her to collect him from the Point. She thought they'd take him to the station. That way there'd be no distractions. She told herself there could be all sorts of explanations for his name change, but her imagination was working overtime. He'd been involved in some of Mantel's illegal operations, she thought. Why else would he want to hide behind an alias? That didn't make him a murderer, but it made him worth talking to. They didn't make a show of waiting, just sat in their car next to the pilot's vehicle until James showed up.

When she saw him walking towards them she had second thoughts. James had been up since the early hours and had that drawn, grey look which is the result of nights of disturbed sleep. She wanted him focused. The way he looked now she could see him dozing off in the interview room, his head on his arm, no good to anyone.

He'd already seen them so they couldn't drive off. 'We can postpone it until later,' she said. 'It's not urgent.'

But James insisted.

'Do you want to let your wife know, then?'

'I'm in earlier than I thought. She'll not be expecting me for a couple of hours yet.'

They were in a room with no natural light, a strip light which flickered, the smell of stale cigarettes. Vera and James sat opposite each other across a table and Joe Ashworth watched them, his chair pulled away so he seemed an impartial observer, a referee perhaps at a chess match. Vera was wearing one of her shapeless, old lady dresses and a cardigan which she'd buttoned up wrongly at the front. James, still in his uniform, was immaculate.

'This is an informal chat,' Vera said. 'Things come up in an enquiry. They're probably not relevant, but they need clearing up. You'll understand.'

He nodded.

'Keith Mantel said he'd met you before. Only then you were calling yourself something different. We had to check.'

'Of course.' Very polite, almost as if he was sorry he'd put them to the trouble of snooping round in his past.

'So I was hoping you'd clear it up for us. Explain what it was all about. And at the same time maybe fill in the background details on Keith Mantel.'

Vera hadn't been sure what to expect. Probably something bland. To be told that it was perfectly legal to change a name by deed poll and that no explanation was required. That it was none of their business. Certainly not this. For James fidgeted briefly with the cap which was sitting upturned in front of him on the table, closed his eyes in a moment of decision and then began to speak, taking them right back to the beginning, telling them, in effect, the history of his life.

'When he was a young man my dad worked on the trawlers. I grew up with all the stories – the storms and the larger-than-life skippers and the big chance catches – but by the time I was at school, he'd come ashore. Maybe the danger and the discomfort outweighed the adventure; already at that time they were having to go further for fish. It wasn't easy money. More likely, I think, my mother persuaded him to give it up. It can't have been much fun for her when he was away.'

Vera nodded, said nothing, waited for him to continue.

'At that time he and my mother ran a newsagent's and sweet shop in the area where they'd both grown up. I was an only child, but there were cousins to play with in the street, my gran to cook my tea when Mum and Dad were busy. It seemed friendly and safe. There was a lot of bitching, of course. You get hurtful gossip in small communities, I suppose. But it didn't touch mc. I remember it as a good time.

'When he was at sea my father was active in the union and he still took an interest in politics after he'd left. You'd have thought he'd be a natural Conservative, a small businessman making his own way in the world, but it wasn't like that. He wasn't a communist. Not quite. But certainly a socialist of the old school. I can't imagine him having any truck with a New Labour government. He'd always been a party member and he had time then to become more active. I remember him canvassing during elections, coming home full of the arguments he'd had on the doorsteps. I don't know what my mother made of it. She probably realized he needed something to stop him getting bored. At first, I think, she saw it as a harmless hobby, like fishing or trainspotting.

'I was halfway through high school when he was persuaded to stand for the council. Not that he took much persuading. By then the marriage was going through a rough patch. They kept things polite for me, managed a show of affection while they were in together, but as I've said, it was a small community and people were only too eager to pass on the gossip. I learned he'd had a number of women. Finally, it seemed, he settled on another party member, a teacher. As I heard it, they were inseparable. I was furious at the time, humiliated. How could he carry on like that and come back at night to my mother? She must have come to the same conclusion, because one night while my father was at a council meeting, she packed up all her stuff and left. She didn't ask me to go with her and even if she had done, I'd probably not have gone. Despite his faults, I always believed I had more in common with my father and anyway he was the more vulnerable. Of the two of them I felt he needed most looking after and that I had a responsibility towards him. My mother could take care of herself. It turned out I was probably right, because, soon after, she set up home with an insurance salesman. She would have had a regular income, at least. She invited me to visit her in their new house somewhere in the suburbs, but I couldn't do it. It was irrational but I was angry on my father's behalf. When I left school, I joined him in the business.'

He paused for breath and again Vera could see how tired he was. 'Can I get you anything, Captain Bennett? Coffee? A glass of water?'

He seemed surprised by her kindness and shook his head. 'I'm sorry to be so long-winded. I suppose none of this is relevant.'

Vera leaned towards him across the table, seemed almost about to touch his hand. 'You tell it in your own way, pet. I'm listening.'

'It must have been around that time that Dad got friendly with Keith Mantel. Keith was a small-time developer then. He'd buy a few properties in rundown areas of the town, do them up and sell them on. The ones on the seafront he tried to let as holiday homes. You could tell he had grand ideas, but Dad probably thought they were in the same league – independent businessmen trying to claw a living in competition with the big boys.'

'Did they meet socially?'

'That's all it was at first, social.'

'Were you involved?'

'Not often. Sometimes Keith would come round to our house. To escape one of his women, he'd say. They'd stay up all night drinking. Dad would start on his stories of life at sea and Keith would provide a willing audience. I tried to keep out of it. Someone had to be up early to sort the papers and anyway I didn't trust the man. Dad was on the council's planning committee. It seemed obvious to me that Mantel wasn't just there to talk about the good old days. He'd be after something.

'Then he took Dad away on holiday. The teacher was off the scene by then and Keith set up a trip to a villa on the Algarve with a couple of young women in tow. It didn't cost Dad a bean. He was so naïve. "Can't you see what you're setting yourself up for?" I said. "What do you think he's going to want in return?" But he wouldn't have it. They were just mates. That's what mates did. They shared around their good fortune.'

'What did Mantel want in return?' Vera asked.

'I'm not sure the first time. I never heard the details. I know that soon after a development of Mantel's passed through the committee on the nod. It was old people's flats, I think. Sheltered housing. There was a grand opening and Dad dragged me along to it. I don't know how he squared it with his conscience. Perhaps they'd have approved the plans anyway. But after that it was always going to be difficult to stand up to Mantel. The crisis came with the proposed building of a new leisure centre. Mantel put in the lowest tender but his plans weren't as good as those of the competitor company. After the planning meeting my father phoned him up to tell him he'd been unsuccessful. I was in the room when he made the call. "Never mind, eh, lad. You win some, you lose some. Better luck next time." He really thought Mantel would have a few beers and put it down to experience.'

'But he didn't.'

'He came round to the house that night. A bottle of whisky in one hand. A big brown envelope in the other. I tried to stick around but Mantel sent me away. I went out for a couple of hours and when I came back he was leaving. My father was sitting on the floor. I'd never seen that before. Men of his generation didn't sit on the floor. All around him on the carpet were photos from the Portuguese trip. Dad in a deckchair with an almost naked blonde sprawled all over him. Dad sitting next to Mantel in a restaurant, laughing at one of his jokes. He was sitting on the floor and he was crying.'

'Mantel had threatened to go public?'

'He said he'd leak the story to the papers that he'd bribed Dad to approve the sheltered housing scheme. He'd bounce back, he said. But Dad wouldn't. Imagine the headlines. *Holiday Romp for Socialist Councillor. Sex and Sangria on the Rates.* In one sense it was true of course. My father had allowed himself to be influenced. He'd been a fool.

'He wasn't only bothered about what his friends in the party would think. It was the people he drank with in the club, and the family. All the aunts and cousins who'd supported him through the divorce because they believed he was something special.'

James paused. The strip light flickered again and faded. Ashworth stood on his chair and thumped the plastic casing. The light returned. James continued as if there'd been no interruption.

'His trouble was that he'd been taken in by his own propaganda. Marty Shaw, champion of the people. He'd believed in that. He didn't like the real man . . . I told him he could resign. Keep a low profile for a bit. People would forget. "People might," he said. "I won't. Nor will you, will you?" I couldn't answer. He'd had a lot to drink and I helped him to bed.

'When I woke up he'd gone and so had his car. I thought he'd just taken off for a few days. It would have been in character, running away. I imagined him holed up with an old friend from his fishing days, feeling sorry for himself and drowning his sorrows. I carried on as usual, running the shop, making his excuses to the customers.'

'But he hadn't run away.'

'Not like that. Three days later his car was reported abandoned.'

'Where?'

'In Elvet. In that car park by the river.'

Where Vera had been with Michael Long the day before. Close to the phone box where Christopher Winter had tried to make his call.

'But he wasn't in it?'

'He'd left a note. At least he'd bothered to do that. Sending me his love. Asking me to remember him kindly . . .' James took a deep breath. 'He must have waited until the tide was high. He just walked out into the river. He'd never learned to swim. He walked until the current took him, sucked his legs from under him, pulled him down. The shore is uneven there, mud and shingle and outcrops of rock. Perhaps he stumbled. I wonder sometimes if he fought it at the last moment. If he tried to hold the air in his lungs when he went under . . . It was nearly a month before his body was washed up. Hardly a body by then. They identified him through his dental records.

'In the docks when I'm working late, I think I see him sometimes.'

'That was when you changed your name?' Vera asked. 'At the time of the suicide?'

'Yes.'

'An extreme reaction.'

'You don't understand. It wasn't just the name. I didn't want to be Marty Shaw's son, associated with backhanders and bribes. I didn't want to run the family business, putting up with the pity, listening to the poisonous gossip of the customers and the family. I wanted to start again.'

'All the same . . .'

'Look, I was young. You do overact at that age. There was a terrible embarrassment. The pictures, Mantel . . . It all seemed so squalid, in such bad taste. I sold stories like that every Sunday to fools who slavered over them, then turned self-righteous. If my father had been involved in a major fraud, insider dealing, something like that, I'd probably have found it easier. Emma calls me a snob sometimes. Perhaps she's right.'

'So you ran away too.'

'If you like. But it was more than that. I felt like somebody different, that I could start from scratch, be the person I was meant to be.'

'You chose to go to sea. That must have been your father's influence.'

'All those stories he told me when I was a child? Perhaps.'

'Why did you move to Elvet?'

'Emma came from here.'

'Did you know that Keith Mantel lived in the village?'

'There was all that publicity when his daughter died. Her murder made it easier for me to contemplate living in the village. I don't think I could have risked running into him otherwise. I mean, I knew then that he'd lost someone close to him too. It was harder to hate him.'

'Revenge?'

'I wasn't sorry she was dead,' he said sharply. 'But I wouldn't have killed her.'

'No?'

'Besides,' he went on, ignoring her. 'By then I had a new life. I could believe I was James Bennett, not Jimmy Shaw. I couldn't let him get to me. And I didn't think our paths would cross much.'

'You moved to Elvet because of your father, then? To remember him kindly.'

'No!' he said crossly. 'I moved there because I found a house that I liked and to be close to my wife's family. It had no more significance than that.'

Vera left it. He was a good story-teller. Plausible. It might even have been true. She organized a car to take him home. She showed him out of the building and stood waiting with him for the car to arrive.

'Why didn't you tell Emma? Didn't you think she had a right to know?'

'It was James Bennett she fell in love with and married. Why would she need to know about a stranger?'

'You should tell her,' Vera said. 'You don't want to put yourself in a position where Keith Mantel could make mischief.'

James seemed to listen to her words and consider them seriously, but he didn't respond.

Chapter Thirty-Three

Vera and Joe were back in the gloomy hotel. The bar was empty apart from a couple of businesswomen who were discussing, in bright staccato voices, a training programme for software advisors. After a couple of beats, Vera stopped listening. The language was unintelligible. How could this place make any sort of profit? she thought. Then it came to her that there was an Agatha Christie book about a respectable hotel which didn't pay. That had turned out to be a front for international crime. She struggled to remember the title, but failed.

On the table in front of her there was a large Scotch. She stared into the liquid and thought it was probably the loveliest colour in the world. She knew she'd had enough to drink already, that she couldn't allow herself another after this. So this one would have to be taken slowly, every mouthful savoured. She lifted the glass to her mouth, sipped.

'What did you make of Bennett?' Joe Ashworth asked. 'Or whatever his name is.'

'Bennett,' she said. 'Legally, it's Bennett now.'

'Living a lie for all these years.'

'Was it a lie?'

'He's told his wife both his parents are dead. His

mother's shacked up with an insurance salesman and lives just down the road. The poor woman has a grandchild she knows nothing about!'

'It's not a crime,' Vera said quietly. 'And we all tell lies.' But righteous indignation had taken over and he wasn't listening. With part of her brain she heard him ranting about how he'd feel if his wife had treated him in the same way. Her mind was following a path of its own. *If someone asked me how much I'd had to drink tonight, I'd knock off a couple of units. It'd be automatic. I'd not think about it. To put myself in a better light. Don't we all do that? Find excuses, justifications? Even Saint Joe Ashworth. He loves his job. He doesn't even mind being separated from his wife and kid. Not really. At least he gets a good night's sleep and a break from the mucky nappies. But what does he tell himself? That it's a sacrifice. But he's prepared to do it to serve the community. Like he's some sort of martyr.*

She realized that Joe had stopped talking and was looking at her strangely.

'Well?' he demanded.

'Sorry, I was miles away.'

'Do you think Bennett killed Mantel's daughter in revenge for his father's suicide?'

'No,' she said. If she was pushed she could come up with a rational argument for thinking that way, but that would be a sort of lie too. Her reply was about trusting her own judgement. Faith, not reason. 'He could have killed the brother, though,' she went on. 'If Christopher had found out about his past. To protect his new identity, the happy family, all that. Yeah, I can see Bennett being prepared to kill to keep that.'

'You think there could be two different murderers, then?' Joe was sceptical, but still polite. He always was.

Do I? 'We can't dismiss any possibilities.' *And I know that's a cop-out because just at this moment I haven't got the concentration to think it through.*

'He'd have had the opportunity,' Joe said. 'I've talked to the witnesses. He could have slipped away from the bonfire. People were coming and going all the time. You were there. Is that how you remember it?'

'Aye,' she said. 'There was some light from the fire but that only lit up the people closest to it. The rest were silhouettes.' She sipped the whisky, held it in her mouth, swallowed it slowly. 'Bennett would have had to know Christopher would be there. He'd have had to arrange to meet him.'

'Maybe it was Bennett who Christopher was trying to phone.'

'Aye,' she said. 'Maybe.' But she'd had too much to drink to focus any longer on the detail. Her imagination was soaring, like one of the goshawks which flew out from Kielder Forest, close to her home in the hills. She felt she should be able to look down on this flat and empty landscape and see the bigger picture.

'What did Abigail Mantel and Christopher Winter have in common?' she asked suddenly, realizing as she spoke that her voice was too loud.

Joe Ashworth looked at her. 'Not much. She was a spoilt brat and he was a screwed-up student.'

'Both screwed up, wouldn't you say?' She shot out the question.

'I suppose.'

'By their parents?' Vera could have quoted Larkin, but Joe would have been shocked.

'Well, the lass didn't have a mother she could remember. But if what Bennett told us is right, her dad wasn't much of a role model.'

'And the Winters? What did you make of them?'

'They're odd,' he said at last. He paused. 'I'm not sure I'd want to grow up in that family.'

'I wonder what Caroline Fletcher's parents are like.' *And Michael Long's. And Dan Greenwood's. And the grandparents. How far could you go back?* The moment of clarity, of seeing the case as a whole, was over. The goshawk had crash-landed. She was left with a headache behind her eye, the knowledge that tomorrow there'd be another hangover and that the glimpse of an answer had probably been an alcoholic illusion.

'I'm off to my room,' Joe said. 'I need to phone home . . .'

'Of course.'

'If there's nothing else, that is . . .'

'No,' she said. 'You get off. I'll be up myself in a minute.' But she sat on, looking into the empty glass, unable to face the square over-heated room with the television fixed to the wall. The businesswomen paused in their conversation for a moment and looked at her with pity. That made her move. She got up, walked past reception and out into the darkness.

The hotel was on the main road out of the village and there were street lights, but no pavements. When a lorry came towards her she had to climb onto the verge and stand with her back to the hedge. She headed towards Elvet with no real sense of why she was there, but enjoying being outside and alone. Her headache started to clear. In the centre of the village, the streets were quiet. The Anchor was still open and through the small window she had a snapshot of two men standing at the bar, their mouths open in laughter, standing beside the giant whisky bottle where they collected change for the lifeboat. Beyond them a barmaid with a diamond stud in her nose. But she continued walking and the picture disappeared almost immediately.

In the Captain's House, the curtains were drawn. Were James and Emma Bennett having a cosy chat by the fire? Was he telling her the real story of his life?

There was a light at the Old Forge. She banged on the arched door. Nothing happened.

'Come on, man. Let me in. I'm desperate for a piss.'

Eventually she heard footsteps and Dan Greenwood shot back a bolt and opened the door. He seemed dazed, as if he'd been woken from a deep sleep, or interrupted from work which took great concentration.

'You're working late, Danny boy.'

'Just as well, if you're as desperate as you claim. The toilet's in the yard out the back.'

She walked through the pottery, but paused by the back door and looked at him before she went through it. He was piling together some papers from the top of his desk and shoving them into a drawer. When she returned the top of the desk was clear.

'Do you always work so late?' she asked.

'A habit it's hard to get out of when you've been a cop. Besides, there's not much to take me home.'

'No woman in your life, then?' She'd remembered the last comment he'd made about that, thought that at this time of night he might be more prepared to talk about it.

He shrugged noncommittally, gave a brief smile. 'Maybe. I'm not sure.'

'That's a bit cryptic for this time of night. What's not to be sure about?'

'I like her well enough. I'm not sure what she thinks of me. Not sure where the whole thing's going.'

'Maybe you should ask her. I always favour the direct approach myself.' Though look where that had got her, Vera thought. There was no man in her life. Hadn't been for years.

He smiled again and she guessed he was thinking the same thing, but was too much of a gentleman to say so. 'What are you doing wandering round on your own after dark?' he asked. 'Don't you read the crime prevention notices?'

'Just restless,' she said. 'You know what it's like.'

'How *is* it going?'

'I'm losing it,' she said. 'Losing the big picture. There's too much going on here. You know what it's like with an investigation this size. All the information. All the detail. Too much to take in. You just get swamped.'

'Aye,' he said. 'I remember.'

'Was it like that with the Mantel case, first time round?'

'First time round it seemed there was just the one suspect. Right from the beginning.'

'But you never thought it was Jeanie Long, did you?'

'It could have been her. It just didn't seem likely.'

'Why not?'

'Sounds daft,' he said. 'Trite. But she just didn't seem the type.'

'Who was, then? You must have had an idea. Someone you fancied for it.'

He leaned back in his chair and stretched. 'No,' he said. 'Not really. I just didn't think it was Jeanie.'

'Could it have been Caroline Fletcher?'

'No! No way. She broke a few rules, cut some corners. And she was besotted with Mantel. But she was no murderer.'

'Fletcher thought Emma Bennett could have been involved.'

'Did she?' He seemed surprised, shocked even. 'She never said so at the time. I never interviewed Emma, but it doesn't seem likely. Even now she seems timid, shy. Then she was only a girl. Caroline must be mistaken.'

'You always think the best of everyone, don't you, Dan?'

He stood up briskly and moved away, anxious, it seemed, to put some distance between them. 'I suppose you want some coffee.'

'Well, Danny, that'd be very civil. And if you could dig out the chocolate biscuits . . . That place we're staying, the size of the portions, you'd think they were feeding bairns . . .'

She watched him go into the small scruffy room with the tray and the kettle. The door swung to behind him. She opened the drawer where he'd stuffed the pile of papers when she'd turned up, demanding to be let in. Underneath a stack of invoices there was a photo album, hard covered, ring bound. She lifted it onto the desk, turned the pages. It was a record of the Mantel investigation. Grainy newspaper articles, snipped out and pasted in. The names of the papers and the date of publication had been written in black biro at the top of each piece. They came from nationals and locals and some had been bought on the same day. If they were too big they were just stuck at the top and carefully folded. They'd often been looked at. In some places the folds were close to ripping. Then there was a faded copy of the forensic report and the pathologist's report. A photo of Abigail lying at the crime scene, and another of her on the stainless-steel table at the mortuary.

On the last page there was a photograph of the girl when she was still alive. A studio portrait, head and shoulders, the body side on to the camera, the face turned towards it. Abigail was smiling seductively. In the background there was a loosely pleated curtain, the lighting could have been filtered, certainly the image seemed soft focused. She was wearing make-up which looked as if it had been professionally applied and her hair was piled onto her head. Her neck and shoulders were bare apart from a pearl necklace. She looked much older than fifteen and it couldn't have been taken much before her death. Perhaps it had been a birthday present from her father, Vera thought. His style. The sort of thing he'd do. But how, then, had Dan Greenwood got hold of it?

In the small room, she heard the kettle click off and the rattle of teaspoon against mug. She folded back the newspaper clippings and shut the book. When Dan came in, carrying the tray, the desk top was clear. She was leaning back in the chair as if she'd been dozing.

Part Three

Chapter Thirty-Four

There is still a wind, but it has turned southerly and is soft and heavy with unspilled rain. Emma sits at her window in the Captain's House and looks out over the street. It is late afternoon. A light is switched on in the forge. She hasn't seen Dan Greenwood for days and is hungry for a glimpse of him. But as she is willing him to make an appearance, her attention is caught by four elderly women who bustle out of the church. They all wear hats shaped like upturned button mushrooms made of felt or fake fur and short woollen coats and they seem to peck at each other as they talk. There has been a service. Mid-week evensong or a meeting of the Mothers' Union. Emma wonders if Mary has been there too, if she's dragged herself out to face the world. She hopes so. She hates to think of her parents stranded in Springhead House, enveloped by the damp and the silence, brooding on the loss of their son.

Emma considered this story for a few moments. Did it need polishing? Redrafting? Did the women coming out of the church really seem to peck at each other? Was that the right phrase? And *was* she still hungry to see Dan Greenwood though she knew now he was an ex-detective, whose response to her had been embarrassment not lust? Certainly, she thought. If anything, *greedy* came closer to describing her feelings. But why? All her certainties were cracking and shifting. The old life, the life of happy families had been founded on secrets and half truths. Now her image of her parents and James had blurred like the outline of a melting candle. Since Christopher's death, the fantasy of Dan Greenwood seemed more real than anything else in her life. It was a comfort. She held onto it greedily. She wanted him more than ever.

She dragged herself away from the window and went downstairs. James was sitting in the living room with a book on his knee. He hadn't drawn the curtains. As soon as she came in he started reading again, but she could tell he was fumbling to find his place. It was a show for her benefit. Before that, he'd been staring into the fire, miles away. She wondered for the first time if he had a fantasy lover too. Or even a real one. It had never occurred to her before. Now nothing would have surprised her.

Usually reading absorbed him. His taste was for the improving and informative, even in fiction. This was a travel book he'd seen reviewed in one of the Sundays and had ordered over the net. He said he'd wasted his first chance at education and wanted to catch up. When he discussed his reading, despite her degree, she felt ignorant in comparison. But recently, since Christopher's death, it seemed nothing held his attention. She wondered if it could be guilt which was eating away at him. He'd never particularly liked Christopher, might even, on that last night, when her brother had been such a pain, have wished him dead.

Perhaps now he was regretting that he'd been so hostile.

She sat on the floor in front of James, her back against his legs, her arms around her knees. She was so close to the fire that she could feel her face turning red. She needed the physical contact. James's bony legs against her back. The heat on her forehead. It anchored her in the present. Without it she'd get lost in her stories. Muddled. It would be like when Abigail was killed. That same sensation of disbelief.

She turned to him. 'Is there anything you want to talk about?'

'Like what?' he asked calmly. He gave up the pretence of reading and set the book aside. There was a picture of a compass on the cover, a big ship's compass in a brass case.

'Like everything that's been going on here. Christopher. Abigail. I can't believe it's happened again.' The words were inadequate. She couldn't explain that she'd lost trust in the everyday, in her own memory.

'Of course we'll talk if you think it would help.' It was clear from his tone that he didn't see how it could be useful. Usually she would have agreed with him. She'd felt that much of the analysis of relationships which had engaged her friends when she was a student was bizarre, an unnatural entertainment. No more than prying and gossip. She'd found James's restraint attractive. After Abigail's death too many people had wanted to discuss her feelings.

'No,' she said quickly. 'It won't bring Christopher back, will it?'

They'd put Matthew to bed and had just finished eating when there was a knock on the door. She was reminded of the night when Christopher had turned up and looked across the table to James, wondering if he'd picked up on the memory, but he was already on his feet, preparing to answer.

She heard a muttered conversation in the hall, then James came in followed by Vera Stanhope and her sergeant. 'Inspector Stanhope would like to ask you some questions,' he said. 'Do you mind?'

She thought James was annoyed by the interruption, but as always with James, it was hard to tell.

'No. Of course not. Sit down.'

'It's about Christopher,' Vera said. 'Not really my job to be asking questions. There's a local team investigating his death now. But you already know us. Better, I thought, that I come along than a couple of strangers.'

'Thank you.' Though Emma thought strangers might be less disturbing than this woman who seemed to dominate the small dining room, who had already made herself at home there. She'd flopped onto one of the empty chairs and was pulling off her cardigan, as if the heat was unbearable to her. Emma felt she should apologize for the temperature, stopped herself just in time. This was their home.

'Did Christopher have a mobile phone with him when you saw him?'

'I don't remember him using one,' Emma said.

'He was seen in the parish council cemetery early on the day he was killed. Near Abigail's grave. The witness thinks he might have been using a mobile, though we didn't find one on his body.'

'Surely you can trace if he owned a phone,' James said.

'You'd think so, wouldn't you? But it's not that easy,

apparently. Especially the *pay as you go* sort. People swap them, sell them. There are no bills, it's hard to get hold of records.' Vera changed tack suddenly, stared at Emma. 'Have you ever visited Abigail's grave?'

'No.' If Emma had thought more about it, she might have been tempted to lie. The bald denial sounded heartless.

'You knew where she was buried though. Did you go to her funeral?'

'No,' Emma said again, adding, 'My parents thought it would be upsetting. And although Keith had wanted a quiet burial, apparently the press were all there. I'm glad I stayed away.'

'What about Christopher?'

'He wouldn't have been there.'

'No? Are you sure? Did you talk about it?'

'There was no need. It would never have happened.'

'He could have slipped out of school. Gone by himself.'

'I suppose so. But someone would have seen him and mentioned it to my parents.'

'Of course.' Vera nodded vigorously. 'A place as small as Elvet, you'd think it would be impossible to get away with anything.' She paused. There was no need to say, *But two murders. Someone got away with that.* 'Christopher would have heard where Abigail would be buried though. It'd have been public knowledge.'

'Yes.'

'He must have visited the cemetery before,' Vera said. 'Our witness said he went straight to her grave that morning. It was still nearly dark, but he knew whereabouts in the cemetery she was buried.'

'I don't know.' Emma felt her head spinning. The questions were coming too fast. She had the dizzy feeling of being only half awake, slipping again into a dream. She had to concentrate hard. 'Christopher was always very private. Even when he was a boy. He'd disappear for hours and no one knew where he was.'

'Do you ever walk down the lane to the river?' Vera had suddenly changed pace. It was as if she was making polite conversation over tea. 'It'd be a nice walk in the right weather. Flat for pushing the pram. Good for a family trip out.' Although the question was directed at Emma, she flashed a sly look at James.

'I've walked there,' Emma said, confused by that look, wondering what it could mean. 'Occasionally.'

'I'm surprised you never looked at the grave. Just out of curiosity. She was your best friend.'

'I've spent my life trying to put Abigail's murder behind me.'

Vera gave her a quick, appraising stare, but let it go.

'I think Christopher might have used a mobile while he was here,' James said.

'Might have. What does that mean?'

'After the meal he went upstairs to the bathroom. I checked on the baby and heard him talking.'

'Did you hear what he said?'

'I don't make a practice of eavesdropping.'

'Don't you?' Vera sounded genuinely astonished. 'I do it all the time.'

'I assumed,' James said, after a moment of disapproving silence, 'that he was talking to someone back in Aberdeen. A girlfriend perhaps. To let her know that he'd arrived safely. Our landline's in the kitchen. We'd have overheard him if he'd used that. I assumed he wanted some privacy.'

'Did it sound like a call to a girlfriend?' Vera asked.

'As I said, I didn't listen.'

'But his voice, was it tender? Intimate?'

'No,' James said. 'It was more businesslike than that.'

Vera pulled a notebook from her bag and jotted down a few scribbled notes. 'We don't understand where he went for the rest of the day,' she said. 'He seems to have disappeared. He was at the cemetery at about eight, then we know he took the lane to the river.'

'How do you know that?' James asked. To Emma the question seemed too loud, too urgent. What could it matter to him?

'We found fingerprints in the public phone box there. You know the one,' Vera said. Again Emma thought this didn't sound right. It was as if the words had another meaning, as if the two of them were talking in a code she couldn't understand, hadn't been let in on. 'We've tested them and we know they are Chistopher's,' Vera continued. 'So what I want to know is where he went after that. We've tracked people who walked their dogs along the shore that morning. No one saw him. There were people about in the village that day. You'd think he'd want something to eat, wouldn't you? A cup of tea, at least. But he didn't go into any of the shops or the bakery. He cut quite a striking figure, apparently. Even if the staff didn't know him by name, you'd think he'd have been noticed. Can you think of anyone who might have put him up? Where he'd have hidden? And who he might have wanted to hide from?'

'No!' she said. 'I feel that I knew as little about him as I did about Abigail Mantel. And I won't have the chance now to know him better.'

'I'm sorry,' Vera stood up suddenly, pulled on the cardigan as she walked towards the door. 'This isn't fair. You've enough to cope with. If you think of anything which would help, you can give us a ring.'

The sergeant, Ashworth, followed. He hadn't said a word since he'd come in, but at the door he stopped, gave Emma a look of such sympathy and pity that she was brought close to tears. 'Take care,' he said. It was as if James was no longer in the room.

Suddenly she was a child again. She was in the house in York, sitting on the stairs. She'd been in bed but something had woken her and she'd stumbled down, half asleep. It had been summer and was still light, the garden behind the open door full of sunshine and birdsong. And her parents' words. They'd been discussing her. She'd heard her name and that had woken her properly and she'd run down to join them. They were sitting on a wooden bench. She'd run out to them. There was a patio made of old flagstones, which were rough against her bare feet but still warm. Her mother had gathered her into her arms. Emma had expected to be included in the conversation, an explanation, for she, after all, had been at the centre of the discussion.

'What were you talking about?' she'd demanded.

'Nothing, darling. Nothing important.'

And Emma had realized that it wasn't worth asking again. She'd been irrevocably shut out. Now, in the Captain's House, she felt just the same.

Chapter Thirty-Five

The next day Emma visited Abigail's grave. She left the baby with James and went alone, only saying that she seemed to have been stuck in the house for days and she needed some exercise. Usually, on his days off, James went everywhere with her. He liked the three of them to be together as much as possible. Liked the idea of it, at least. Today he let her go without comment, without seeming even to listen to her explanation, and she wondered again what was preoccupying him.

Christopher wouldn't be buried next to Abigail. Although they didn't know yet when the body would be released, Mary and Robert had already decided that he would be cremated. Mary had said she couldn't bear the idea of strangers coming to stare at his grave; these days even civilized people seemed to turn into voyeurs whenever a violent crime was reported in the media. Emma hadn't been consulted over the matter, and she thought that was only right. Of course she was sad that Christopher was dead, but she wasn't devastated. She wasn't overwhelmed with grief as you should be when a brother has been killed. She wondered what was wrong with her.

Emma felt guilty too because she'd had so little contact with her parents since Christopher's death. She could do something about that and she promised herself she'd go soon to Springhead to see how they were getting on. She realized she had viewed their retreat into isolation with something like relief. It meant her father wasn't turning up on the doorstep every five minutes to offer moral support and guidance. She didn't have to play at dutiful daughter.

When she reached the cemetery she wasn't sure why she'd bothered coming. After so long, her presence was probably a meaningless gesture. At the last minute she wished she'd brought flowers. It would have given the visit some point. She tried to fix a picture of Abigail in her mind, but whenever she remembered an occasion they'd spent together, the image of the girl slipped away from her and she was left with the background to the scene. So, there was that time when Abigail had told her triumphantly that she'd finally persuaded Keith to ask Jeanie Long to leave. Friday night. Youth club in the church hall, which Abigail usually turned her nose up at, but which Emma was forced to attend. A couple of pool tables and a ghetto blaster in the corner playing music she'd never heard before. The smell of steamed fish left over from the old people's lunch club. A stall selling crisps and Cash and Carry cola and cheap sweets: chews, lollipops and twisted bits of brightly coloured candy she'd never seen in proper shops. Emma knew Abigail had looked stunning in a sparkly green top – she could remember the pang of envy which had shot through her when Abigail had sauntered into the hall – but she couldn't *see* her. She could picture the faces of all the lads in the room looking wistful because they'd known she was way out of their league. Including Christopher's, because he'd been there too. He'd been playing pool and had straightened up from the table and stared intently for a moment. But not Abigail's. Emma couldn't remember at all what Abigail's response had been to all that attention.

Standing at the grave, her focus shifted. Instead of being part of the background, Christopher took centre stage. This was where he'd last been seen. And if the inspector was right, it was a place he'd visited many times before. She could picture him quite clearly – the long flapping anorak, his lank, untidy hair. The face drawn through lack of sleep and a hangover. But she had no idea what had been going on inside his head. She felt the desperation of missed opportunity. If only she'd been more sympathetic or more assertive. If only she had persuaded him to tell her what he knew.

Her attention was caught then by a flurry of activity around the farm buildings across the field. A minibus had arrived in the yard and a gaggle of police officers got out. There were a couple of dogs; she heard shouted instructions. The officers waited, then a car pulled up and two figures, sexless in white paper overalls and white caps, emerged. Someone must have had a key to the house because they went inside. The rest of them stood by the bus, looking at the junk, the piles of rusting machinery, as if they didn't know where to start. Emma thought Vera Stanhope might turn up and didn't want to be caught by her at Abigail's grave. The detective might think it was her comments of the night before which had prompted Emma to come. Emma didn't want her to have that satisfaction.

As she turned to leave, Emma saw Dan Greenwood leaning against the railings. He must have been watching her. He smiled and raised one hand in greeting. She felt her face flush, a sick excitement in the pit of her stomach. There was still a thrill of connection. That was what made James different, she thought. She never really felt connected to him. He was just a character in one of her stories.

'What do you think they're doing?' She nodded towards the figures in navy, who had started to organize themselves into groups. One of the parties filed through a gap in the hedge into the field nearest the river.

'They want to find out where Christopher spent the day he was killed. The cemetery was the last place he was seen and the farm's empty. He could have been in there. They'll be checking if he left any trace of himself behind.' He didn't speak as if he was guessing. She supposed he must still have friends in the service who kept him informed.

She walked out through the gate to join him. He smelled of the tobacco he rolled into cigarettes; she stepped away until it was lost in the background scent of dead leaves. Safest not to get too close.

'You haven't got the baby with you today, then?' he said.

'No.'

'You must feel you need some time to yourself occasionally.'

'Yes,' she said. 'I do.'

'Let me walk back to the village with you. I don't like the idea of you being out on your own.'

She thought again that James hadn't bothered about that. 'I can't see there'd be any danger. Not with all these police around.'

He didn't answer, but moved over, so he was closest to the road, and fell in step with her. Despite the misty drizzle, he wasn't wearing a coat, just a jersey of coarse navy wool, and the damp smell of that overlaid the tobacco. She felt awkward, clumsy.

'What made you decide on the pottery when you left the police?' she asked, for something to say.

He didn't speak for a moment. 'It took me a while to decide on anything. I'd had a sort of breakdown. Stress. I knew I wanted to do something creative. When I first left the service I went to art school for a couple of years, but I couldn't get my head round most of it. Conceptual art. What was that all about? Some of it I liked though. The craft side. Ceramics, producing something concrete for people, something useful.' He paused. 'Not making much sense, am I?'

'Yes, you are.'

'I had a bit of a pension from the police. Enough to get me started. Then my mother died and left me the money I needed to buy the forge.'

'Is that why you left the police? Because the stress was getting to you?'

'I suppose.' He smiled to make a joke out of it. 'Too sensitive for my own good, I daresay. I couldn't forget the victims were real people.'

They walked on in silence until they reached the village. At the door to the forge they paused. Emma knew she should carry on walking, cross the road, let herself into the Captain's House. James might be looking out for her.

'I don't suppose there's any chance of a coffee,' she said. She could feel the colour rising in her face. 'As you said, I don't have the chance to get out much without the baby. I'm not sure I can face the house again just yet.'

'Of course.'

She couldn't tell at all what he made of her request. Did he think she was going mad? Put it down to grief? 'But perhaps you're too busy,' she added. 'Perhaps I should go.'

'No.' The door had warped and caught at the bottom against a flagstone. He put his shoulder against it to push it open. 'I'll be glad of the distraction.' On a bench just inside the door there was a row of jugs he'd hand painted, swirling patterns in intense blues and greens.

'They're lovely,' she said. 'They make you think of water, don't they? You feel you're drowning in the colour.'

'Really?' He looked genuinely pleased. 'When they're glazed you must have one.'

The sick excitement came back.

They sat in the small room she'd seen on her first visit. He made the coffee, apologized for the chipped mug, the lack of fresh milk.

'What were you doing at the cemetery?' she asked suddenly. It was hot. She felt ill at ease. Now she was here, she couldn't carry off the situation with polite conversation. She wished she could do the joking banter which had come naturally to her colleagues at the college. 'Were you there to visit Abigail's grave?' She remembered what he'd said as they'd walked back to the village. 'Was it because even though you'd never met her, Abigail Mantel was a real person to you?'

He seemed startled by the question. 'No,' he said. 'Nothing like that.'

'I'm sorry. None of my business.'

'I'd heard the lads were starting a search on Woodhouse Farm and even after all this time it's hard not to be curious. I suppose I miss the police in a way. The friendship, certainly. I keep in touch with some of the lads but it's not the same.'

It seemed sad to her, the thought of him watching his former colleagues working two fields away.

'Did you ever meet Abigail while she was alive?' She didn't know where the question had come from, regretted it as soon as it was spoken.

He looked up sharply from the coffee he was cupping in his hands. 'No. Of course not. How could I?'

'I'm sorry. It's brought it all back. Christopher dying.'

'I did meet *him*,' Dan said. 'That afternoon you found the girl's body, I was talking to him in the other room, while my boss was in the kitchen with you and your mother.'

'If he'd seen the murderer he'd have said, wouldn't he?'

'He answered all my questions. I didn't have the impression he was keeping anything back. Did he ever say anything to you?'

'No.' She set down her mug. It was still almost full. 'I should go. Taking up your time like this.'

'There's no hurry,' he said. 'It's a lonely business this. Tell you the truth I'm glad of the company.'

'You should find yourself a woman.' She spoke lightly and was quite proud of the jokey tone. It would make him realize she had no designs on him.

'Maybe I've already found one. But things aren't working out quite how I'd hoped.' He stared at her and a ridiculous thought came into her head. *He wants me to ask what he means. Is he talking about me?*

'Look,' she said. 'I must go now. James will be wondering where I am. I don't want him worried.'

'Come back,' he said. 'Whenever you want to talk.'

She didn't know what to make of that and left without answering. Outside she stood for a moment, trying to recover her composure, before going home. On the other side of the road, the bulky figure of Vera Stanhope appeared in the bakery door. She crooked her finger and beckoned for Emma to join her. Like the witch, Emma thought, out of *Hansel and Gretel*, tempting her into the gingerbread house. And like the children, she felt compelled to obey.

'What have you been up to?' Vera asked.

'I went for a walk. Bumped into Dan. He invited me in for coffee.'

'Did he now.' There was a pause, loaded with a significance Emma couldn't guess at. Then Vera added lightly, 'At your age you should know better than to go off with strange men.'

'Dan Greenwood's not strange.'

There was another pause. 'Maybe not. All the same, just take care.' The same instruction Joe Ashworth had given at their last meeting. The inspector turned away with a little wave and Emma was left with the impression that she'd been warned off.

Chapter Thirty-Six

Michael Long hadn't seen Vera for days. Not to speak to. He'd glimpsed her across the street, and once he'd approached her, but she just gave a friendly wave and continued on her way as if she was too busy to talk. At least he thought that was the impression she'd wanted to give and he didn't think it was fair. He deserved better than that. Not only was he Jeanie's father, he was the man who'd pointed Vera in the right direction when it came to Keith Mantel. And he was an important witness, the last person to have seen Christopher Winter alive. Michael would never have put it that way, but he felt like a jilted lover. He wanted Vera to take some notice of him again. He stayed at home in case she called. Whenever there was a knock on the door, he hoped it might be her.

Then he thought, *Sod it*. He wasn't going to hang around for any woman. He'd do his own research, collect his own information and he'd show her. He imagined presenting her with a fat file on Mantel, all organized and typed. It would provide her with everything she needed to show the man was a murderer. Because that was what Michael wanted to prove to her. Mantel was a monster who'd killed his own daughter and the young Winter lad. And Mantel was to blame for

Jeanie being locked up all that time, for her desperation and suicide.

He got the bus into the town up the coast where Mantel had first made his money. He knew it had a decent-sized library. The high school was there too and he shared the bus with kids on their way in. He told himself this was a nuisance and indeed the noise of shrieking girls and boys locked in continual mock battle irritated him to distraction. He muttered under his breath about feckless parents and bringing back national service. But it had its compensations. The bus was full and he was squeezed on a bench seat which faced into the aisle. Beside him was a girl of fourteen or fifteen, with a white powdery face and narrow eyes lined in black. She seemed too dignified for the chaos surrounding her and was annoyed as he was by the shouting and chucking of missiles. She sat with her legs crossed at the knee and her bag on her lap. 'Why don't you just grow up?' she snapped at a lad with a face scarred with acne when a pencil sharpener missed its target and hit her arm. Then she turned to Michael and rolled her eyes conspiratorially, as if they were the only sane ones there.

When they got off in Crill, in the windswept square close to the seafront, he was reluctant to let her go. He was tempted to follow her, just for the pleasure of watching her walk. She had a straight back, long legs, a haughty tilt to her head. But he told himself he had work to do. In the square, council workmen were erecting Christmas lights from a truck with a hydraulic lift. The library was a grand building with pillars in the front and wide stone steps leading to a double door. It was shut and wouldn't open until nine thirty. His irritation returned. He ranted under his breath about the idleness of the staff. He could have walked with the girl as far as the school, after all. Then he told himself it wouldn't do to get into a state. Peg had always warned him he would get into serious bother one day if he didn't learn to calm down.

He asked one of the workmen where he could get a coffee and he was pointed down a narrow street. The place was called *Val's Diner* and was full of noise and steam. It reminded him of the cafe on the Point. The bacon in his sandwich was just as he liked it – crisp and brittle – and his temper improved. These days, he thought, it took something that small to alter his mood. He wondered if he'd always been like that and if everyone was the same.

He knew the woman who ran the local history library. She was called Lesley and she was efficient and jolly with a loud voice, which made the readers in the reference section look up and tut in disapproval. He'd first met her just before he'd retired. He'd started to get nostalgic about what he was giving up. Lesley held the archive of the lifeboat station and the pilot office on the Point, and he'd come in to look up the history. There'd been one photo, he remembered, of the house where he'd lived all those years with Peg. It had been taken in the twenties, and the Point had been quite different then. The dunes had stretched further and the two cottages and the lighthouse had been the only buildings. Outside their cottage, a man with a large grey moustache had been leaning against the wall by the front door, glaring out at the camera.

Lesley was sitting at her desk and looked up when she saw him approaching. He could see from her face that she'd read about Jeanie in the papers, but she didn't say anything. She didn't even show that she recognized him, which he found upsetting, because when he'd been doing his research into the Point, he'd thought she liked him. He explained that he was interested in the back issues of the local paper going back twenty, even thirty years. 'They are available?'

'Oh yes,' she said, and she smiled. 'Are you after anything specific?' Because she was still sitting at her desk, she seemed to be squinting up at him.

'No! Nothing like that. Just general interest.' Immediately he was sorry that he'd been so sharp, but she hadn't seemed to have noticed. She sat him in front of the microfiche machine and showed him how to use it, repeating the instructions patiently when he asked her to.

'If you need anything, just give me a shout.' Her voice carried across the large room and she could have been talking to any of the customers there.

He started at the time of Abigail's murder and worked back. At first he found himself distracted by other stories. Not the murder. He moved quickly past that and when he came across a photo of Jeanie he shut his eyes. He couldn't bear the thought of her captured in the machine where anyone could come and stare at her. It was the less dramatic stories which caught his attention. The largest container ship ever to come into the Humber. Cows wandering across the river at low tide and becoming stranded on a sandbank. A festival of tall ships in the estuary. When he looked up at the clock on the wall it was nearly eleven and he'd found nothing useful. He forced himself to move on more quickly and began to find mentions of

Keith Mantel. Flashes in words and photographs. Michael began tracking him back in time. It was like watching a jerky old film played in reverse.

The most recent reports, the ones he came to first, were positive and he had to stop himself from sneering out loud. There was a picture of Keith Mantel standing beside a giant cardboard cheque, Mantel Development's donation to a charity which provided respite care for disabled children. A beaming girl reached out from her wheelchair to hold the other end of the cheque. Keith Mantel with a group of others, appointed as NHS trustees for the local hospital. Keith Mantel in wellingtons, planting a tree in the wildlife garden of a junior school. Michael muttered under his breath about the gullibility of the public, but looking at the smiling, confident face, he thought if he hadn't known any better, if he hadn't tangled with Mantel in the village, he'd have fallen for it too. He'd have believed in Mantel, the entrepreneur with a social conscience.

As he followed Mantel's story back, his memory was wakened. Occasional references triggered a recollection of incidents he'd investigated before, when his only reason for disliking Mantel was that the businessman was an arrogant sod who'd tried to undermine his position in the village. A brief report about the grand opening of a leisure centre took him back to a conversation with an old friend. They'd been to school together, but Lawrence Adams had been promoted within the family business and suddenly turned gentleman. He'd taken up golf and got himself elected as Tory councillor. A couple of big contracts had been awarded to Mantel and Michael had been sniffing around to find out why. They'd met, at Lawrence's request, in a small, rundown pub near Hull prison. It had seemed a strange place for a rendezvous, not Lawrence's usual sort of haunt.

'Why here?' Michael had asked.

'No one will recognize me here.'

And Michael had liked that. He'd realized that this was a kindred spirit, someone else to share his paranoia about Mantel.

'Mantel can't get at you, can he?' He'd thought Lawrence had too much money to be corruptible.

'He can get at anyone. Just keep out of his way.'

And then he'd rambled about the leisure centre, not making too much sense, so Michael thought he'd been drinking before he'd arrived. 'It should never have gone to him. We came to a decision at the planning committee. All sorted we thought. Then suddenly the preferred contractor withdrew. No reason given. So it went to Mantel in the end.' Lawrence had looked up from his beer. 'You know how he started, don't you? How he first made his money?' That was when Michael had heard the story of the old lady leaving Mantel her house, the story he'd passed on to Vera Stanhope when she'd knocked at his door. And he still wasn't sure how true it was.

As they'd left the pub to head for their cars, too drunk to drive legally, but reckless, Lawrence had said, 'I mean it. Stay away from him. Look what happened to Marty Shaw. He was no friend of mine, but I'd not wish that on anyone. Mantel was behind it, you know.'

Michael hadn't heard of Marty Shaw and had no idea what Lawrence was talking about, but he'd made enquiries, found out that he was the man who'd been washed up on the riverbank. Michael had heard about that. Some poor sod from Crill who'd walked into the river and drowned himself. It had been all they'd talked about in the Anchor the day he'd been found. He hadn't realized at the time that there'd been a link with Mantel, or he'd have taken more notice.

It hadn't been difficult to pick up the rumours. Michael had had friends everywhere then. He'd been sociable, famous for it. Not like now, when he hid away in his bungalow built for sad old people, drinking alone. Then there'd hardly been a pub on the peninsula where he'd not been known. Everywhere he went there'd be people he'd gone to school with, or served on the lifeboat committee with, or done a favour for. He sat now in the quiet library staring at lines of print through the microfiche machine. They told one story. The memories of those conversations of years before fleshed out the details.

Back again in time. He found the report of the inquest into Shaw's death. Suicide. He'd left a note so the verdict was inevitable. They hadn't said what had driven him to it. Poor stupid bastard, Michael thought now. Then he'd been less charitable. He'd always thought suicide was a coward's way out. The report said the dead man had left behind a wife and a son. Michael couldn't remember if he'd picked up on that at the time. It felt suddenly grubby, this digging around in the past, and he was tempted to give up. Then he looked out through the long window across the square at the men who were still trying to string up the tacky lights and thought he had nothing better to do.

He almost missed the significance of the photograph. It seemed at first like the more recent stories. Keith Mantel as local hero. This showed the opening of a sheltered housing complex for elderly people. The sort of place Michael would end up living if he didn't take more care of himself. The picture was taken in a courtyard, paved with plants in tubs. Behind the party the brick building looked brutally new and hard-edged. In the centre the mayor, a plump middle-aged woman, held a pair of scissors to cut the ribbon strung across the front door. Beside her stood Mantel, but around them were crowded a number of councillors and their families. There must have been a free lunch, Michael thought, to have brought so many people out. He read the names idly, putting off the time when he'd have to leave the comfort of the library. *Councillor Martin Shaw. James Shaw.* James stood next to his father. It was obvious that they were father and son. The resemblance was striking. Marty Shaw's face seemed familiar and Michael thought perhaps he'd seen pictures at the time of his death. Then an image flashed into his mind of the man in uniform. A pilot's uniform. Not Marty of course. But Marty's son.

Then the old paranoia took over and he imagined Keith Mantel and James Bennett working together, a web of conspiracy, which took in Jeanie's suicide, his own enforced retirement from the pilot service and two murders.

Chapter Thirty-Seven

The psychiatrist was a pompous bastard. As soon as she walked into his office in the big new general hospital, Vera saw this would be a waste of time. He seemed too young to be a consultant, with his dark hair and his clipped black beard which looked as if it had been painted on. There wasn't a trace of grey. She spent a moment wondering if it had been dyed. He looked up from his desk.

'Inspector Stanhope.' He was a man who liked rank. He'd call the nurses *sister* or *staff nurse* just to put them in their place. 'My secretary said it was urgent.'

'I'm leading an enquiry into the Abigail Mantel murder case.'

'Yes.'

'One of the detectives working on the investigation was a patient of yours.'

He said nothing.

'Daniel Greenwood,' she said. 'Is he still your patient?'

'You know better than that, Inspector. I can't discuss individuals.'

But he was interested, she could tell. He'd been hooked by the drama of a famous murder case, just like the people who slavered over the same story in the tabloids, then said how disgusting they found the publicity. Murder had a glamour all of its own.

'Of course not.' She settled comfortably into the leather chair. She might as well take the opportunity to take the weight off her feet. 'I was after more general advice. The benefit of your expertise.'

He smiled, pulling his narrow lips back from his teeth. There was a gold crown on an upper molar. She found it hard not to stare. 'Anything I can do to help the police, which doesn't compromise me professionally, Inspector . . . Of course.'

'I'm interested in . . .' pausing, an attempt to find the right words, '. . . a person with an obsessive personality.'

'Yes?'

'I'm talking a stalker. Someone who is fascinated by a young woman. Follows her maybe . . .'

'Such a man could be dangerous.'

The psychiatrist smiled again. Under her polyester trousers, Vera felt her flesh crawl.

'It would be a man?' she asked suddenly.

'No, no. Not necessarily.' He stroked his beard very slowly. 'There have been many recorded cases of women taking an unhealthy, delusional interest in a man. Often an ex-lover. Most commonly, they refuse to believe that a relationship is over.'

Jeanie Long never accepted Mantel didn't love her, Vera thought. She wasn't mad.

'But if the object of the obsession was a young woman?' Vera said.

'Then the stalker is more likely to be a man,' the doctor conceded.

'In what way could the obsessive become dangerous?'

'His fantasy would be that the object of his desire
shared his feelings. If the fantasy was shattered, he
could resort to violence.' He looked at her. 'We are talking still in general terms here. I must make it clear that
I have no evidence of such behaviour in any of my
patients.'

*What does that mean? That you suspect Dan Green-
wood of stalking and killing Abigail Mantel, but you have
no evidence for it? Or that he wouldn't hurt a fly?*

She contained her impatience. She knew he would
only enjoy it if she lost her cool. 'Is there such a thing
as a serial stalker?'

'In what sense?'

'Suppose the scenario you've described were
played out. The obsessive killed the young woman and
got away with it. Is it possible that he could transfer his
attention to another victim?'

'Certainly it would be possible.' He paused. She suspected he enjoyed making her wait for the rest of his
answer. 'He could have been excited, aroused by the
violence. While that might have been unintended in
the first instance, it could become an integral part of
the fantasy in the second.'

'So he'd dream of killing her? That would be his
intention?'

'As I've said, it's possible. Certainly not inevitable.
As I'm sure you're aware, very few mentally ill people,
not even those who are seriously disturbed, commit
acts of violence.'

'Would I know if I met him?' Vera demanded.

'What do you mean?'

'If it was someone I met in the street, or socially, or at work, would I realize he was mad?' She threw in the last word as a provocation. He didn't rise to the bait.

'In the street, almost certainly not.'

'Would someone be able to function normally, hold down a regular job, and still behave in this way?'

He considered for a while and still couldn't come up with a satisfactory answer. 'I'm not a forensic psychiatrist. This isn't really my area of competence.'

'Give me an opinion.'

'It would take considerable control. The separation of the fantasy life and the everyday. It would be exceptional.'

'But not impossible.'

'No. Not impossible.'

Driving back to Elvet, Vera thought she'd made a fool of herself. She should never have gone to the hospital. It had been a spur of the minute impulse, an excuse to get out of the village. She'd over-reacted to Dan Greenwood keeping a few momentos of his last major case. It wouldn't do to start rumours that Dan was some sort of weirdo. A place like this, that was the last thing he'd need.

She drove through the square and saw that he was working in the forge. She was tempted to stop. Why not just ask him why he'd kept the material on the Mantel case and how he'd come into possession of the photograph? But she continued on the road towards the coast until she came to the crescent of small houses where he lived. She pulled her car into the verge on the main road and walked towards his home. The street was quiet. In one house an elderly woman was watching a game show on the television in her front room. She sat with her swollen legs on a footstool, a Zimmer frame within easy reach. When Vera walked past she kept her gaze fixed on the screen.

Vera stopped before Dan's place and went up to his neighbour's front door. She rang the bell. There was no reply. She did the same thing at the house beyond. The street was only built on one side. It curved round a small children's play area. Satisfied that no one was looking, she approached Dan's. The door was locked as she knew it would be. She looked under the mat. No spare key. One of his larger pots containing a small evergreen shrub stood next to the doorstep. She shifted it. Nothing. The bedroom window at the front was open, but she didn't have the build or fitness for climbing drainpipes.

There wasn't much of a garden, just a square of muddy grass and a low privet hedge to separate it from the houses on each side. No hiding place. Because the Crescent was a terrace, the only access to the back gardens was from the fields. She was about to give up. She wasn't in the mood for shinning over farm gates or wading ankle-deep in muck. Then she returned to the shrub in the pot and felt around the wood chippings scattered on top of the soil. One mortise lock key. She wiped it clean on her jumper and opened the door. She slipped off her sandals and put them sole up on the carpet. She closed the door behind her and padded barefoot into Daniel's home.

It's a skill to search without leaving a sign of the intruder. It takes time. But Daniel's house was easier to look through than most. He had few possessions and he kept them ordered. Vera started at the top of the house. There was a small bathroom, probably renovated in the eighties, with an avocado suite and black mould in the sealant around the bath. In the mirror-faced wall cabinet, she found a packet of paracetamol and a bottle of antidepressants. These had been prescribed by his GP, not the hospital consultant. Daniel's room contained a double bed, neatly made with sheets and blankets. No duvet. There was a pine bedside table. He was reading a novel by James Lee Burke, a paperback with a black and purple jacket. In the drawer she found a couple of packets of condoms. Unopened. Wishful thinking? Or had he found a girlfriend? Some secret woman prepared to take him on? He had admitted to bringing Caroline Fletcher home for a drink, after all. Perhaps there was more to that relationship than he'd let slip. His clothes were all folded and neatly hung in a white plastic fitted wardrobe. The laundry basket in the corner was empty. If he had killed Christopher Winter, there would be no forensic evidence to link him to the scene.

The second bedroom was at the back and smaller. The curtains were closed. They were heavily lined and when Vera first entered she could see nothing. She switched on the light. In the second before the room was lit, she felt breathless, frightened for what she would find. But at first it seemed there was nothing out of the ordinary. Under the window stood an ornate dressing table, with three mirrors, angled, all surrounded in cheap gilt. Then, next to the wall, a narrow single bed covered in a floral quilt. On the dressing table there was a photograph of a woman. From the style of hair and clothes it had been taken in the early fifties. She was young and smiling into the camera. Daniel's mother, perhaps? The woman who'd died and left Daniel enough money to buy the forge and set up his business. On the bed lay a pair of women's panties. Black. Tiny. A heart in sequins sewn on the front. Not the sort of garment Caroline Fletcher would go for. Too brash and downmarket. Vera could see the label inside from where she stood. The garment had come from a chain store which catered to younger buyers. It should be possible to find out when they'd been produced, Vera thought. She hoped they were a recent addition to stock, that they hadn't been part of the range ten years previously.

Downstairs she found nothing of interest. She was meticulous although she was aware of time passing. Did she want Daniel to find her, so she could confront him and give him a chance to explain? Certainly she took her time, sorting through the CDs in the living room and the drawers in the kitchen, emptying the small freezer compartment in the fridge so she could feel to the back.

At last she was satisfied. She opened the front door and looked out. Still the road was quiet and the playground empty. She put on her sandals and stood on the doorstep. She locked the door and replaced the key. A few bark chippings fell from the pot onto the concrete path. She picked them up and threw them into the gutter as she walked to her car.

Chapter Thirty-Eight

Michael knew it was no good going to see Vera Stanhope yet. His mind was fizzing, the thoughts chasing each other, becoming wilder and more fantastic, but he was sane enough to realize that she'd need more than theories and accusations. At the moment she'd see him as a barmy old man with a grudge. Why should she listen to him?

He left the library in a hurry, hardly taking time to thank Lesley, not waiting to put on his bulky coat, gathering it instead under his arm. In the square the men had finished putting up the decorations and were testing the lights. There was nothing magical about them, Michael thought. He couldn't see the point of all that effort. A whole morning's work, for what? The bulbs were as big as you'd find in domestic light fittings, but with garish colours, pink, lime green and a sulphurous yellow. There was a snowman which had been cut out of grubby polystyrene and hung from a wire strung between two lamp posts. Its grin leered at passers-by. Michael found the crooked smile disturbing. It followed him down the street to *Val's Diner*, where he drank a cup of coffee and tried to order his thoughts. He needed to plan what to do next.

At the bus stop there were a couple of women

who'd come into town from Elvet to do their shopping. He heard them talking from a distance. 'Only a month until Christmas. Fancy.' They wore little fur-lined suede boots, identical, and there were piles of white carrier bags on the pavement surrounding them, so each was stranded in her own island of plastic. Michael knew them. If he'd allowed himself a moment to think about it, he'd have remembered their names. They'd been friends of Peg's. But he was still racing after the ideas which seemed to be galloping away from him and nothing else mattered. He stood behind them to form a queue, became suddenly aware that he was being spoken to.

'It's nice to see you out, Michael. In town on a bit of business?' It was the shorter one with the white bubbly hair. He looked at her sharply, wondering for a moment if there was anything sinister in her question. It even occurred to him briefly that she might be a spy for Mantel. That was the extent of his anxiety. Then he told himself that he was letting his imagination run away with him. He'd spent too long brooding on his own. Still, it was as well to be careful.

'No. Just here to visit the library.'

'You couldn't find anything that you liked, then?'

'Sorry?'

'Books. You've not got any books with you.' She spoke very slowly, then looked pityingly at her neighbour.

'No. I wasn't there to borrow. I wanted to look something up in the reference.'

'A shame,' she said. 'It can be very healing, a good story.'

He was saved the necessity of replying because the

bus arrived, spluttering and spewing out diesel fumes from the exhaust into the cold air. Michael had to pay full fare because he'd never bothered to get a pensioner's pass and half the way home he had to put up with the Elvet women telling him how to go about applying for one. The bus dropped them all outside the church and Michael stood there for a moment to give the women time to move away.

He looked across the street at the Captain's House. He could see there was a fire in the grate in the front room. Emma Bennett came out and closed the door behind her. She paused for a moment then walked up the street. She looked very smart in a long black coat, and he wondered where she could be going. She didn't have the baby with her and he thought James must be inside. It was tempting just to knock at the door and confront him with the questions he had to ask. At least that way they wouldn't still be inside his head. But James had always intimidated him, even when they'd worked together every day. He thought he'd have to find another way. He couldn't face the bungalow and started walking out of the village, towards the sea.

When he'd been living on the Point with Peg, there'd been nights when he'd walked home from the Anchor. Not because he was scared of getting done for drunk driving – once in a blue moon you'd see a cop in Elvet then. It wasn't like now. Since this latest murder every other person you saw was a stranger and you could tell, even if they weren't in uniform, that they were police. No, he'd walked then for the pleasure of it. A good night and a belly of beer, then the walk down the Point with the river on one side and the sea on the other, and knowing that Peg would be waiting for him in the big, soft bed. Just the starry sky and anticipation. That was how it had been, hadn't it? He hated the thought that his memory might be playing tricks.

He'd started out on foot just because there was a relief in the exercise, though the walk seemed harder and longer than he remembered, with a stiff breeze from the south blowing into his face. But it helped him think more clearly too and he saw what he should do. He'd talk to Wendy, the coxswain of the pilot launch. She'd been friendly with James Bennett from the start, before he was so highly qualified, before he'd moved to Elvet. Before he'd married. Michael had even wondered if there'd been more between them than friendship, though he hadn't been around to find out. He'd only worked with Wendy for a few weeks, a period of handover before he'd retired. If James Bennett, usually so stiff and reserved, had confided in anyone about his past, it would have been Wendy.

It was mid afternoon before he reached the pilot station and the light was starting to go. Stan, the second coxswain, was on duty. He was sitting at the desk, his legs in front of him, reading the paper and drinking tea. When Michael walked in you'd have thought he'd seen a ghost. 'Eh, lad, what are you doing here?'

Michael thought it had been a fair few years since he'd been called a lad.

'Just a bit of a constitutional,' he said. 'You're busy, I see.'

'Another half hour and I'll be out to collect a pilot.'

'Which one?'

'A new man called Evans. You'll not know him.'

'Do you know if Wendy's around?'

'Her day off. She'll be in the cottage if she's not out gallivanting.'

'Does she do a lot of that these days?'

'More than she used to. I think there's a new man in her life, but she'll not let on.'

Michael went back outside before Stan could ask what he was after. The grey bulk of a tanker was moving up the river, approaching the mouth of the estuary. It had started to spit with rain.

It was odd to knock at the door of the cottage after so many years of just letting himself in. There was a light on upstairs and the sound of music so he knew she was there. He knocked again more loudly. At last there were noises inside – water in a drain, someone clattering down the stairs – and she opened the door to him. She was wearing a dressing gown and her hair was wrapped in a towel. She recognized him at once and was surprised. If it had been someone else, he thought, she'd have been angry about being disturbed. One good thing about being bereaved. People felt they had to be kind to you.

'Sorry,' she said. 'I was in the bath.'

Her feet were bare and he couldn't stop staring at them, at the feet and the smooth legs which disappeared into the towelling robe. He imagined her lying in the bath, shaving them. Her toenails were painted silver. Who was there to see them this time of year? It wasn't the weather for sandals. He stared at the painted nails, couldn't stop.

'Can I help you, Michael?' she said, trying to keep the impatience from her voice. He realized she'd been waiting for him to explain why he was there.

'Maybe I should come in. You'll be catching your death standing there with the door open.'

She nodded, giving in to the inevitable. 'Just give me a minute. I'll get some clothes on.'

She let him into the kitchen and left him there. In Peg's day he would have taken off his shoes before going in, but now there didn't seem much point. He would never have recognized it. He could tell that underneath the mess nothing much had changed. They were the same cupboards and benches Peg had chosen from the MFI on the ring road. But everywhere there was clutter. Dirty washing spilling out from a basket, a pyramid of shoes and boots, mucky plates and pots, drying cat food on a purple plastic dish. He didn't know what to make of it. He tried to work up some indignation, told himself Peg would have a fit if she could see it, then thought it didn't really matter. When Wendy came back in, dressed in tracksuit bottoms and top, slippers too big for her, she cleared some clothes from a chair and sat down.

'Now then, Michael, what can I do for you?' Not unfriendly but brisk, making it clear she couldn't give him much of her time. No offer of tea either, and after the walk he was gasping.

Now, he wasn't sure how to start. On his way he should have planned how to go about it. He shouldn't have let his mind wander back to the good times.

'It's about James,' he said. 'James Bennett. How well do you know him?'

'What are folk saying?' She narrowed her eyes, seemed to curl back in her chair like a cat ready to spring.

'Nothing. Nothing like that.'

'Only you know what it's like, one woman working with men, people make up all sorts.'

'No,' he said. 'But I thought he might have talked to you, that's all.'

'What about?'

'His childhood, where he grew up. That sort of thing.'

'Why would you want to know?'

He felt the room swim around him as he grasped for an explanation which would satisfy her. 'I thought I might have known him when he was a lad.'

'Oh.'

Again the spinning panic. 'Did he go to the Trinity House School?'

'No, he's not a Trinity House lad.'

'Local, though?'

'I don't think he's ever said. He's not one for chatting. He doesn't give much of himself away . . . Michael, what is all this about?'

'Like I said, I thought I knew him. Came across an old photo. It was the spitting image. But he wasn't calling himself Bennett in those days. Shaw, that was his name. I wondered if he'd talked about it to you.' He realized he was gabbling. She was looking at him as if he was one of those mad old men let out into community care, who rant to themselves as they walk down the street. He wondered, as he had that day talking to Peg in the cemetery, if that was what he'd come to in the end. Perhaps that was what he'd come to already.

'Why would he change his name?' she said reasonably. 'You must have made a mistake. You can't really tell from an old photo, can you? Why don't you ask him next time you see him, if it's troubling you.'

344

'He must have said something about his family, what he did before he joined the pilotage. You know how you get chatting while you're waiting for a ship.'

'James doesn't chat,' she said. 'He's always pleasant and polite, but he likes his privacy. And so do I.' She stood up and he saw he'd have to go.

'I'm sorry to have bothered you. You're right. It must have been a mistake. You'll have to forgive me. I'm not myself at the moment.'

Then she felt sorry for him again. 'Look, how did you get here? Give me a minute and I'll take you back to the village.'

'No, I'll not trouble you. Stan said he was bringing in a pilot. I'll get a lift back with him.'

They stood awkwardly. She was blocking his way to the door and moved to let him out. At exactly that moment there was a sound upstairs, a slight creak. One of the floorboards in the bedroom had been loose even in his day. She saw that he'd heard it.

'Must be the cat,' she said.

'Aye.' Though he knew it wasn't any cat. It wasn't just the sound from upstairs, which had more weight behind it than the heaviest cat. It was the way she looked as she said it, furtive and excited at the same time, as if she was playing a secret game. After she'd shut the door behind him, he stood in the small garden and looked upstairs where the light had been, but now the curtains were drawn and he couldn't see anything. The single car parked behind the cottage he recognized as Wendy's.

The launch was out and he waited beside the office for it to come back to the jetty. He didn't feel he could just let himself into the office any more. The boat

345

nosed back through the gloom and he felt the stab of nostalgia which he'd expected to feel in the house. Later, he stood with Stan looking out towards the river while the pilot made a call to the data centre.

'Who is it that Wendy's taken up with? You live next door, man. You must have seen him go in and out.'

'Never. He must be like the Invisible Man.'

'There'll be rumours. I know what the gossip's like round this place.'

'One thing's obvious.' Stan touched the side of his nose with his finger. 'He's married, isn't he? Why else would she keep him secret?'

Chapter Thirty-Nine

They sat in church, in their usual places. Mary and Robert, Emma with the baby on her knee and James. At Mary's feet the dreadful fat handbag which Emma hated and which was always full of rubbish. A splash of sunlight shone through the glass, coloured the dust which swirled in the draught from the door and stained the surplice of the priest who walked down the nave to shake the hands of the congregation as they shared the peace. He reached across James to touch Emma's head. 'Peace be with you, my dear.'

The sun had shone briefly in just the same way on the morning of their wedding. James remembered sitting on the front pew, next to Geoff, the colleague he'd persuaded to be his best man. It had taken some persuasion, he thought now. Not that Geoff hadn't been pleased to be asked, but he'd been surprised, unable to hide his bewilderment. 'Of course I'd love to. But usually it's family, isn't it? Or some mate you've been to school with. Someone you've known for years at least.' James had said there wasn't anyone. No one he'd rather have than Geoff.

So, he'd been sitting at the front of the church, surprisingly calm, knowing absolutely that this was the right thing to do. The music had started. Not *'The*

Wedding March.' They'd decided against that. '*The Arrival of the Queen of Sheba*'. He'd known Emma was on her way, but he'd not looked round, not immediately. He'd waited a few beats before turning. And just at that moment the sun had come out, bleeding the colour from the stained glass onto the ivory satin of her dress. She'd caught his eye and smiled nervously, and it had come to him, like the melodramatic ending of a romantic novel, that everything had worked out for the best. His father's death, the shame and the scandal, everything that followed, had all led to this moment, to his taking this beautiful young woman to be his wife.

The intensity of the sensation had quickly passed. The procession – Emma on her father's arm, two small bridesmaids in a state of imploding excitement – had moved on towards the altar and he had to focus on getting the ritual right, but he was left with an optimism which had remained, unshaken, until the recent drama.

Now, sitting in the church, as the sun shone through the window and the elderly priest took his hand, the sense of well being returned. There was, after all, nothing to be concerned about. The unpleasantness of the last few weeks would pass, and things would go back to normal. He would continue to bring boats safely up the river, then return home to his wife and child. Nothing would disturb the equilibrium of their lives.

He had thought Mary and Robert would be unwilling to face the scrum around the coffee pots and plates of biscuits in the church hall and they did pause for a moment in the porch.

'Would you rather go straight home?' Robert asked

his wife. James had always thought of him as a strong and reliable man. The sort of man to hold his family together. And even immediately after Christopher's death it had seemed he was still playing that role. Today though he appeared indecisive, vague. He wanted Mary to tell him what they should do.

'No,' she said. James saw that Springhead was the last place she wanted to be. 'We'll have a coffee first, shall we?'

Inside the hall she seemed embarrassed to be a customer and was all for rushing into the kitchen to find an apron and begin the washing-up.

'Sit down,' James said. 'I'll bring your drink over.' He stood in the queue and looked at them, holding each other's hands across the Formica table, not speaking. They looked old. Around them the parishioners circled like birds of prey over a carcass, eager to make contact, to give their condolences. To get news.

Emma had stayed in the church after the rest of the congregation had left. She'd whispered to James at the end of the service that she needed time to herself. He respected that. She was very young to have suffered so much. Now she walked into the hall, oblivious to the sympathetic glances, her face pale and still, without expression. He had never been able to tell what she was thinking, and since Christopher's death she had become more distant from him. He disliked violent displays of emotion. There had been too much shouting and raving, too many tears, when he was young. But now he wondered if he should have encouraged her to weep, if when she had asked if they might talk, he should have made it easier for her to confide in him.

He set the cups of coffee in front of his parents-in-law. Two women had plucked up sufficient courage to approach them and Robert seemed to have recovered his spirits under their attention. James went to Emma, who was standing by the window, looking out over the churchyard, twisting a strand of hair around her finger.

'I'd like to invite Robert and Mary to lunch,' he said. 'Would you mind?'

'No.' She seemed surprised to be asked, as if usually he would have made the invitation without consulting her. And perhaps that was true, he thought. Throughout their marriage she'd been so passive that he'd always taken her consent for granted. Had he been more like a father than a lover to her?

In the Captain's House he insisted on preparing lunch. He sat Mary and Robert in the living room and threw some logs onto the embers of the fire. The logs were dry and the bark caught immediately, curling back from the wood and sending sparks up the chimney. The couple stared into the grate, mesmerized, only moving when he handed them a glass of sherry each. Still they weren't talking. Emma was upstairs settling Matthew into his cot for a sleep. A little later he heard her come down. He thought she would join her parents, but instead she came into the kitchen. She came up behind him and kissed his neck.

'Thank you for being so kind to them.'

She slipped away before he could respond and he heard her voice, no more than a murmur, in the other room.

This is who I am, he told himself. A kind man who cares for his family. Perhaps even a good man. There is no deception here.

At the table Robert became more himself again,

brightening as he had earlier, surrounded by people, in the hall. He said grace and complimented James on his cooking. He drank more than he usually did and James was reminded of Christopher's last meal in the house. He had never thought father and son had much in common, but now he could detect a resemblance. A dramatic quality. The possibility of excess.

'Why don't you both stay here for the night?' Emma asked. Mary didn't like driving Robert's car and James saw she thought her father was already over the limit. 'You can go back early tomorrow.'

'No,' Robert said. 'I need to get home. I'd like to go into work tomorrow.'

'Is that wise?' James had never questioned Robert's judgement before and felt rather brave. 'I'm sure they'd understand that you need more time. You could have until Christmas at least. It's hardly worth going back for a few weeks.'

'I'd prefer to be at work. I brood too much at home.' But Robert reached out for the bottle of wine and topped up his glass.

'Besides,' Mary said suddenly, 'if I don't go home today, I'll never face it.' She saw that she'd shocked them. 'I know it's foolish, but that's the way I feel. I'll never be able to walk through the door.'

'Why don't I drive you back later this evening?' James said. 'Then you can stay for a while, relax, have another drink. I'll pick Robert up first thing in the morning so he can collect his car.'

Emma smiled at him and brushed her fingertips over the back of his hand.

Later there was an old film on the television. The room was hot. Robert and Mary both fell asleep. Mary had her mouth slightly open and snored occasionally. Matthew lay on his stomach on the rug surrounded by toys.

'I think the doctor gave them tranquillizers,' Emma said. 'They seem spaced out, don't they? Dad especially. But a bit more relaxed, at least.'

When they woke she made tea for them, and James toasted crumpets in front of the fire. He crouched and held his arm outstretched because the embers were still so hot.

'Comfort food,' Emma said. She watched with satisfaction as Mary finished a mouthful then licked the butter from her fingers. James thought Emma had worn the same expression when she'd persuaded Matthew to take baby rice from a spoon for the first time.

'We should go,' Robert stood up. The tray was still on the floor, the toasting fork lying on the hearth. 'Are you ready, my dear?'

Outside, on the other side of the road, someone was waiting under the bus shelter.

'He'll be there a long time,' James said, hoping to lighten the mood. 'There are no buses on a Sunday. Do you think I should tell him?'

The man turned and stared at them though he couldn't have made out the words. His face was lit by the orange glow of a street light.

'It's Michael Long,' Robert said. James had recognized him at the same instant. 'Perhaps it would be better to leave him alone.'

James went into Springhead with them. He'd always liked the house despite its discomfort and inconvenience. It was where Emma had grown up and there were reminders of her everywhere. School photos, books with her name in, her wellingtons just inside the door. Now, as he stood awkwardly in the kitchen while Robert and Mary fussed with the lights, he wondered how they could bear the gloomy paint, the threadbare carpets, the piles of slightly damp books. He was irritated that they'd never organized the improvements which were needed.

'Will you stay here?' he asked. 'You won't move?'

'Of course not!' Mary spoke as if he'd suggested something unthinkable. 'Where would we go?'

'I'm not sure. You could get somewhere smaller. In the village perhaps. Close to the shops and to Emma . . .' He tailed off as he saw her reaction.

'Impossible,' she said.

'It's just that earlier you seemed reluctant to come back . . .'

'It's painful. But this place is all we have of Christopher now.'

She didn't speak to him again and he thought he'd offended her. Then, as he was getting into his car in the yard, she came running out to him, still in her slippers, a coat thrown over her shoulders.

'Thank you for this afternoon. For lunch. For looking after us so well.'

He wondered if the medication had worn off because she seemed desperate, rather manic.

'No problem. You know you're always welcome.'

'I'd like to do something for you. For you and Emma. She was looking so pale today, didn't you think?'

'It's been a dreadful time for you all.'

'Let me have Matthew for an evening. So you can

353

spend some time on your own together. Go out for a drink perhaps. I'd like to. If you'd trust me.'

'Of course we trust you. Have him whenever you like.'

'Tomorrow then. Bring him here.'

She rushed back to the house and James wondered if Robert had even realized she'd gone.

When James drew up outside the Captain's House, Michael Long was still standing at the bus stop, his hands in his pockets, muffled in his coat. He watched James climb out of the car, held his glance, a sort of challenge. It was too far for James to shout and he started to walk over the road towards him. The church clock began to strike the hour. Michael stood his ground for a moment, then he turned and hurried away towards his bungalow.

Inside Matthew was in bed and Emma was loading the dishwasher.

'Were they all right?' she asked.

'I think so. They're so self-contained, aren't they? It's hard to tell.'

'I thought that's what you admired in them.'

'Perhaps it's not always a good thing.'

'Can we go to bed?' she said.

He felt nervous as if it was the first time. Afraid of doing something wrong, something which would upset her, spoil the mood.

'Of course.'

He was in the bedroom before her, went to close the curtains. Michael Long was back at his post under the bus shelter. He was looking up at the window.

Chapter Forty

Vera Stanhope liked Dan Greenwood, had done since the first time she'd met him at one of those dreadful training days her boss had forced her to attend. All keen young officers behaving like corporate managers, fighting amongst themselves to be most enthusiastic, most positive. No negative talk allowed there. Dan Greenwood had looked at her helplessly across the conference room, with its beech-effect tables and chairs, as if he'd been thrown into the middle of a game and he didn't understand the rules. As if she was the only one there on his side. She'd thought, looking at him, that he shouldn't be caged inside a building at all. Looking at him, scruffy and feral, you'd have thought he should be a gamekeeper, someone used to being outdoors. Perhaps he'd thought that was what the police would be like, keeping things ordered, tidying up vermin.

'Don't worry, pet,' she'd said to him over coffee. 'They don't *mean* any of it. All that positive talk. Back at the station they'll be griping the same as you and me, sloping home early and coming in late.'

'What's the point, then?' he'd said, and she'd thought that he really didn't understand. He had no

355

ambition and no desire to impress. She'd thought then that he was incapable of deception.

That was before she'd seen the file on Abigail Mantel, which he kept in his desk and pored over, like some pervert slobbering over downloaded porn.

Pride had stopped her acting immediately. She couldn't bring herself to believe that she could be *that* wrong about anyone. Then she'd stood in the village and watched him walking with Emma Bennett up the lane from the river, attentive and careful, and she'd seen the way Emma had looked at him. This was another bonny young lass. Not as young as Abigail had been when she'd died, but there were some days when Emma still looked like a teenager. And she'd known Abigail, found the body. Perhaps there was a thrill in that for Dan. You could never tell how some people's minds worked. Not even the psychiatrist could manage that. Or perhaps he wanted to get close to Emma to find out how much she remembered. If he'd had any sort of relationship with the dead girl, he'd want to know if she talked about it before she was killed.

Pride was a terrible thing, Vera thought. It had always let her down.

So she swallowed her pride and went to see Caroline Fletcher. She did it properly too, calling in advance to check if it was convenient. There was no fuss this time when she stood on the doorstep of the desirable executive home, no show.

Caroline had changed from her business suit into jeans and a baggy jumper which reached almost to her knees. The boyfriend was nowhere to be seen and Vera didn't ask after him. He'd be playing squash, she thought. Or staying late at the office. Something normal. In the living room there was a bottle of white wine standing in a cooler on the floor by the armchair, one glass taken out of it. Caroline had been holding the glass when she opened the door.

'Would you like some?' she said, seeming ready to build bridges herself.

Vera preferred red, but it would have been churlish to refuse.

'What's this about?' The woman's voice was cautious but not unfriendly.

'Dan Greenwood,' Vera said.

'What about him?'

'What did you make of him?' Caroline looked at her without answering and Vera was forced to elaborate. 'You worked closely with him. Did you ever have any concerns? I mean, did the breakdown come out of the blue?'

'I'm not a doctor.'

'As a colleague. A friend.'

'I wasn't expecting it,' Caroline said. 'He seemed to be holding it together. Perhaps, though, it was inevitable. He let things get to him, took them to heart.' She paused. 'I don't think he's stupid, but he wasn't really up to the job. The politics, the games you have to play. The rules you have to keep to or bend. He says what he means and he can't understand when other people don't do the same. He talked about resigning at the same time as me. I shouldn't have discouraged it.'

'You'd resigned before he went on sick leave?'

'Yes. Getting Jeanie Long to court was the last thing I did.' She paused. 'Everyone said I was going out on a high.'

'How soon after the court case was Dan's illness?'

'I'm not sure. It's hard to judge time when you look back from this distance. It all becomes a bit of a blur. Not long though. A couple of months. Six at the most. You could check. Personnel might still have it on file. Someone there would probably remember better than me.'

'I don't really want to make it official. Not yet.'

Vera sipped the wine which was still cold and very dry. Caroline looked at her over her glass. 'What's all this about?' she said again, more forcefully, meaning, *Cut the crap, lady. I've played these games too in my time.*

'Are you sleeping with him?' Vera asked, matter of fact.

'No!' Caroline gave a hoot of laughter, so spontaneous and joyful Vera knew it was genuine. 'Where did you get that idea?'

'We all get daft notions in our heads from time to time.'

'You didn't come out here just to ask me that.'

For a moment Vera didn't respond. In this investigation, she'd started off thinking she couldn't trust this woman as far as she could throw her. It came hard now to pass on information she hadn't even shared with Joe Ashworth.

'Dan Greenwood has a file on the Mantel case. He keeps it in his desk at the pottery, takes it out and reads it every now and again. It could mean anything. Guilt because he didn't stand up to you over the Jeanie Long arrest. Nostalgia for a time when he was part of a team and he had friends – he seems a bit of a loner now. Or it could be more sinister. Some sort of trophy, maybe. It could mean he killed her.'

Caroline listened carefully. She didn't dismiss the

idea out of hand. She knew what it had cost Vera to be there.

'What's in the file?'

Vera shrugged. 'I didn't have much of a chance to look. Duplicates of the case papers and the investigation log. A duplicate of the post-mortem report. Post-mortem photographs. A glossy picture of the girl before she died, looking dressed up and glamorous.'

'We might have asked Keith for a photo for publicity,' Caroline said quickly. 'An appeal through the media asking for witnesses to come forward. It doesn't mean Dan knew her before she died.'

'I thought you didn't bother much with that sort of publicity. You took Jeanie Long into custody pretty quickly.'

'It doesn't mean we didn't make other plans at the beginning . . .'

'Do you remember asking Keith for a photo?'

'No, but I wouldn't after all this time.'

'Strange, anyway, Dan holding onto it for ten years.'

'Yes,' Caroline said. 'Perhaps.' She poured herself another glass and waved the bottle towards Vera, who shook her head. She'd wait until she got back to the hotel, then have a proper drink. They sat again in silence.

'What happened to the clothes Abigail was wearing when she died?' Vera asked.

'God knows. After all this time . . . Why do you want to know?'

'No reason.'

Caroline looked at her suspiciously, but didn't push it. 'Dan was a bit of a loner even then. I mean friendly enough, a part of the team, no one ever minded being partnered up with him, but not really one of the lads. Do you know what I mean?'

Vera nodded. He wouldn't get pissed with them. He wouldn't swear about the bosses, or get sentimental and pour out his heart.

'Has he ever been married? I didn't check that either.'

'God, no.' Caroline considered, then added. 'I don't know why that should seem so unthinkable. I suppose he didn't seem the type. And he never mentioned anyone.'

'Gay?'

'No.' Then after more thought, 'At least I don't think so.'

'He fancied you, didn't he?'

'Probably, but you get used to that. A woman in a team of men who feel the job's screwed up all the other relationships in their lives. After a while it's not flattering any more.'

I'd be flattered, Vera thought. *Trust me.*

'You never felt threatened by his attentions?'

'Not once.'

'Is there any way he could have got to know Abigail socially?'

'I can't think of one.'

'Perhaps you invited him to one of Keith's parties?'

'None of my colleagues knew about Keith. We were very discreet.'

'Dan guessed. During the investigation.'

'Did he? He never said.' Caroline seemed amused rather than surprised.

'Where was Dan living when Abigail was murdered?'

'In Crill. He had a flat in one of those big terraced houses on the seafront. I picked him up from there a couple of times.'

'Did you ever go in?'

'Once or twice. Sometimes he wasn't ready if I was early to collect him for a job. Once he asked me in for a beer at the end of a shift.'

'What was it like in there?'

'Bloody cold,' she said. 'It had old sash windows that let in all the draughts.' She looked sharply at Vera. 'There weren't any photos of naked schoolgirls on the walls, if that's what you mean.'

'Did you see inside his bedroom?'

'No. I've told you. We weren't on those terms.'

Well then, Vera thought.

She said, 'Abigail was at school in Crill, wasn't she?'

'Yes, and the bus took her straight there and brought her straight back in the evening.'

'Except when she bunked off.'

'What are you saying?' Caroline demanded. 'That Dan Greenwood picked her up on the street and had sex with her?'

'I'm investigating possibilities.' Vera stretched out and put her empty glass on the table. There was a moment of silence, then she said, 'Is he that sort? Into young girls?'

'Most of the men I've ever known have been that sort. They see a schoolgirl walking down the street, fifteen or sixteen years old, face plastered in make-up, uniform, short skirt, they look. It doesn't mean they do anything.'

'Did Dan Greenwood look?'

'I don't know!' Caroline was losing patience. 'I'm just saying.'

'What sort of family does he come from?'

'What!'

'Humour me.'

Caroline looked at her as if she should be locked up, but answered anyway. 'He's an only child. I think his parents were getting on when they had him. His father was already dead when he joined the team. He was close to his mum, but I think she's died since. Money from the sale of her house gave him the cash to start the pottery. Is that enough for you?'

'Aye,' Vera said. 'It'll do.'

'He was a good policeman. Sometimes I thought he took it all too seriously. You could imagine him going home and thinking about work all evening and dreaming it at night. A bit intense, I suppose, and that worried me. He saw everything in black and white. But he worked on other cases involving young girls and I never had any concerns about how he handled them. There was no talk among the team, no complaints from the public.'

Vera hoisted herself to her feet. She should have been pleased. Caroline had told her what she wanted to hear. But still she felt bad tempered, edgy.

At the door Caroline started talking again. It was as if she had continued thinking about Dan and like Vera felt that there were still things to say.

'I'm not very good at summing people up,' she said. 'I mean it's so hard to tell. You look at someone and they do something a bit odd, but they could be shy or weird or dangerous. How do you know? The most dangerous man I ever met looked as if he wouldn't hurt anyone.'

'I'd have put Dan Greenwood down as harmless,' Vera muttered. 'So what does that mean?'

'I could imagine him killing someone,' Caroline said. 'If he thought it was the right thing to do. The lesser of two evils. But I'd say the same about most of the men I worked with.'

She shut the door then. Vera stood for a moment on the step, looking down the sloping front garden into the street. In the house opposite the curtains were still not drawn and two children were lying on their stomachs in front of the television. In the distance a car alarm was ringing. Standing there, considering Caroline's words, she had another sudden goshawk moment, a brief glimpse of the whole picture. She walked on slowly to her car.

She and Joe Ashworth had dinner that night in the hotel. They'd only managed it a couple of times before. Usually the restaurant was already closed when they got in and they'd made do with takeaways in the car or bags of chips. Tonight they only just made it in time. Everyone else was already onto puddings or coffee and the room emptied as they ate. There was no one to overhear. The waitresses were in end-of-shift mood and stood by the desk chatting and giggling. The sweet trolley had been reduced to three sad profiteroles, some browning fruit salad and half a trifle.

Vera told him about finding the Mantel file in Dan Greenwood's desk. 'I'm sorry, I shouldn't have kept it to myself.'

'Do you want to get a warrant? Have a proper look round?'

She sat for so long in silence that he was about to repeat the question. 'No,' she said at last. 'No need. I had a bit of a poke about myself.' She explained about her search of the house in the Crescent, felt like a guilty kid.

Ashworth looked at her as if she should know better. 'How do you want to handle it?'

'We'll keep it to ourselves for the time being. No need to tell the Yorkies. We don't want the rumours flying if there's nothing to it. There's nothing to link him to the Winter case. But we'll keep an eye on him. I'll go and have a chat tomorrow. See if I pick up on anything.'

'What do you want me to do?'

'I've got something special for you. A bit of a fishing trip. An away day. You'll love it.'

Chapter Forty-One

Emma drove Matthew to Springhead. Arriving at the house, she sat for a moment in the car, reluctant to take him inside. She wasn't sure now that she wanted to let him out of her sight. Would her parents be able to cope with him?

Inside though, Mary was looking out for them. She must have heard the car and the kitchen curtain was pulled aside. Emma saw her silhouetted against the yellow light and imagined her peering into the darkness. She gathered Matthew into her arms and prepared to be cheerful. Inside, her parents were drinking tea, pretending not to be waiting.

'I've expressed some milk so I don't have to hurry back,' Emma said in a jolly voice she hardly recognized as her own. She handed the baby to Robert. She wanted to say, *He's only a loan. Not a replacement for Christopher. Not yours to keep.* But that would have been foolish.

Back at the Captain's House, she and James sat awkwardly at the kitchen table. She thought there was a peculiar restraint between them, a shyness. They were like a couple in a Victorian novel who had escaped the chaperone, though Matthew could hardly count as a chaperone. Now they were alone they weren't quite sure how to proceed.

'What would you like to do?' James asked. 'I could cook for you. We could go out for a quiet meal.'

'I'm not sure I want quiet,' she said. 'There's been too much of that recently. Noise would be good. Music. Talk. Would you really hate it if we just went for a drink in the Anchor?'

'People will want to ask about Christopher,' he said. 'You know what they're like. You won't mind?'

'No. I think I'd like it. It seems healthier somehow than pretending it didn't happen. There might be people who knew him there. Friends from school.'

'It could be a sort of wake?'

'Yes,' she said gratefully. 'Exactly that.'

She went upstairs to run a bath. The oil she used had sandalwood in it and patchouli. He'd teased her when she first used it, called her a hippy, but she'd never been the sort to camp out at Glastonbury and hadn't known what he was on about until he explained. On his way to the bedroom to change, he stopped on the landing and looked in on her. She'd propped open the door to let out the steam. The bathtub was old, made of a hard, stained enamel. It was very deep. She'd lit candles on the window sill and their scent mixed with the bath oil. She'd already washed her hair and tied it in a thin silk scarf in a knot on the top of her head. She lay back in the water, allowing her legs to float and her eyes to shut. Then she opened her eyes and saw him there, staring at her.

'Come in,' she said. He seemed poised to make an announcement. There was a long silence. She thought he was composing a sentence in his head and wondered what he could have to say. Suddenly he seemed to lose his nerve.

'I'll leave you in peace,' he said. 'Let you relax.' But the moment was spoilt for her and she climbed from the tub.

She made special preparations to go out, although they were only going across the road to the pub and she wasn't dressing up. She'd already put jeans and the striped jersey she'd bought on her last trip to town on the chair. She came into the bedroom wrapped in a big bath towel, and sat in front of the dressing table. She used straighteners on her hair after drying it, her eyes fixed on the mirror. The towel slipped when she raised her arms above her head and she had to fasten it again. Then she took time to apply her make-up. Throughout, she was aware of James sitting on the bed and watching her.

She waited for him to come behind her and touch her, but he sat, quite still, watching. She felt breathless, light-headed. *Let's stay here*, she was tempted to say. *Let's not bother to go out. I'm making all this effort for you.* But the same shyness prevented her and anyway she thought she would enjoy the anticipation, being in the same room as him surrounded by people, aware of his eyes on her, knowing that soon they would come back here.

She caught his eye in the mirror and smiled.

'Well?' she asked. 'Will I do?'

'You're fishing for compliments.' Now he did stand behind her. He reached out and stroked her neck. She caught her breath, but didn't give herself away.

'No, really. I've never been sure I'm doing it right and I'm out of practice.'

'You look lovely,' he said. 'Really.'

'It's warpaint, of course. I'm quite nervous about facing people. I need something to hide behind.'

'Hide behind me,' he said. She caught his eye again and they laughed together at the soppiness. She felt herself relax.

By the time they arrived at the Anchor all the regulars were there. James opened the door to let Emma in first. She paused when inside to see if there was anyone she recognized. A group of kids had gathered around the pool table. She thought she'd seen them waiting for the school bus. Certainly they didn't seem old enough to be drinking, but in these country towns what else was there for kids to do? Of course she'd never had the option of the pub. She remembered long, boring evenings at Springhead. Until she'd gone away to college her only entertainment had been the church youth club under the watchful eye of her father.

Their entrance had been noticed. Some of the lifeboatmen were playing darts and they stopped for a moment to nod towards James. Veronica behind the bar smiled at Emma, trying to hide her surprise. Veronica was familiar to them both. She came to church, not as a regular worshipper but on special occasions, Easter Sunday, midnight Mass on Christmas Eve. She always donated a couple of bottles for the summer fayre. Her son had been to school with Christopher. They'd been in the same class. Emma struggled now to remember his name.

'How's Ray?' It had come to her suddenly.

'He's fine.'

'What's he doing these days?' Emma wondered how

she was performing. She wasn't used to this sort of conversation any more.

'He's joined the fire brigade. Leeds. Of course he was never as clever as your Christopher, but we're very proud of him.' She paused. 'I'm so sorry about what happened, love. We all are.'

'I know,' Emma said. 'I know.'

'Have the police got anyone for it yet?' Barry had appeared suddenly from the back. He stood with his hands flat on the bar and he stared at Emma. The question shot out, without politeness or preamble.

'They haven't said.'

'It's a disgrace,' Barry said and Emma couldn't tell whether he considered the murder a disgrace, or the police's inability to find a suspect, or the lack of communication.

One of the darts players who'd come to the bar for another round muttered his agreement.

'Have these on me,' James said. 'In memory, you know, of Chris.'

Half an hour later and there was as much noise as Emma could have wished. The kids had put something on the jukebox and in the other bar they were watching football on the wide screen and occasionally the cheers and groans were loud enough to swamp the music.

She sat by the window chatting to one of the lifeboatmen's girlfriends. Someone else who'd been to school with her. She heard the woman talking about a new bloke, a whirlwind romance, a proposal, but all the time she was aware of James, standing at the bar, looking at her. What does he want from me? she thought. What does he want to say?

Then the door opened and Michael Long walked in. He let the door swing to behind him, but there was so much noise that no one took much notice. He walked with a swagger to the bar. Emma couldn't hear the conversation, but guessed James was offering to buy the man a drink. She thought he had already been drinking. He looked dishevelled and unsteady.

'You've got a nerve.'

She could just make out the words and sensed the hostility; it was palpable, like a smell. She watched, horrified. The chatter beside her continued. James obviously hadn't heard and must have asked Michael to repeat himself.

Michael opened his mouth wide and roared, so everyone could hear him, even above the racket. 'I said, you've got a bloody nerve.'

The conversation faded. On the jukebox the record came to an end and no one replaced it. From the other bar there was a round of sarcastic applause as a penalty was missed. Michael seemed pleased to be the centre of attention. He turned to them all with a theatrical gesture. 'You wouldn't be drinking with him if you knew what I know.'

Veronica leaned across the bar. 'You're not well, love. Maybe you should get yourself home.'

Michael appeared not to hear her. 'Do you know who you're drinking with? Do you? You all think you know him, don't you? Family man, pilot, church-goer. Well his whole life's a lie. Even the name's made up.' Michael began to speak more quietly, almost as if he and James were alone together in a small room, but Emma could hear him. The bar was silent. Everyone was watching and listening. He didn't need to shout. 'It shouldn't have happened like this. I was going to get more evidence then go to that inspector. But I couldn't stand it, seeing you in here, laughing and talking. Everyone feeling sorry for you.'

'The inspector already knows,' James said. 'I told her.'

For a moment Michael couldn't take that in. He stared, open-mouthed, a fleck of saliva on his lower lip, trying to convince himself that James was lying.

'Why hasn't she arrested you, then?'

'I've done nothing wrong. It's not illegal to change your name.'

'But you were a friend of Mantel's. I've seen photos. The two of you smiling together.'

'My father was Mantel's friend,' James said. 'He was nothing to do with me.'

Michael shook his head as if it would take violence to clear his thoughts. 'You killed the girl and got my Jeanie locked up.' His voice was desperate. 'You must be involved. Why would you live a lie like this if you didn't have anything to hide?'

'I've reason enough to hate Keith Mantel,' James said, 'but I didn't kill his daughter.'

Veronica had come out from the bar and now she came up to Michael and put her arm around his shoulder. 'You're not yourself, love. Not surprising all the things you've been through. Come into the back with me. I'll make you a hot drink and we'll get the doctor to have a look at you.'

Michael allowed himself to be led away. Behind the bar, Barry's eyes were darting from one person to another, glittering with pleasure.

Emma was frozen. Her reactions had slowed, shut

down. She watched James approach her but she couldn't move.

'Come home,' he said quietly. 'We can't talk here.'

This is what happens, she thought, when you let down your guard. How can I make a happy ending out of this?

'Come home,' he said again. She felt the staring faces and prying eyes. She stood up and followed him out. But once they'd crossed the road she stopped on the pavement and faced up to him. Branches from the tree beside their house blew across the street light and threw moving shadows onto her upturned face.

'Was any of that true?'

'Some of it. I changed my name when I was twenty-one. Legally. There were reasons. I can tell you, if you want to know.'

'What about your family? Are they really all dead?'

'Not all of them.'

'So you lied to me from the beginning.'

'No. By the time I met you, this is who I was.'

'Did you kill my brother?'

'No,' he cried. 'Why would I?'

'Why would you lie to me?'

She couldn't face it. She needed the comfort of a familiar story. She turned suddenly and ran back across the street towards the forge.

Emma runs across the square and, keeping to the shadows in case the drinkers in the Anchor are still watching, she reaches the forge. She pushes open one of the big doors which form an arch, like the door of a church, and she stands inside. The roof is high and she can see through the curved rafters to the tiles. She feels the heat of the kiln and sees the dusty shelves holding unglazed pots.

At first, it seems that the pottery is empty. Everything is quiet. She shuts the big door behind her, still making no noise. It stands a little ajar, but a person walking past on the square outside would see nothing but a strip of light. She walks slowly forward. She knows that Dan is here. She can sense it. Soon he will come out. He will take her into his arms. He will come with her to Springhead so she can be with her baby. She can't face all this alone.

'Dan.' The word is strained, like a whimper, but still it echoes around the high space. 'Are you there, Dan?'

From the little storeroom there comes a scrabbling. Hardly human. It makes Emma think of rats nosing through rubbish.

'Dan,' she says again, and then he does appear, as she has always imagined, crumpled and untidy and eager to see her. She stands very close to him and can smell the clay on his hands. She waits for him to touch her. As she looks up, she sees someone else framed in the storeroom door. Not the inspector this time. Someone altogether unexpected.

Chapter Forty-Two

After seeing Ashworth off on his fishing trip, Vera went to the pottery. The doors were closed and padlocked. It was still early so she drove to the little house on the Crescent where Dan lived, but when she knocked on the door, no one answered. A young woman, with a toddler in a buggy, came out of the house next door. Just as well she'd been out the day before, Vera thought.

'Mr Greenwood won't be in at all today,' the woman said. 'A trade fair. Harrogate. He left very early and he's not back until this evening, then he'll have to go to the pottery to unload.'

'Oh,' Vera said. 'Right.' She was surprised that Dan had given away so much. She'd always thought of him as being very private. The woman was attractive in a pale, washed-out way. Perhaps they were more than neighbours. Perhaps she wore black sequinned pants, though Vera couldn't really picture it.

'Is it business?' the young woman said. 'I can always take a message.'

'No, no message. I'm an old friend. I'll call again.'

She spent the rest of the day at headquarters in Crill. She breezed into Holness's office. 'Can I borrow one of your people for an hour or two. A bit of research.'

He looked up from a desk piled with paper. Worse than hers, she saw with satisfaction. 'Is it urgent?' He was probing for information on the Mantel enquiry. Well, he'd get nothing from her.

'It'll not take long. A few phone calls, a bit of sniffing around.'

'I'll need more than that before I release someone,' he said.

'Bugger off then, I'll do it myself.' She flashed him a grin and he didn't know how to react.

She walked into the incident room, responding to the stare of the officer at the nearest computer with a wave. 'Don't mind me, pet. You'll not know I'm here.'

She found herself a spare desk and a phone and began a lot of fruitless conversations with the manufacturers of ladies' underwear. At the same time she was eavesdropping on the Winter enquiry. The way she saw things, they hadn't much to go on. They were still trying to trace the details of Christopher's mobile, but he hadn't bothered registering it, and they hadn't found anyone in Aberdeen who had the number. He'd never given the number to Emma, or to his parents, which Vera thought was odd. After an hour she got bored and went back to pester Holness. She leaned on his door frame and looked into his office.

'Did anything come of the search of that farm by the cemetery?'

'The lad was there,' Holness said. 'There was a fingerprint on the door of the stable.'

'Did you find anything to suggest he met someone?'

'A couple of other prints both left by one other person. No one known to us. Might be useful if we ever get as far as pulling in a suspect.'

'And he wasn't seen all day?'

'We think he must have hidden out in the farm until it got dark. Otherwise he'd have been noticed. Elvet's that sort of place. Nosy.'

Halfway through the afternoon she cracked and phoned Ashworth. She'd been thinking about him since he'd left in the morning. It was clear he couldn't talk without being overheard. He sounded pleased with himself, though, and she wished she'd taken on the job. Delegation was supposed to be about shipping out the crap, but she'd never seemed to have got the hang of it. Usually she was left with that stuff herself. She went back to the hotel, had a long bath and tried to contain her impatience.

Her phone rang at about eight thirty and she snatched it from the bedside cupboard, thinking it would be Joe Ashworth at last with some news. It was Paul Holness and disappointment made her lose concentration for a moment. She missed what he was saying because she was wondering what could have happened to Joe.

'Sorry,' she said, 'it's a terrible line. Would you mind repeating that?'

'We've just had a phone call from Veronica Lee, the landlady at the Anchor. It seems Michael Long's made some sort of scene there. He's in a bit of a state, she says. Wants to speak to you. We could send one of our lads if you like, but I thought you might want to go. Jeanie's dad, isn't he? Nothing really to do with us.'

'Yes,' she said. 'Probably best if I do it. He knows

me.' She thought she was a sad old bat, because a phone call like that could suddenly make her come alive.

She parked in the square and noticed that there was a light on in the Old Forge. She hesitated briefly, tempted to go there first to talk to Dan. But that could wait, she thought. He wouldn't be leaving the village again tonight. She'd best see what had rattled Michael's cage first. There was no sign of drama in the Anchor when she went in. Half a dozen kids were gathered round the pool table, a few middle-aged couples sat at the tables in the window, two large-bellied men were playing darts. They stared at her, then looked away. By now everyone in the village knew who she was.

'Veronica about?'

The barman was thin and spotty and scarcely looked more than a boy himself.

'She's out the back. She said to go on in.' The short side of the bar was hinged. He lifted it for her to go through. She felt a sudden thrill to be there, standing behind the bar between the taps and the optics. It was like going backstage at a theatre. She imagined herself retired, running a small pub in a village in the hills, but knew it would never happen. She'd offend the customers and drink all the profits.

She'd thought the door behind the bar would lead through to the landlady's living quarters, but she emerged into a kitchen where, earlier in the evening, bar meals had been cooked. The sink was full of dirty pans. Michael sat at the table looking dazed. A half-drunk cup of tea, with a film already forming on the top, stood in front of him. Veronica was looking at him anxiously. A man with pebbly eyes stood leaning against the counter looking down at them. He was eating a cheese roll and his mouth was half full.

'You'd best go back, Barry,' Veronica said. 'Someone needs to keep an eye on the bar.'

'Sam'll manage.'

'No,' she said. 'He won't. I'll not be long myself. Michael doesn't need an audience.'

Barry seemed inclined to argue again, but she shot him a look and he slouched off, still clutching the cheese roll.

'What's all this about, then?' Vera said. She realized she was speaking as if Michael was an invalid or a naughty child and tried again. 'They said you wanted to talk to me.'

He looked up and seemed to recognize her for the first time.

'I found out about that pilot. He used to know Mantel, changed his name. I imagined all sorts. You know the way your mind can work. He was in here tonight with that young wife of his.' The words tumbled over themselves. He looked at her fearfully, anticipating her disapproval. She saw that he'd fallen apart since she'd last seen him. Jeanie's death had finally caught up with him.

'Did you tell her what you'd found out?' she asked. 'Don't worry. It wouldn't be the end of the world.'

'He told the whole bar,' Veronica said. 'Made a bit of a scene. I should have realized what sort of strain he was under. I thought he was coping. I've called the doctor.'

Vera took a seat beside Michael. 'You should have

come to me. I'd have explained.' *But what?* she thought. *What could I have told him?*

'It was Mantel, wasn't it?' Michael said, desperately. 'He was behind it all.'

Again, she didn't know what to answer. 'It won't be long now,' she said. 'This time tomorrow we should have someone in custody. It'll not bring Jeanie back . . .'

He finished the sentence for her. 'But I'll know . . .' For a moment he seemed to be more himself. Veronica reached across the table and took his hand.

Out in the square, Vera stood to collect her thoughts. A dog or a fox had been at a bin and scraps of rubbish blew across the street. They wouldn't like that, the respectable people of Elvet. They liked their muck firmly shut away. She walked to the Captain's House and banged on the door. James opened it almost immediately. At first she misinterpreted his anxiety.

'Sorry,' she said. 'I should have thought before making that noise. I'd forgotten there was a baby in the house.'

'No, Matthew's not here. Robert and Mary are looking after him. I thought you were Emma.'

'Where is she?'

'There was a scene in the pub. She ran off.' He hesitated. 'You were right, of course. I should have told her myself.'

'Where's she gone? To her parents?'

'No. The car's still here.'

'And you just let her go off by herself?' *In the dark? A week after her brother was murdered?*

'She's quite safe,' he said. 'I saw where she went. She ran over to the forge. Dan will look after her.'

'Why did she go to Dan?'

'I suppose she needed someone to talk to. He's my friend. Perhaps she thought he'd understand, make her understand. Perhaps she thought I'd discussed it with him.'

'Are they close, the two of them?'

'No,' he cried. 'Not like that.'

'I'll go over,' she said. 'See what's going on.'

'I'll come with you.'

'Best not. Give her a chance to think about it. Mind, I work for the police, not marriage guidance. I'll not try to persuade her either way.' *If she's there. Alive and safe.*

Back on the pavement she saw at once that there was now no light in the forge. She thought there had been when she'd left the pub, but she'd not heard a car leaving when she'd been talking to James. Standing just inside the hall, the door still open, she'd have heard, might even have heard the big doors being shut to, the snap of the padlock. She remembered what Dan's young neighbour had said about his unloading after the trade fair. Perhaps there'd been a van parked in the yard in the back. Perhaps they'd left in that. But where would he take her?

All this she was thinking as she hurried across to the pottery, and then came the fanciful thought that she was like a piece of rubbish, blown backwards and forwards across the square.

The doors were bolted inside, but not padlocked. She banged on them with the flat of her hand, rattling them until her palms were stinging, but there was no reply and she moved on down the street, looking for a way into the yard at the back.

Access was through a tunnel, which cut through a terrace of houses. It led to an alley where domestic cars were parked. At the end of the alley was a set of wooden gates, now propped open, and the yard at the back of the pottery. There were no street lights in the alley, but it was lit from the windows at the back of the houses. This was considered private space and many hadn't bothered to shut curtains. She had brief glimpses of ordinary lives: a mother hanging nappies on a radiator, an elderly man washing-up. In another room a young couple sat after a late supper, the kitchen table transformed for romance with a paper tablecloth, a candle and a bottle of wine.

The yard behind the pottery was empty. If Dan had been there with a van, he'd already gone. He must have Emma with him, unless he'd left her inside. Vera had a picture of her in the dusty storeroom, tied perhaps, scared, but she couldn't bring herself to believe it. Was she dead already? Strangled like her brother and her best friend? Vera shook her head, trying to clear away the nightmare. She wiped dust and cobwebs from the narrow windowpane with her sleeve and peered in, but it was dark inside and impossible to see. There was a small back door. She tried that, but it was locked. The paint was peeling from it, but the wood was sound and she wasn't sure she'd have the strength to break in. She leaned her shoulder against it and shoved. Nothing moved. She thumped on the door then put her ear to it and listened. There was no sound. She gave up.

James was watching from his window. As she

approached the house the curtain fell back into place but she'd seen his white face pressed against the glass and the door opened before she knocked.

'She's not there, is she? I can tell the place is all locked up.'

'Has she got a mobile phone?'

She watched panic flash across his face. 'Like Christopher, you mean? You think there's some connection?'

'No,' she said. 'Not like Christopher. You could call her. Find out where she's gone.'

He gave an embarrassed laugh, lifted the phone in the hall and dialled. Vera realized they were both holding their breath, that she was straining to hear Emma's voice. From the kitchen came an electronic tune. Something lively which she recognized. Something from an old film. *The Entertainer.* Slowly James replaced the receiver. 'That's her mobile,' he said. 'She must have left it here. Probably thought she wouldn't need it in the pub. She knew I had mine with me.' He paused, made an effort to hold himself together. 'She'll be all right with Dan, though. He used to be a policeman.'

'Yes,' Vera said. 'I know.'

She left him in the house. Someone had to be there, she said. Emma couldn't come home and find the place empty. Besides, Dan might talk some sense into her. She would probably phone.

She sat in the car, knowing that James would be watching and expecting immediate action. People were coming out of the pub though it wasn't quite closing time. Every time the door opened, there was a blast of music like cold air. She didn't know where to go or what to do. There was the baby to think of too. It wasn't like her to be indecisive and the lack of direction made her anxious, the first stage of panic. Her phone rang and she punched the button, glad to be distracted for the moment at least.

It was Ashworth. 'You were right,' he said. 'But then you always are.'

No, she thought. *Not any more. My judgement's worth nothing these days. I thought I was sure about Dan Greenwood. Once.*

'Where are you?' she asked.

'On my way to the house. That's what you want, is it?'

Is it? 'Yes.'

'I'll see you there, shall I?'

'Yes,' she said again, more quickly, glad that the decision had been made for her.

'Are you all right?'

'Of course,' she said. 'Of course.'

Chapter Forty-Three

Ashworth was sitting in his car at the end of the drive to Springhead. Vera pulled into a gateway leading into a small patch of woodland and walked down the road to join him. There was a smell of wet leaves and cows. She felt better, though anxiety about Emma had settled at the pit of her stomach, a dull ache. She couldn't cope with breaking more bad news. And she couldn't cope with being wrong about what had happened here. She climbed into the passenger seat. Joe was listening to the radio. Classic FM. He was doing an evening class in music appreciation. She reached over and switched it off.

'Well?' she said.

'I did as you suggested, talked to the neighbours. It wasn't very useful at first. Most of them had moved in since the Winters left. It's one of those classy areas where everyone's too busy to wonder what's going on behind closed doors. Big houses, lots of garden. Then I tracked down one elderly woman who remembered them. "A lovely family," she said. "Such a shame when they moved."' He put on an old lady's voice, high pitched, with a BBC accent. Vera thought he'd be good in the local panto. He could play the dame.

Joe went on. 'She was a widow even then and she

used to babysit for the Winters when the kids were small. Until they stopped asking. She'd been upset by that, wondered if she'd done something wrong, if the children had taken against her for some reason. It troubled her so much that she went to see Mary. "Of course I was worrying quite unnecessarily. One of Robert's colleagues had a daughter who needed the money. It was only natural that they should ask her instead."'

'Ah,' Vera said. A sigh of relief and satisfaction.

'The colleague's name is Maggie Sullivan. There'd only been four of them working together. Three architects and someone to run the office. Two of them – an architect and the office manager – had been close to retirement, a bit old to have teenage daughters, so it wasn't hard to work out she was the most likely. She's still working in York. When I explained what I was there for, she was only too pleased to see me. She felt guilty because she hadn't gone to the police when it happened.'

'And what, exactly, did happen?'

'Robert Winter became obsessed with the daughter. He followed her around, waited for her outside school. Made a real nuisance of himself.' Ashworth paused. 'How did you know?'

'I didn't. Not really. But there had to be something to make them change their lives so dramatically.' *And there was something about him, something that made my flesh crawl. And the psychiatrist said someone sufficiently controlled could get away with it.*

'To make him turn to God?'

'Aye, I suppose . . .' She nodded towards the house. 'What's happening in there?'

'I don't know. It's been quiet while I've been here.'

'You've not seen Emma Bennett go in?'

'No, but I've only just arrived.'

'She's had a row with her husband and gone missing.' Vera explained about Michael Long and the scene in the Anchor. 'Probably nothing, but I've got a nasty feeling about it.'

'It can't be significant, can it?' He turned to her easily. He thought he knew now exactly who'd killed Abigail and Christopher. She didn't answer immediately. Now it came to it, she wasn't sure any more.

'Maybe not.'

'How do you want to play it?' he said. 'We could wait until morning, get a warrant. The boy's mobile has still not been found. If that's in there, we've got a result.'

Vera thought she couldn't stand to wait until morning. She hated this case. She hated all the pretending, the unfinished grieving, the foul, flat country. She wanted to be home. Besides, there was Emma and the bairn to consider.

'Why don't we go in?'

'Now?'

'No big deal. A few informal questions. And we've got an excuse. We're looking for Emma.'

'What if we scare him away?'

'I don't think that's likely, do you?'

Ashworth considered for a moment. 'No,' he said. 'Someone like that, he wants to be caught.'

Vera didn't think Joe had got that quite right, but she was still hoping to persuade him to bend a few rules, so she didn't say anything.

Ashworth reached for the key to turn on the engine, but she stopped him.

'We'll walk in. Don't want to give any warning.'

And she needed time to work it all out. Not so much that, to psyche herself up, to believe again that she was up to the job. To forget that moment of panic outside the Captain's House. They walked up the straight, flat drive to the house and their eyes got used to the dark, so after a while they didn't need Joe Ashworth's torch. It was a clear night. It might freeze later, like the night Christopher was killed. Would Robert and Mary be looking out at the stars, remembering? There was enough light from the traffic passing on the road and the moon. To their right, the coast was marked by the red lamp on the pilot mast and ahead of them were two orange squares, one above the other. One downstairs and one upstairs window in the ugly square house. Another sort of beacon.

The curtains at the kitchen window weren't drawn, and Vera stood, pressed against the wall so she couldn't be seen from inside, looking in. Robert and Mary were sitting at the kitchen table. Mary stood up, took a pan of milk from the Aga and poured it into mugs. Only two mugs, Vera saw. Something of the panic returned. Where was Emma? From another room there came a noise, a howl.

Then Emma walked in and Vera felt her pulse slow. She was carrying a screaming baby on her hip and her eyes were red from crying. Mary offered to take Matthew from her, but she held onto him. She paced up and down, rubbing his back until the cries subsided, then she took her place at the table. Immediately Robert started to talk to her.

All this talk, Vera thought. Everyone sitting around telling stories to justify themselves or shift the guilt. She wondered what could have happened. Had Emma been to the pottery at all? Perhaps Dan had given her a lift. Another story, Vera thought. More explanations. Emma had come to Springhead to collect the baby of course, not to talk to her parents. She'd never confided in them.

She continued to stand there in the yard looking in. Outside was the huge winter sky, which made you dizzy just to think of it, inside a small family drama, a soap opera. And she was in the middle. Even if they'd been able to make out her shadow in the darkness, she thought they wouldn't have noticed. They were engrossed in conversation and she could hear everything which was going on. Springhead House had never run to double glazing.

Mary was talking now. 'I don't understand,' she said. 'Why would James do such a thing?'

'I don't understand either. He lied to me. What else is there to know? If Mr Long hadn't dug up his past he probably never would have told me.'

'Shouldn't you ask him?'

'Perhaps he lied because he killed Abigail. I don't want to hear that.'

'That's ridiculous,' Mary said. 'James changed his name. It doesn't make him a different person. He didn't lie about anything important. And you married him, you had his child. It's not something you can just walk out of. You can't run away.' She was clutching the big patchwork bag on her knee as if she had a baby of her own.

'Why not? Isn't that what he did? He didn't like who he was, so he ran away.'

'You should phone him,' Robert said. 'He'll be worried.'

'Good.' Emma could have been fifteen again, defiant, determined to get her own way. Vera thought she must have had exactly that expression before she set off to meet Abigail in the Old Chapel, venting her fury in her battle against the wind. 'I hope he's desperate with worry.'

Vera walked away from the window and knocked on the kitchen door. Not too loud. The state of their nerves, she'd give them all heart attacks. But they'd probably think it was James. She imagined them staring at each other, trying to decide who should answer. Eventually, Emma opened the door. That would be what the parents had wanted, Vera thought. They always knew what was best for her, and they always got their way. The young woman stood in the doorway, still holding the baby, glaring out at them.

'I can't believe James got you involved with this,' Emma said. 'It's not police business. Nothing to do with you.'

'He was worried,' Vera said mildly. 'It'd do no harm to let him know you're safe. Are you going to let us in?'

'What do you want from us at this time of night?'

'A few questions. As you're all up anyway.'

The fight seemed to leave Emma suddenly and she became passive again, wan, girlish. She stood aside to let them past. *Why does she do it?* Vera thought. *Why does she turn into a child every time there's trouble? That little-girl look. The big sad eyes. Is it conscious?*

*Does she think it'll keep her out of bother? Make Dan
Greenwood love her?*

'How did you get here?' Vera asked. Emma, in this
mode, made her want to lash out and the question
came out brutally.

'I got a lift.'

'Where is he now?'

'Who?' But already Emma was blushing. It started
at her neck and ears and moved up her face.

'Dan Greenwood. You went to see him. He gave
you a lift here. Don't mess me about. If I ask you questions, it's because I need information.'

'I don't know where he is now.' Emma seemed on
the verge of tears. Vera could sense Ashworth behind
her, winding himself up to be chivalrous. Any minute
now he'd be offering the lass his hankie. He was
always taken in by a pretty face and a sob story. She
moved through to the kitchen where the Winters were
sitting just as they'd been when she'd watched them
through the window.

'I hope you'll forgive the intrusion,' she said.

Nobody spoke. They stared at her.

'I've just told Emma, there are a few more questions.' And then, she thought, with a bit of luck she'd be
away from this place and these people. They were getting under her skin. She could almost believe that they
were the cause of the allergy on her legs, the itching
and scratching. It was the people, or the stagnant water
in the ditches, or the rotting weeds in the set-aside
fields. Then she told herself not to be so daft and get on
with the job.

'An investigation like this,' she said, 'we have to dig
deep. People have secrets . . .'

'Are you talking about James?' Robert interrupted. 'Emma has already explained about that. There was no need for you to come all the way out here.'

'No,' Vera said. 'Not James.' She stopped, turned to Emma. 'But why don't you phone him? Put the poor man out of his misery.'

'What other secrets can there be?' Emma said.

Vera didn't answer directly. 'Phone James. Listen to what he has to say.'

'Why do you want me out of the way?' Emma said. 'I'm not a child. You can talk in front of me.'

Vera looked at her sadly.

'Sergeant Ashworth has been doing most of the leg work. He spent the day in York.' Robert Winter was sitting opposite her. She was watching for a reaction, but none came. Perhaps he'd been expecting this. Perhaps he'd been waiting for it from the time news of Jeanie Long's innocence was released. Beside her, Mary, who had been restless all evening, was becoming even more agitated.

'We don't need to discuss this now, do we? It's late. As you can tell, Inspector, we have our own family problems. Emma's very upset.'

'Mr Winter?'

'What do you want to know?' His voice was professionally courteous, with just a hint of a threat. *I hope you're not here with allegations you can't substantiate. We're victims. You should treat us with respect and compassion.*

'I spoke to your former business partner, Mrs Sullivan.' Joe Ashworth was still standing by the door. They all looked up at him. At one time it would have made him awkward to be the centre of attention. Vera was proud of his new confidence, liked to think she had something to do with it.

'Maggie and I parted in rather unfriendly circumstances,' Robert said. 'She felt she'd lost out financially. I don't think you should depend on her version of events.'

'She told me you developed an obsession with her teenage daughter.'

'Ridiculous.'

'She said that she was the one to dissolve the partnership. She felt she was forced to break professional links with you, because she was so concerned about your relationship with Zoe.'

'Look,' Robert said. He put a smile into his voice, sounded like a politician at his most sincere. 'Maggie Sullivan's husband left them when Zoe was still a baby. I was a father figure. I admit I took an interest in the girl, but I thought I was helping.'

'I'm sure that was how it started. She was almost a part of the family, wasn't she? She spent a lot of time in your home and she helped with your children.'

'She was an only child,' Robert said. 'She loved them.'

'Then you started phoning her when you knew her mother wasn't in the house. You took to waiting for her outside school, following her home. You wrote her love letters. Mrs Sullivan described you as a stalker. She threatened to go to the police, but disliked the idea of her daughter becoming involved in a court case.'

'You make it sound so squalid,' Robert said. 'It wasn't like that.'

'What was it like?' Vera asked, as if she was just curious, as if it was a bit of gossip over the tea table.

'I suppose I was going through a crisis in my life. Everything seemed pointless. I was very depressed. Helping Zoe gave me some sense of worth. I believed I could make a difference. Bring some love into her life. It's easy to be cynical about something like that, but it was how I felt. It was at that point that I discovered the importance of faith. It was all meant, you see. The misunderstanding with Zoe and Maggie, the problems at work, they all helped to bring me to Christ.'

His voice was calm and reasonable. He could have been presenting evidence about an offender in the magistrates court. There was a silence. For a moment even Vera could think of nothing to say. She considered laughter to be the only response to such a distortion of the truth, but she'd seen Emma's face, which was pinched and white, and knew that this was no laughing matter.

Robert stared round at them. 'You do understand, don't you?'

Nobody replied.

Chapter Forty-Four

There was a brief, intense silence and then the phone rang. No one moved, but it continued to ring. Mary got to her feet, walked into the hall and answered it. They could hear her words quite clearly. 'She's here, James. She was just going to ring you. Yes, she's fine. Perhaps you could collect her. Not immediately. Give her half an hour.'

She came back into the kitchen and took her place without a word. Vera looked at them, waited for someone to speak.

'You lied,' Emma said to her father. She seemed more in control. Her voice was as calm as his had been. 'You're no better than James.'

'You were very young. It was complicated.'

'I remember Zoe. They're good memories – a barbecue in the garden. Her helping me with piano practice. She was musical, wasn't she? She played the flute. It's one of my clearest childhood memories, sitting in the garden in York, listening to her practise. I wonder what she's doing now. Do you know?'

She looked around at her parents, but they both ignored her.

'I wondered why she stopped looking after us.

Chris missed her more than I did. She understood his projects. They were very close.'

'What did you make of it, Mary?' Vera's voice was very quiet. They could have been alone in the room.

'Of Robert's fondness for Zoe? It was a difficult time. He blamed me for the friendship. If I'd been a different sort of wife it would never have happened, he said. If I'd been younger, more attractive, more attentive . . .'

'You didn't believe that?'

'I didn't know what to believe. When she first started coming to the house, I'd watch them together, and see that she made him happier than I ever could.'

She looked at Robert, but he said nothing to contradict her.

'Then, when he became a Christian, I was relieved. I thought things would change. He'd been very low. Sometimes he talked about suicide. I tried to persuade him to see a doctor, but he wouldn't go. I felt responsible. For him and for poor Zoe. I thought I could hold the family together and make it work. Pride, I suppose. I didn't want to admit that we weren't as close as we appeared.'

'It wasn't your fault,' Emma said. 'None of it.'

Mary didn't answer. 'I believed the move to Elvet would be a fresh start for us all. A wonderful new beginning. And no real harm had been done after all. We still had a chance to put things back to how they'd been. But that was never really possible. We were different. We'd all been affected by what had happened in York, even the children, although they were really too young to notice what was going on, and we tried to protect them. I suppose it was inevitable.'

'Did anything change?' Vera asked.

'Yes, of course! At the beginning! Robert loved his work. He felt fulfilled and valued. We had the structure of our life in the church. I began to relax. I thought everything would turn out well.'

'Then what happened?'

She didn't reply and Emma answered for her. 'He fell for Abigail. For the red hair and the short skirts.' Again her voice was calm, matter of fact. 'I can remember when he first met her. That time on the Point, when the sun was shining and we were all eating ice creams. Then at youth club. He told me that he'd never met Abigail, but it wasn't true. I should have remembered the club. That was one of the first things he did when he arrived in Elvet, he set up the club. He can't have really changed, can he? If he'd really changed that would be the last thing he'd do. Put himself in a position where he'd meet young girls. I'd forgotten all about that until recently, forgotten that Abigail was ever there. She wasn't a regular, but she did come occasionally, showing off, making the rest of us look pathetic. Dressed up in her smart clothes. The first time she came was for a disco, wasn't it? I'd asked her and I was so excited when she agreed to come. It was the last meeting before the summer holidays. Dad was sitting on the stage watching the dancing. I remember. He couldn't take his eyes off her. I was so stupid. I thought it was because she was a good dancer. Then Keith got held up and couldn't take her home and Dad gave her a lift back. Chris and I came back to Springhead with Mum.' She looked at her father for the first time. 'Is that when it started?'

'Mantel was never a real father,' Robert said. 'She needed someone to talk to.'

'Like Zoe?' Vera asked. 'Did you pick Abigail up from school too? Meet her when she bunked off lessons?'

'I never encouraged that. I tried to persuade her to go back. I acted like her social worker, that's all.'

'My God,' Emma said. 'You had sex with her.'

'No! She wanted to. The opportunity was there. I admit I was tempted, but we never had sex.' He looked at Mary. 'You must believe me.'

Vera had a sudden picture of Bill Clinton. *I never had sexual relations with that woman.* But perhaps Robert was telling more than the literal truth.

'Is that when the blackmail started?' she asked. 'When you refused to sleep with her. We know she was a very mixed-up young lady.'

'Yes,' he said. 'She threatened to tell the whole village that we'd been lovers. "We could announce it at the youth club. Deceit's a sin. We should stand on the stage, holding hands, and tell the world." Then she'd burst out laughing, as if she'd been drinking or she was mad and I never knew whether or not she was serious. I tried to stay away from her, but I couldn't stop thinking about her. I thought I was the only one who could save her.'

'Then you killed her,' Emma said in a whisper. 'You strangled her, and left her out by the ditch for me to find.' There was a moment of silence, of horror. 'Did you kill Christopher, because he'd found out?'

They were all staring at Robert, waiting for an answer. He said nothing and Emma continued talking.

'I think I've always known. I think I even knew at

the time. Not about Zoe, not the details at least, but even then I knew something was wrong. I couldn't believe the miraculous conversion. There was one night when I couldn't sleep, and I came downstairs. You were in the garden talking about it. There was a smell of honeysuckle. You were planning how you could leave York. I must have heard something . . .

'And Abigail must have wanted me to know. What a game it would have been for her. There was the way she talked about my father, all teasing and secretive. How many hints had she dropped? And I never picked up on them. Or I didn't want to. She'd have told me eventually, of course. She'd have loved it, made out that it was for my own good, that she felt I had a right to know the sort of man my father was. And I'd already guessed. I just couldn't admit it to myself. I didn't want to believe it.'

Vera, watching, heard the self-dramatization, thought she couldn't wait to get away from them all.

'Did you kill her?' Robert asked.

Emma looked at him as if he was a fool. 'Me? Of course not. Do you really think I could do that?'

He didn't answer.

'Get out,' she said.

Robert stood up and seemed about to say more. She looked away from him.

'I'll phone James,' he said. 'Tell him to come now.' It was as if he hadn't spoken. He looked around, expecting a response. Even Mary seemed unaware of his presence. He left the room. Ashworth slipped out after him.

Chapter Forty-Five

Vera cleared her throat. She'd heard enough. It was time for her to take centre stage. It was usually a position she loved, but somehow tonight, she couldn't get into the mood.

'Robert didn't kill Abigail,' Vera said. 'At first I thought he did, but it wouldn't have been possible. Not physically. You all described that Sunday to Caroline Fletcher. Her records aren't brilliant, but she made a note of that. Emma, you and your father were together in here, washing-up.' She paused. 'How did Christopher get out of helping?'

'He probably claimed he had homework to do. Some project. He could usually dream up something urgent for school after Sunday lunch. Something to get him out of domestic duties.' Emma watched Vera warily across the table.

Vera stared back. 'Christopher would have been upstairs, then?'

'Yes.'

'And your mother would have been in the living room, reading the paper. That was the Sunday routine. She cooked the lunch and then she was allowed some peace. Nobody would have disturbed her.'

'She deserved some time to herself. We all appreciated that.'

'Oh, we all deserve some peace.' *Even me. Even an old cop, who spends her life meddling in other people's business.* Vera looked at the women, thought suddenly that she'd made a terrible mistake, that she'd got the whole case wrong. Then her confidence returned as suddenly as it had deserted her. *This is it,* she thought. *Let's get it over. Then I can go home.*

'But there was no peace for you that day, was there, Mary? You waited until Robert and Emma were washing-up and then you left the house by the door into the garden. You'd arranged to meet Abigail. How did you manage that, Mary? Did you send her a note, pretending to be Robert?'

'I didn't think that she'd come,' Mary said.

'What happened to the note? It was never found.'

'She had it with her when we met. She was waving it at me, taunting. I snatched it from her hand.'

'I don't think for a moment you intended to kill the girl. You thought you could reason with her. You'd explain that Robert was a good man with a lot to lose. You only meant to protect him. You were more like a mother than a wife, weren't you? It doesn't seem fair that you had to live like that. Holding the family together, keeping up appearances in the parish. You'd never all have survived another move.'

For the first time that evening Mary was quite still. She could have been carved from wax. She stared ahead of her and she didn't answer.

'But Abigail was never reasonable. She was disturbed and wilful. She liked to create trouble. She would have been delighted to see you. Someone else to be her audience. Did she gloat about her power over Robert? It would all have been a game to her. Did she laugh?'

'Yes,' Mary said. 'She laughed.'

'And she wouldn't stop?'

At first Vera thought Mary would refuse to answer, that she'd made a terrible mistake, coming here so late, provoking a confrontation. The silence seemed to last for hours. Then Mary spoke, her words as considered as always. She wanted her story told in her own way. 'It was so loud. Louder than the rooks and the sound of the wind. Even there, miles from anywhere, I was afraid someone would hear.'

'You wanted her to be quiet.'

'Yes,' Mary said. 'I wanted the noise to go away.'

The door opened and Ashworth came quietly into the room. Mary didn't notice.

'Perhaps we should talk about this later,' Vera said. 'Somewhere else. When there's a lawyer to look after your interests.'

'Let me tell you now.' Her voice was urgent.

'I should warn you that you'll be charged and that you don't have to say anything . . .'

'I know all about that,' Mary interrupted impatiently. 'But I want you to know. Before anyone else puts words into my mouth . . .'

'Let her speak,' Emma said. 'I have to know.'

'Go on.'

'Abigail was laughing. Suddenly it felt so undignified, standing there, shouting at the girl. I reached out to make her stop, so I wouldn't have to yell. I caught both ends of her scarf and pulled them. To make her listen at first. Just to make her take me seriously. Then she was quiet and limp and I could hear the rooks again and the wind. I left her and I went home. I took off my wet shoes and my jacket and put them in the cupboard under the stairs. I went into the kitchen. No one had missed me. I didn't really believe she was dead. I thought I'd given her a fright, she was young and fit, and she'd run back to the Chapel.'

'You can't really have believed that,' Vera said. 'Because you followed Emma out.'

'I wasn't sure. I didn't want Emma to find Abigail and be alone. I suppose I thought I might have killed her.'

'You never told Robert?'

'He didn't realize I knew he was seeing her. He thought it was a big secret.'

'Weren't you angry that he was making a fool of himself over her?' Emma asked. 'Jealous?'

'He couldn't help himself,' Mary said. 'And he had so much to give. So much good work still to do.'

There was another silence. Vera knew she should move on. It was one of the rules she'd passed on to Ashworth. *Don't let them get to you. Whatever they've done, you can't take it personally. You'd go crazy.* But she allowed herself one unnecessary question. 'How could you let Jeanie go to prison?'

'I couldn't think about it. I had Robert to look after and the children. They wouldn't have survived without me. She was young, strong. I thought she'd be out in a few years.'

Vera said nothing. She thought of the prison on the top of the cliff, Jeanie Long protesting her innocence, facing the parole board and refusing to play the game which would have got her released.

'If you had children,' Mary said, 'you'd understand.'

'Did Christopher see you out in the field that afternoon?'

'No. No one saw me.'

'Why did he have to die?'

'He didn't have to die. Of course not. Do you think I wanted to kill him?'

'I don't understand. You'll have to explain.'

'That summer, he was obsessed by Abigail Mantel too. It was as if she'd cast a spell over the whole family, over Emma and Robert and Christopher. I was the only one who could see through her. That first day, when we'd ridden our bikes to the Point and we were eating ice creams, and she turned up with her father in that fast car, I could tell then that she resented us. We had a closeness that she missed. Her father was out with different women, tied up with work. She wanted to be like us but she couldn't and so she had to spoil things.'

She was a child, Vera thought. *Screwed up and miserable*. But she let Mary go on.

'Christopher saw Robert and Abigail together. He didn't say anything then. Perhaps it didn't mean much at the time. He'd had the afternoon off school. A dentist's appointment. He saw them together in Crill. Then he watched her. I think there were other occasions.'

'Did he ask you about it?'

'No. Of course not. He was a secretive boy and children seldom confide in their parents.'

'How do you know, then, that he saw Abigail and your husband together?'

'He told me when he came here last week.'

'The day that he died?'

403

'Yes.'

'The day that you killed him?'

There was a long pause. 'Yes.'

'Did he phone you that morning?'

'Robert had left for work. I started later in the library, and I was on my way out when the phone went. It was Christopher, calling on his mobile. He sounded dreadfully upset, almost incoherent. He was in that derelict farm near the parish cemetery. He was accusing Robert of killing Abigail. He said he should have realized, said something at the time. I didn't know what to do. I thought we were safe. Robert was working hard. He'd put the nonsense of Abigail Mantel behind him and nothing of the sort had happened since. We had a new family, Emma and James and the baby . . .'

'More people for you to be responsible for.'

'Yes,' Mary said gratefully. 'You see, you do understand.'

'Did you go to see Christopher at the farm?'

'No. I needed time to consider what I should do for the best. I told him I'd ring him later, that we could meet. I hoped he'd get bored with waiting. He was very easily bored. I didn't think he'd make a scene in public. I hoped he'd just go back to Aberdeen and forget. Later, when I'd had time to put together a proper explanation, I'd go to visit him and make him see. I understood then why he'd been so reluctant to visit us, to be a part of the family. I thought if I had time, I could make it right. That we could be close again.'

'Easy-going,' Vera said. 'Relaxed. Like other families.'

'Yes,' Mary said. 'Exactly.'

So the second set of fingerprints at the farm hadn't

belonged to the murderer. Another false lead. Vera thought there was probably little forensic evidence connecting Mary to Christopher. But now they had a confession. And she wouldn't go back on that, whatever her lawyers would tell her. The role of martyr suited her.

'Was killing him one of the options you considered?'

'Of course not.' She was horrified. 'He was my only son.'

'What did you do with his mobile phone?'

'It's upstairs. In my drawer in the bedroom.'

Vera knew she should be triumphant, but looking at the dumpy woman with the untidy ponytail, she only felt sick. No doubt Mary would end up in Spinney Fen too. *She* would be a model prisoner. She'd volunteer for the groups to tackle offender behaviour. Robert and Emma would visit. Robert wouldn't be able to work there any more, but the probation service was supposed to be compassionate. They'd find him something else.

'Why did you arrange to meet him in the lane outside the Mantel house?'

'I didn't. He must have made his way here. Hoping to make a scene perhaps. Some sort of confrontation. James and Emma must have mentioned the fireworks. When he came here and the house was empty, he crossed the fields to the Chapel.'

Taking the path Abigail had used ten years before.

'When I went to fetch my coat, he was waiting by the car. It was a terrible shock. It was as I told you. I switched on the headlights and there he was. He was very cold. He'd been waiting for a long time. He looked like a tramp. I hardly recognized him. He said his father had killed Abigail. I told him that was ridiculous, that it wasn't true. He got out his mobile and said he was going to phone the police. I had to stop him. Of course I didn't mean to kill him.'

Didn't you? thought Vera, no longer convinced. *Was it really another accident? Like Abigail? It's much easier to love a dead son, than a live, inconvenient one.*

'He was your son,' she said, forgetting again the rule about staying detached. 'Yet afterwards, you kept to your story. When we talked to you the next day you were very calm.'

'It was the greatest sacrifice a woman can make,' Mary said. 'I did it to protect Robert, to keep the rest of the family together. I couldn't let the sacrifice be in vain.'

Bollocks. You panicked and you did it to protect yourself. 'What did you hit him with?'

'There was a torch in the car. Long, very heavy. He turned away to make the phone call. I hit him. He fell into the ditch. He fell awkwardly. All you could see was that horrible anorak. I moved him so that he looked more peaceful. He wasn't breathing. I checked. There was nothing anyone could do to save him. And he wasn't happy any more. He wasn't happy as he'd been when he was a boy, living with us.'

'What did you do with the torch?'

She seemed surprised by the question. 'It had blood on it. I wiped it on his anorak. That was dirty anyway. Then I put it back into my bag.'

And I let you carry it away, Vera thought. I knew we'd have to search your car, but we didn't search you. I thought you were too distressed to bear it. How long will I have to live that one down? She was already wondering if there was some way that could be left out of the final report.

She realized then that Emma was crying. She wasn't making any noise, but tears were rolling down her cheeks.

Chapter Forty-Six

Vera caught up with Dan Greenwood in Wendy's cottage on the Point. She thought she deserved some light relief before she left for the north. It was the next morning. She hadn't been to bed. The night had been a blur, a nightmare. She remembered Robert standing by the kitchen door at Springhead as they'd led his wife away into the freezing night. 'One day, Mary, I hope I'll be able to forgive you.' What had all that been about? A grand theatrical gesture which meant fuck all. She'd have liked to charge him too, but Ashworth had persuaded her that they had no grounds. Winter had never had sex with Zoe Sullivan. The mother had been quite clear about that. Probably not with Abigail either. Two murders and nothing but a sad, middle-aged man's fantasies as a reason for them. A sad middle-aged man and a mad middle-aged woman. He'd be back at church on Sunday and no doubt the old ladies would rally round, offering him home-made soup and sympathy.

Wendy opened the door. She was in her dressing gown.

'I want to see Greenwood,' Vera said.

Wendy hesitated.

'Don't piss me around. I know he's here. Emma Bennett saw you together last night in the pottery.'

'Poor Emma,' Wendy said. 'I think she had a bit of a crush.'

'Don't tell Danny boy that. You don't want to flatter him. He's not in any bother. I'm just here to say good-bye.' She raised her voice. 'Come on down, Dan. Decent or not.'

She followed Wendy into the cottage. She wondered if she was wearing knickers under the dressing gown. Black knickers with a sequinned heart. Of all the places in Elvet, this was the house where Vera felt most at home. She loved the untidiness, the view over the water. Danny emerged down the stairs. He was still pulling a jersey over his head. 'How long's this been going on?' she demanded.

'I don't know. A couple of months.' Wendy was grinning, couldn't help herself. She perched on the arm of the chair where Danny was sitting, could hardly stop herself from touching him.

'Why did you keep it quiet?'

'Wouldn't you? A place like this?'

'Aye, maybe.' She stood by the window, looked out. 'It's all over,' she said. 'There's someone in custody.'

'Who?' Danny asked.

'Mary Winter, the mother of the lass who found the body.'

'My God!' He sat quite still for a moment, trying to take it in. 'Why did she kill them?'

'God knows,' Vera said. 'She says she thought she was acting for the best, but I'm not sure I believe her. Simple jealousy perhaps, because the lass was young and bonny and the husband fancied her. That's for the lawyers to fight over. But it'll make no difference to the verdict. It's over.'

'A bit late for Jeanie Long.'

'Not for you, though. Time to set it behind you.' A tanker was easing slowly up the river. 'I found that file in your desk.'

'I wondered if you'd seen it.'

'For a while I wondered if you'd killed her.'

'No,' he said. 'That was a different kind of obsession. I thought one day I might be able to put it right. Find the real murderer. Not that I did anything about it. Just took the file out every now and again to rub salt in the wound.'

'What will you do with it now?'

'Burn it.'

'Good luck,' Vera said, 'with everything.'

'Thanks.'

'Right then. I'm off.'

'Home?'

'Aye,' she said. 'North of the Tyne. Civilization.' She smiled broadly. 'No offence.'

She had to drive through the village to pick Ashworth up from the hotel. She was forced to slow down at the Captain's House to let a couple of kids run across the road and saw that Emma Bennett had returned home to James. She was sitting in the bedroom window, looking out over the square, apparently lost in thought. Like the heroine of some Victorian melodrama, Vera thought.

It was about time she got a life.

Author's Note

TELLING TALES is set in a fictitious landscape east of Hull. There is no village called Elvet and though the Point is geographically similar to Spurn, there are significant differences. The coxswains of the pilot launch don't live there, for example.

The pilots have moved out of their old office in Hull, but to my knowledge it has not been sold for development.

I would like to thank Ray and Val Eades for their invaluable advice about pilotage on the Humber. Any mistakes are mine.

HIDDEN DEPTHS

The third novel in the Vera Stanhope series

Julie stared at him, submerged beneath the bath water, his hair rising like fronds of seaweed towards the surface. She couldn't see his body because of the flowers . . .

On a hot summer night on the Northumberland coast, Julie Armstrong arrives home to find her son strangled, laid out in a bath of water and covered with wild flowers.

The stylized murder intrigues DI Vera Stanhope, and then another body is discovered in a rock pool, the corpse again strewn with flowers. Vera must work quickly to find a killer who is making art out of death.

As the local residents are forced to share their deepest, darkest secrets, the killer watches, waits and plans to prepare another beautiful, watery grave . . .

Turn the page to read the first chapters

Chapter One

Julie stumbled from the taxi and watched it drive away. At the front gate she paused to compose herself. Best not to go in looking pissed after all those lectures she'd given the kids. The stars wheeled and dipped in the sky and she almost threw up. But she didn't care. It had been a good night, the first with the girls for ages. Though it wasn't the girls that had made it so special, she thought, and realized there was a great soppy beam on her face. Just as well it was dark and there was no one to see.

At the door she stopped again and scrabbled through the eyeliner pencils and lippy-stained tissues and loose change in her bag for her key. Her fingers found the scrap of paper which had been torn from a corner of a menu in the bar. A phone number and a name. *Ring me soon.* Then a little heart. The first man she'd touched since Geoff had left. She could still feel the bones of his spine against her fingers when they'd danced. It was a shame he'd had to leave early.

She snapped the bag shut and listened. Nothing. It was so quiet that she could hear the buzz of the evening's music as a pressure on her ears. Was it possible that Luke was asleep? Laura could sleep for

England, but her son had never seemed to get the hang of it. Even now he'd left school and there was nothing to get up for, he was usually awake before her. She pushed open the door and listened again, slipping her feet out of the shoes that had been killing her since she'd got out of the metro hours before. God, she hadn't danced like that since she was twenty-five. There was silence. No music, no television, no beeping computer. Thank the Lord, she thought. Thank the fucking Lord. She wanted sleep and sexy dreams. Somewhere on the street outside an engine was started.

She switched on the light. The glare hurt her head and turned her stomach again. She let go of her bag and ran up the stairs to the bathroom, tripping halfway up. No way was she going to be sick on the new hall carpet. The bathroom door was shut and she saw a crack of light showing underneath it. From the airing cupboard there came the faint gurgle of water which meant the tank was refilling. And wasn't that typical? It took hours of persuasion to get Luke into the shower in the morning, then he decided to have a bath in the middle of the night. She knocked on the bathroom door but there was no urgency about it. The queasiness had passed again.

Luke didn't answer. He must be in one of his moods. Julie knew it wasn't his fault and she should be patient, but sometimes she wanted to strangle him when he went all weird on her. She crossed the landing to Laura's room. Looking down at her daughter, she came over suddenly sentimental, thought she should make the effort to spend more time with her. Fourteen was a difficult age for a girl and Julie had been so caught up with Luke lately that Laura almost seemed like a stranger. She'd grown up without Julie noticing. She lay on her back, her spiky hair very black against the pillow, snoring slightly, her mouth open. It was a bad time for hay fever. Julie saw that the window was open and, although it was so hot, she shut it to keep out the pollen. The moonlight splashed onto the field behind the house where they'd been cutting grass.

She returned to the bathroom and banged on the door with the flat of her palm. 'Hey, are you going to be in there all night?' With the third bang, the door opened. It hadn't been locked. There was a smell of bath oil, heavy and sweet, which Julie didn't recognize as hers. Luke's clothes were neatly folded on the toilet seat.

He had always been beautiful, even as a baby. Much lovelier than Laura, which had never seemed fair. It was the blond hair and the dark eyes, the long, dark eyelashes. Julie stared at him, submerged beneath the bath water, his hair rising, like fronds of seaweed, towards the surface. She couldn't see his body because of the flowers. They floated on the perfumed water. Only the flower heads, not the stems or the leaves. There were the big ox-eye daisies which had grown in the cornfields when she was a kid. Overblown poppies, the red petals translucent now. And enormous blue blossoms, which she had seen before in gardens in the village, but which she couldn't name.

Julie must have screamed. She heard the sound as if someone else had made it. But still Laura slept and Julie had to shake her to wake her. The girl's eyes opened suddenly, very wide. She looked terrified and Julie found herself muttering, knowing that she was lying, 'It's all right, pet. Everything's all right. But you have to get up.'

Laura swung her legs out of bed. She was trembling, but not really awake. Julie put her arm around her and supported her as they stumbled together down the stairs.

They stood like that, wrapped up in each other's arms, on the doorstep of the neighbour's house and the silhouette thrown on the wall by the street light made Julie think of people in a crazy three-legged race. One of those pub crawls that students went in for. She leaned against the bell until the lights upstairs went on and footsteps came and she had someone to share the nightmare with.

Chapter Two

It disturbed Felicity Calvert that she'd become so pre-occupied with sex. Once, in the doctor's waiting room, she'd read a magazine which claimed that adolescent boys thought about sex every six minutes. Then she'd found it hard to believe. How could these young men lead a normal life – go to college, watch a film, play football – when they were so frequently distracted? And what of her own son? Watching James playing on the floor with his Lego, it had been impossible to imagine that in a few years he would be similarly obsessed. But now she thought that an interval of six minutes between sexual daydreams could be a conservative estimate. In her case at least. For a while now an awareness of her body and its responses had been with her whatever she was doing, an uneasy, occasionally pleasurable background to the stuff of everyday life. For someone of her age this seemed inappropriate. It was as if she'd attended a funeral wearing pink.

She was in the garden picking the first of the strawberries. She lifted the net carefully, sliding her hand underneath between the mesh and the straw bedding. They were still small but there should be enough for James's tea. She tasted one. It was warm from the sun and very sweet. Glancing at her watch she saw it was almost time for the school bus. Ten more minutes and she'd have to wash her hands and walk down the lane to meet him. She didn't always go. He claimed he was old enough to make his own way to the house and of course that was true. But today he'd have his violin and he'd be glad to see her because she could help him carry his stuff. She wondered briefly whether it would be the old bus driver or the young one with the muscular arms and the sleeveless T-shirt, then looked at her watch again. Only two minutes since she'd last considered sex. The thought returned that at her age it was quite ridiculous.

Felicity was forty-seven. She had a husband and four children. She had, for goodness' sake, a grandchild. In a few days Peter, her husband, would be sixty. The bubbles of lust surfaced at random, when she was least expecting them. She hadn't talked about this to Peter. Of course not. He certainly wasn't the object of her desire. These days they seldom made love.

She got up and walked across the grass to the kitchen. Fox Mill stood on the site of an old water mill. It was a big house, built in the thirties, a coastal retreat for a ship owner from the city. And it looked like a ship with its smooth, curved lines, the mill race flowing past it. A big, art deco ship, stranded quite out of place in the flat farmland, with its prow pointed to the North Sea and its stern facing the Northumberland hills on the horizon. A long veranda stretched along one side like a deck, impractical here where it was seldom warm enough to sit outside. She loved the house. They would never have afforded it on an academic's salary, but Peter's parents had died soon after he and Felicity had married and all their money had come to him.

She put the basket of strawberries on the table and checked her face in the mirror in the hall, running her fingers through her hair and adding a splash of lipstick. She was older than the mothers of James's friends and hated the idea of embarrassing him.

In the lane the elders were in flower. Their scent made her head swim and caught at the back of her throat. On either side of the lane the corn was ripening. The crop was too dense for flowers there, but in the field which they owned, close to the house, there were buttercups and clover and purple vetch. The pitted tarmac shimmered in the distance with heat haze. The sun had shone without a break for three days.

This weekend it was Peter's birthday and she was planning what they might do. On Friday night the boys would come. She thought of them as boys, though Samuel, at least, was as old as her. But if it stayed like this, on Saturday there could be a picnic on the beach, a trip to the Farnes to see puffins and guillemots. James would love that. She squinted at the sky, wondering if she could sense an approaching cold front, the faintest cloud on the horizon. There was nothing. It might even be warm enough to swim, she thought, and imagined the waves breaking on her body.

When she reached the end of the lane there was no sign of the bus. She hoisted herself onto the wooden platform where once the churns from the farm had stood to wait for the milk lorry. The wood was hot and smelled of pitch. She lay back and faced the sun.

In two years James would move on to secondary school. She dreaded it. Peter talked about him going to a private day school in the city, to the school which he'd attended. She'd seen the boys in their striped blazers on the metro. They'd seemed very confident and loud to her.

'But how would he get there?' she'd said. This wasn't her real objection. She didn't think it would be good for James to be pushed. He was a slow and dreamy boy. He'd do better working at his own pace. The comprehensive in the next village would suit him better. Even the high school in Morpeth, where their other children had been students, had seemed demanding to her.

'I'd take him and bring him back,' Peter had said. 'There'll be lots going on after school. He can hang on until I've finished work.'

That had made her even less favourably disposed to the plan. The time that she had with James when he arrived home from school was special. Without it, she thought, he would be lost to her.

She heard the bus growling up the bank and sat upright, squinting against the sun as it approached. The driver was Stan, the old man. She waved at him to hide her disappointment. Usually three of them got off at this stop – the twin girls from the farm and James. Today a stranger climbed out first, a young woman wearing strappy leather sandals and a red and gold sleeveless dress with a fitted bodice and full, swirling skirt. Felicity loved the dress, the way the skirt fell and the exuberance of the colours – the young today seemed to choose black or grey even in summer – and when she saw the woman help James off the bus with his bags and violin, she was immediately drawn to her. The twins crossed the road and ran up the track to the farmhouse, the bus drove off and the three of them were left, standing a little awkwardly, by the hedge.

'This is Miss Marsh,' James said. 'She's working at our school.'

The woman had a big straw bag strung by a leather strap over her shoulder. She held out a hand which was very brown and long and bony. The bag slipped down her arm and Felicity saw that it contained files and a library book.

'Lily.' Her voice was clear. 'I'm a student. This is my last teaching practice.' She smiled as if she expected Felicity to be pleased to meet her.

'I told her she could come and stay in our cottage,' James said and set off up the lane, unencumbered, not caring which of the adults carried his things.

Felicity was not quite sure what to say.

'He *did* mention I was looking for somewhere?' Lily asked.

Felicity shook her head.

'Oh dear, how embarrassing.' But she didn't seem very embarrassed. She seemed to be remarkably self-assured, to find the incident amusing. 'It's been such a nightmare travelling from Newcastle every day without a car. The head asked in assembly if anyone knew of accommodation. We were thinking of a B&B or someone wanting a paying guest. And yesterday James said you had a cottage to let. I tried to phone this afternoon but there was no answer. He said you'd be in the garden and to come anyway. I presumed he'd discussed it with you. It was hard to say no . . .'

'Oh yes,' Felicity agreed. 'He can be very insistent.'

'Look, it's not a problem. It's a lovely afternoon. I'll walk into the village and there's a bus from there into town at six.'

'Let me think about it,' Felicity said. 'Come and have some tea.'

There had been tenants in the cottage before, but it had never quite worked out. In the early days they'd been glad of an extra source of income. Even with the money from Peter's parents the mortgage repayments had been a nightmare. Then, with three children under five, they had thought it might house a nanny or au pair. But there had been complaints about the cold and a dripping tap and the lack of modern convenience. And they hadn't been comfortable having a stranger living so close to the family. They'd felt the responsibility for the tenant as an extra stress. Although none of them had been particularly troublesome, it had always been a relief to see them go. 'Never again,' Peter had said when the last resident, a homesick Swedish au pair, had left. Felicity wasn't sure how he would feel about another young woman on the doorstep, even if it was only four weeks until the end of term.

As they sat at the table in the kitchen, with the breeze from the sea blowing the muslin curtain at the open window, Felicity Calvert thought she probably would let the young woman have the place if she wanted it. Peter wouldn't mind too much if it was for a short time.

James was sitting beside them at the table, sur-

rounded by scissors, scraps of cut paper and glue. He
was drinking orange juice and making a birthday card
for his father. It was an elaborate affair with photos of
Peter taken from old albums and stuck as a collage
around a big 60 made out of ribbon and glitter. Lily
admired it and asked about the early photographs.
Felicity sensed James's pleasure in her interest and
felt a stab of gratitude.

'If you live in Newcastle,' she said, 'I suppose you
wouldn't want the cottage at weekends.' She thought
that would be another point to make to Peter. *She'd
only be here during the week. And you work such long
hours you wouldn't notice she's around.*

The cottage stood beyond the meadow with the wild
flowers in it. Besides the garden, this was the only
land they owned. Viewed from the house the building
looked so small and squat it was hard to believe that
anyone could live there. A path had been trampled
across the field and Felicity wondered who had been
here since the grass had grown up. James probably.
He used it as a den when he had friends to play,
though they kept the building locked and she couldn't
remember him asking for a key lately.

'Cottage makes it sound more grand than it is,'
she said. 'It's only one up and one down with a bathroom built on the back. The gardener lived here when
our house was first built. It was a pigsty before then, I
think; some sort of outhouse anyway.'

The door was fastened by a padlock. She unlocked
it then hesitated, feeling suddenly uneasy. She wished
she'd had a chance to look around the building before

inviting the stranger in. She should have left Lily in the kitchen while she checked the state of the place.

But although she was aware at once of the damp, it was tidy enough. The grate was empty, though she couldn't remember cleaning it after her youngest daughter and her husband had been here at Christmas. The pans were hanging in their place on the wall and the oilskin cloth on the table had been wiped down. It was pleasantly cool after the heat in the meadow. She pushed open the window.

'They're cutting grass at the farm,' she said. 'You can smell it from here.'

Lily had stepped inside. It was impossible to tell what she thought of the place. Felicity had expected her to fall in love with it and felt offended. It was as if an overture of friendship had been rejected. She led the woman through to the small bathroom. Pointing out that the shower was new and the tiles had recently been replaced, she felt like an estate agent desperate for a sale. Why am I behaving like this? she thought. I wasn't even sure I wanted her here.

At last Lily spoke. 'Can we look upstairs?' And she started up the tight wooden steps which led straight from the kitchen. Felicity felt the same uneasiness as when she'd paused at the door of the cottage. She would have liked to be there first.

But again, everything was more in order than she had expected. The bed was still made up, the quilt and extra blankets folded neatly at its foot. There was dust on the painted cupboard and dressing table, on the family photographs which stood there, but none of the rubbish and clutter which usually remained after her daughter's stay. A jug of white roses stood on the wide window sill. One of the petals had dropped and she picked it up absent-mindedly. Of course, Felicity thought. Mary has been in although I never asked her. What a sweetie she is! So unobtrusive and helpful! Mary Barnes came to clean twice a week.

Only when she was closing the padlock behind them, did Felicity think that the roses couldn't have been there for more than a few days, and Mary, an unimaginative woman, would never have thought of a touch like that without being prompted.

They stood for a moment outside the cottage. 'Well?' Felicity asked. 'What did you think?' She caught a falsely cheerful note in her voice.

Lily smiled. 'It's lovely,' she said. 'Really. But there's such a lot to think about. I'll be in touch, shall I, next week?'

Felicity had intended offering her a lift, at least as far as the bus stop in the village, but Lily turned away and walked off across the meadow. Felicity couldn't bring herself to shout or run after her, so she stood and watched until the red and gold figure was lost in the long grass.

Chapter Three

Julie couldn't stop talking. She knew she was making a tit of herself, but the words spilled out, and the fat woman wedged in the Delcor armchair that Sal had got from the sales last year just sat there and listened. Not taking notes, not asking questions. Just listening.

'He was an easy baby. Not like Laura. She was a real shock after Luke. A demanding little madam, either asleep or crying or with a bottle in her gob. Luke was . . .' Julie paused trying to find the right word. The fat detective didn't interrupt, just gave her the time to think. '. . . restful, peaceful. He'd lie awake all day, just watching the shadows on the ceiling. A bit slow talking, but by then I'd had Laura and the health visitor thought that was why. I mean, she was so bright and taking up all my time and sucking my energy, that Luke had got left out. Nothing to worry about, the health visitor said. He'd catch up as soon as he started nursery. Geoff was still living with us, but he was working away a lot. He's a plasterer. There's more money in the south and he went through one of those agencies, ended up working on Canary Wharf . . . It was a lot to cope with, two kids under three and no man around.'

Then the woman did respond, just nodding her head a touch to show that she understood.

'I started him at the nursery at the school in the village. He didn't want to go at first, they had to drag him off me, and when I went back an hour later he was still sobbing. It broke my heart, but I thought it was for the best. He needed the company. The health visitor said it was the right thing to do. And he did get used to it. He used to go in without screaming, at least. But all the time looking at me with those eyes. Not speaking but the eyes saying, "Don't make me go in there, Mam. Please don't make me go."' Julie was sitting on the floor, her knees pulled up to her chin, her arms clasped around them. She looked up at the detective, who was still watching and waiting. It came to her suddenly that this woman, large and solid like rock, might once have known tragedy herself. That was why she could sit there without making those stupid, sympathetic noises Sal and the doctor had made. This woman knew that nothing she could say would make it better. But Julie didn't care about the detective's sadness and the thought was fleeting. She went back to her story.

'It was about that time Geoff came home from London. He said the work had dried up, but I heard from his mate that there'd been some row with the foreman. He's a good worker, Geoff, and he won't be pissed about. It was a difficult time for him. He was never one for sitting around and he was used to making big money. He put in a new kitchen for me and did up the bathroom. You'd never believe what this place looked like when we first moved in. But then the cash ran out . . .'

429

Sal had made tea. In a pot, not with bags in the mugs as Julie always made it. Julie reached out to the tray and poured herself another cup. It wasn't that she wanted one, but it gave her time to sort out what she wanted to say.

'It wasn't a good time. Geoff wasn't used to the kids. When he was working in London, he had only one long weekend a month at home. Then it was a novelty for him being there. He'd make a fuss of them, bring presents. We were all on our best behaviour. And every night he was out at the club drinking with his mates. When he came back for good it couldn't be like that. You know what it's like. Baby clothes drying on the radiator and toys all over the floor. Mucky nappies . . . There were times when he lost patience, especially with Luke. Laura would giggle and play up to him. Luke seemed to be in a world of his own. Geoff never hit him. But he'd shout and Luke would get so scared you'd think he *had* been battered. I used to shout all the time but they knew I never meant it. They'd get their own way anyway. It was different with Geoff. Even I got scared.'

She was silent for a moment thinking of Geoff and his temper, the gloom which lingered over the house after one of his outbursts. But she couldn't keep quiet for long and the words started again.

'Luke was no bother in the infants' school. He even seemed to like going. Perhaps he was used to it, because the nursery was in the same building. He had a lovely teacher in the first class, Mrs Sullivan. She was like a grandma to them, sat them on her knee when she was teaching them to read. She told me he had problems – nothing serious, she said – but it would be best to get him checked out. She wanted him to see a psychologist. But there was no money, or the waiting list was too long and it never happened. Geoff said the only thing wrong with Luke was that he was lazy. Then he left us. He said we got on his nerves. We were dragging him down. But I knew fine well that he'd been having a fling with a nurse from the RVI. They ended up living together. They're married now.'

She stopped again for a moment. Not because she'd run out of things to say, but because she needed to catch her breath. She thought Geoff had known all along that there was something wrong with Luke. You could tell by the suspicious way he'd stare at him when he was playing. He just didn't want to admit it.

It was eight-thirty in the morning. They were still sitting in her neighbour's house, in Sal's front room. Outside the postman walked past, staring at the cop standing by her front door. The kids further down the street were chasing and giggling on their way to school.

The fat woman detective leaned forward, not pushing Julie to continue, more showing her that she was content to wait, that she had all the time in the world. Julie sipped the tea. She didn't tell the woman about the way Geoff had looked at Luke. Instead she moved the story on a year.

'The tantrums started when he was about six. They came out of nowhere and you couldn't control him. Mam said it was my fault for spoiling him. He wasn't in Mrs Sullivan's class then, but she was the only one at that school I could really talk to, and she said it was frustration. He couldn't explain him-self properly and he was struggling with his reading and writing and suddenly it all got too much for him. Once he pushed out at this lad who was teasing him. The lad tripped and cracked his head on the playground. There was an ambulance and you can imagine what it was like waiting to pick up the bairns that afternoon – all the other mams pointing and whispering. Luke was dead sorry. He wanted to go and see the lad in the hospital, and when you think about it, it was the other lad who'd started it with his teasing. Aidan he was called. Aidan Noble. His mam was all right about it, but his dad came round to the house to have a go at us. Mouthing off on the doorstep so the whole street could hear.

'The head teacher called me in. Mr Warrender. He was a short plump man, with that thin sort of hair that doesn't quite cover the bald patch. I saw him in town the other day and I didn't recognize him at first – he's taken to wearing a toupee. He wasn't nasty. He made me a cup of tea and that. He said Luke had behavioural problems and they weren't sure they could cope with him in school. I showed myself up. Started crying. Then I told him what Mrs Sullivan had said about it being frustration and if they'd pushed for Luke to see a specialist earlier on then he might not have worked himself up into such a state. And Mr Warrender seemed to listen because Luke did see someone. They did tests, like, and said he had learning difficulties, but he should be able to stay in school with some support. And that was what happened.'

Julie paused again. She wanted the fat woman to understand what it had felt like, the relief of knowing that the tantrums and the moodiness weren't her fault. Her mam had been wrong about that. Luke was special, different, had been from the beginning. Nothing she could have done would have altered the fact. And the woman seemed to know how important that had been because at last she allowed herself to speak.

'So you weren't on your own.'

'You don't know,' Julie said, 'how good that felt.'

The woman nodded in agreement. But how could she know, when she'd never had children? How could anyone know, if they hadn't had a child with a learning disability?

'I could put up with people talking about us and the whispering at the school gate about the special help he was getting, because it was out in the open and most people were dead kind. There was a class-room assistant who came in just to help him. And Luke did all right. I mean, he was never going to be a genius, but he tried hard and his reading and writing came on, and some things he was good at. Like, any-thing to do with computers he took to really quickly. They were good years. Laura had started school too and I had some time to myself. I got a part-time job in the care home in the village. My mates couldn't understand why I enjoyed it so much, but I did. It made me feel useful, I suppose. Geoff was never very interested in seeing the kids, but he was OK about money. I mean, nothing exciting ever happened, no holidays or wild nights out, but we managed.'

'It can't have been easy, though,' the detective said.

'Well, maybe not easy,' Julie conceded. 'But we coped. Luke started getting into bother again when he moved to the high school. Other kids saw he was an easy touch and took advantage. Set him up to act out in class. He was always the one that was caught. He started getting a reputation. You must know how it happens. You must see it all the time. The police were called when he was caught thieving from a building site. Plastic drainpipes. What would he want with those? Someone had offered him a few quid to take them, but it wasn't that. He wanted people to like him. All his life he'd felt left out. He wanted friends.'

You could understand that, couldn't you? Julie thought. She didn't know how she'd have managed without her friends. The first trouble with Geoff and she'd be on the phone to them. Sharing her worries about Luke when he'd been ill. And they'd be straight round with a bottle of wine. Keen for the gossip of course, but there for her.

'He did have one special friend,' she went on. 'A lad called Thomas. They met up when Luke started at the high school. He was a bit of a scally. In and out of trouble with the police, but when you talked to him you could see why. His dad had been in prison for most of the time he was growing up and his mam never seemed to bother with him much.

'I'd never have chosen Thomas as a friend for Luke, but he wasn't a bad lad, not really. And he seemed to like spending time in our house. In the end he was almost living with us. He was no bother. They'd be up in Luke's room, watching videos or playing on the computer, and while they were there they weren't thieving, were they? Or taking smack like a lot of their mates. And they got on really well. Sometimes you'd hear them laughing at some daft joke and I was just pleased that Luke had a friend.

'Then Thomas was killed. Drowned. Some lads were messing about on the quayside at North Shields. He fell in and couldn't swim. Our Luke was there too. He jumped in and tried to save Thomas but it was too late.'

Julie paused. Outside a tractor and trailer with a load of bales went past. 'Luke wouldn't talk about it. He shut himself in his room for hours. I thought he just needed time, you know, to get over it. To grieve. He stopped going to school, but he was fifteen by then and he wasn't going to get any exams, so I thought I'd just let him be. I'd talked to the lady who runs the care home and she said she might be able to find some work for him there when he was sixteen, helping in the kitchen. He'd come to work with me a few times and the old folk really took to him. But I should have realized he needed help. It wasn't normal the way he carried on, but then our Luke never really was normal, was he? So how could I tell?

'He stopped washing and eating and he was awake all night. Sometimes I'd hear his voice, as if he was talking to someone in his head. That was when I got the doctor. He got him taken into St George's. You know, the mental hospital. They said he was very depressed. Post-traumatic stress. I hated visiting him in there, but it was a relief not to have him at home. I mean, I felt guilty thinking like that, but it was true.'

'When did he come home?' the fat woman asked. Her first question.

'Three weeks ago and he seemed better. Really. I mean, still sad about Thomas. Sometimes he'd burst into tears just thinking about him. And he was still seeing the doctor at the outpatient clinic. But not crazy. Not mad. This was the first night out I'd had in months. I really needed it, but I wouldn't have gone if I hadn't thought he'd be all right. I never thought he'd do something like that to himself.'

The woman leaned over and took Julie's hand, covered it in her great paw.

'This wasn't your fault,' she said. 'Luke didn't commit suicide.' She looked at Julie to make sure that she'd taken that in, that she really understood. 'He was dead before he was put into the bath. He was murdered.'

NOW A MAJOR BBC DRAMA
Shetland
STARRING DOUGLAS HENSHALL

Ann Cleeves

Ann Cleeves
RAVEN BLACK
'A RIVETING READ'
Val McDermid

Ann Cleeves
WHITE NIGHTS
'A MOST SATISFYING MYSTERY'
Peter Robinson

Ann Cleeves
RED BONES
'ELEGANTLY WRITTEN,
SLOW-BURNING INTRIGUE'
Peter James

Ann Cleeves
BLUE LIGHTNING
'THE DEFINITIVE
DETECTIVE THRILLER'

Ann Cleeves
DEAD WATER
A HIDDEN PAST WITH
UNDERCURRENTS OF MURDER

Ann Cleeves
THIN AIR
A KILLER WHO LEAVES NO TRACE
A VICTIM WHO VANISHES INTO

extracts reading groups
competitions books new
discounts extracts extracts
competitions events
books new discounts
reading groups
events extracts
books interviews
new titles reading groups
extracts
events extracts
discounts events
new books events books
events new events
discounts extracts discounts

www.panmacmillan.com

extracts events reading groups
competitions books extracts new